THE VISITORS DESCEND

With awe, Irtuk-saa watched the huge construct lower itself to rest. This was the intruders' *small* ship? Irtuk awaited what would come.

A hatch dropped open and a ladder descended. A being emerged: hindlimbs first, then trunk and forelimbs; finally a head. Wrapped in coverings that left only head and grasping extremities exposed, the biped clambered slowly down, encumbered by various objects attached to harness straps. Two more of the creatures followed, each differing in some ways from the first.

She stepped forward to greet the creatures who had come so far. And hoped they meant her well.

Other AvoNova Books by
F. M. Busby

ARROW FROM EARTH
ISLANDS OF TOMORROW

THE TRIAD WORLDS

F.M. BUSBY

AVON BOOKS • NEW YORK

THE TRIAD WORLDS is an original publication of Avon Books. This work has never before appeared in book form. This work is a novel. Any similarity to actual persons or events is purely coincidental.

AVON BOOKS
A division of
The Hearst Corporation
1350 Avenue of the Americas
New York, New York 10019

Cover art by Eric Peterson
Published by arrangement with the author
Library of Congress Catalog Card Number: 95-96053
ISBN: 0-380-78468-8

First AvoNova Printing: June 1996

AVONOVA TRADEMARK REG. U.S. PAT. OFF. AND IN OTHER COUNTRIES, MARCA REGISTRADA, HECHO EN U.S.A.

Printed in the U.S.A.

RA 10 9 8 7 6 5 4 3 2 1

To Joe and Patti Green

I

The ship approaching Magh came not from Eamn; of that much, Irtuk-saa was satisfied. As premier bearer of the Saa holding and senior of the Nearer Archipelago bearers' council, she had studied and correlated reports gathered throughout the council's domain. Their initial evaluation, she was certain, would prove correct: Chorm's outer moon could mount no such device.

The renegade colony was, she knew, better healed of their ancient war than Magh, the world of common origin. The two achieved conjunction roughly ten times in eleven of Magh's days—its tide-locked orbits, inside Eamn's, around massive Chorm. Simple observation indicated renewed industrial capability on Eamn: radiations not of natural origin, areas of increased heat where no volcanic activity could occur. But no specifics, nothing that might hint of new attack on the mother world.

Yet Eamn ships had come, not long since and wholly unexpected, to Maghren skies—nearing, circling Magh, then receding in return to Eamn. Crude by comparison to those shown in old records, let alone the unfamiliar color-flaring construct now approaching from the system's outer reaches, still Eamnet presence in space caused alarm. Suspecting no such progress, Maghren councils had put no thought to regaining capability of offworld travel; as Irtuk herself maintained at the most recent plenary gathering, "Once plagued, suffices."

Literally as well as figuratively, her words spoke true. In that long-past war, Magh's only such conflict since its primitive bands first united under one rule, none fought limb to limb: ships raided and surface defenses sought their destruction. Shipborne weapons devastated the two worlds, but it was plague that destroyed both civilizations: Magh's, and that of its abominable offshoot the Eamn colony.

Generations later, no one really knew who originated the pestilence. Magh tradition blamed Eamn—but among the enemy, Irtuk surmised, all onus lay with the mother world.

The reality of Eamnet return to space brought alarm; the former colony's intentions could only be mistrusted. An emergency plenary meet mandated full mobilization of study, labor, and resources. And quickly.

Now, though, as Irtuk in the absence of Paith the Elect sat acting head of councils, progress toward Maghren space capability had to wait. First she must allay nascent panic, must put the newer, unexplained sighting into perspective. Certain though she was that no Eamnet effort could have produced the new-seen ship, the true facts might be yet more dire.

She did not know the young seeder, wearing ornate though well-worn harness, who rose to speak, nor the adaptive who accompanied him. By their Tsi insignia they hailed from Tajakh Island at the rim between Chormside and farside, where Chorm sat moveless at the horizon. And they were the pair who had first sighted the new spacecraft and made detailed observations.

The speaker was, thought Irtuk, a prime specimen of his gender: smooth-plated and evenly colored on limbs and sides, with a tawny central mane reaching from forehead to and down the back to cover the tail, now tucked decorously forward between the lower limbs and then up, to shield genitor and excretor as was proper to the occasion. Large, wide-set eyes emphasized the bold curve of his narrowing jaws, and to either side of his upper lip, the epaulets of fur lay neatly trimmed.

". . . with no thrust flames," he was saying, "nor ion trail, such as propelled vessels made here or on Eamn in times past. Instead, as it slows from speeds never before observed, ahead flow streams of color. And to the sides also, though lesserly, as its aim changes." Digits splayed, one forelimb gestured. "We did hark to records, some cycles back, of the ship that came from Shtai the Forerunner and returned there. A vessel which showed similar activity."

"And you found . . . ?"

"This one's aura spreads farther, stronger and more intense. Speeds and changes of speed occur in much greater magnitude. And unlike the previous unknown, it approaches directly from far outward of Magh's path, as we accompany great Chorm about our star Jemra."

"From outward, yet not from Diell the Companion." The visitor from Shtai a time ago, circling Chorm and passing closely to both Magh and Eamn, had also been sighted earlier, a faintly seen object nearing the system from Companion Star's direction. That one had first vanished behind Chorm when Shtai, also, was so hidden, and did not reappear on its original predicted path. It was deemed to have landed upon Shtai, remaining for a time before the later reconnaissance.

Those events, raising the concept of sentient life from some world circling Companion Star, had shaken the basic assumptions of Maghren thought. Less so, perhaps, than finding that Eamn held life-forms not dissimilar to those of Magh, though none on the outer moon had developed near to sentience. To learn, then, that another star's worlds harbored beings capable of thought, of building—this had been not so great a leap of belief.

"Not from Diell, no," the seeder responded. "The two incoming vectors, in fact, stand almost perpendicular."

"So it is yet another new thing." Munching on a podnut from farside, Irtuk nodded, then paused. Midday neared—and with it, on this Chormward side of Magh, the short dark. "Let us adjourn here until after midmeal." Again she addressed the young seeder. "I should like you to share it with me. Your co-speaker, also."

And perhaps, she thought, to share more than that.

A brief time later, leading the two across the enclave's central oval, Irtuk in her peripheral vision saw Jemra edging behind Chorm as the pale sky darkened. Underfoot lay scattered leatherleaves, long and narrow, fallen this morning from the slim trees gracing the open area. In another two days there would again be enough to gather, to be compressed and tanned into the utile sheeting that gave the tree its name.

As Irtuk noted the quick, sure movements of the two younger Maghrens, pleasurable anticipation stirred. Most propitious would be that the adaptive were in nonprogenitive stage. Or at least unseeded. To the best of Irtuk's knowledge she held no womb in receptive mode, but given the confusions of travel, she could not be certain. Of her six lifecradles, however, three were already in process. To quicken another would exceed the normally accepted limit.

Still, conceiving an adaptive or seeder unscheduled would constitute only minor deviance in any case—and in hers must figure an allowance for the one, a time back, that had issued unready. But not until next Chormcycle was she authorized to bear another of her own kind, longer lived by half than the other two. The proportion of bearers in Maghren society must always be kept in proper balance, and although her own bearing period had not a great many Chormyears left to it, no one kept truer vigilance, with regard to that balance, than did Irtuk.

So her enjoyments, at this time, might well be limited.

Sometimes, thought Sam Gowdy, patience does pay off. When the Habgate winkled him off Earth to take command of *Roamer*, the ship six months and an eighth of a light-year short of the Whitey system, slowing at one gee and down to half of c, prospects hadn't looked like much. Smack in the middle of Whitey's habitable zone rode Big Red, nearly Jupiter's size and even more massive. Such giants allow no stable orbits near their own, no place for a smaller world with H_20 in liquid form.

So Gowdy had braced for disappointment. The alternate goal lay nearly twenty light-years farther on. Someone else, a few cadres from now, might bring *Roamer* to a useful world and have the great luck of founding a new colony. Not Sam Gowdy, though.

But as *Roamer* entered its final week of decel, at two percent of c and a billion miles to go, the clutter of debris in Big Red's visual area revealed not one but three prospects: two good-sized moons, plus a scout at lead Trojan in Big Red's 1.35 A.U., 504-day orbit.

E-days, that was. Scout's own rotation ran to twenty-eight hours and some loose change.

It was all in Gowdy's report. One last time before sealing the envelope, he glanced through the pertinent sections.

> . . . both moons smaller than Earth, but not by much. Acey circles a bit over a quarter of a million miles out, in something like forty hours; we guess its gravs at point-seven-three gee. Deucy orbits at roughly a million and a quarter in sixteen and a half E-days, and pulls nearly point-eight-seven. Most likely the inner one's tide-locked to Big Red, but the other should rotate normally.

His figures were highly approximate; Ol' Man Mose had more exact data tabulated in Appendix I, for any who cared to search through that fat sheaf. But a quick scan . . .

> Then there's Scout, the Trojan world. It's bigger than either moon, maybe nine thousand miles across and about one-point-two gee.
>
> We're still too far out to detect signs of habitation, let alone technology—but somebody's nosing ships around Big Red's subsystem, blowing chemicals, that sort of thing. And locals are as good a bet as any.

He hadn't mentioned the sensings that looked mighty much like Traction Drive, proceeding more or less toward the major planet. First, because Mose wasn't sure. And second, the faint traces came from well outside Big Red's path, where nothing swam but gas giants and assorted minor clutter.

So until the info jelled, its reporting could wait. Gowdy sealed the envelope and reached to his intercom switch.

Two minutes earlier and the call would have ruined Skeeter Cole's whole morning. He was just breaking off a wrap-up kiss, rolling free of Alix Dorais, when the intercom beeped and a voice said, "Skeeter? Gowdy here."

With a final caress he ruffled her short red hair and reached for the switch. "Yes, captain." Due on watch in ten minutes, Skeeter hoped this wouldn't take long.

It didn't. "I'm in quarters. On your way to control, could you stop by and run a report to Earthgate for me?"

"Sure thing, sir."

So he and Alix still had time for a quick shower together.

* * *

Frowning, Sam Gowdy checked the time. Watch change in three minutes. Skeeter would need to hurry; Sydnie Lightner never turned a watch over until the entire relief group reported, and she didn't take kindly to being relieved late.

Not that she'd be in any rush to join him here at quarters. These days, she didn't seem to take kindly to much of anything.

The door chime broke his train of brooding; Skeeter was going to make it after all.

The exchange didn't take long. Gowdy settled back to study more of the ship's visual log, over forty light-years of travel recorded at a time dilation of ten to one. Viewing on high speed, since outGating he'd covered nearly three-fourths of it. And found very little of interest.

He wanted to finish by orbiting time, when ship's facilities must be reoriented for zero gee. Because he hadn't decided yet, just what to orbit.

It was time he did.

Behind the radiant field of its Traction Drives in decel, *Roamer* resembled a sharpened pencil stub, blunt end leading. Fifty meters wide, length one-twenty: seventy of cylinder, fifty of cone. In feet, call it one-sixty-five by four hundred, overall. But the designers all spoke metric.

No streamlining: at relativistic speeds, the interstellar gas wouldn't have noticed.

Three concentric cylinders made up *Roamer*. Of the twenty-meter innermost, the forward half including the sharpened tip comprised the Deployment Vehicle, the only part of *Roamer* that could ever land; the rear carried major cargo items. The intermediate tube measured forty meters across: water storage in the tapered forward section, amidships three concentric decks of working space, and at the rear the Traction Drives and major Gate-fed facilities: fuel tanks, life-support systems, and ship's supplies. The midtube's outer deck held control gear and the Habgates; the middle one provided drive mode quarters oriented to the one-gee axial thrust of accel and decel, plus storage for ship's supplies, the necessities of daily living. Racks for a variety of ancillary circuit equipment filled the inner deck.

Five meters of radius remained for the outer tube. The forward cone's outer rim provided ramps from the control deck to the transfer ring which gave access to the ship's rotating belt, crew quarters for zero gee. And behind the belt were stored the major structural components of a macroGate, the device that would permit ships to Gate directly to or from Earth.

Or if Whitey's worlds didn't prove out, the unassembled parts would be carried on to *Roamer*'s new destination.

The more Sam looked at the data, the more it seemed the Whitey system was doing his deciding for him. Moons and all, Big Red was nearing the end of its orbit's right-hand limb; Scout, on the other hand, was halfway back to its passage behind Whitey. Sam checked orbital velocities; depending on the positions of the moons when *Roamer* arrived, he'd be catching one moving six to thirty miles a second away from him. Compared to *Roamer*'s current pace, those figures were small stuff—but closer and slower, even a minor mismatch would cost time. Now if he caught Acey on its own right-hand limb, going away . . .

As he fed in the numbers he heard the door close. "Hard at work, I see," commented Sydnie Lightner. "Diligent, aren't we?" And then, flat-voiced, "In some matters, at least."

He didn't ask was anything wrong, let alone what; he'd heard enough versions of "If you have to ask . . ." Instead, "I think we'll orbit Acey. Or maybe go Trojan with it." *Your move.*

"You've actually made a decision? Perhaps we should mount a celebration; I could use one. Assuming you have champagne on ice." Her voice sharpened. "Have you?"

He turned to face her as she stood, head thrown back and one arm forming a graceful arc to the bookcase beside her. Slim, an inch shorter than his own five-ten, she had a model's poise and the face to match. Now, with the longish dark blond hair skinned back into a coil, her cheekbones and jawline made a sculptor's dream. The slight showing of teeth could almost be a smile—but the full lips lay absolutely straight, and the lids of her long hazel eyes half-closed. *Panther mode.*

Against his will he wanted her. "If you'd like . . ." But he hadn't thought of it by himself, hadn't foreseen her wishes. He was so sure of her answer that at first he didn't hear it; by the time he did, the bathroom door had closed behind her.

"Johnnie will have some. Maybe enough for all night."

Gowdy shook his head; if there were any way out of this kind of trap, he'd purely like to know it. Trying without much luck to ignore his frustration, again he ran the numbers for his orbiting options. Yes, Acey was the key.

He moved to call control, then stopped. His conclusions could be explained perfectly well over the intercom, but just for now he needed not to be here. He punched for a readout, tore off the hard copy, and moved to the door.

Stacked into an annulus three meters wide and ninety-four in median circumference, formed of pullout bulkheads and accessed by fold-down staircases, drive mode quarters were definitely the low-rent version. In the stairwell he shared with the digs of his exec Carlene Doyle and Habgate specialist Ellis Vardigan, Gowdy climbed to a level with access to the next outer tube. The nearest hatchway opened into control.

All hands present and accounted for. Mosu Tuiasso in charge as pilot/navigator, the big Samoan overflowing any standard chair. Skeeter Cole at the sensor console, and Johnnie Rio's pairmate Inga Kuikken checking drive status monitors. All as should be. Gowdy held out his readout sheets. "Look through these, Mose? I want to match vee with Acey. Possibly orbit. Our approach was set with decel to spare. How soon should we start cutting it, and by how much?"

Running fingers through his bushy, gray-shot hair, Tuiasso frowned—indicating, Sam knew, that the man was thinking it over. "How about two percent for six hours? Then we'll check."

"Yes." Gowdy nodded. "We don't want to push more than one gee. Or have to do turnover again, to add speed and catch up."

"Gotcha."

With the system ahead displayed on forward screen, the four talked, chatting easily. Time for midwatch snack caught Gowdy by surprise; he hadn't thought to stay this long.

He knew his personal problems needed attention. Still, back

in quarters he felt relieved to hear Sydnie rummaging around the bedroom, not yet gone but not out here in his face, either.

When it came to women, Samuel Hall Gowdy wasn't exactly a novice. Fresh out of college at the peak of the Liij Environ Crisis, he entered space training and was commissioned as a copilot in the Environ supply relief effort. During training he'd caught the fancy of Alain Harter, deskbound in Operations and four years his senior. Her brunette charm and obvious admiration bowled Sam over; after his first trip in the supply ship *Mako* to the Environ and back, they were married.

What there was of the marriage had been quite pleasant, producing one daughter and one son. The catch was the Environ's growing distance and velocity out of the solar system; by an ever-increasing factor, the trips lengthened. He simply wasn't home enough to maintain continuity; following the *Tarpon* incident he returned to find an empty apartment and divorce papers.

Poised on the edge between a medal and a court-martial, he had to leave family matters on hold. Sam got the medal; Alain got the divorce and soon remarried. She said the romance hadn't begun until the decree was final; knowing Alain, he believed her.

Enrolling in the stringent *Starfinder* training program, Sam wrote the marriage off and wished her well; for his own reasons he put his entire bonus from the *Tarpon* escapade into the kids' trust fund. He might never see them again, but they'd have reason not to forget him completely. So then he concentrated on what he hoped would be a new career.

Waiting for a starship berth was a long haul. He enjoyed several promising romantic liaisons but nothing permanent; near as he could tell, no hearts were broken on either side.

He made *Starfinder*'s cadre 3-A as junior watch officer and pilot/navigator; by then, the sensation of Irina Tetzl's takeover bid had faded to scuttlebutt. Gowdy's shipwife Mona Campbell was another brunette, taller than Alain and his same age. In their ship's year they became good friends and friendly lovers, well suited to each other. But back on Earth—well, only a third of shipside pairings survived homecoming; theirs didn't.

Very little, in fact, endured well for Sam Gowdy. His Environ trips hadn't racked up enough t/t_0 differential to cause problems, but *Starfinder*—plus two Gatings—aged him only one year to Earth's fourteen; family and friends couldn't seem to cope. Polite enough, mostly, but not really connecting; he felt like some kind of impostor, and gradually withdrew from contact.

Mona snagged a promotion and shipped on an *Arrow*-class ship macroGating to Tetzl's Planet (and how had Old Iron Tits recouped her status enough to merit a discovery berth?). Gowdy had a fling at Oort Cloud mining, then a spell of sheepdogging influng comets, nudging trajectories to fit intended orbits. Jobs like that. When he got the offer to command *Roamer*'s final leg to destination, he'd almost forgotten putting in his bid.

For a time he'd been mostly away from women. But he hadn't forgotten the lessons they'd taught him. Except that with Sydnie Lightner, most of what he knew didn't seem to apply.

Like all starship crews, *Roamer*'s was nominally joined in group marriage, not to encourage promiscuity but to allow for the seemingly inevitable pairing changes without legal clutter. Some crews shuffled more than others: 4-B, relieved by Gowdy's group, had been quite volatile; 5-A, his cadre's present complement, had made few changes, usually temporary. But the eight members of Gowdy's 5-B, once paired, proved to be remarkably stable.

Not that he'd laid on any strictures to that effect. Until now. When Sydnie came out wearing a light robe, her hair turbaned in a towel, he said, "Do you actually plan on nighting with Johnnie Rio?"

Her gaze slanted. "And why would you need to know?"

"So I can have your things moved there. Or shall I assign you separate quarters?" Only until 6-A arrived could that order hold; its twelve members would fill all remaining crew space. But if you weren't one jump ahead of Sydnie, you'd never catch up.

"What do you mean?" And: why, she was only—this was well within their shared agreements—he had the same right—it wasn't as if—and who did he think he was, anyway?

"The captain. Whose shipwife doesn't sleep around."

Her eyes flared open. "Or?"

"Or she's not, any longer."

"Oh, come off it, Samuel. Captain Sebring didn't . . ."

True. Sebring's pairmate Claudine Whatever-her-name-was had gone the rounds, with enthusiasm, of both 4-B and 5-A, and during cadre overlap had made a good run at 5-B. Mose the third officer, chief instrument tech Skeeter Cole, Owen Tanacross the galley chief, even Sam himself: none of the four cared to risk their relatively new pairings for a quick flyer. But Claudine took her best shots—and to Gowdy's knowledge, Sebring made no attempt to stop any of it.

Nonetheless, "Captain Gowdy does."

In silence she dressed and groomed herself. At the door she paused and looked at him, then gripped the latch decisively. He could read her face as she remembered it wouldn't slam, anyway.

Frustrated, Sam tried to think matters through. Back on Earth, as 5-B settled into pairings, Sydnie Lightner had been a woman to dream of. Not only the beauty of her, nor even her almost-frightening capacity for passion: from the start she'd seemed to sense all Gowdy's needs and feelings, and to appreciate his efforts to meet and match her talent.

He'd never been able to figure what drew her to him in the first place. At 145 he was skinny for five-ten, and certainly no beauty king. Though not exactly Herkimer Gooch, either. Well, add it up. Rebellious sandy hair, freckles, mouth widish for his lean face, eyes Alain had called hazel but in some lights shone green. Whatever, apparently the package appealed to Sydnie; all through those first months he couldn't do a thing wrong, and it felt great.

Now, though. Try as he would, he could do nothing *right.* As all too often lately, he found himself second-guessing his own actions. How had he screwed up?

The hell of it was, he had no real idea. And of what to do about it, even less.

Except—now that he thought back, past the glow he'd lived in at the time, he did know. The sharp edges, that now made life with Sydnie a series of unexpected painful jolts, first surfaced the day they outGated aboard ship and he took command.

When he showed her his duty roster she'd pointed to her name, listed as junior watch officer. "Number four? But . . ."

The choice was not discretionary. 5-A's Carlene Doyle held seniority, then Johnnie Rio. Though Mosu Tuiasso of Sam's own group had good claim to outrank both. But reassured by "Ol' Man Mose" that the big Samoan didn't much care either way, Gowdy had decided to avoid the appearance of cadre chauvinism.

On the face of it, Sydnie was plainly the least qualified of the four. By experience, that was; on performance he'd back her know-how against just about anyone's. Ship maneuvering, sensor interpretation, navigation—and of course, decisiveness. She had it all, and he told her so.

"But then why . . . ?"

"Playing favorites, it'd look like." And would be. But he didn't want to say that. Try a carrot: "Six months, Syd. When 6-A relieves our other cadre, I can bump you up."

"To . . ."

"Third." At her look, he said, "The new exec takes first; that's S.O.P. And no way in hell can you top Mose. Few could."

She didn't pretend to like it. She dropped the subject, but it left a mark. Increasingly her clear disappointment showed; whatever Gowdy said or did, somehow he missed the boat, failed to understand, lacked sensitivity, betrayed her expectations, belied the promise she'd seen in him earlier. Sam the fuckup . . .

Well, either they'd get straightened out or they wouldn't.

Idly he looked at his roster and considered the changes to come. With 5-A he'd lose officers Doyle and Rio, his Gatemeister Ellis Vardigan, drive tech Inga Kuikken and Meiko Omata on instruments, plus Shelby Kane the all-purpose handyman and galley backup. Well, replacements at two to one would surely fill every job. Setting the list aside, he tackled the rest of the sensor log. Still finding nothing much that merited reporting . . .

A half hour later the intercom sounded. "Gowdy here."

"Sam!" Sydnie's voice. "Come on over. Johnnie says he's

uncomfortable, outnumbered by all us women.''

So he went up one staircase and down another, to the rooms Rio shared with Kuikken. Johnnie wasn't all that swamped: just Sydnie and quiet Meiko and freckled, brindle-haired Molly Abele.

Sydnie Lightner's real message came clear enough; having thought it over, she wasn't calling the captain's raise. Yet.

A time later, both rosy with champagne but tracking fine, they returned to quarters. It was some while since they'd made love without the rough edges of discord—but now they did, and the afterglow lasted until sleep.

His last thought was, *if only things could stay this way!*

For a time they did, superficially at least. Whatever else, his pronouncement of criteria for sharing captain's digs put a lid on her stretching of the acceptable behavior envelope.

Gowdy didn't push it. As long as she was willing to play nice, so was he. For domestic peace and enjoyment, the last week before hitting orbit was the best he'd had aboard *Roamer*.

Slowing, the ship swung starboard of Whitey in pursuit of Big Red, then edged a bit farther out. As Acey crossed the face of its primary, *Roamer* eased to match orbits. But it didn't take a genius to see that with Acey so close to Big Red, Gowdy would need practically an air-hugging orbit for any semblance of stability. And maybe not even that would suffice.

So, fiddling decel up and down, he coasted ahead of the inner moon and brought his ship to ''rest'' at its leading Trojan position, close enough to show only minor libration. Of course he'd need to make corrections every time Deucy came by. . . .

Rising from the console, Sam found he'd lost the feel of movement in zero gee. And so, it seemed, had others. At least no one looked like getting spacesick.

He turned to Carlene Doyle. ''Your watch. When you have time, point us north.'' From the ecliptic, that was. ''Put the main scanners on Acey, hi-mag, and start 'em mapping. If we're quick we can shoot the whole forward hemisphere in full day, on this pass.'' Assignments made, Sam left control.

Reacclimating to Velcro soles, he felt pleased; the operation was on track.

Meanwhile he had his own work cut out. Get the rotating belt brought up to speed and start people moving onto it. And the big chore of repositioning control functions, Habgates and such, to zero-gee operation. In control the deck would now become the rear bulkhead, as seating and equipment underwent a right-angle transposition and hullward became "down."

He hoped the new cadre wouldn't start arriving until most of that work was done. Either way, he needed some sleep first.

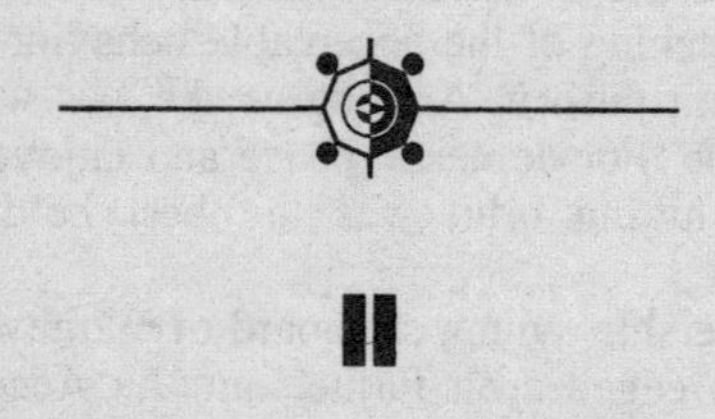

II

With the reinforcement ship from Yain now within days of arrival, soon to ride alongside *Tayr*, the first-come vessel in Yamar's sky, T'phee works to consolidate es new Stewardship of the colony. So it were blessing, not bane, that T'phee's genitive matrix has proved unready, that er has not, at this growthseason's blooming of the *cruance*, realized es expected get. The burden of new life ripening at one's chest, lying between and against the forethighs, gradually impedes movement and agility. Particularly when the developing neck-trunk frees, so that the get can learn, feed independently, and grow to survive separation. An administer must be active and so impress others; even this much of added burden could badly hamper es effectiveness.

Not that any seek to obstruct T'phee's assumption of es new position, merely that there is much more to its workings than er had realized. Even after two of Yamar's long years as apprentice to Cejha, who had served as Steward since their ship left Yain and who still holds ready for T'phee to consult at need.

Long go the days here, also; one of Yamar's to nearly two of Yain's. Nearly as disproportionate are the respective years, with two of Yamar's exceeding three of the home planet's.

Now entering into middle life, T'phee has no personal recall of that world. Less than a homeyear before the launch of Yain's first interstellar venture did er begin life; es parent Tadsh had carried en aboard still unshed, even es necktrunk's organs yet uncovered.

Half a lifetime, that voyage consumed—though not of those who rode the ship. For them time slowed, almost to stopping, its pace hobbled by pushforce generators set to produce such effect.

So while the greater force units took the ship *Tayr* to a speed one-tenth that of stellar radiation, before shutting down until voyage end brought need for reverse thrust, similar though lesser machines maintained the lowest feasible rate of entropy in all living areas.

Once *Tayr* reached proper cruising state, designated crew members needed only to make periodic checks of the control area. Between the two entropic habitats, therefore, timelocks acted. Analogous to airlocks, these—although there within the ship, neither environment required artificial aidings.

Because excursions into normal time were both brief and infrequent, crew members performing regular watch duties aged only slightly more, overall, than those who did not. When, on decision of Steward Cejha, the ship came to orbit about Yamar, T'phee had aged only a homeyear aboard ship. While Tadsh the navigationalist, es own carrying parent, by dint of watch duties performed after T'phee was shed, experienced half another.

Hard to conceive that Yainstar's reddish light reaches Yamar only after five homeyears. And *Tayr*'s passage endured ten times that. . . .

The choice of Yamar as haven world, Cejha insists, had been no easy one. First considered was the Parent and its two Get, the group ever following Yamar's path around this brighter star, always a sixth of orbit behind. Accreted from the same primordial mix, those bodies are equally rich in the minerals needed to replenish *Tayr*'s fuel reservoirs. For a time that service kept the ship's three lander-carriers busy indeed. Now, but for bringing *Tayr* supplies and duty reliefs, they are used largely in traffic across the distances of Yamar itself.

In any case, on Get and Yamar alike the star's whitish glare, harsh to Yainan eyes, would be the same. Well in advance, darker-tinted eyeshields had been prepared, and for windows here on Yamar, transparent sheetings of similar properties. As Cejha reminds es students, other factors governed the choice.

"The Parent's two life-bearing Get," er admits, "exert worldpulls less than that of Yain." While the pull of Yamar is over a fifth greater. But its stronger, quicker-burning atmosphere maintains Yainan strength and energy at near normal. Or so Cejha affirms; again, T'phee has no comparative experience.

"Yet it was seen," the elder continues, "that both those worlds are peopled, the inner more so, but both to notable degree. Too much so, perhaps, to willingly offer haven. Hostile welcome could not be risked." And *Tayr*'s journeying to the Parent group for closer scrutiny had been no more illuminating.

Cejha's neckskin ripples—in self-deprecation, T'phee assumes, rather than disclaimer. "We could not know that some from the outer Get had come here also; even between the two, so near together, we saw no evidence of transport. And on this world no constructed works showed from afar. Nor even at orbit."

Nonetheless the Emmans are here, and with some of their world's biota. Only in village strengths, along a temperate shore of Yamar's second largest land mass and living by the most primitive of agriculture and husbandry. Showing no hostility, posing no threat; among the Yain they arouse only the urges to learn and to aid.

Although auditory ranges of the two species overlap well, language at first comes difficult. But with contact over time, each finds understanding of the other's speech. And given the chance, the get of either kind develop bilingually.

Odd-seeming, this similarity of minds. For except that each can utilize some foodstuffs native to the other's world and to this one, the two species show little commonality.

As: Emmans are of three types; to perpetuate the species all three are required. Whereas, regarding reproduction, no Yainan differs from any other. After a season of melding genitive secretions with a variety of donor-receptors, thoracic matrices conjoining in bliss of warmth and moistness, the bloomdust of *cruance* triggers zygote coalescence in every Yainan of fully ripened matrix, and the get develop. Normally, once viability and divestment have proceeded, the parental matrix regrows to ripeness within two seasons—three at most. But here on Yamar neither regrowth nor *cruance* blossoming are so predictable.

The Emmans, though. Taller by half again than Yainans, all are bipedal with grasping forelimbs. Strange-seeming to T'phee with es four short, sturdy legs, muscular neck-trunk normally reaching high above the thoracic braincase but fully retracting in rest or sleep, and quartet of manipulars immediately below the sensory cluster and vital orifices at the necktrunk's tip. Nor are Emmans encloaked with dense multibranching fur; except for a narrow dorsal mane the bipeds display integument of joined flexible platelets, softly colored in patterns T'phee finds pleasant to see and consider.

Emman seeders and adaptives are slimly built; but for the interrupted stripe of fur above each seeder's feeding orifice, they appear much alike. Bearers, though, each equipped with six incubative chambers coming to readiness in turn, grow to be much sturdier, more bulky. And their "heads"—foreshortened sensory clusters which actually house the brain!—project wider and less sharply curved than those of the two slighter forms.

Incredibly to Yainan prejudicion, each type may genitally conjoin with any other. As instance, seeder conjugation with a gamete-receptive bearer yields always a seeder as get.

Congress between seeder and adaptive results only in a more complex gamete. Vented while yet viant into a receptive bearer, by the adaptive's genitor in evertive mode, the zygote will become a bearer. But the normal gamete of an unseeded adaptive, likewise genitally transferred, brings forth another adaptive.

"It is the bearers," T'phee's teacher has explained, "who traditionally controlled the matings, to regulate proportion of each type get. But long ago, in the colony on the outer Get, the lesser genders rebelled, enslaving the bearers. The schism, these Emmans here maintain, caused the unprecedented war that ended their peoples' capability of interworld travel."

"And here on Yamar, which types hold precedence?" asks a fellow-student.

The teacher's neckskin ripples. "None. Or perhaps all. Unable to maintain skills of knowledge, scrabbling for bare survival, these remnants give little thought to relative dominance. Thus achieving a quite amicable society."

"As have we," T'phee comments. "But we did not need a war to do so."

"We should not assume superiority. Perhaps our genomic character is not burdened by such provocations."

The Yainan burden lies outside the species; its name is extinction, its executor the Comet Swarm. Twice in known times, swinging in past Yain's orbit to dare the fringes of its parent star, the Swarm has pelted that world and destroyed much. Twice the race has been crushed near to barbarism, yet somehow it endured, and eventually rebuilt.

Within a life-span comes the next such scourging. And rather than a grazing passage as during the earlier ordeals, Yain will meet the Swarm at dead center. No one could hold serious hope for species survival. So when Yainan research developed forcedrive, Yainan will and effort built and launched starships. Here to Yamar is *Tayr*, the first. Two later ships, at stars near enough to reach, found no sanctuary for Yainan life without need of artificial environment. Both are in return to Yain, for what service they may render there.

One more, *L'lit*, lay in reserve, to join and reinforce the first to find haven. On reaching Yamar, Cejha deployed powerful surface-based signal facilities and messaged es discovery to the homeworld; in time came word of that ship's bringing more Yainans to es support. And of the Tricouncil's directive toward building greater vessels—greater, and of need, slower—to ferry the largest possible number to the new haven Cejha has found.

But what a pitifully small fraction that will be!

Faced with doom's onset, Yainans have curtailed breeding, reducing their number to the minimum required for a workable society and viable gene pool.

Even so: for each who can be rescued, a multitude remain to die. Not for a single day can T'phee forget the fact.

Sitting with the eleven others of cadre 6-A waiting for Habegger transmission to starship *Roamer*, Kayo Marlin watched the Gate tech take his own sweet time with the paperwork. She'd Gated before, to Tetzl's Planet where she'd spent three years cataloging plant and animal life of much the same mental capacity. Where she and Larry Corcoran began a marriage that went fine until they came back to Earth, then sank like a rock.

Three years later her ID read Age 28, Ht 5-7, Wt 130 (plus a few since the cadre's good-bye feast). Eyes Gr for gray; she had no idea what stood for green. Hair Bl: hers shone pale, tended to curl, and currently lay trimmed fairly close, helmet fashion. Mouth stubborn, but the card didn't say that. Nor how her colorings derived from a Nordic father and half-Tlingit mother; Mendel's dice must land on edge sometimes.

In the eye blink while a Habegger Gate's flare of color deposited you at the far end, the rest of the universe rolled up roughly two years. Not much use for the short haul; where Gates came in handy was between star systems. Or on starships, as in crew rotation and provision of supplies.

Kayo's first Gating had been a whizzer. Not the mere interior of a Gate alcove going iridescently translucent, but all ambient space around the ship she rode, within an eight-hundred-foot macroGate ring. Her return, back here to the Glen Springs crewing center, had been considerably less spectacular.

So as to the jump, now, she knew what to expect. At the far end, maybe not. For one thing, no one knew whether there'd be any more use there than at Tetzl's for her specialty, the highly speculative field of algorithm-assisted xenolinguistics.

For another, she'd barely heeded the group's tentative pairing maneuvers. Now she and Jethro Blaine and Simone Leopold and Dan Quillan were the only ones not into the doublesnugglies. Come to that, drive chief Blaine and executive officer Leopold were showing signs. Which left Kayo and Quillan looking at each other—and not comfortably.

Danny, the number two Deployment Vehicle jockey, was

a nice enough kid, a few years the younger but not enough to matter. And considerate: right now he was off finding Kayo a sandwich, to tide her over the unforeseeable length of this delay.

At twenty-three or so he wouldn't be much in bed. But to start with, neither had Larry. Maybe she should have given Dan a try, see how it went. It wasn't as if she considered herself a sacred vessel or something.

Emotional symbiosis was the tough part. Second quarter at university, the city a little scary after childhood in Ketchikan, Alaska, she'd somehow let Hec Palmer talk her into moving in with him. She was finally emerging from a bad case of the adolescent chubbies; just being chosen carried a lot of clout.

It wasn't all bad, but one quarter sufficed. Her ideas were awfully cute, but of course Hec knew better. And he took such pride in terminating her virginity so pleasurably, she never had the heart to tell him of Charlie Pechuk from Metlakatla, back in the safely semipubertal winter of seventh grade. Oh well . . .

And her marriage, fine on Tetzl's but not back home, still hurt. No, Kayo Marlin was really in no hurry for a shipspouse.

Refusal could make things awkward. Bunking twenty, *Roamer* usually carried two cadres of six each. But 5-B, Gating away nearly two hundred days earlier to join *Roamer* in mid-decel, numbered eight; 6-A's dozen would fill the paired quarters.

The hell with it; need be, she could doss down in the rec lounge. If off-duty socializing got too noisy, that's what earplugs were for. If she did indeed turn him down . . .

Anyway, here came Dan with the sandwich, his cheeks and ears pinkening from the Gate tech's glare. Now the tech started down his list: alphabetical rather than by rank, so instead of Simone Leopold the exec, Jethro Blaine stepped first to the Gate recess.

The operation moved right along, colors blooming to hide the vanishment of each in turn. Seventh up, Kayo barely finished her snack as the tech announced, "Marlin, Katharine Olivia."

Grasping her carry-on, Kayo stood. Time to go.

* * *

From Tetzl's, Kayo had Gated home by way of *Starfinder*. Now, as iridescence died in *Roamer*'s Earthtush, she found the sister vessel's look familiar. As was zero gee. So the ship had come to orbit, and should be mostly reconfigured from drive mode.

Moving gingerly on Velcro soles, Kayo shook hands with welcomers and tried to register names. The lean man with sandy hair and faded, vestigial freckles was Gowdy, the captain; the rest she'd have to nail down later.

A large Asian man took her arm. "Mosu Tuiasso," he said. "Ol' Man Mose. Would you like to see your quarters?" Indeed she would. In case he'd missed it, she repeated her own name.

They walked to the ship's forward circumferential passage and down a ramp to its outmost level. At a large pair of sliding doors, Tuiasso's touch of a green button revealed a transfer car about thirteen feet high and deep, twice as wide, and sharing the curvature of the ship's outer cylinder.

Mosu punched closure; Kayo felt both sidewise acceleration and centrifugal pull. As the former died away, the latter built; the cage locked to the ship's rotating segment, and she recognized its nominal one-third-gee pressure.

At the cage's rear another door opened, showing corridors painted in shades of green rather than the neutral tones of the working areas. "This way." Ahead of her, he left the cage.

One thing about shipside life, she'd forgotten. Stepping out to walk along the corridor, Coriolis force set her feet not quite where she intended. After a moment, though, she caught up.

They passed an open door. "Our rec lounge." Inside she saw bright colors, comfortable furniture, a good-sized holovid, snack counter with coffeemaker, and minibar. From a table a man and woman waved hello, then resumed conversation.

Down the hallway Tuiasso stopped just short of the rear transverse passage. "Number five. Your luggage should be inside by now." She thanked him; handing her a key, he nodded and left.

As the door's opening brought up the basic room lights, Kayo looked around. Not bad: living area separated by a counter and hanging cabinets from the kitchen and dining alcove behind, and alongside them a short hallway to bedroom and bath. The decor ran to soft light colors, nothing that would get on her nerves.

And plenty of room. Sheer luxury, for shipside. Even with her luggage spread around the floor, she had room to walk past and look around more thoroughly.

Except . . . the luggage wasn't all hers. And the big carryall directly in her path bore the tag "Daniel B. Quillan."

I might have known.

First things first. Kayo located the makings for coffee and set a pot going. Her larger travel case disgorged a bottle; finding a glass and ice, she stepped past Quillan's duffel to the cushioned lightwood sofa, and sat.

Her mind kept avoiding the problem: the sofa would be more convenient over *there*—but that was a tool chest job; on the belt as well as in zero-gee spaces, all furniture sat firmly secured.

Bourbon in small doses was good for thinking; she sipped. By default, all quarters full and no one saying anything to the contrary, she was moved in with Dan Quillan. So: did she accept the situation? Or, if she had to, kick up a row?

Pretty hard on young Dan, that would be, and none of this his fault, really. All right; what *were* her objections?

Nothing about "love"; shipside pairings could include it or not, and nobody else's business. So what else? Physically he seemed nothing special, but okay. Personality pleasant enough, no major irritating traits. A good set of brains, with humor: tell a joke, usually he got the point.

Then what? Not the five years of physical age difference. But how about the four others, the two Gatelags? The body didn't age, but folklore had it that somewhere deep down, the mind knew. Nine years, not five. Still, that shouldn't be too much.

Another sip, another insight. Their childhoods, hers and Dan's, were out of step: trends, attitudes, in the schools, the media, inevitably the home also. Building different mind-sets.

Young Kayo had acculturated on such acerb humor as the holotoon Barkinghams: doggie daddy with three puppies, piggy mama with three little shoats. Crafty and conniving, the pups tormented their naive stepsiblings—and generally managed to outsmart themselves. Innocence prevailed, usually, but with a liberal dose of tongue in cheek. Kayo rooted for the pups.

She still had an old holocap. But back at Glen Springs when she'd played it for Danny, he hadn't liked it. Not a bit.

"Too quarrelsome," he said. "Too much stress. Silly kid stuff, but still it makes me uncomfortable. Now what *I* used to like . . ." Before he said it, she guessed—and groaned inside. She'd been twelve when Sloopy the Seagoing Sloth premiered in all his syrupy blandness. Even the *sharks* were cuddly. . . .

The toons were merely a token. What it came down to: she enjoyed hard edges on things sometimes, and he didn't.

Still and all, what was she going to tell him?

Kayo preferred the left side of the bed; being here first, she took it. In the closet and drawer space alongside, she soon had her things unpacked and stowed, empty bags and all.

Coffee came ready; she broke an irradiated cream cap into her first cup and sat again. Tasting, she nodded in approval.

Her bourbon glass still held half an inch; the tastes went well together. Soothed, Kayo felt ready to tackle her situation.

The door opened. *Well, ready as I'll ever be.* "Hello, Dan." And why did he always have to blush?

He went to his largest travel bag. "I guess you're already settled in. I'll get my stuff out of the way now." As he laid clothing into drawers, his talk kept speeding up. ". . . lots of room here, we'll be really comfortable, don't you think? I—"

"Dan? Shut up a minute."

Gaping, he stood, shirts dangling from his grip. "What . . . ?"

Brows drawn down, Kayo made her tone severe. "Quit blathering, will you? And say what's really on your mind."

His hands clenched, doing the smallclothes no good. "All right then, are we pairing here or aren't we?"

Not very romantic, but to the point. "Depends on what you mean." He looked blank; she gestured. "We can share quarters. Bed and all. Sex when we both want to. Be friends as much as comes naturally." *Sloopy the Seagoing Sloth.* "Does that suit?"

"Well sure. I mean, what else . . . I don't expect you to

love me right away; that takes time. But we'll be . . ."

". . . apart more than together. You're on the DV and my major job is downside. But more important—it's all temporary, until one of us runs out of contract and goes home. Or we both do—but you know the stats on shipside pairings, after. So don't get yourself invested in it, is all I'm saying."

Too rough; she could see him folding inside. "Look, Dan. My whole life, I've been with only two men." *And one boy.* "Both times I went for keeps, but it lasted just the short haul. I'm not climbing back on that hayride. Not here."

It helped; he was looking better. "I've never had anybody at all." Again he reddened. "Not long enough to really count. There was a girl at summer school, an honors add-on after we graduated—but we only got together the last month, and then . . ."

Turning away, he stuffed the abused cloth into a drawer. Then, facing her again, "There were a couple of others; same song, different choruses. But I've never had the chance before, to live with anybody this way."

Oh for God's sake. She finished her coffee, saw she'd drained the little shot glass without noticing. She stood. "You think the shower might be a good place to start?"

She thought he was going to turn red again, but he didn't.

At last the Overgrouping recognized Nsil's right to speak. Intent on making address to these who spoke for all Eamn, the seeder had waited long. As the first of Eamnet decisioners to correlate sightings of the new sky intruder, to chart its path and determine its destination, he had given much thought to what should be said here.

Now he rose. "No longer can we doubt; the strange ship has chosen to side with Magh, against us. Where it hails from, how the pact was made, none of this matters. It has come and it is there, hovering near Magh. We . . ."

Tral spoke—an adaptive much given to quibbling for little cause. "What of the earlier visitor?"

Nsil shook his head. Unlike many of his colleagues he had quickly come to terms with the evident fact that thinking life could arise elsewhere than Magh. "The ship from Diell the Companion, which made survey of Magh and Eamn alike, has not stirred since returning to circle Shtai the Forerunner.

Its doings are another matter, not for this assembly's concern."

Not unusually in Eamnet Overgroupings, dissent arose. Nsil waited; only when consensus began to shapen did he make sign to speak again. "I agree; reconnaissance of Magh must ensue. But—not only from its sky. For the first time since the Great Dying, Eamnets must set presence on the world that tried to destroy us."

The means were clear enough; their sufficiency was yet to be proved. "Our first small skyship remains intact and functional. As does the second and larger, though in this venture I see no part for it. But the new, still greater one, recently completed and now outfitting to set forth . . ."

Nsil spread the digits of his forelimbs, then cupped them together. "If it were to carry the smallest near to Magh, that one could descend and land, then later rise to be retrieved and returned here." He paused to allow a swelling murmur to pass. "From that landing a force would deploy, to search out and bring back what evidence can be gathered of our enemies' planning and intent. Along with samples of their current weaponry."

Against a tide of comment mixed with protest Nsil continued. "This is a thing we can do, which at this time the Maghrens cannot. If we wait, their new allies may redress the balance. We must not allow the opportunity to fade unused."

"There is risk," said Tral, recalcitrant as always. "Safer to remain offworld and let fall explosives, pyrogens, airborne poisons. In that way—"

"No!" Impatient, Nsil cut short the adaptive's protest. "As yet Magh has made no attack. If we strike, inflict death and harm, assuredly we provoke retaliation. I say we scout and learn. Then shall we know whether attack is merited."

Consensus, though slim, resolved in Nsil's favor.

Back to his home nesting, Nsil fretted. Too long fixated on this day's purpose, he cast about for means of release. At feeding, with his five fellow seeders and six concomitant adaptives, he felt impatience—their narrow focus and predictable responses reminded him of all too many recent Overgrouping sessions: sheer surmise aimed toward no clear endpoint.

His aftertreat unfinished, he rose; without leave-taking he strode away, through curtained passageways and along bush-lined paths to his holding's confinement dome. On the low-growing splaybushes, olive-tinted bulbs swelled and darkened toward brown ripeness; soon they would be prime for picking, for the enjoyment of the potent gases inside.

Reaching the dome's doorpost he rapped for entry; from inside came answer. "You have welcome."

He entered, almost immediately beginning to relax in appreciation of the rich scents and handsome wall drapings. The bearer Scayna, nominal servant and factual center of Nsil's householding, lounged slanting by her soakpool in impressive bulk. Beside her lay two pet smofs, small animals native to Eamn itself. Scayna nodded; her broad mouth eased to show tonguetip where lower teeth slanted apart. "So your task at the Overgrouping has completed. Is it well?"

For comfort, he edged one pet away and moved to lie against her; unfazed, it snugged to him instead. "You may judge."

When he was done relating what had occurred, he waited, again tensing, for her commendation. Scayna gnawed a fingerhorn, then said, "It was my kind, I am told, who began the first great slayings. Will it be your part, now, to order the next?"

"I seek only to protect us all!"

"Yes. Well. Let us hope you succeed."

Stung and still dissatisfied, Nsil asked, "Are you womb-ready?" Three of her six, he knew, stood in process, engrowing one seeder and two adaptives. The others, though . . .

"I am. But another seeder to the householding . . . ?"

"No. I had hoped you were not. Scayna, I will go now."

Tirys, the adaptive who shared his chamber, lacked all interest in the issues that made up Nsil's public life. But in matters such as concerned him now, Tirys was ever a joy.

Nsil walked faster.

Once Sydnie got the hang of it, holding on in unfamiliar ways to maintain contact, sex in zero gee was something she wished she could have tried a long time ago. Johnnie Rio was ringing bells she hadn't felt lately.

But she couldn't have, not with Sam making like a dunghill

rooster. Until now, Johnnie leaving in a few hours so no chance she'd be tempted to keep the affair going and maybe get caught. There wouldn't even be time for her and Rio to give themselves away, looking at each other wrong or saying anything stupid, maybe getting herself dumped out of captain's digs.

She'd risked worse, but not of late—different times, different ways. It wasn't her life on the line now, only her lifestyle. But that was plenty. This better be worth it . . .

So Sydnie Lightner kept her moves slow and slowed Johnnie also. This was their third go-round, inship in one of the few drive mode quarters units not yet dismantled, eight hours of safe privacy with Sam on watch. Sydnie wanted to make it last.

Too soon they'd all be seeing Johnnie and Inga off at Earthmouth, along with the rest of 5-A. And at the farewell party, if she or Rio did make a slip, everyone would be too wound up to notice.

She'd kiss him on the *cheek*, f'Chris'sakes. And let's see Sam Gowdy try to make something of it. . . .

III

Eamn had seen many Chormyears since Scayna, at bearer maturity, was posted from the householding of her birth to this one, then led by the adaptive Fsar. Not sufficient, though, for her to forget the pain of loss, nor her youthful anxiety.

Now Ilrin, Scayna's oldest bearer-child still in residence, neared completion of her tenth Chormyear and soon must go. And Ilrin's dread was plain to see.

Seeders and adaptives, Scayna supposed, felt much the same when at full growth, which they reached even earlier, they too were subject to abrupt transfer. Yet those of her bearing she sent off routinely, with the best of wishes but no qualms.

Young bearers, though, were different—if only because they went to virtual isolation from their own kind. Although in recent years bearer visitation had become permitted, the strictures of the great rebellion were slow to ease.

And now came Ilrin's time. In these matters Nsil, like Fsar before him, showed consideration. Scayna's bearer-children were placed in establishments whose bearers, failing in fertility, yet remained to guide and comfort their successors. Ilrin was now pledged to the seeder Arnt; both he and the aging bearer of his householding were long known to Scayna, and trusted.

Still, Scayna sought to give Ilrin help and reassurance. Now in the sanctuary of her confinement dome, long since become the epicenter of Nsil's domain, she counseled. "Twice in any Chormyear, Ilrin, I may visit you; Nsil has so specified. Or on one of those occasions you may come here instead; the choice would be yours."

"Yet we are slaves," the younger bearer said, flat-voiced. "Or at best," tweaking one little smof's pinkish brown topknot as the other nuzzled for attention, "pets like these."

Had smofs attained cognition, the analogy might have held. Minor in Eamn's ecology, they constituted this world's nearest approach to sentience. Quadripedal yet capable of standing and moving erect, they could recognize and solve such things as latches. But while each forelimb's forward digits seemed capable as an Eamnet's, the two opposables, fused together into one stubby mass, gave only limited potential for grasp.

The little animals did suggest miniature Eamnets—and thus, Maghrens as well. But heads and bodies were rounded, limbs shorter in proportion, and in lieu of dorsal manes grew only fluffed topknots and plumed tails. Psychologically, perhaps, they served as surrogates for lately borne Eamnet young—though certainly less troublesome and more ingratiating!

Reaching to tease an ear, Scayna said, "Perhaps so by rule, but no longer in fact. Oh, we observe the forms, the confinement and isolation—which, at times, I can almost cherish. But within those, no one exerts undue sway on us. Quite opposite, in truth. Though I have no voice in the grouping, I need none; I speak with Nsil, and often in council he speaks for me. Thus, while I am unheard, it is not unusual that my thoughts prevail."

"Tell me once again," said Ilrin. "Tell how it was for us on Magh, and why it all changed."

Passed down from bearer to child, likely the story had altered greatly; Ilrin knew this as well as Scayna. And over the years, in bits and pieces she had heard the most of it. Still, "Of old, bearers in council ruled Magh; all were welcome to advise, but bearers' decisions governed. Thus was controlled the balance of genitive types, and therefore the management of population growth, maintaining sufficiency while avoiding glut."

"But then we reached Eamn," Ilrin prompted. "Why did the dynamics here become so different? How were they changed?"

The matter did not favor brevity. Pinching a splaybush bulb off a cut stem that carried several, Scayna bit down and inhaled deeply. Yet unripe, it yielded only traces of its heady vapor. With a *snff* of resignation she began to compose her thoughts.

Biology, Scayna first cited. Maghren bearers' cycles were someway tied to Magh's changing relations to Chorm and its star Jemra. On Eamn all differed: Chorm's influence lessened greatly, and the periodic swing between it and Jemra came at vastly greater interval. Most disturbant, Eamn itself rotated, light and dark alternating between two and three times as often as on the homeworld. The cycles of indigenous lifeforms had grown of these conditions, under Eamn's heavy atmosphere and greater worldpull; the newcomers' had not. Clearly, disruption of bearers' cycles should have come as no surprise.

Nor should its effect. As wombreadiness came less often and lost regularity, bearing dropped by almost half. Resentment at exploitation by the homeworld had already brought a clique of seeders and adaptives to advocacy of bearers carrying more than three wombs in process—perhaps even all six. So that Maghren emigration limits could not stifle colony growth.

Steeped in tradition and wary of increased physical burden, Eamn's bearers stood adamantly opposed. Instead they urged study of the factors governing the cycles of native life-forms. Although the little smof bearers alternated only four wombs, the principles of trigender reproduction should be similar; such studies might prove fruitful. And meanwhile . . .

"Our bearer ancestors strove for conciliation with Magh and wholly underestimated the cabal." With five Maghren skyships standing at Eamn's major port, the rebels struck, capturing four. One attempted flight; with engines poorly readied, it crashed.

In the same coup all Eamnet bearers were taken in custody, their householdings dispersed. Families consisted of three to five bearers, five to six times as many seeders and adaptives, offspring tended by all adults in common. These now split into smaller units, each with one bearer only, kept isolated from others of her kind. "As, for the most part, we are today," Scayna added. "I have sometimes wished . . . but what is, is."

She twitched a massive shoulder. "The war, now. We have it that Magh first attacked, its ships spewing blast and fire. Equally likely is that the cabal essayed a preemptive raid on Magh but did not achieve its goal."

In either event war erupted, bringing carnage to both worlds. Early the Eamnet rebels held such confidence of victory that one ship, greatly augmented, set off to claim and explore Shtai the Forerunner. And though the matter was little known in these times, signals had told of its safe arrival, and of the new world's hospitable nature. "But then," said Scayna, "came plague. Not to Shtai; those aboard that ship escaped before it struck. But to us, and to Magh also."

No need to tell of that: regardless of origin, it left less than one of six alive. Or of twelve, perhaps; who could know? Old, grim tales spoke of the wasted age before Eamnet society could even begin the struggle to form again.

"In those times, Ilrin, bearers were truly slaves, put to breed on demand; no womb stayed idle past minimum recovery. All thought of balance died; only bearers bore, so produce more bearers." Seeing the young one's distaste, Scayna added, "They had little choice: build a greater populace or settle for scrabbling a bare living from the dirt. The arts of manufacture require more than a handful of householdings for sustenance."

Long past need, such practice held; only when Scayna's collateral ancestress Klar the Sacrificed mounted a rebellion of bearers did the ruling seeders and adaptives concede as much and relent. Bearers regained the older, time-honored breeding limit. Yet the right to select gender of offspring remained with the householding's leader, not the bearer herself.

Ilrin worried another matter. "What of those on Shtai? Free of plague, could they not build as we did, and come to aid us?" The eyes widened. "No one speaks of this."

"The question lacks point. Signaling requires complex devices; we lost the knowledge to build them. When it was regained, ears turned to Shtai. But that world lies silent."

Ilrin posing no further diversion, Scayna resumed. "Let us now consider the tactics of policy. For example: should a subordinate seeder or adaptive seek your affirmation in complaint against the holding's leader, what response might best serve?"

No rest for the weary. With the residence belt up to speed, equipment reorientated for zero gee, and drive mode quarters largely deconstructed, Sam got cadre 5-A partied to the Gate and off to Earth. In time to greet 6-A and see all twelve of it shepherded to digs on the belt. You'd think a hardworking captain could take a break. In Gowdy's case you'd think wrong.

On balance he liked his new exec. Simone Leopold's record shone. The dark-complexioned woman stood slim and moved well; strong features somehow complemented her soft voice. And if she ever did anything with all that hair except pile it up, the result might be worth seeing. Just now, though, she wanted a lot of complicated answers when Sam Gowdy needed to go lie down.

"Why do we sit so far out from the inner moon? Wouldn't the L-2 point between it and the planet be more convenient?"

"Yes," chimed in Marthe Vinler. Blond and sturdy, the young tech radiated gung ho energy. "Where the gravities cancel."

"Not the same." Gowdy shook his head. "Equigrav positions are inherently unstable. Anyway, Lagrange points are different.''

Keep it simple. ''At L-2, Big Red's pull one way and Acey's the other give the same effect as Big Red's alone at Acey's distance. So you get the same period around Big Red.''

Leopold wasn't done yet. ''And what's wrong with that?''

Oh well. ''Too *busy*. We can't eliminate libration about an L-point, but out here we have a longer sight line. Don't have to be quite so precise with our corrections.''

Then how, she asked, would he manage closer reconnaissance? Deadpan, Gowdy said, ''That's why we brought the DV. Look; we're not out all that far; the seeing's pretty good from right here.'' With that, he got away. In his new digs—and was he ever glad of the move!—he showered and went to bed. Sydnie had the watch, so he didn't have to make chat. Or figure why she felt so obviously one-up, lately, and made little effort to hide it.

Skeeter Cole's sharp-featured big-eared elfin look didn't fool Sam. If Skeets said he was trading information with Acey, Gowdy believed him. ''How far have you gotten, so far?''

The procedure was Handbook routine. Acey radiated signals, so flood the visible hemisphere with similar frequencies, keyed in repetitive patterns. If a response came, switch to counting with dot groups and then proceed to more complicated games. If nobody answered, put the Handbook back in the drawer.

Acey was definitely a first case. Unlike Scout; from there, no pay at all. Well, maybe when the nomads arrived, with the wake that looked like Traction Drive except weaker. For sure, now, the unknown ship's course aimed toward the Trojan world.

''It's going pretty good, sir,'' Cole replied, ''ever since they recognized we were counting and took it from there. We ran a series of odd numbers, they came back with evens. We went to sums and differences, products and quotients. Using simple dot-dash combos for operational signs. We stayed with each category until they fed back examples that correlated. Hey, when we sent a string of squares, they upped the ante to cubes.'' Skeeter grinned. ''These guys are no dummies.''

''And the current status?''

''Confused. We sent the first twenty prime numbers, one through sixty-seven. But what came back didn't match anything. They've rung in operators we can't figure out. Yet.''

Gowdy thought about it. ''Maybe they're overestimating us.''

''How's that?''

''Some series only make sense in terms of specific logical premises. You know; like the posers in IQ tests.''

''Maybe. But if I'm going to test my IQ, I'd just as soon get to know the language first.''

Which could, of course, be part of the test. Or maybe the locals were just plain showing off. . . .

''Well, stay with it. And keep me advised. Anything at all from Scout?''

''Nope. Still sending the dit-dah, but nobody's biting.''

They hadn't tried Deucy yet. Its rotation, plus orbital discrepancy with *Roamer* and Acey, made contact skeds hard to figure. Eventually Sam meant to pull a satellite from the main central hold and position it for steady relay to the outer moon. Or maybe when time allowed, send the Deployment Vehicle.

No hurry. Because whatever communication Skeeter achieved with Acey, its natives would likely pass on to the other moon as a matter of course. So why duplicate the effort?

On Yamar all Yainans celebrate arrival of the ship *L'lit*. None aboard began life before *Tayr* departed the homeworld; no personal acquaintance between the two groups is possible or expected. Yet once met, it is as with long-known neighbors. Inside the common meeting hall, with lighting more friendly, news and greetings are exchanged across the welcoming board.

Especially gladdening is the circumstance that *L'lit* carries larger than expected supplies of *cruance*, both seedlings and grown shrubbings. Yamar is not kind to the plant, and before best care measures were determined, much of *Tayr*'s original bringing has succumbed—to an extent that threatens efficacy of Yainan breeding. In *L'lit*'s bounty T'phee foresees relief.

To Nahei, preceptor of *L'lit*, T'phee feels immediate warmth. After the overall greeting ceremonials they two retire to T'phee's resting spaces and partake of special viands prepared by resident servitors. Afterward they share bliss and genitive exudations, Nahei being informed of the yet-unready state of T'phee's matrix but finding this lack no bar to pleasure.

Later, with other forethinkers of *L'lit* and of Yamar, plans and prospects are discussed: for the many left on Yain, what hope? In this matter, little cheer is found. True, T'phee can report several of the great life ships launched from Yain since Nahei's shipborne receptors lost signal from home. And remind that these announcements are from over five Yainyears past: ". . . Yain's efforts may now prosper better than we can know."

But although the building of ships—along with needed ancillary activities—dominates those efforts, the ratio of savable to doomed is a limit that breeds only despair.

By fortune, T'phee has another topic to offer. Addressing Nahei in particular, er asks, "Has any told you of the new sighting, the ship come to rest in the Parent grouping?" None has; smoothing es neckskin with a lower manipular, er begins.

Since learning that interworld traverse in the Parent-Get system restrains itself to infrequent forays from the outer Get to circle the inner and return, utilizing primitive mass-ejection devices for propulsion, Cejha and now T'phee have placed low priority on observation of those bodies.

"In future time we will seek acquaintance, but the need is not yet." At now, images of Parent and Get are recorded at set intervals, and scanned when a respectable body of data accrues.

"So that when a strange ship approached, from a direction in which no nearby star exists, we did not become aware of it until it came near to resting. Where now its path leads the inner Get as Yamar leads the Parent system itself."

But that is only half the marvel! T'phee has wonders yet untold. "The earliest appearances show a rate of motion several times that attainable by *Tayr* or *L'lit*. And its facility of slowing denotes pushforce doubling our best twice over—near, in truth, to Yain's own worldpull."

"Our own vessels," says Cejha, "could do as much. But only briefly, until fuel exhausts itself."

A murmur passes through the gathering; T'phee clicks manipulars to quiet it so that Nahei, questioning, may be heard. "Vast, this ship must be, to hold such fueling?"

T'phee waves nullment. "Here exists a puzzle. The strange ship, which emits a monotonous rote signal pattern when it passes this side of the Parent, bulks only moderately greater than our own *Tayr*, or your *L'lit*."

"Then either its fuel is incomparably potent, or utilized for far better yield than even our best theorists can conceive."

Discussion blossoms. While none here can claim to know the truth of what is hypothecated, all find it of lively interest.

T'phee is content; for this time, at least, the doom of Yain is gone from the forefront of minds present.

As T'phee expects, the group from *L'lit* find the Emmans a source of wonder. Led by Nahei, six of the newcomers trek a distance with T'phee, coping with the unaccustomed heavy worldpull and squinting behind unfamiliar tinted eyeshields against the glare of this world's star, to meet those who speak for Threewaters village.

Bretl-kai, a bearer near to past the age of that function, sits accompanied by two seeders whose names elude T'phee's recalls, and an adaptive called Endri.

As elder, as well as by fluency in Yainan, Bretl derives precedence of speaking. Es questions hold urgency. "Many more of you, then, will come? Ship upon ship?" The bearer looks at the reed-grown point where two streams meet, then up to the low ridge behind which lies a small lake, the third water of the village name. "So many. Can there still be place for us?"

"Ever, your steadings remain yours," T'phee gives assurance. "To do with as you choose." In es own mind er makes comparative estimates and flicks the tips of a manipular in affirmation. "Even if all Yainans could come to Yamar . . ." *And would that it were so!* The greatest land mass lay unexplored. And Emmans utilized only a portion of this continent's coastal plain. But T'phee added only, ". . . we could have no cause to encroach."

Though having earlier heard much, from T'phee, of Emman folklore, Nahei queries further—and fails signally to hide shock at Bretl's calm telling of the Getworlds' mutual slaughter.

"From all signs," Bretl concludes, "we had come to believe both Magh and Eamn to harbor none but the dead. Until your first great ship drove to their vicinity, and returned to tell of settlements visible from high above. And that Eamn—the outer Get as you call it—again raises ships toward our old enemy."

Er moves a limb in forlorn gesture. "Always we had hoped against belief, that aid would come. But then we knew the truth; Eamn survives, and has abandoned us." Er turns to Nahei and to T'phee. "I say again, we are no longer a part of them. We would be of your people, and that you be of ours."

As best er can, T'phee reassures the distraught Emman. On the long return walk to es own residing spaces, er confides to Nahei, "Like our young get, they seek nurture. With beings of such size, is it irrational of me to find their need disturbing?"

Kayo knew a little about Deployment Vehicles, but hadn't yet been inside one. "Time you did," said Danny Quillan, "before you ride it. And we can put your lingo hardware aboard, too."

So on the next checkout tour Kayo followed him and senior pilot SuZanne Craig inship. The good news was Quillan toting part of Kayo's gear; even in zero gee it was too bulky for one. Muscular and ripe-figured, her stubby thick black braids jouncing at each step, Craig moved ahead. From the control deck a series of ramps and hatches led to *Roamer*'s dimly lit central cylinder. Forward lay the DV's berth, major cargo holds aft, with a five-meter gap between to facilitate inboard loading.

A railed catwalk-cum-ladder extended to the axially located DV portal. Its first hatch opened into an airlock chamber; the second revealed the rear of the smaller vessel: a central hatch inside the triangle of three Traction Drive nodes and matching trio of landing legs, now folded in against the stern.

SuZanne motioned Dan ahead. "More airlock practice." He opened the outer portal; when all were inside he closed it and undogged the final one, into the long axial tunnel of the Vehicle itself. At no stage had the lighting improved.

Twenty meters thick, forty meters of cylinder capped with

a twenty-meter cone, the Deployment Vehicle lacked many of its parent ship's features. No Habgate supply, no rotating belt: strictly in-system transport, designed to accel forward, decel tail first, and land standing up. Forward, the operating deck lay circular and crosswise; under drive, aft was always down. The tunnel's far end was ringed with a safety rail; Dan and SuZanne and Kayo in turn gripped it to swing past and around, planting Velcro soles solidly on the deck. Reorienting took Kayo a moment; then she was all right.

Quillan found a lighting control; for the first time since leaving *Roamer*'s control deck, Kayo enjoyed decent illumination. As she stowed her gear away in the lockers Craig indicated, the others strapped into the pilots' consoles, opposite the major viewscreen across the tunnel's mouth, and began to run operating simulations. Lesser screens sat nearer, and ordinary shipboard chairs formed a second rank around the pilots' couches. Observer positions? Passenger seating? For zero gee and maneuvering, of course, passengers would mostly stay in their own couches.

Her working gear put away, Kayo looked around to take inventory. The deck measured ten meters across, a little less. Peripherally, one side held minimal food preparation and dining facilities, at the other were two latrines: drive mode and zero gee. Along each of the two stretches of bulkhead between those installations, hinged panels hid five double-deck, fold-up bunk sets. Twenty cots, then, that doubled as accel couches.

She craned her neck to look up. Toward its top the cone's inside surface curved inward, until at the center it bulged down. To house a forward Traction node, for counter-accel if needed.

Around that bulge sat a gaggle of smaller ones, trailing cables along the hull's interior. The forward sensors, those would be; the yaw thrustors lay farther back, one four-unit array just behind the cone and another near the tail end.

SuZanne was telling Dan, "A full tank gives us two weeks of one gee, total delta vee about four percent of c. We're stocked to feed six people six months, austerity style. Water to match, and air renewal would outlast all of it. When Kennealy's *Tarpon* lost power, comm and all, heading out on an Environ run . . .''

Kayo knew the story, part of it anyway; tuning out, she began to prowl. The bunks, now: how comfortable would they be? Starting toward the nearest, she noticed that at the seam between one pair of panels hung a scrap of cloth.

The handle turned easily; swinging out, the panels displayed tiers of shallow drawers on their inner sides.

The wrinkled cloth was part of the folded lower bunk; Kayo pulled it down and found an unmade bed, definitely used. Stains told what it had been used for, so the earring beside a pillow came as no great surprise. An engraved teardrop of carnelian, stippled with insets of onyx and banded with red gold. Picking it up, Kayo marveled at the delicate carving. This was valuable.

Show and tell. ''Look what I found,'' and gestured toward the bunk. ''Somebody's going to be glad to get it back.''

Craig's eyes narrowed. ''Maybe. Might not be a good idea to let on *where* you found it.'' She cleared her throat. ''Why not let me have this? I can probably take care of it with no fuss.''

''Whose do you think it is?''

''You don't want to know that.'' Abruptly Craig began shutting down the simulations. ''Hell, *I* don't want to know.''

Reluctantly Kayo reached to hand over the ornament. Then she stopped. Since when did she need SuZanne Craig to tie her shoes for her? ''Never mind. I can handle this myself.''

Briefly glowering, SuZanne shrugged. ''You'd better be right. Because if you're wrong, you're wrong all by yourself.''

Without further comment the woman completed shutdown, then shepherded the others ahead of her, back into the ship proper.

Showered and fed, Kayo entered the lounge, greeted Skeeter and Mose and the captain and a few more, fixed a drink, and sat alongside Leopold the exec to watch some holie. At the bar, though, she was clumsy. When she straightened after picking up her dropped ice cubes, a flash of gold and carnelian peeked from under the minibar's corner.

It was like fishing off the pier, sitting beside granddad on one of Ketchikan's rare sunny days; you dropped your bait and then you waited. Kayo's drink got warm long before it ran low; she sat with it, because getting a refill would somehow obligate her to wait longer. And dammit, she could really use a refill.

So she sat, nursing her dregs in indecision, when Sydnie Lightner stalked in, freshly off watch. At the bar she sloshed spirits over ice and turned away, then peered searchingly around the room before going to one knee, reaching back without looking, and rising again. The bauble wasn't there now.

Lightner sat alongside Sam Gowdy. She didn't show him the earring, or appear to mention finding anything at all.

Nor did Kayo, later, feel called upon to report what she'd seen. SuZanne asked questions; Kayo said only that the matter was taken care of.

Maybe so, but not in her own mind. Days later, when she reboarded the DV for a ride down to Acey, she still wondered.

"It's out of the question, Jules! And I told you not to call me here." Sydnie Lightner glanced nervously toward the bathroom door; Sam wasn't given to showering at length.

"But why can't you meet me?" Even with the volume turned down, the intercom made Jules Perrone's voice louder than she liked. "Look, Sydnie. It's not easy for me, you know, getting clear without Maril wondering. So when I do manage, you—"

"Oh, stop whining. You know how careful I have to be." She heard the shower stop. "Sam's coming. Good-bye. We'll talk—but *don't* call here again."

She cut the circuit. How could he be so short on judgment, on understanding? Was this the man she had trusted? What had gone so wrong? And what had pushed her to take such a stupid chance for so little gain? She knew better and always had.

It wasn't Sydnie's fault, of course. She'd hankered for a sympathetic shoulder, and out of the entire new cadre, drive tech Jules Perrone seemed to hold the most promise. She really hadn't intended things to go this far—not so soon, at least.

Slim and dark, soft-voiced and sleek-haired, Jules caught

her fancy the moment he stepped out of Earthtush. Returning handshakes and greetings warmly, he paid special heed to hers. Sydnie knew a roving eye when she met one.

At the welcome-aboard gathering in the lounge she'd sat near him. When his pairmate, the thin, blondish comm and instrument tech Maril Jencik, left for their quarters to start unpacking, Sydnie chatted the man up. Three days later, he on duty and she off, Perrone invited her to operate the Virtual Thrust test for him while he checked out the Deployment Vehicle's drive.

She hadn't planned on winding up in bed; still, that outcome didn't surprise her greatly. What did was the earring she knew she must have lost in that bed, turning up under the minibar in the lounge. The bad part was, it hadn't got there by itself; somebody knew more than they should, and Sydnie had no idea who. The good part was that Sam hadn't noticed anything.

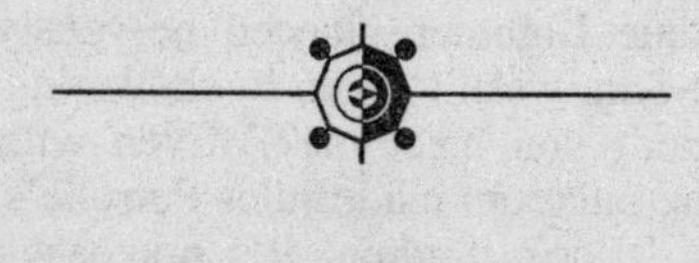

IV

With no Tsi bearer to lend their views authority, the seeder Duant-tsi and adaptive Triem gladly accepted temporary aegis from Irtuk. Her own retinue, understaffed due to the abruptness of the councils' summons, welcomed the additions.

Triem-tsi had indeed been seeded when they first met; only after discharge of the compound gamete did Irtuk conjugate with the adaptive. Meanwhile, Irtuk's wombreadiness having passed, she and Duant explored those aspects of each other's ways.

Returning as head of councils, Paith the Elect freed Irtuk from the burdens of presiding, which had irksomely circumscribed her activities; her normal working seemed almost like a time of rest. Now at the onset of longdark she lounged in her personal chamber, lightly robed, to enjoy a beverage after latemeal and talk with those of her following who were not busied elsewhere.

What of the new ship, come from a direction displaying no feasible origin? Enigmatically the newcomer had passed by Magh without pause, slowed behind its own flared emissions, and assumed station far above Magh's leading rim. "We know," said Duant, "how it holds position: by leading Magh around Chorm just as Shtai leads Chorm, and us with it, around Jemra."

Triem spoke. "It would seem that Magh, not Eamn, is its prime concern." Addressing Irtuk, "Does it pose a danger? And were it to attack, what could we do?"

"Against this ship," Irtuk counseled, "those we had before the Great Dying would be useless. And now we lack even those."

Duant *snff'd*. "Why assume threat where none is manifest? We should seek to know of those who bring the ship—and to that end, observe it in all ways possible."

"I am told," said Irtuk, "that it emits radiation in discrete groupings. Might these carry meaning?"

"They do," Triem said, "but only of numerical import. And elementary, awkward even for simple counting. Though we are progressed somewhat further. Yet those aboard seemingly lack the concept of position in a series as a measure of magnitude."

The seeder Waij-saa spoke. "Not likely; without such usage, complex calculation becomes prohibitively difficult. And these intruders construct and utilize devices far beyond our own understanding—as does the ship from Diell the Companion."

"And this one to even greater degree," Irtuk acknowledged. "I suspect, Waij, that your view is correct, that some other disparity impedes comprehension."

Waij-saa showed pleasure. And well he might; his perceptive comment reminded Irtuk how intuitive he could be in more intimate ways. While his attention was to her, she made the signs of eye and lip that announced him chosen for this night.

Her meaning was clear to all, and Duant showed dismay.

She had not intended him disappointment; it was merely that enrapt by his novelty and Triem's, as always with intimants who had learned the nuances differently, seemingly she had allowed the pair to overestimate their primacy in her life. Belatedly she signed to both a reassurance of her approval.

Always, Irtuk strove to avoid being unkind. But kindness and spontaneous response did not always fit the same mold.

Cadre 6-A was too big for Sam to assimilate all at once. When the next wave hit, he was still pinning names to faces. But here came the downside evaluation team led by Barry Krsnch, and then Pia Velucci's macroGate crew. Both ahead of time. Far from ready to send an advance group to Acey or to unship macroGate components for assembly, Gowdy wasn't braced for extra people. And this tandem influx almost tripled the number aboard.

With helpers greener than himself, new supplies chief Milo Vitale got out mattresses and such, cleared space in storage areas on the belt, and soon had all the fresh troops camped out.

Along with the arrival of personnel came increased food supplies. Helped by three newcomers volunteered whether they liked it or not, Owen Tanacross managed to keep the galley one jump ahead of the appetites. His face got redder but his voice stayed quiet. All in all, logistics kept up with demand.

If Pia Velucci had any patience worth noticing, she kept it well under wraps. Muscling into a seat across the table, she started in on Sam again. Where was he going to site the macroGate? And when? Why not break out and assemble some segments, to be towed into position later? Index finger pinning his attention: "What's your holdup here, captain?"

Ordinarily he didn't mind sharing info, but this woman rubbed him crossways. Her stained and sloppy jumpsuit, the soup bowl haircut that screened her eyes but showed a lot of thick neck, the heavy features unmoved by any effort to look pleasant, her frenetic urgency—but most of all, the way her voice grated when she wound it up. Nonetheless . . .

"We want to get the evaluation team down on Acey, but not before we improve communication with the natives. Skeeter had a breakthrough today, but it still takes time. Leaving here to set up your macroGate might set the process back to reboot. The catch is, both jobs use the DV and it can't be two places at once.'' He glared at her. ''Do you understand that much?''

Her laugh rang harsh, too. ''Stubborn doesn't mean stupid, Gowdy. All right, you're giving native relations priority over expediting major transport from Earth. Maybe a board hearing will see it your way and maybe not.''

Even sipping coffee she made noise. ''And can't we at least get some assembly going, outside? You're not going to move ship hard enough to break a towline.''

He shook his head. ''No towing. Inertia could bang things together, or against the ship. Too much chance of damage.''

Velucci huffed a deep breath. ''Try this. Everything we assemble, we lash solid to fittings on the hull. And yes I know to keep clear of the drive fields and sensor clusters.'' She leaned forward. ''How about it?''

What won her the argument was, she forgot to rasp her voice. Sam let himself grin. ''Tell you what: give your people some suit drill. When they're ready, I'll pump one of the Gate holds down for opening. Just ask first, before you pull any stern plates.''

It felt good, not having to be pissed off at her. ''Siting the macroGate took some thought.'' Velucci looked puzzled; Gowdy continued. ''Any orbit tied to Acey or Deucy, before long the surrounding space gets just too damn *busy* for heavy traffic. You've seen what a hoodoo's nest the near-Earth Gate cluster turned out to be. We need a different approach.''

Pia shrugged; the effect was impressive. ''So?''

''It's sort of a copycat trick, but whatever works. I intend to site you in Big Red's own orbit, trailing Trojan. Like Scout, you know? Only behind, L-4 to Scout's L-5.''

After a moment she nodded. ''Sounds all right. I never did understand how Trojan works, but it does and that's good enough.''

Sam felt the same way; he knew the basic setup but had never plowed through the math to prove it. And probably never would.

Velucci stood. ''It's not a bad haul from here. If you ever get your shorts in gear and haul us out there.'' A true compromise, Gowdy mused, leaves all parties less than satisfied.

Turning away now, she said, "Enjoy your lunch, captain."

He was already trying to decide whom to saddle with bird-dogging her operation. Just so long as it wasn't him.

Barry Krsnch, leading the downside team, posed a different problem: how in hell did you get sensible answers out of him?

Five years younger and two inches taller, Krsnch had maybe forty pounds on Sam. Even so, at times Sam purely wanted to hand Barry a fat lip. That wasn't his style, though, so forget it.

At first Krsnch came across well, and his effect on some of the women amused Gowdy more than not. His dark, slaty complexion, curly hair, a *dimple* for Pete'sakes: only strong brow and jawlines redeemed the face from pretty boy status.

The pretty was all outside; whatever sat inside was hard to figure. Take the initial quarters assignment: strictly off-the-cuff and everyone making do, Sam in the interests of hospitality made an offer. "If you'd like your group rooming together, give us a little help and we can clear the whole rear storeroom."

Freezing, Krsnch said, "We'll quarter as it may fall."

"But . . ." Questions got Sam nowhere, so he shut up.

On galley skeds he tried again. Tanacross had Sam's and Velucci's people set up, but not the landing crew's. Sam asked, "Hey, Barry; want to slot your team in on the meal roster?"

Walking, Krsnch made an abrupt halt. "My team will dine together at all times. Adjust the rest of it however you like." And moved on as if there had been no interruption.

You'd think the man's whims came on stone tablets. Oh well.

For a while he gave Gowdy no real problems, and why sweat the small stuff? But now came time for the DV to make landing. One by one Sam got his party on line. Milo Vitale and part of the macroGate group suited up to boost supply crates outship for lashing to the DV's hull. Kayo Marlin already had her special gear aboard, and Skeeter Cole his comm equipment, which except for the antenna arrays would ride inside and warm. And calm on the outside but Sam knew better, pilot SuZanne Craig saw to it that the Vehicle itself lacked nothing needful.

So as not to miss the show, Gowdy planned to ride copilot himself, alongside Skeeter at the comm. On the fold-down bunks, Dan Quillan and Kayo, Maril Jencik and Marthe Vinler in aid of Cole groundside, Jinx Lanihan and Alix Dorais and Feodor Glinka for all-around backup, and senior drive tech Jules Perrone.

Odd about Perrone; he'd been Sydnie's idea. "You shouldn't go without a drive tech. How about Jules?"

Jules, is it? "Why him? I didn't know you were buddies."

Her voice tightened. "We've talked. With Chief Blaine staying aboard here, Perrone's your next best bet. And why shouldn't he go with Maril? You have some other couples listed."

And some not: Craig and Vinler were going solo, and Sydnie hadn't offered to keep *him* company.

But what the hell? "Okay, he's in."

Leaving the DV with twelve empty bunks; at lunch Sam asked Krsnch which of his team should ride the first landing run.

Abruptly, with one hand the man made a chopping motion. "My team goes in together. If not this time, then on your second trip." Why, the damn fool didn't even know the DV wouldn't hold all his people at once if they flew it by themselves!

Sam had started to sit across from the team chief; now he stood again. "Have it your way. We'll go without you."

And left before he said what he really wanted to, which wouldn't have done at all.

Skeeter Cole wasn't a blusher like Dan; Kayo couldn't figure why he always looked sunburned. Now, in the control room he and Marthe Vinler worked at an aux screen displaying a table of arbitrary symbols. "We've been trying to edge from math into language. Quite a few items on here, you might call words."

"Invent your own pronunciation," said Vinler. She was really young, Kayo thought: young and blond, a little chunky. Pleasant enough, and openly eager on the job. "Plus and minus lead to increase and decrease, up and down. Moving along a series gives forward and backward. Things like that.'' She pushed long bangs off her forehead; they didn't stay pushed.

''I guess you got past the math hang-up, then,'' Kayo said.

Skeeter nodded. ''Positional notation. They call it backward: units first. When they thought to spell it out as polynomials, everything clicked.''

''Uh . . . A plus ten B plus ten-squared C equals there you go?''

''Except, they use twelve. That was another hang-up.''

Yes, it would be. ''Language, though,'' Kayo prompted.

Skeeter gave it thought. ''We can compare things: bigger, smaller, and so forth. But we can't name the things. Or anything they *do*. What we have, basically, is auxiliary parts of speech. What we can't peg down from here is nouns and verbs.''

''Because . . . ?''

''We need pictures. Something to point at, demonstrate with, make motions. Without common reference points, which usually means visual, you can't name things. *Or* actions.''

He anticipated her next question. ''We're beaming down video sigs: test pattern, nothing fancy. But the odds are bad.''

Kayo waited; Marthe said, ''They don't use those frequencies; we haven't caught anything much above thirty megahertz.''

If you say so; electrochatter wasn't Kayo's long suit.

Skeeter added, ''For vid you need lots higher freqs; I guess they haven't invented the right gadgets yet, downside.''

Pointing to the screen, Kayo took a deep breath. ''So what you have here is all we're going to get?''

Almost synchronized, the two instrument experts nodded, as Skeeter said, ''We can add more trimmings, but that's about it.''

''Then I'd better go tell the captain it's show time.''

The show began sooner than Kayo expected; two days later she was aboard the DV and buckled in. From her lower bunk, to the left and slightly behind the control couches, she had a slanted, foreshortened view of the main screen; with the bunk's head cranked all the way up, she could see without craning.

Unexpectedly, the Vehicle was full after all. Only a few minutes short of Go, six of Krsnch's group arrived, led by his secundo Libby Verdoorn and overloaded with gear. Looking both pleased and irritated, Gowdy rawhided the six into getting things stowed immediately, then returned to his accel couch.

From Kayo's right, Dan Quillan made low-voiced comments as SuZanne and Skeeter and Gowdy checked off. "Virtual Thrust okay," Craig was saying. "Easing down from redline max." Pause. "Force equivalent zero; switching to operational. Readout."

Sitting copilot, Gowdy spoke. "All indicators nominal."

"Landing legs unlocked," Skeeter reported. "Levering out; holding at notch two for emergence."

"Now they break the seal, forward," Dan whispered. "It's magnetostrictive," which Kayo already knew, "and . . ."

Shhh! As Craig announced, "Supercooled loops interrupted, solenoid currents decaying." Then, "Fields essentially zero."

She cleared her throat. "Firing propellant."

As the Vehicle moved, inching forward in short jerks, reverberating vibration drowned all speech. Behind, gasses underwent catalytic ignition, propelling the DV out where its Traction Drive emissions would clear the ship.

Sure enough, "Drive activated," said SuZanne Craig.

From the screen Kayo couldn't tell what the DV was actually doing. Craig said, "We're clear, *Roamer*; drift minimal. Landing legs to full lock, as fenders for loading operation."

Comm spoke: Tuiasso's voice. "Starting flip for rear contact. Try to hold position." Because it was easier to pivot the ship than to take the Vehicle the long way around.

The wait extended; had something gone wrong? A brief surge of negative weight nudged the DV backward toward the ship. "Enough," said Mose; then a few seconds later, "And stop her . . . *now*." A touch of plus gee pushed Kayo against her couch.

For a time nothing happened except desultory talk at the control consoles with Tuiasso chiming in on the speaker, and clumping noises as though large animals worried the hull below. Once Pia Velucci was heard, cussing in the tinny voice that meant relay from her suit comm. The captain grinned. "Oh, sure; she'd have to be out there herself, bossing the job."

Not much later Mose announced, "External cargo secured." Then, "MacroGate personnel inside." And finally, "Cargo hold closed. Vehicle, you're free to leave."

Onscreen a few stars wheeled, the rim of Big Red appeared briefly, then Whitey showed enough bright edge to trigger the safety circuits, dimming the visual display.

"We were pointing ecliptic north," said Dan Quillan, as if Kayo didn't know. While the DV oriented into the ecliptic plane, then aimed to apply delta vee out from Big Red and slightly retrograde, he went on to exposit. "We coast out a way, slowing so Acey can catch up, then let Big Red pull us down to match speeds again. With a little juggling, of course."

"Nice trick if it works," grumbled Kayo. In zero gee she hadn't noticed the wrinkles in the stiff fabric she was lying on, but under normal thrust they chafed. And even at only one gee, Regs said passengers stayed strapped in for maneuvering.

Then the pressure eased. "Drive off," Craig announced. "You can unstrap now; zero gee until further notice."

Kayo could eat and sleep without gravs; even the toity was feasible if you'd read the manual. But with all this company, limited space, and no privacy, Acey seemed a very long way off.

"Our venture progresses well," said Nisl, gesturing in appreciation of the delicacies Scayna offered. Truly, she had as deft a touch with sauces as with conjugation. With her next upcoming wombreadiness yet in abeyance, they had again this day enjoyed that intimacy and then shared dining also. Now in all concurrence they put thought to greater matters.

"Our new skyship, then, can indeed lift the small one with itself?" Cast it loose at Magh, to land and return? Then, once more united, ground safely home again? "How certain can you be?"

Splaying foredigits in deprecation, Nisl said, "Limitations

are more strict than we had thought, but plans adjust. Our small ship One must rise separately to join the larger Three. Near to Magh, fuel chambers replenished, One descends to our enemy world while Three waits circling until One lifts and they reunite."

Stroking Scayna in the sensitive nook below an ear, Nsil continued. "At return here, if both cannot come to ground as one they may again need to part. So much fuel is squandered to raise only a little, that after One has dropped to Magh and risen from it, we cannot be certain what amount remains for safe return."

Reaching to her another morsel, also he took one for himself. "If both ships cannot in any way safely ground, all crew must gather in one and cast the other adrift. To save the larger would be preferred, but either can bring all home alive."

"And in this, their lives hold first importance?"

"As always, Scayna."

Her next touch came unexpected. She said, "Should you wish to remain further this day, Nisl . . ."

Now the Overgrouping heard the voice of Nsil without delay. So often had his words proved true that earlier dissent melted away. He strengthened voice to reach all extremes of the domed, softly-lighted hall. And told of what his skywatchers had only this day reported, that had brought him here in abrupt haste.

The out-system ship leading Magh in orbit had launched a lesser-flaring shiplet outward and retrograde, for the pull of Chorm to draw again toward Magh. "By design," said Nsil, "its initial burst of impulse will, with little further use of driving force, bring it to proximity at which landing will be possible."

"It is as you said," cried Gvan, leader of a major holding. "The new ship seeks alliance with Magh. I am convinced, Nsil, and freely offer our support to advance the timing of your plan."

That night Scayna awaited Nsil without fulfillment. For it was decided: at earliest capability, ships One and Three would rise. Though the venture's details had grown in complexity, its essence conformed to his initial plan.

If only Nsil himself could pursue this mission . . . !

* * *

Word to Duant-tsi and Triem-tsi from Tajakh Observatory, confirmed by the nearer and larger installation at Denaize Shore and reported to combined councils by Irtuk-saa, created much alarm, shrillness of comment, and unbridled speculation.

With steady voice, Paith the Elect set better example. "Let us speak of what is known, not what is imagined. Irtuk, the new intruder ship itself still circles Chorm before us?"

"It does. And now sends only rote signal patterns. Or rather," the bearer corrected herself, "that function is transferred to a smaller object that has left the ship." How and why, no one knew. The thing had not been seen before; even now, reports of visual sightings lacked precision. But the signal source had moved, outward from Chorm and back past Magh, lost to Tajakh and tracked only marginally by farside stations.

Until now. "In its present movement," Irtuk continued, "the envoy vessel—or so we hope it to be—has returned inward, toward Chorm and toward ourselves. With respect, Paith the Elect, I suggest it seeks to approach our own signaling source."

Thus, Irtuk and her assignment group became detailed to Denaize Shore. Since turbulence barred floatship flight between now and longdark, Irtuk procured airfoil transport sufficient for the number assigned. Now, jounced and pummeled by Magh's cyclic winds, the noisy machine jangled Irtuk's thought.

The small ship: where had it been hidden? Even an object no larger than her present conveyance would be prohibitive, in terms of cargo and fuel space, to store within a vessel of reasonable size. Yet no such construct had been secured to the ship's hull. Even at its distant position, that much could be ascertained; orbital progress gave the ship an apparent rotation as viewed from Magh, yet its silhouette did not alter.

No matter; all of that would be clear soon enough, if indeed the small ship intended landing. What type of creatures, Irtuk mused, might emerge? On a mission amicable, or hostile? But if the latter, surely not to come in such small strength. Making a deep *snff*, Irtuk lay back into her cushions.

A long way yet to Denaize; even so, the airfoil machine

would reach there well before longdark. Would the newcomers arrive before her? Sleep eluded Irtuk-saa.

Responding to Nahei's request for conference, T'phee finds *L'lit*'s preceptor disturbed of mind. "Observe you the unknown ship's doings?" T'phee has not, and awaits clarification. "It dispatches a smaller vessel to the inner Get. Similar to our own lander-carriers but of greater bulk." Nahei's neckskin tics. "And greater capability, it would seem. Much greater."

Yainan auxiliary vessels are utile only in ventures of a few radii from a world's surface, a mere fraction of the distance involved here. "True," T'phee acknowledges. "But already we knew the ship itself to far exceed either of ours, in every observable function. What new urgency incurs?"

Rocking absentmindedly from front limbs to rear, Nahei mulls. "We must have nearer vantage," er says. "One of us must take a ship near the inner Get. Perhaps even make known our presence—both to the Maggens, enemies of our Emmans here, and to those who have come in the new ship."

"Put a lander-carrier to ground, there?"

"We must, I feel. Uncertain now remains only one point of choice. Shall it be you, or I?"

T'phee pauses. "I require time to consider."

"Of a surety. And to attend one other premise. That in any event, Bretl-kai and some few of es grouping symbiotes will wish to accompany."

"To es enemy world?"

"Enemy or no, Bretl holds entitled concern. Er has hinted to the matter a time and more, since our visit at es holding."

"I will speak with en," says T'phee. "Too much lies in balance at such a meeting, to risk it running astray. In unthought pursuit of old hatred."

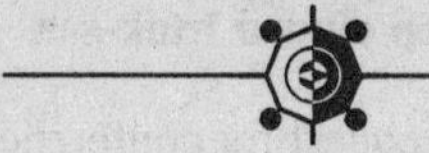

V

One thing Sydnie Lightner learned early on. No man ever lived up to his initial promise.

Her father. Lacking her mother Oreadna's finely tuned sense of outrage, Sydnie didn't understand how George Lightner changed from Mister Wonderful to Mister Rotten. All she knew was, Mommie got mad at him a lot but maybe pretty soon she'd get over it.

Sydnie was eight when the façade cracked, the clay feet crumbled, the roof fell in and the dam broke. Shouting woke her, loud from the kitchen. Trembling, Sydnie softwalked to the lighted room; both parents turned to her.

"I'm scared."

"It's all right." Glaring at her husband, Oreadna came to the child. "Come on, I'll tuck you in again."

"Yes," said her father. "I—I'll see you in the morning."

He was talking to Sydnie, but her mother looked back and said, "No you won't. Pack!" Sydnie never saw him again.

With bitter comment, Oreadna read his letters aloud. If the support money came late, he didn't care about Sydnie. Timely payment proved only that he was trying to buy her love.

Either way, he shouldn't have taken a promotion clear across the country, away from Oreadna's family and old friends.

Not that Mommie ever had friends for long; they always let her down. But then she'd find new ones, mostly men.

One after another, men lived with Oreadna and Sydnie, some longer than others. Mark and Hayden and Frederich, Oreadna married. Duke and Seymour, and finally Kegger, she didn't. Each began as the nicest and most perceptive man Oreadna ever met, and Sydnie would hope that *this* time . . .

But sooner or later Oreadna came to realize he didn't truly understand, didn't care about her needs, was just a big fake and always had been.

So Sydnie grew up knowing what was what. A man's job was to find out what a woman wanted and see that she got it. But once they were onto a sure thing, they never delivered.

At barely sixteen, which made her legally adult, Sydnie left home. Four months after Kegger moved in, and from the start he had her scared. Copping feels, peeking in the shower and taking his time at it, catching her changing clothes, always an accident and Oreadna believed him. She still had hopes with Kegger.

One day Oreadna was out but Kegger got home early. In a light robe with the house to herself, Sydnie brought in the mail.

She was opening an envelope addressed to her personally when Kegger came in. Thirty seconds later the robe was half-off and his boozy tongue pushed at her teeth while a hand groped toward what he was really after.

She got a finger up his nose and dug the nail in, hard. "Let me go!" When he jerked back, blood spurted. Still holding the envelope she ran to her bedroom and bolted the door.

Ten minutes Kegger's leaky nose kept him busy before he came and yelled. "Lemme in you little bitch or I'll kill you!"

Shaking as Kegger smashed at the door, Sydnie hefted her Little League bat. Just one chance: swing straight for his head.

If she missed, she was roadkill.

Twice more he hit, then his cussing trailed away. The front door slammed, and she heard him rev up his cycle and smoke out.

Finally she got to look in the envelope. Her father had set up this trust fund; now she was of age, she could go claim it. She packed two suitcases as full as she could carry and started out, then paused. On Oreadna's Skedmaster she called up the month's Household Accounts file; Kegger wouldn't think to look there even if he knew how. For today's date she entered:

> Whatever that pervert says he got his nose hurt when he was out to rape me. If its not him its the next one so

I wont be back. Im ok for money and will call or write soon.

S.

She knew about punctuation, but keyboards differ; on this one a lot of the markings were worn off, so she didn't bother.

She didn't call or write, either.

Eight years later Sydnie Lightner passed the entrance exams for Gayle Tech; no high school diploma appeared in her file, but she made her grades anyway. On graduation she entered space training and worked up to courier pilot, on runs short enough for ships that lacked Habegger Gate fuel feed.

Her bid for the starship program came with a good record. Her private life drew no mention, nor did any entries document the eight years prior to her tenure at Gayle Tech.

In her own mind Sydnie couldn't erase those years so easily. She tried, though. Especially with regard to Jorge Aroka the Spider Prince, and what she'd had to do to get free of him.

When *Roamer*'s cadre 5-B opened for applications, she was ready. Only Earth's second starship, *Roamer* was due to reach destination orbit just about the time 5-B would outGate aboard.

So instead of being stuck with the same small crew for an entire voyage, as on later ships, she'd go straight to a new world. And with a lot of others Gating in, to generate a colony.

Sydnie always liked a little elbow room.

When 5-B was cut to its final octad, the pairings began. Sydnie Lightner never cared for second-best; she cut Sam Gowdy out of the herd, lavished her unique brand of understanding on him, and wound up solidly in captain's quarters.

Until she saw the roster, she thought it might work. But like all the others, Sam only talked a good game; when crunch time came, he let her down. *Fourth* watch officer . . . ?

So, Jules. She hadn't meant to get involved, but instinct moved her toward the next highest rank available, she forgot to put the brakes on, and now he thought there had to be more to it.

Which made him a risk, if he kept after her openly. So she made her pitch for Jules to go on the DV, and Sam bought it.

Was Jules ego-dumb enough to stake claim on her, to Sam? She'd shoot him down: reproach Sam for lack of trust and insist that a lustful, frustrated Jules made the whole thing up.

Oh my, yes. What she could do with *that* situation!

Gowdy hadn't noticed when Acey changed from out there to down there, until sounds and tremblings hailed the edges of atmosphere. Now all hands strapped in for maneuvering.

As Skeeter punched speed and distance vectors onto the main screen, SuZanne Craig called her moves. "Atmo contact; speed suborbital, maintaining shallow angle." She touched buttons. "Starting one-eighty flip." Sam felt the familiar play of lateral forces as yaw thrustors began and ended the turnover.

Acey slid offscreen; Cole switched to rear sensors and found it again. Tail first, the DV eased down around Acey's forward side. The signal source on Skeeter's monitor gave Craig a target: about sixty degrees west, by Earth usage, of the point facing Big Red, and twenty north of the equator. Gowdy found no pattern to the signal dots; maybe the locals were into calculus. The Vehicle took a wiggle and jump; SuZanne called, "Decel coming." Pressure hit: less than a gee at first, then building. Not steady for long. As sunlight crept around Acey's rim, warming air masses churned up new and violent winds. Lips drawn back grinning, Craig fought weather and gravity, cutting airspeed to save the outside cargo from friction effects.

Gowdy envied her every tension-filled move. *Roamer* was a fine ship, but not like flying one of these little hornets. In training, back during the Liij Crisis, he'd loved whipping the battered old trainer around like an express courier.

Assigned as second pilot on a ship running supplies to the humans lodged precariously in the departing Liij Environ, Gowdy kept such urges under wraps. Until his last run, anyway.

* * *

Pushing the supply ship *Mako* out from loading orbit in his new rating of acting chief pilot, Sam felt mostly cheerful.

Not entirely. NewsComm said Ironhead Kennealy's *Tarpon* was still missing. An old freight shuttle jockey retired against his will, Ironhead had stretched cash and credit to buy *Tarpon*, an agency castoff, and gone into the Environ supply business on contract. Never mind that Ironhead had never been farther out than the asteroids, or that his financing had diddly squat left over for maintenance. *Tarpon* made it to the Environ once and back without major disaster; naturally, Ironhead went out again.

Went out, yes; got there, no. And neither drive trail nor signal had been spotted past Beacon Six, close to a month ago.

With most ships, Gowdy wouldn't be into serious worry yet. But Ironhead's credit probably wouldn't carry anywhere near the standard emergency stores of food, water, even air. After a month, Kennealy would be in truly deep.

He was.

Whatever causes of disaster Ironhead later reported to the underwriters, the results were clear: power plant slagged, drive nodes fried just short of crisp, life support on backup, and about enough comm power for across the street. If Gowdy hadn't nursed his detectors on the edge of positive feedback, he'd never have spotted the tenuous signal; *Tarpon* would likely be lost and gone, space-cold all through. Sam didn't know Morse, not even SOS, but the signal was keyed and it came from *thataway*.

His crew protested. Chief engineer Slats Jason outranked any second pilot—but acting or no, Gowdy pointed out, a chief pilot could overrule all the sonofabitching seniority there was.

"And back it up at a board hearing?" said Jason.

"If necessary, yes." Sam cut accel and swung ship. Two days later he found *Tarpon*, and learned that ship-to-ship access tubes are a bitch to set up but they do work. He had guessed right; air was scraping minimum, water severely rationed, and cannibalism a serious and imminent possibility.

After Kennealy's eight had a meal, Gowdy said, "We can give you a lift, Ironhead. It'll be crowded, but—"

"Lift, hell! What about my *ship*?"

Tarpon was junk when Kennealy bought it and downhill from there. But if he could get it back to Earth, the old cowboy might save his butt. Or even the cargo: but *Mako* had no room, and if salvagers found it first, Ironhead could crap in his hat.

There was also Sam's own cargo. He decided to fasten the two ships together and go on to the Environ. Not a popular idea, but the best he had.

They caught the Environ. Far past Gowdy's target point, and only by straining *Mako*'s drives did he come that close.

Cargoes offloaded and signed for, with penalty deductions for late delivery, Gowdy headed home. Still lugging *Tarpon*, and his own drives bucking for premature overhaul.

Since *Tarpon* could not be kept habitable, both crews had to crowd in together. It made for a long trip, and if Sam's bunch had been pissed with him earlier, that term was now too mild.

Still two days out, *Mako* blew a drive node; limping on a fudged trajectory, the ship arrived at orbit later than even the twice-extended schedule allowed. But putting such concerns aside, Gowdy took leave and headed downside, for home.

Except that home wasn't there any longer. The place was, but Alain and the kids were gone. She'd left the divorce summons on the kitchen table.

He had no time to deal with that shock; as Jason had predicted, a board convened. Items: *Mako* had been diverted from schedule, was assessed penalty for late arrival, had squandered more than twice its fuel allotment to return at a time when it should be halfway out on its next trip, was unfit for service until thoroughly overhauled at considerable expense, all these financial damages inflicted on the parent agency by the unauthorized decisions of acting chief pilot Samuel Hall Gowdy.

Further, said acts redounded only to the benefit of private contractor Ira Ned Kennealy whose own negligence had placed his ship *Tarpon* at some inconvenience, which Mr. Gowdy had on his own initiative seen fit to remedy.

"*Inconvenience*, you say?"

"Silence, Mr. Kennealy! We are recessed until tomorrow at oh ten hundred, at which time judgment shall be rendered."

Gowdy did not sleep well; when the hearing reopened he

sat waiting for the axe. The chairman rose. "In the matter of the agency ship *Mako*, acting chief pilot Samuel Hall Gowdy is granted an honorable discharge with suitable bonus and awarded the agency's Distinguished Service Medal for outstanding initiative."

Sam clung blindly to Kennealy's arm. "How the hell . . . ?"

Ironhead either coughed or laughed; sometimes it was hard to tell. "You don't watch much holie, do you?"

"No. Why?"

"I know this old babe, see? Down at the All BS newsroom."

"All-Broadcast Systems?"

"I guess. Anyway, I fed her the story and last night on the late news she ran with it. Drew a whole lot of calls."

So much for the merits of the case. Now, mercifully or perhaps not, Alain's divorce suit didn't take long. Her imminent remarriage took care of any alimony problems, and of his own accord Gowdy settled the unexpected bonus on his kids.

At loose ends, Sam applied for the *Starfinder* program. Oddly enough, the publicity from *Tarpon* seemed to work in his favor. And then he had things to do, active things, to divert his mind from past misfortune.

But now, as SuZanne Craig bullied the Vehicle down through wrenching jet streams to quieter strata, Gowdy had to sit passive and watch her do the job.

She's done this before. Under her breath Kayo repeated the comforting mantra. Shuddering, the DV pitched and dropped, Traction Drives slowing its fall in jerky increments.

On the main screen the ground below, sidelit as its sunstar lowered, expanded to nearness. At one side lay a smooth-curving beach; to the other, a cluster of buildings. Directly below, Kayo saw living beings scuttling to get safely clear. They had plenty of time; the drive nodes weren't even kicking up dust yet.

Dan grunted; Kayo realized she was squeezing his hand hard enough to draw juice. She eased her grip. "Sorry."

"It's okay. Gets you the first time, doesn't it?"

As swirls of dust obscured the screen view, Skeeter Cole

switched to the outer rear visuals; SuZanne could see all around the landing site but not the spot itself.

With less jar than some of the wind shears had made, the DV grounded. Abruptly, Kayo's breathing came a lot easier.

With awe, Irtuk-saa watched the huge construct lower itself to rest. This was the intruders' *small* ship? Larger, she knew, than those Magh raised so long ago to Eamn. Through the roiling dust she saw a few loiterers scramble to safer vantage. Now, flanked by Menig-dre and Staon-tal, senior bearers of the observatory staff, Irtuk awaited what would come.

A long wait, until at the bottom of the vessel's hull, central to its three support beams, a hatch dropped open and a ladder descended. A being emerged: hindlimbs first, then trunk and forelimbs, finally a head. Wrapped in coverings that left only head and grasping extremities exposed, the biped clambered slowly down, encumbered by various objects attached to harness straps. Two more of the creatures followed, each differing in some ways from the first.

As that one reached ground and straightened to an exaggerated degree of erectness, Irtuk motioned to Menig and Staon to remain where they were. Accompanied only by Duant, who held a small tone projector, she stepped forward to greet the creatures who had come so far. And hoped they meant her well.

"Atmosphere check." With the Vehicle down, Sam leaned back in the comm seat and took charge.

"Pressure's a bit light," said Skeeter Cole, "about like five thousand feet back home." And this was sea level, or near it. "Partial pressure 0-two in nominal proportion, no toxics. Particulates—well, the dust's still settling—slight traces of organics. Pollen, maybe? Temperature eighteen Celsius."

"Right." Gowdy stood. "Cole and Marlin, with me. We'll carry breather tanks and masks, just in case. Kayo, your field recorder; get a start on language. And your bleeper, Skeets; let 'em know right off, we're the folks who sent the numbers."

As the three equipped themselves, SuZanne Craig pointed to the screen, its composite picture showing the surroundings below. "Look at some of the stuff that crowd's packing. Weapons?"

"Maybe," Sam said. "Wouldn't you? But we're taking nothing of the sort. What good would it do us?" Feeling less confident than he hoped he sounded, he climbed over the safety rail and started down.

Less than three quarters gee made the tunnel descent easy work. Inside the airlock, Gowdy closed the upper hatch. "Here goes." As the lower hatch opened, air pressure fell. He dropped the ladder, jounced on the top rung to test its footing, and descended. Halfway down he was pleased to find that the air tanks wouldn't be needed. But it was too late to go put them back.

When he had both feet on the ground and not before, he turned to see the welcoming committee. They stood on two legs but slightly crouched; fully erect, the ones in the foreground might have topped Sam's height a few inches.

No clothing as such; harnesses hung with totally unfamiliar gear covered very little of the creatures' bodies. Smooth, delicately colored integument was articulated into flexing segments, interrupted only by a central ridge of mane from brow to tail. At first the tails fooled Gowdy; then he saw that the apparent flap of fur at lower abdomen was only the end of that appendage, curled forward between the legs and up again.

The heads, with their large and wide-set eyes, resembled no animal he knew of—but still, somehow, looked familiar.

Before he could define the quality he sought, another datum struck him. Skeeter said it first, though. "Did we land at a school or something? I mean, it looks like just three grownups and a lot of kids."

And as two natives approached, Gowdy saw that the leader, as well as two who stayed behind, was much larger than any of the others: not only half a head taller, but bulking hugely wide.

Size wasn't Kayo Marlin's concern as she grasped Sam's arm. "Look out! That little one; what's he doing?"

Only a few yards away, the smaller local raised and aimed a compact device. As Gowdy wondered whether he'd made a really bad mistake, the thing began to chirp at them.

Skeeter Cole pulled out his own bleeper and started counting numbers right back. Only louder.

VI

Clothing sweat-streaked, Kayo Marlin clambered over the safety rail onto the DV's operating deck. "Whew! I'm baked. Thank heaven for the daily eclipse." Not that two hours' break made much dent in a day's twenty-odd. Even the late breeze, sometimes prelude to cooling storm, felt like oven breath.

From the pilot console Sam Gowdy looked up at her. "Making any more points with Maghren syntax?"

She grinned. "A few; nothing earthshaking." And headed for a cool shower.

Twenty, now, of Magh's fortyplus-hour orbits. Ignoring the turmoil when SuZanne Craig fetched Barry Krsnch and the rest of his team, Kayo plied her algorithm compositer in sessions with Irtuk and Duant and Triem. Skeeter's mathematical efforts had laid good groundwork—giving her, as he'd said earlier, the equivalent of several auxiliary parts of speech.

Now that she and Cole were able to point, act out, and speak and hear, Kayo had ample grist for her algorithmic mill.

Not that it had been all smooth sailing.

She'd never forget that first meeting, when everyone thought the bearers were the only adults. By now Kayo had the Maghren genders at least partially straight. Enough to realize that all Magh's history and politics were *based* on these peoples' strange modes of reproduction.

Done showering and nominally clothed, Kayo fixed herself a cooler and rejoined the captain. She sipped. "The good part is, they learn our words as fast as Skeeter and I pick up theirs. The bad is, it still takes us hell and forever."

"Funny thing," Gowdy said. "Our first impression wasn't so far off, at that. Those big ones, the mothers . . ."

"Bearers," Kayo put in.

"Whatever," said Gowdy. "They really do act like parents. Nobody else does anything without Big Mama's okay."

"And that's what seems to have caused their old war. An upheaval at the Eamn colony, a reversal of traditional roles. The word they use translates as heresy. Or abomination."

Sam grunted. "Sounds familiar. Well, keep on it. We'll talk when I get back." Kayo nodded; with peaceful relations established, next priority was putting the macroGate together. Even ahead of getting the Earthgates off *Roamer* and working.

So that soon now, there'd be other ships from Earth. And a bunch of Johnnie-come-latelies could barge in and take over.

But what the hell? Kayo knew that before she joined up.

As cycles passed, strangeness yielded to familiarity and Irtuk-saa found herself more comfortable with the Erdthan yumins. Duant also was losing his initial wariness, though Triem still appeared to hold reservations.

What was the factor, among adaptives, that resisted change? That in the basic acts of reproduction they alone filled two disparate roles—as surrogate bearer to seeders and as seeder to bearers? So that in other aspects of their lives they felt need for constancy?

The hypothesis brought no conclusion. Nor did it account for the apparent unease of Menig-dre and Staon-tal in dealing with the yumins. Now, as Irtuk labored to improve speakings with the two called Kayo and Skeeta, her fellow-bearers squatsat well back from the group, their mistrust evident—though not so clear, Irtuk hoped, to the yumins themselves.

"This Gate you build," Irtuk said, "in the sky. Your kind can come through it from your home? Tread in, tread out? No need for ships to travel long and long?"

Before Kayo spoke, Irtuk recognized the yumin's look of indecision. "The macroGate, so we call it, is to bring entire ships through. But with it *or* the lesser Gates it's not just go in and come out. Time passes." Kayo turned to Skeeta. "How many Maghdays? Or would Chormyears be easier?"

"Maghdays," the other answered. "Um—three base–squared, almost exactly."

Irtuk thought, then nodded. "And in relation, a cycle of Chorm is seven parts of ten, to the time of a Gate passage."

Skeeta nodded. "Near enough." Then he—for Skeeta was in the yumin way a seeder—said that this time elapsed only *outside* the Gates, not for those utilizing them. And more greatly incredible, the time related not to distance; whether from star to star or only between holdings, it would not vary.

Had any Maghren raised such a premise, Irtuk would have *snff'd* it to scorn. But these were Erdthans, saying of Erdth devices. And of a surety they had come here from another star; if they could do so much, then why not this marvel also?

As to why they came, Irtuk's thought was yet unclear. Kayo, who claimed to be a bearer though she lacked proper bulk and could not possibly have even one womb in process, said it was because yumins sought to learn all that was. But if that were true, they were as lately borns; experience brought realization that such a task transcended possibility. Yet perhaps Kayo's thought was less grandiose than Irtuk perceived it.

While Duant and Skeeta sought to reconcile discrepant interpretings of a question, Irtuk's thinking drifted. All Erdth yumins yet seen were either seeders or the absurdly small individuals claiming bearerhood. When Irtuk asked of yumin adaptives, Kayo said no such existed—that with no adaptive intervention whatsoever, normal seeder emission might produce within a bearer either of their two types.

As an exercise in imagination, Irtuk found the concept most interesting. In practice, however, she felt it would sadly curtail the range of possible intimacies.

What a pity! A species so skilled with devices, yet doomed to such limitation in one of the more rewarding aspects of life.

Climbing down, past the wail of Feodor Glinka's saxophone from a cargo hold, Sam came groundside; through warm drizzle he headed for the mess tent. A woman of Krsnch's group, showing none of that man's resentment at having to share such chores, cheerfully zapped a luncheon packet and poured fresh coffee.

"Thanks." Finding a nearby table, Gowdy munched away. He wasn't pleased when Jules Perrone brought a glass of iced tea and sat across from him, but nodded anyway. "Hi."

Sleek as always, the drive tech smiled. "You'll be glad to get back to the ship." And so? "I expect you haven't been *too* lonely, though. With Craig and Vinler here, and the group marriage and all." He paused. "Or should it come to Maril, I'm not exactly the jealous type." A grin, now. "How about you, captain?"

Deliberately, Gowdy stared until the other man looked away. "I would not advise you to make that any of your business."

Quickly standing, he disposed of his utensils and sloshed his way to the comm tent. Fuming. What the hell?

Needing to finalize his plans for departure, Gowdy sat in the tent and stewed. Shorthanded and no help for that, was he leaving the right mix here, to get the job done?

Kayo and Skeeter had the communication project going well, and Maril Jencik could backup for Cole on the equipment side. Third Officer Feodor Glinka was to take charge; his pairmate Jinx Lanihan doubled in ship's maintenance and as a competent galley hand. *Roamer* would run shy on instrument techs, but at in-system speeds and gentle accel, vernier-grade accuracy wasn't needed.

So much for contact and communications. As for testing and classifying everything about this world, Barry Krsnch and Libby Verdoorn had the down team hopping: analyzing soil and sea and air, life-forms from all three as fast as Verdoorn's biosearch squad could nab them, maybe even Big Red's weather patterns. Already the team learned that humans could safely eat most local fruits and vegetables (but watch out for purple veins or orange nodules!), and vertebrate life was edible. With invertebrates, if it had legs, let it go. In the cluster of pre-fabs down by the shore, Krsnch had his project well up and running.

Fine—except for Barry's idea that *all* downside ops were his pigeon. "Your group," he said now, "can hand their reports to Libby; I'll add the important parts to my own daily messages."

Before Sam could frame a diplomatic answer, Skeeter Cole cut in from the comm desk. "*You'll* decide what's important? What makes you the authority on our business?"

The bigger man smiled; if he intended to look friendly, it didn't come across. "You're working downside now. That's my area, so . . ." He spread his hands.

"Wrong," said Sam. The hell with tact. "Nobody's in charge of my crew but me. Your reports will route through *my* comm gear, so you hand them to my duty watch, for Gating to Earth." Krsnch glowered; Gowdy gave him a flat deadpan stare. "In full, I might add; none of us will presume to edit your work."

He paused. "Any more questions?"

In silence, Krsnch turned away and left the tent.

"What gets into that guy?" Cole sounded plaintive.

"Empire fever," said Kayo Marlin. "The more he can take over, the bigger slice he can cut when we're assigned colony status." She frowned. "Except, we won't be. We're only visitors here, not discoverers. Instead of establishing a colony, we'll be asking permission to set up an enclave."

"Right." And so much for Gowdy's Star or Gowdy's Planet; maybe Sam could find himself a good comet. "Okay, the roster here. Feodor and Jinx, Maril, and you two; that's solid. Maybe Jules, too; you could use some help moving crates around."

Cole and Marlin went quiet; Gowdy said, "I know, it leaves you two the odd ones out. But I need my number two DV pilot."

Sunburn or no, Cole's face certainly flared now. "You're leaving your number one drive tech. Why not Alix, instead? How do Jules and Maril rate over us? For being together, I mean."

Helpless against the man's resentment, Gowdy tried again. "Well, like I said, the muscle. Two men didn't seem quite enough for the grunt work. And . . ." He trailed off.

"And you don't want us having to beg favors of Barry's crew," Kayo added. "C'mon, Skeets. It makes sense."

"If you say so." But Cole wasn't really buying it.

He had a point, too. Not that it changed anything: Perrone would stay because Gowdy was fed up with the slick sonofabitch and wanted rid of him.

Anyway, it was time to check in with *Roamer*.

* * *

"... really no point in our making a rendezvous, captain," Tuiasso reported. Flare emission from Whitey made visuals useless; the circuit was voice only. "I doubt you could tie on, anyway. With Velucci's Gate segments sticking out all over, our hull looks like an artichoke screwing an eggbeater."

Sam gave one laugh snort. "Just so it doesn't shed any leaves when you hit the push."

"That's another thing. Pia has the stuff secured, but it's none too strong in its own right. I plan to hold thrust down to about a quarter gee."

Gowdy thought about it. "Yeah. With no sudden moves, you shouldn't have to secure the residential belt. Of course you still need to stow all the jounceables."

Funny ha-ha; no one ever managed that task. But too often the results weren't funny at all. Tuiasso said, "If you were to get out there first and peg the Trojan point for me, I could zero in a lot easier. Avoid any high-thrust corrections."

"Good point. Okay, tell you what; we'll take off midway on a retro leg of our orbit." Subtracting Magh's orbital velocity from Big Red's would save some fuel. Not much, but a little.

"Right," said Mose. "I intend to leave the same way. We hit that spot in about six hours, so we'd better snap to."

"Fine." Cutting the circuit, Gowdy realized he needn't move the DV for a time yet; why sit out there and wait?

He felt good. While Mose had to herd the big ship slow and easy, Gowdy could put this little bucket through its paces. Like on his old training ship, except this one had more legs to it. And he hadn't done turnover since the freight haul days.

For this course he didn't need computer readouts. Just stay in plane with Whitey and Big Red and Magh—or maybe Scout, for a longer sighting leg. Back off to where the star and major planet lay sixty degrees apart, fudge sideways until Scout sat smack in the middle, and fiddle the fine tuning from there.

If an easier navigation problem existed, Sam hadn't heard of it. Still, he'd double-check his sightings against the readouts, until the DV sat librating exactly where it should. If librating and exactly really belonged in the same sentence. . . .

* * *

Longer than Nsil or his supporters expected, preparation for the Magh raid dragged on. Originally the plan seemed so simple, its implementations so elegant—but first one and then another segment posed problems neither quickly nor easily resolved.

Fuel was the key: how to lift enough to power the mission. The two ships, Three the carrier and One the scout, could not launch as a unit. Even raising separately, the margin would be debatable. So the midsized ship Two must lift to fixed-position orbit, where it would serve to refuel both others.

Following its single reconnaissance of Magh, however, Two had not been reconditioned for further use. Thus, additional unforeseen tasking had created even greater delay.

With the Overgrouping's full support, successive reliefs of planners and workers provided continuous effort; soon now, all three ships would be readied. But liaison and connection between the three, high above Eamn, required protective garments known only from old records. Now these must be reinvented and fabricated. And there could be no mistakes, Nsil insisted; all such devices must operate correctly the first time.

"Not precisely so," Scayna protested when Nsil complained to her. "Can you not construct a testing chamber?" Why not, indeed? While total airlessness lay beyond achievement, surely Eamnet skills could produce an approximation suitable for these purposes. Accordingly, Nsil ordered such a program begun.

And so, and so. The suitings, the fittings and grappling devices for connection between ships in free space, many and more omissions discovered in the plan, each to be remedied.

And then fewer. Until finally the liftings could have a time assigned, in immediacy. For the most part, then, Nsil felt both exhilaration and relief.

But in one matter, neither. For now Scayna must be told of his decision.

"It is necessary; I cannot send others to a peril I do not face also."

From the tension she could sense in him, Scayna knew that Nsil believed deeply in what he said. Tonguetip worrying the central V-shaped gap between her lower teeth, she pondered on what to answer. Tentatively, "Your feeling speaks of honor, as all who know you would expect. And yet . . ."

"You find my thought wanting?"

Her forelimb digits, tangled in the mane just behind his head, tugged gently. "You misread my hesitation; I see no lack on your part." No lack, but excess, Scayna wished to curb. How, though? Ah . . . "It is only that—what if—I dread the peril to *Eamn*, Nsil, should you go to Magh and be lost there."

For moments she hoped him convinced. But unlike most, Nsil had largely overcome the self-importance so typical of seeders. Head to one side, he demurred. "False praise, Scayna. Well meant, I credit, yet still based on fallacy. Gvan, for instance, could take up any tasks I might leave uncompleted. Or others . . ." Silent for a moment, he said, "Well, certainly Gvan."

"Then you are determined?"

"I am. But I could not go without first being here with you." He reached to the base of her neck, around to the place where touch brought shivers of delight.

Against the impulse he aroused, she said, "You have not asked of wombreadiness."

"And I shall not. Whatever may ensue, has my validation."

From his earliest days, thought Scayna, bending to his touch, there had always been a special quality to Nsil.

Directing the foray, Nsil strove to participate in all its aspects. As ship Two fought its noisy way to orbit, he rode alongside Feln and Tasr, its veteran controllers. Once the ship was up, circling Eamn at a distance that kept the launching site stationary below, lack of weight first dizzied him, but soon he adapted and could maneuver around the interior well enough. His quasimate Tirys, among others, experienced greater difficulty.

The ship's position would not hold for long; Chorm's mighty pull disturbed the calculated path. Yet drift was slight; Two would be near proper place until its first chore was done. And for its second, the provision of landing fuel to the returning ships, predetermined locus of rendezvous need not be so precise.

Even diminished by the hull-piercing vision tubes, the sight of Eamn below, more than twice its diameter distant, awed Nsil. So did the far vaster yet lesser-seeming bulk of Chorm, fully lit by Jemra, and in black sky the unwinking stars. Anticipating the total strangeness of this situation, Nsil had braced to combat fear—and was greatly pleasured that it did not materialize.

Eamn now lay sunward of Chorm; against the glare of Jemra, no Maghren device should detect the ships here. As the other two rose, then jockeyed to proximity, Magh passed behind Chorm. Ship One had no difficulty, but the larger, more sluggish Three suffered overcontrol a time or two before meeting succeeded.

Now, as Nsil and others donned the protective suits, came a greater hurdle. Well tested though the suits had been, only one fact was proven: that they had not failed *as yet.* Hiding his misgivings as best he could, Nsil led the way into the evacuable chamber and then, trailing a flexible cable tethered to the ship's hull, ventured out into nothingness.

By the time One and Three were fully refueled, then fastened side to side for the voyage to Magh, that world had circled Chorm and was near to disappearing once more. Entering ship One, Nsil and Feln were greeted by their fellow-members of the landing party, and shortly the engines of Three, now directed by Tasr, began driving the united pair Chormward. After a time, when their projected velocity was reached, the engines fell silent.

Their course, planned to hide them in Jemra's brightness for as long as possible, was necessarily inefficient; this need further magnified the fuel requirement. Over a time, then, and weightless more often than not, the Eamnet crews learned to live and function in their unnatural environment. In particular, Nisl and the rest found excretion and its containment a most unpleasant chore; over the cable linking the two ships, Tasr reported the same problems on Three. In future, Nsil promised himself, more practical facilities must be devised. Though Feln, who had circled Magh in Two, denigrated the newer spacefarers as little smofs, needing their excretors dabbed and powdered.

At last the joined pair neared Magh, as that world moved toward passage between Chorm and Jemra. Crew members from Three emerged to free the lesser ship. After their return inboard, Three left to seek orbit, higher than old wartime surface weapons might threaten but well within range when One should lift again. Then, as controller, Feln turned ship One to drop toward Magh.

Until the need came to slow and land, One's vision tubes monitored the surface below. And as its course began to curve around to Magh's Chormward side, now entering its night period, Nsil saw flaring color as the smaller out-system ship, straightly risen to well above a boiling surface storm and now commencing to turn, built speed. Strangely, it seemed bound not for its parent vessel but into emptiness. Even Shtai the Forerunner lay opposite to its heading. What could be its goal?

No time for speculation; from an area lying between a body of water and a range of hills, near the apparent start of the departing ship's rise, Nsil detected signal radiation. Behind those hills, then, One would essay to ground. From there, the storm granting safe alightment, Nsil's force could reconnoiter.

Here waited the crucial passage; no longer could Jemra shield the ship—and from Maghren detecting instruments, the storm might or might not protect. Turned to drop backward through Magh's thinner air, finally its engines roared thrust ahead to slow the turbulent, jostling fall.

Here vision tubes lay useless; only signal-echo devices told of One's decreasing distance to the world below. Soon now, Eamnets would again tread the soil of Magh.

Or at any rate, come to meet with it.

Sam didn't lift the Vehicle; SuZanne Craig wanted to give young Dan the practice and Gowdy saw her point. Not to be second-guessing anyone he watched on aux screens as the DV rose into rainy darkness and jolted through a storm cloud layer. In moments Big Red, until now a dim patch of light on cloud, loomed clear; near the glowering disk's center, Acey's shadow appeared.

As the DV began to turn away, something on a screen jarred Sam to alertness. "Hey!" He hit the proper Record button. "Something going in, off to starboard—and back of us, now. Chemical drive, looks like."

Frowning, Craig shushed him. "Later, dammit!"

All right; Quillan didn't need the distraction. Until they

were straightened out and the heading set, Gowdy shut up. Even then he waited until SuZanne asked, "All right, what was it?"

"Let's see." He ran Reverse, then played what he had. It wasn't much; nothing to give any indication of scale, and not very good focus. But some tin can had come in, blaring flame ahead, toward hope of landing. The image dwindled and died before that hope could be realized or denied; Gowdy stopped the replay. "Our own natives aren't flying anything yet, are they? So this has to be from Deucy—Eamn, they call it."

"They're enemies," Alix said. "Aren't they? And couldn't that be dangerous? For *our* people."

SuZanne shook her head. "How many troops could one ship carry? Against a whole world. Still, it couldn't hurt to pass the word."

"Right," said Gowdy. "I'll call down, tell our folks to be on the lookout. And if necessary, head for safe cover."

He didn't feel he could justify following his first impulse: to turn back immediately and make sure everybody was okay.

"Some kind of *ship* landing?" As Kayo watched and listened anxiously, Skeeter Cole shook his head.

Scratchily from the speaker, as the screen showed random hash, Sam Gowdy's voice came again. "You didn't see anything? Or hear it? Should have been one helluva blast."

Kayo leaned forward. "It's really come up a storm here; if anything did land, we probably took it for just more thunder."

"Well, it wasn't. Tell your Maghren friends they have company. If they haven't noticed already."

"Will do, skipper," said Cole. "Anything more?" No, so he signed off. "All right; who gets to go tell Irtuk?"

"In this weather?" Involuntarily, Kayo shivered. Then she stood. "Oh, well. If it has to be . . ."

Skeeter blinked. "Wait'll the storm dies; these things don't usually last long. Right now I'll give Feodor the news."

So she sat again. It seemed a little strange, sharing the comm tent with Skeeter Cole. But they did work together, mostly, and it was handy living where all their gear was kept.

Jinx and Feodor had a tent to themselves; so did Jules and

Maril. Pitching a solitary cot in one of the supply tents didn't strike Kayo as the essence of cozy.

So on balance she felt fairly comfortable with the platonic setup. And certainly Dan Quillan hadn't batted an eye when the idea was broached. Well, he wouldn't.

She was surprised how much she missed Dan. In his own retiring way the kid was *fun*, not to mention easy to get along with. As to sex he was eager but too shy to get pushy; after a time she'd had to tell him it was okay to ask. One of these days his skills might even match his consideration. If they ever got to bunk where privacy wasn't so scarce. On the DV, for instance, there simply hadn't been any. What you'd call a really dry run.

Meanwhile she sat waiting for the other shoe to drop. In minutes Cole returned, saying that Glinka agreed Irtuk should be notified but the need wasn't immediate.

Later, when the storm eased, Skeeter relented. "I'll go." By his grin Kayo saw he'd meant to do this all along.

But she was already parka'd up. "Let's both. It's not too good an idea, being out there alone." So off they trudged, into rain driven by shifting winds that reminded Kayo of what the Gulf of Alaska could do to her uncle Pete's fishing boat.

She didn't like it any better now than she had then.

The stone walk to Denaize Observatory's outlying guest quarters lay slick with mud from the sudden runoff. Sliding and skidding, Kayo and Skeeter found the entrance they sought and cranked the unfamiliar knocker; after a long shivering time, one of the smaller Maghrens admitted them.

By repeating Irtuk's name they gained escort to the bearer. In a room with two others she gave greeting, asking what brought them here at such an hour and in such discomfort.

"A ship landed," Kayo began, "and it's not one of ours."

Astonishment: had she seen it? Then how could she know? Told from her own ship, now departed? And had those aboard seen the landing, specified its location? Pause. But then how . . . ?

Trying to get a spacegoer's viewpoint across to one who'd never been upstairs, Kayo found the job next-door to impossible. Finally Irtuk agreed, "At the end of longdark we will set search, and determine if your ship observed truly."

Kayo checked her watch, gimmicked by Skeeter to Acey

time: six more hours before Whiteyrise. To Irtuk she said, "Any way we can, we'll help." And to Skeeter, "Let's drag ass home."

Outside, the wind was gone but the mud wasn't. Back in the tent, Kayo truly missed the DV. Sponge baths would never replace the hot shower. The exploration team had showers and even a tub, but she didn't feel like going outside again, this night.

Or being patronized by Barry Krsnch for needing to use his group's facilities. Better to suffer the minor embarrassment of Skeeter's conscientiously turned back as she sponged and toweled.

With due regard to weather and terrain, Feln brought ship One to ground most admirably. True, it stood overshadowed by broken, flame-scarred trees in a cavernous ravine rising over twice its own height. But firmly set, though perilously aslant.

A few paces one way or another and it could be toppled, perhaps exploded, in any case rendered unable to rise ever again. In main, then, Nsil credited the controller with skill beyond reasonable expectation.

The deep gulch hid the ship well from discovery, but also blocked communication with any scouting party; the signal units for such use operated on line-of-sight frequencies. Nsil sighed; no advantage came without restrictions.

The storm's worst had passed; as Feln moved the outer hatch a barest crack ajar, air from Eamn whistled forth, scattering raindrops before it. Aides now unfolded the jointed ladder; as director, Nsil climbed first down to stand on Magh.

Thinner air meant lesser endurance, but bred and grown on heavier Eamn, Nsil's muscles handled this reduced weight with ease. Over the generations, Eamnet physique had shortened and become more stocky. Stronger, thus, than Maghrens. Yet in conflict limb to limb, Eamnet aim must be swift resolution, ere fatigue eroded that superiority. Were such conflict to arise . . .

Now, upon inspection Feln assured that One could lift from this degree of tilt; in accordance the controller tasked a maintenance team with readying the ship to do so at Nsil's need.

When Three next passed overhead, Feln messaged affirmation of successful grounding and was assured of information relay to Eamn. Only then did Nsil, he and nine followers provisioned and accoutered for the venture, undertake the long, steep climb out of the ravine, toward the hills that hid their goal.

VII

From the first flaming rise of Nsil's ships until Tasr's report of ship One's safe descent to Magh, Scayna kept restless vigil. Nsil's authorization of personal access to all public procedurals provided her an open link to Gvan, who in the Overgrouping now stood stead for Nsil.

Only when assured of Nsil's safety did Scayna return to the confinement dome for a well-earned time of warmbathing, food and drink, and intimate indulgences. Her cycle having proceeded beyond wombreadiness, she could now indulge freely with favored seeders or adaptives alike, and without care as to the seeded or unseeded state of the latter.

Soon she would know, and could inform Nsil by way of ship Three, whether their own latest intimacy had begun a new seeder.

Custom notwithstanding, Scayna rather hoped that it had.

A bit short of forty hours out, Gowdy swung the DV through turnover and began decel. The little can was agile, all right; even watching his indicators, it was hard to avoid overcontrolling. But a little fudging got it on line, stern first toward Big Red's trailing Trojan point.

When Acey's tide-locked orbit brought the base back into contact, Skeeter reported from Irtuk: nothing seen, heard, or located. "If anything did come down, the storm covered it. Irtuk laid on a search, along the shore both ways and well up into the hills, but they found diddly, so she called it quits.''

When the Vehicle caught and passed *Roamer* there was still no solid info. And as signal lag grew with increasing distance, chat for its own sake was hardly worth it.

Simone Leopold did have other news. ''There's a ship circling Acey, well upstairs. Molly Abele made the sighting, fiddling around on hi-mag. No idea what it thinks it's doing.''

Too bad the Vehicle couldn't spot small stuff at such distance. ''Okay; thanks. Let me know if anything develops.''

Nothing did. As Gowdy began to maneuver the DV for Trojan positioning, he wished *somebody* could give him a clue.

As Nsil had adjudged, in short term the Eamnet musculature overbalanced the disadvantage of thin air, while over a longer period the reverse obtained. Clambering up the canyon wall, through dense growth of the water-loving leatherleaf trees, the group took frequent restings; once up and out, the lesser hillside slopes allowed more progress between pauses.

At the canyon's rim, Tirys served as relay to Feln and his seven on ship One. Besides a tone signal unit the adaptive carried a short-range talker; aimed downward, its emissions would not be detected here above. The addition was Feln's suggestion; realizing his own limited cognizance in such matters, Nsil welcomed the controller's advice.

Nsil found Magh less strange than he had anticipated. Its scant air and lesser weight burden were known aforetime. And with less atmosphere to refract Jemra's light, the darker hue of daylight sky followed as natural consequence.

The hillsides held only scattered trees; dense brush clumps, themselves impenetrable but separated enough for easy passage, stood higher than Nsil's head. Lesser growth presented a mix of plant forms, some familiar and some not; also, many he knew at home were absent here. Only a sampling of Magh's bounty had been taken to Eamn, where now it grew among native forms, the distinction forgotten by all but specialists in such matters.

The same factors held for animal life. Any smofs found here would be descended from pets brought back by traders, as colonists had taken spiny-backed hunting zhigas to Eamn. Those zhigas, though—what few there may have been—had fallen to the Great Dying. Eamnet museums displayed specimens of the rangy beasts; Nsil hoped that here they still thrived. And also the free-roving untamed cousins to Magh's draft and meat animals, some of whose descendants now grazed on Eamn.

The top of yet another hill marked the cresting of the overall range. Now came tumbled slopings to a narrow plain, ending at a great bay bounded by distant headlands and now gleaming brilliant under Jemra's light.

Before that bay a cluster of buildings sat, and near them ground vehicles, two floaters, and one airfoil. Shading his eyes from the water's glare, Nsil could see Maghrens, seeming small as crawling plant pests, as they moved throughout the settlement.

If any who followed Nsil thirsted and hungered as he himself did, respite was well past due. Accordingly he called a pause; squatting together with the adaptive Vyorn and seeder Knad, he spoke of the next phase.

They would descend to the plain's edge, wait for Jemra to leave the skies, then explore this center of habitation.

"But we enter no buildings and confront no one; we are not to be seen. For this occasion, we gather only facts."

Artifacts could await their next incursion.

Overwork, Sam decided, made Pia Velucci much less of a pain. Now on an aux screen he saw her directing an assembly move, as the DV towed one end of a macroGate arc to position while the other was winched to accurate juncture with its mating segment.

When the primary fasteners were in place she'd send the DV to its next assignment, inspect the unit now in assembly, check skeds to ensure that components were coming offship in proper sequence, pop inship for an "oil change" (coffee in, pee out), and come back to holler where the hell was the DV and why not.

Work had taken most of the lard off; for a stocky woman, Velucci looked trim. Best, though, was that with real work at hand she forgot to rasp except when thoroughly exasperated.

Back at Acey the supposed Eamn ship still held orbit. Also, Mose reported one moving from Scout's position. But the angle was bad; he hadn't yet pegged its course. With signal time from Acey now steady at a bit over eleven minutes, Sam didn't bother to query. If Cole and Marlin learned anything, they'd pass it on without need for asking. He couldn't afford to worry about it.

Now he watched Velucci wave the DV off, tie lines trailing, and allowed himself a grin. He *deserved* one, maybe even needed it. And here in control seemed to be his best bet.

Quarters sure as hell wasn't. Whatever Sydnie had up her nose this time—his puzzle to figure out and he never had yet—it was certainly stuck there. All he knew was, at rendezvous when he and the others tubed aboard and hit the lounge for a welcome home drink, Sydnie seemed okay until she looked the returning group over. Then she did her instant freeze trick, and so much for his hopes of rollicking reunion on a mussed bed.

Now she spoke to him only in Cryptic, which she knew damn well was beyond his grasp. They still shared quarters, and obviously she begrudged him even that. So be it: when Pia's crew took residence on the macroGate, he was moving Sydnie out.

As he reaffirmed that thought, she entered control. And not even due on watch yet. "You're early."

Her dark blond hair hung loose today; now she pushed the left side back. "I was bored. You're relieved, if you like."

"I do like." It was no real favor, certainly not meant to be one. So he didn't say thanks.

How long until the big Gate was ready? Four days? Five? Not over a week, surely, that he'd be stuck here on *Roamer*.

Sam could hardly wait.

Sydnie didn't give two farts in a bucket how Sam Gowdy felt. While he was offship she'd considered how best to exploit the situation, once he and Jules returned. It shouldn't be too hard: fuel Sam's jealousy, orchestrate a confrontation, and let the two men destroy each other's credibility in front of witnesses.

She'd laid some groundwork. Vetting the many reports that went to Earth, Sydnie had inserted obvious minor errors in the versions she forwarded—errors that did not appear in *Roamer*'s log. And followed up with corrections, also unlogged, in her own name. Maybe she was looking too far ahead, but at some future review hearing, a little spin could make a big difference.

But Sam Gowdy, that sorry bastard, had left Jules behind on Acey, sinking her plan without a trace. She wasn't about to forgive him that unwitting ploy.

If it *was* unwitting. For now, she could let him stew, while she reworked her thinking. Meanwhile, time to check with Acey; Glinka was a hopeless drudge, but maybe Marlin or Cole had something she could use to keep the captain off-balance.

The *current* captain, Sydnie reminded herself. And along with that possibility of change she considered another factor. Soon there'd be colonists arriving. When that happened, the seat of authority would shift from *Roamer* to Acey.

And on that world she knew a man with a taste for power. The kind of man it was easy to manipulate, because he kept so busy jerking other people's strings, he wouldn't even notice.

"No, still nothing new," Kayo reported. "Sorry, Mose. If we pry anything out of Irtuk I'll advise soonest." Afterthought: "Tell Dan hello for me, would you please?" She really missed him, but how to say so through a third party? "Marlin out."

She was checking her notes of the call when Skeeter barged in. "Hey, Kayo. Irtuk says there's a mystery ship moving in!"

"*Another* one?" But if Eamn was sending reinforcements, she asked, what was so mysterious about that?

"No. From Scout—Shtai the Forerunner, they call it." Late afternoon winds had Cole's sunburned look at its glowing best.

After a moment she remembered. "And not the first time; right? But they think both ships came originally from Whitey's companion star. How far is that?"

Cole shrugged. "Four light-years, a little less."

"Not much of a haul, there."

"With our drive, no," he conceded. "But according to Irtuk those ships came in considerably slower than we did, and took a lot longer to kill what speed they did have. This one's using awfully light decel, if that proves anything."

"Traction Drive, chemical, or what? Do they know?"

"Traction, from what their observers say. Flaring a comparatively weak corona, though."

Kayo frowned—not annoyed, just querulous. "But any Traction unit that can move a ship at all . . . you'd think . . ."

Skeeter's eyebrows rose. "Fuel. If your supply's limited, you trade time for it. The way the DV would, in a lifeboat situation and trying to stretch distance."

She nodded. "Without Habgates for your fuel feed . . ."

". . . and crew rotation and the rest of it." Cole gestured emphasis. "Can you imagine riding *Roamer* all that way without Habgate capability?"

She could indeed. "We'd have arrived very old. And very very hungry." Suddenly the grim logistics came real to her. "Skeeter—how do you suppose they did manage it?"

"I'm not sure I want to know. But we'd better pass the word out to *Roamer*." Cole brought the transmitter up online.

Fully crewed for the first time since arrival at Yamar, *Tayr* builds movement—backward along that world's path toward the great Parent, to seek position near its inner Get. Nahei and skilled mechanicians from *L'lit* ride in accompaniment to *Tayr*'s, as does the Emman Bretl and seven of her own retainers.

Of greater height than Yainans, Bretl's Emmans find *Tayr* less than comfortable. They must walk its passageways stooped, touching a forelimb to the deck for balance. A storage area of greater clearance is equipped for their residency: water supply and heating, with means for bathing and excretion. And the operating dome itself rises enough for Emmans to move freely, saving only that they touch no instruments or controls.

Emmans adjust well to the reduced downpull given by *Tayr*'s pushforce; only during its cessation, as the ship swings ends to slow again, does Bretl admit difficulty. T'phee and Nahei feel relief; the thought of eight nauseous Emmans is a daunting one.

Although T'phee leads this endeavor, Nahei with experience of es own ship in flight serves as preceptor of Tayr, having left his surrogate Ornd in oversight of *L'lit*. And in

T'phee's absence, Cejha resumes Stewardship of Yainan affairs on Yamar.

Such matters T'phee puts behind en; ahead lies enigma deep enough to raise es necktrunk from midsleep in confused wariness, seeking to fixate fleeting images that hint of peril.

Waking, er speaks not of such vagrant seemings. Yamar will turn eightfold during this voyage; why should T'phee fall prey to errant, unformed concerns before need arises?

It is Nahei, in watch at a vision tube focused for farsight, who reports intruder ships moving, their purposes unevident.

"The smaller unknown has raised from the inner Get; with the larger it proceeds away from the Parent and from Yamar alike. Having achieved their aims, do they now return to their source?" Nahei's necktrunk bobs. "Further, two reaction-mass vessels from the outer Get, united as one, have come from it to the inner. The smaller goes to ground while the other, unpowered, follows a chosen circuit. But what these movements portend . . ."

"The Emmans attack?" T'phee's speaking is comment, only.

"With one small reaction ship?" Nahei's sensory cluster waggles briefly, a negating gesture. "One which, by appearance, might or might not be capable of again leaving the surface?"

"But on the journey," T'phee notes, "the small ship used no fuel. Any such vessel must be able to lift and later alight; doing these things in opposite order poses no greater demand."

Alongside looms Bretl; the Emman says, "There may be no intent for that one to rise again."

With one forelimb Bretl makes a grim sign. "Perhaps Eamnets return the dire blow struck by Magh in the old war. They may seek only to bring back plague, whence so long ago it came." Er grunts. "To do so while Magh has yet no means to strike back."

Plague? T'phee's neckskin twitches. Never since *Tayr* reached Yamar has contagion passed between Yainan and Emman. But lack of occurrence does not preclude possibility.

T'phee decides. "Before we risk a lander-carrier to that surface, we learn more. Nahei, can you seek us a resting position well away from the Emman vessel?"

* * *

At a point between the Parent and its inner Get, Nahei brings *Tayr* to uneasy rest. Gently but inexorably it weaves about that point, bound by the pulls of both worlds in relation to *Tayr*'s movement around the greater.

With affirming stroke of a manipular to Nahei's necktrunk, T'phee tells en "Well conducted," and offers a handcup of euphoric. "We lie safe away from Maggen reach," er assures Nahei. "And to detect *Tayr*, they must distinguish it against the vast colored face of the Parent."

"True," says Nahei, partaking of the liquid. "Yet we ride near enough that our lander-carriers, returning, should find no difficulty in making rendezvous."

Tayr carries three of the smaller vessels; its position lies well within their lifting range. Initially T'phee plans to take only one to the surface. Having often moved one such from Yamar to *Tayr* and back, as well as between surface locations, er will do so now also, leaving Nahei as ship's preceptor.

Paramount, however, is the venture's safety: first T'phee must ascertain the absence of contagion, and that Maggens view es mission to be cordial. As es mechanicians match parameters with detected Maggen signals, T'phee prepares to initiate discourse.

Er alone will speak. Bretl stays near to explain or interpret if need be, but T'phee mistrusts the displaced Emman's balance in dealing with es ancient foes, and has laid strictures on es participation.

Somewhat to T'phee's surprise, Bretl makes no dissent. So with Nahei also beside en, T'phee utters Emman words. "Maggens! We who come first from Yain of the nearest star, and most lately from that world you call Forerunner, would meet with you directly. May we come in safety, with no harm dealt by any?"

Er makes repeatings, pausing between, but no response ensues. T'phee goes to rest; others replace en as speaker. After almost a half turn of Yamar er returns, and has barely resumed es efforts when reply comes.

"Denaize Shore speaks. Who calls here, claiming provenance of Diell the Companion and of Shtai the Forerunner?"

* * *

Kayo had never seen Feodor Glinka excited. With angled eyes under heavy brows, broad nose between high cheekbones, and stolid mouth immobile, more than not he resembled a crudely hewn statue. Now bushy hair stuck out like last year's faded straw as he gestured. "The ship from Scout, is it? Who's aboard?"

Skeeter Cole answered. "Yainans, they say. From outsystem, originally. The observatory picked them up first, then Irtuk called us. Just to monitor, now, but Kayo's convinced Irtuk that having a starship ourselves, we might be some help later."

From the console a voice came; it could, Kayo thought, be a Maghren with a really bad accent. Glinka frowned. "I am not fluent in the local patois. Do you understand any of that?"

"Sort of," and Skeeter nodded agreement as she said, "Like a Londoner new to the Deep South, or vice versa. Wait a minute . . ."

She listened, then said, "Confirmation, gang. They saw a ship from Eamn come in to land somewhere near here."

"So the captain was right," said Glinka.

"Apparently. And—they want to know if it brought plague. Because they'd like to send a delegation down here, but not if anything contagious is running loose."

From another speaker came Irtuk's voice. "Over several cycles since the purported landing, no evidence of contagion has been found. And if plague were sown, anywhere on Magh, we would by this time know the sorrow of it."

After a delay the offworlder spoke again. "You have others there, not of this star system. Are they of good intent?"

Gratifying Kayo no end, Irtuk gave "the yumins" good marks. "They seek knowledge and bring it also; we and they learn together." The bearer *snff'd.* "Will you come here, then?"

Transmission lag seemed endless; finally the voice resumed. "We so intend. But with us are several Emmans, come to the Forerunner a great time past. Perhaps before your conflict, or near its onset. Long before our own arrival, in any case. Now they are of few numbers and live simply. Will those with us be welcome at our meeting?"

"So these *are* from the other star," Glinka commented. "Now what d'you suppose they'll be like?"

As Irtuk said, "They may come, yes. We accept your assurances for your own conduct; why not for theirs also?"

"Well, Feodor," said Skeeter, "I guess we'll find out."

It would be a big relief, Sam thought, when he could set the growing macroGate structure free of *Roamer*. Or, by now, 'tother way around; although outmassed by the ship, the skeletal Gate structure's sheer extent gave it considerable moment of inertia. Any residue of momentum put torque to the combined mass. Gowdy had given up correcting his orientation with the yaw thrustors; now *Roamer*, Gate and all, turned slowly about some random axis.

Well, Velucci had the last major components outship, was seeing to the assembly of the final two arc segments, and had bet Sam she'd have the outsized circle closed within thirty hours.

Much interior work still remained. While the primary wiring, for instance, was laid inside structural members during manufacture, connecting the junction boxes where arc segments met would be no small chore.

But given closure and pressurization, the rest was in-house work. Velucci could operate without the DV, moving supplies through the oversized tube now in place between ship and Gate. Might take a little longer that way, but it would free the Vehicle; Gowdy could take it back to Acey.

He truly wanted to be there, see what was going on with Eamn and with the ship from Scout. To be in the middle of it all.

Sam snorted. Why kid himself? What he wanted most was to be away from Sydnie. Lately she took undue pleasure in passing him bossy notes from Barry Krsnch. "He'd like an answer ASAP, if you can find the time," that sort of thing. Gowdy wouldn't put it past her to abet this new annoyance—but he couldn't prove it.

He scanned Barry's latest version of the same stupid demand: the macroGate should be at L-2 between Big Red and Whitey, and Gowdy should move it there. Copy to Earthbase, and Sydnie had Gated that flimsy off before showing him the original.

We'll see about that. He hit the intercom to Exec's quarters. "Simone? Sam here. From now on, officer Lightner is not authorized to Gate anything to Earth. Any items she wants transmitted, she will turn over to you for thorough inspection. And I mean word for word. Any questions?''

Leopold's usually smooth voice showed tension. ''Sam? Is there some problem I should know about?''

What to say? ''More crap from good ol' Barry, and she passed it through without my okay. I don't want that to happen again.''

Her answer came slow. ''If this is personal, it's none of my business.'' No argument there. ''But to single her out . . . why not simply have all reports go through you for clearance?''

Never mind that no other watch officer *needed* checking on. ''I won't be around. As soon as the DV's available I flag ass back to Acey. So it has to be your pigeon.''

Part of her idea was good, though. ''I guess it *would* be better if everyone routes through you. Not just Lightner.''

''Do you want a staff meeting?''

And give Sydnie a forum for her grievances? ''Definitely not. You just draft the notice and I'll sign it for posting.''

To Sam's relief, Leopold agreed. There'd be more to it; he had to tell Mose why the extra red tape, and little chance he'd evade a dose of Sydnie's patented guilt. But with luck he might have the DV away before she could get her tactics online.

''Okay then, Simone. And I'll catch you for a full briefing before I leave.''

''You'd better!''

''Hey, that's a promise.'' Cutting the intercom, he drafted a memo to follow Krsnch's complaint to Earth. He didn't call Barry an ignorant fugghead; he merely pointed out that the man's L-2 scenario would mean fifteen percent more solar heat for the Gate to pump away, along with its own thermal excess, and would Gate ships deeper into Whitey's gravity well in the same wasteful proportion. *Bureaucrats . . .*

Gowdy checked the time. With luck, he might catch Pia on a meal break about now. On the off chance of nailing down a solid time frame for release of the DV, he headed for the galley.

For that matter, he'd built some hunger on his own account.

* * *

From his first reconnaissance Nsil derived some knowledge and a spirit of confidence, but no firm plan. In this settlement no safeguards were evident, nor recognizable weapons. The few seeders and adaptives he had seen in the dimness stood rangier and slimmer than their like from Eamn—no match, limb to limb, for his raiders.

A bearer, though, would be—and more. On his next foray, then, Nsil and his followers would carry the new dazers. Combining a pulsed glare of light with blasts of sound reaching both above and below audible frequencies, the device stunned mental faculties while leaving the subject ambulatory.

Or so its providers claimed. From a shielded room Nsil had viewed tests, and certainly the volunteer subjects seemed rendered wholly docile.

They would need to be. Any plan Nsil might now devise must include taking Maghrens to Eamn. His early thought, to obtain proofs of Maghren intent, now seemed impractical. Tasr's report, the ship from Shtai hovering between Magh and Chorm, gave no time for laborious searchings. But captives he could come to know, could question—at length though preferably not harshly—and thus eventually learn more than from his own weight in documents.

The few scattered objects he had accumulated told him little or nothing. In most ways they could have been Eamnet. The only true unfamiliarity lay with the out-system creatures left behind by their smaller ship, and those Nsil had yet to view at close range. He had not estimated so many of them. Nor their strangeness, the stiff vertical bodies hidden under wrappings of some sort, and rounded heads with minimal jaw structure.

The wrappings made him wonder, did these beings come from a chiller world? Were he to abduct one or more of them also, could they subsist on Eamnet provender? Or must he release them here?

For that matter, would the dazers properly affect them? Conferring, he and Feln could not reach decision. Until Tasr gave call from Three as it passed above.

"Those from Shtai approach," er announced. "A small vessel, leaving the larger in place, applies power constantly, thus will reach surface alarmingly soon. With respect, Nsil and Feln, you may wish to abandon the mission and return here.''

The decision was Nsil's. ''We will essay forth once more, and do what may be done here. Then we rise to rendezvous, and all return to Eamn.''

With dispatch he set tasks, leaving Feln two helpers to raise ship at last resort. Tirys again would mount relay at the canyon's rim. ''Should we be trapped, Feln, I shall give word. If possible, you will wait for Tirys to join you. But if not . . .''

Nsil hunched his neck muscles. ''If taken, we will state the truth—we have sought only to learn of danger to Eamn, that we might avert it. And all remember, we use no weapon other than the dazers, which give no lasting harm. So the Maghrens may have naught to hold against us, save that we are Eamnet.''

No more to say, then, excepting, ''We must go now.''

When all were equipped, the party set out. Fortune lay with Nsil; they would reach the plain almost as dark arrived.

VIII

Pia Velucci finished the macroGate shell and won her bet; Gowdy had never been so glad to lose one. Already he had a team loading the DV with hardware for Magh—especially the matrices and peripherals for the colony's overdue Earthgates.

He asked Pia, ''Anything you need before we go?'' Because he was still concerned with this end of the show, too.

''No. We'll use our trim thrustors to stop this rotation and align our axis. For ferrying small stuff, outship, we're setting up the sleds.'' Velucci grinned. Sweating in a suit had left her face leaner, too. ''Didn't want to use 'em while the DV was horsing big stuff around, but now they'll do us just fine.''

The sleds, right. DV trimmer Traction units, fuel tanks good for longer than the operator's air tanks, graphite/polymer laminate steering deflectors, all on a sturdy load-bearing framework. Gowdy had never jockeyed one of the little scooters, but they might be fun. An idea came. "Could you spare me one?"

Velucci nodded. "Sure; I'll have it loaded on for you."

"Thanks. And good work, getting the Gate up. Now then: Simone's in charge—but either of you, call me if you need to."

A bit later he shepherded his picked team through the joined airlocks, into the Vehicle. Now that Dan Quillan had some solid DV experience, SuZanne Craig could stay with Mose again; she was shaping up as a good watch officer. Alix Dorais could rejoin Skeeter, and along with apprentice linguist Marthe Vinler would come her short, dark pairmate Milo Vitale; when the Earthgates opened up, a good supplies man would be worth a bundle.

Sitting copilot, Sam monitored the DV's release; once clear, Quillan got it oriented and hit Go, bringing thrust up to a standard gee. Vinler sat comm. Until thrust steadied, Milo and Alix took accel couches; after that they could move around.

Sam didn't; he kept Marthe bird-dogging for signals. He knew there was an Eamn ship in orbit, maybe one downside. Chemical drive, but adequate in the circumstance. Plus the wild card, out from the Forerunner, last seen at L-2 between Magh and Big Red. All this could be either an okay mix or dangerously not. And six of Gowdy's own were stuck in the middle of it, along with several times as many of Barry Krsnch's.

More than a day into accel, Marthe caught signal. Skeeter Cole's voice: ". . . the ship at L-2 dropped something. DV size or smaller. Irtuk's instruments . . . accurate enough . . . ETA, but . . ."

The signal hashed out. Gowdy stewed but it got him nowhere. Finally as Quillan prepared for turnover, the circuit came alive.

Feodor Glinka calling. But what he had to say, nobody liked at all.

*   *   *

Searchlights outlined the landing area. At its edge and breathing faster than she meant to, Kayo Marlin squinted upward as the Shtai vessel dropped flickering through the probing beams.

First came its Traction flare, paler than she expected. Then the ship itself, nodes brightening with increased thrust, until it grounded. Jouncing, but safe down speaks for itself.

Obviously this can wasn't a patch on *Roamer*'s auxiliary boat. Which was probably about halfway back here by now.

Kayo and Skeeter were in comm when the seeder Waij brought Irtuk's summons. Now, flanking the bearer, they watched the new arrival stop jiggling. Nearby stood other humans, ship's and exploration team both; Kayo was crowded by Barry Krsnch who didn't seem to notice. She moved away; then, as dust settled, followed Irtuk's group toward the newcomer.

Squinting at it, Kayo made some estimates. Maybe half the DV's size and much its same look: a cone-topped cylinder braced on three landing legs, stumpy in proportion. The light ramp now extending from a lower hatch didn't have far to drop.

Hardly breathing at all now, Kayo stared at the creatures who minced carefully down it. Each torso, furred to roundness, moved on four short, sturdy legs. Forward, a long tapering neck, held high and bobbing slightly, bore near its tip two pairs of digited grasping members. That tip didn't look much like a head, but amid a cluster of unidentifiable features she saw a mouth and two wide-set eyes. Speechless, Kayo shook her own head.

Skeeter Cole gave a low whistle. "Yainans, huh? Mix up one king-size dachshund, one giraffe, a touch of Persian cat . . ."

Unusually subdued, Krsnch said, "Uh-oh! This must be one of the Eamnet exiles." Crouching as it backed down onto the ramp, an unmistakable bearer emerged. Straightening to the normal angled posture, it too descended.

Bearer yes, Maghren no: the newcomer stood shorter by a head than Irtuk and bulked considerably stockier. First to speak, she said, "Maghren sister! Is there peace between us at last?"

Seemingly disconcerted, the lead Yainan jerked its neck

toward the bearer. "Bretl! You were to observe, only, at this time." Kayo recognized the voice she'd heard earlier; without signal distortion she found it a lot easier to understand.

Whatever Irtuk said, then, was lost to insane chaos: blinding strobe bursts and deafening cacophony. Staggered, Kayo reached to Skeeter. But a heavy arm grasped and propelled her past the ring of landing lights to the rougher ground beyond it.

She barely made out even that much; blasts of glare and din tore at consciousness itself, as her captor moved her faster than her legs wanted to accept. And moved and moved and kept moving.

Even when the assault ended, its effects raged in mind and senses. As captors forced Kayo stumbling on, time lost meaning; a confused jumble of sensation was all she knew.

Fatigue, and thirst, the onset of cold wet rain and herself slipping in the mud it made. And that she really had to pee.

Treachery. Lured into capture and now pulled along by cunningly looped ropes, T'phee finds es strugglings useless. Except among very young get, physical contention is foreign to Yainans; T'phee resigns enself to passivity until advent of opportunity to essay reason, always es preferred tactic.

Wet, dark, and mud dim es senses, but as they recover from the ordeal of excess stimuli, er peers about. Even through cloud the Parent's glow illumines to Yainan eyes. Looking past es colleague V'naet, also unresisting, T'phee sees not only the unmistakable figures of Bretl and the welcoming Maggen bearer but also two wholly unfamiliar shapes. These two, sheathed in coverings and moving with trunks almost at vertical, must by logic be those arrivals the Maggen Irtuk names as yumins.

T'phee's thought changes. Betrayal comes not from Maggens, nor yet the unknown yumins; these may prove to be of help; er must strive to gain their accord. In consequence, these who push and haul en along wet and sticky ground must be Emman.

One question lies in painful doubt: to what *purpose* do es rude and forceful abductors ply this discourtesy?

* * *

Blood pumping with vigor, Nsil hardly noticed chill of rain or impediment of mud. He had done it! Not only a Maghren bearer and seeder taken but also a bearer from the lost Shtai colony, two creatures come there from Diell the Companion, and two also of the strange, stiffly erect race whose provenance was yet unknown. His dearest hopes had not envisioned so much.

Only by fortune had he brought sufficient helpers, two to aid with each of the seven taken. But he faced another dilemma: were so many crowded inside ship One, could it yet lift? Landing had shown that One's loading already edged the safety limit.

Past the hills' crest, Nsil signaled a pause for recuperation. To Vyorn he said, "A detachment must remain on Magh. To observe and signal reports to Eamn, and to undertake action against this alliance that forms against us."

"And so that these we escort may be lifted away." As Nsil hesitated, Vyorn said, "It is true; the plan is necessary."

Seeing that the adaptive understood, Nsil continued. "While I shall bend all effort to retrieve the contingent, I cannot assure success. Knowing this, are you willing to lead it?"

Hesitantly, Vyorn touched Nsil's forelimb. "I am honored."

"And I, most grateful. All supplies and materials not needed for rendezvous will be left for the use of you ten." Although, Nsil emphasized, certain devices for infliction of damage should be used only in extremity.

Summoned and apprised, the seeder Knad agreed to serve as second voice to Vyorn. Torn between gratification at their loyalty and bereavement of leaving two such favorites behind, Nsil summoned fortitude to resume the journey.

Whole-minded, Irtuk-saa could not be held and herded by a mere two seeders or adaptives, even these sturdier ones from Eamn. Nor by the noose about her neck, tugged now and again by the one behind. But the onslaught of light and sound left her confused, unable to form purpose. Now as sense and thought returned, curiosity came more readily than firm intent.

Rain and darkness limited her vision, but over a time she espied at least one yumin, the Yainan pair and the bearer

Bretl, and her own Duant-tsi. A varied catch, these Eamnets had made.

She shifted heed to the seeder who attended no one prisoner but prowled back and forth along the moving line, seeing to one and then another. As he paused just ahead, Irtuk listened. Nsil, this one was called; she would remember.

He held himself unlike any seeder she had known. After a time she felt she understood it. No Maghren seeder, even highly positioned, related quite the same to bearers as to the other genders. A kind of deference intervened, so subliminal that until now, seeing its lack, she had not realized its existence.

Irtuk was not at all sure she found that lack tolerable.

Now the seeder approached, saying to the Eamnet beside her, "This bearer proceeds without difficulty?"

Irtuk spoke. "This bearer answers for herself. Nsil."

"Your ears are well arched. We will exchange information later, in warmer and drier surroundings."

"If your good fortune continues, we may." Enjoying his puzzled look, she said, "To escape my people, you need only raise ship. But against yumins or Yainans? You have taken some of each; what might they do, if need be, to retrieve them?"

As Nsil went silent and turned away, Irtuk felt warmth despite the chill rain.

Below the canyon's rim, the rocks outjutted largely free of mud. Preoccupied with the Maghren bearer's veiled warnings, Nsil put little heed to footing. At least, he thought, he had gained a name to put to the far-come strangers. Yumins . . .

Arriving at the bottom to relieved greeting by Feln and his two cohorts, Nsil explained what was needed. Offered food, some captives did not accept, though water was welcomed by all. A final opportunity to excrete more conveniently than would be possible aboard the ship was also declined by several; glumly, Nsil expected to share their later regret for that decision.

Notwithstanding, he had the group brought aboard One and variously secured, as seemed advisable in each case.

* * *

After speaking with Tasr on ship Three, Feln with Nsil's approval began readying One's engines for operation. While Nsil saw to unloading of foods and matériel as he had promised Vyorn, making certain that items such as the packets for molten heat would be at prudent distance when the ship's nozzles flamed.

Soon all came ready. Nsil bade Vyorn farewell, saw the ten move safely away, then secured the hatch and went to his place.

"When you are prepared, Feln, let us proceed."

With firm touch Feln built the engines' racketing until the ship shuddered free of ground. Weight force grew painful, then steadied and dropped away. As did the engines' roar.

Only small sounds of metal contracting disturbed One's weightless flight. Lacking function at this stage of the venture, Nsil looked with interest at his silent captives.

Chilled and spent, Kayo Marlin moved passively. As an escort gestured, she stopped with the rest, short of the ship ahead. Given water she took it gladly, but shook her head at the offer of food, doubtful that she could keep it down. She heard the word for "excrete" and saw others squatting, so followed their example; better here than zero gee.

Directed, Kayo climbed up through an airlock. Near the ship's nozzles a stench affirmed the chemical nature of its engines. She didn't need the directing gestures; she understood the seeder's orders (and noticed that the Yainans did, too). But she was simply too stubborn to give away any info the raiders didn't have already. And hoped Skeeter felt the same way.

Inside and up a long central shaft, the interior didn't look like much: crowded, cramped, and uncomfortable, with pairs of strap-in bunks crowded around the rim of the tilted control deck. Kayo allowed herself to be tied to one bunk; alongside, an adaptive knotted bindings to secure a Yainan, its short legs folded under to show only the front extremities, like cat's paws.

Bearers, she noted, rated a pair of bunks each, and double lashings to hold them.

* * *

After a lot of Eamnet talk and fuss, from below rose a raucous thunder; Kayo reminded herself that chemical rockets did work sometimes, but her tensed muscles paid no attention.

Unseen metal rattled; the deck pitched, then began to push at her. Merging with the noise that filled the place, thrust built to more gees than she'd ever felt; how had the early spacers *endured* this? Then it stopped; she lay weightless, only the bindings holding her as her ears rang with absent roar.

An adaptive held out some sort of plastic pouch and expelled from it a small bead of water. All right; Kayo reached and the Eamnet held it so she could drink. One swallow was enough.

A second pouch extruded a bud of pulpy, brownish gray substance that smelled like cheddar with a hint of liverwurst. Why not? She mouthed the nozzle and gave the pouch a squeeze.

Not bad. Finished, she beckoned for more water, but took only a sip. Even if Eamnets had zero-gee johns, they wouldn't fit humans. Eventually she'd have to go. But preferably later.

At the Yainan's turn, sure enough it spoke, low-toned, with the Eamnet. When that one left, suddenly Kayo found the Yainan's necktip within inches of her face. "Have you Emman words?"

For the chance to learn, Kayo forgot about stubborn. So, in the Maghren/Eamnet language, "What would you know?"

Taffy, the Yainan's name sounded like; it rendered hers as K'yo. Then, "Your ship of great power: where lies its origin?"

Inside this metal box, direction meant nothing. Distance, though: start with lightspeed and count numbers on your fingers. Once they had put Yain's and Earth's years both in terms of Shtai's, Kayo could give a horseback guess: she was about eleven times as far from home as Taffy was.

Taffy's reaction surprised her: a loud insuck of breath, then gestures of the whipcord grasping appendages. "But in ships hardly larger than our own, how is there sufficient fuel, food, or gases for breathing? And yourselves! Can your lives endure over so lengthy a venture?" Even though, the Yainan noted, K'yo's ship was first seen at greatly higher rapidity than any Yainan construct had achieved. "How do such things be?"

Strapped to a bunk in zero gee, riding a can of explosives as prisoner of aliens whose motives she didn't know from fruitcake, Kayo didn't feel up to explaining Habegger Gates.

And maybe she wasn't supposed to. If anyone had said what should or shouldn't be told to other species about Earth tech, Kayo didn't remember hearing it. Rather than lying, she hedged. "I am not expert as to the means of dealing with those problems."

Relativity, though, hadn't been secret since Einstein. "Up near the speed of radiation, you know, time slows. So we . . ."

"Ah! You achieve such rates of movement? We have not. Our way of slowing time differs greatly."

Tech talk wasn't Taffy's long suit, either. What did emerge to clarity were Yainan reasons for coming to this system, and those reasons left Kayo shaken.

"Your homeworld, then, cannot survive?"

"The world, yes—but not ourselves, those who remain there."

A conversation stopper if ever there was one . . .

Nsil pondered: bound and weight-free, likely his unwilling guests were of no mood for serious questions. He had assigned bunk pairings for greatest isolation: bearers apart, the larger yumin with the Maghren seeder, the smaller beside a being from Shtai, and that one's cohort with Tirys who now moved among the bunks with pouches of water and softfood.

Impatient, Nsil waited. He found no amusement in the captives' awkward dealings with excretion into thick fabric absorbances; the odors varied but all were noxious.

When ship One came to meet with Three, again the two were joined for travel, and the smaller resupplied.

Now the long ordeal until ship Two was reached and decision must be made. How many of the ships, would it transpire, could be landed safely? And which?

All else aside, One must have priority. No suitings were at hand, nor means to fabricate any, to protect bearers or members of the two new species from airlessness; they could not be moved. And of all his foray's trophies, these held most importance.

Slowly, it seemed, the paired ships edged toward Eamn.

* * *

Kayo gone, and Skeeter! Irtuk and Duant, two Yainans from Companion by way of Shtai, and a squat, heavy bearer from who knew where. ". . . this huge blare, captain, all sound and light; it stunned everybody." Nearer now, Glinka's voice came solidly, with no wavering. "When it cleared, they were gone."

"You didn't see them?" Gowdy waited through signal delay.

"Felt them, more. One ran me over, marched right up my back. No sir; none of our people got much of a look."

"All right, Feodor. Best you can, compare notes with the Maghrens—and try to keep fences mended until we get there."

Gowdy signed out. No point, he decided, in holding off turnover and going to higher decel; it wouldn't save enough time to make up for the added strain. And eventually Dan sat the DV down at Denaize Shore.

Sam got ready to ask some questions.

Groundside he and Glinka conferred with Menig-dre and Staon-tal, bearers who had worked most closely with Irtuk. "From Eamn they were," Menig said. Marthe Vinler translated, though Gowdy's grasp of the lingo was improving rapidly. "Their scent," said the bearer, "like our own yet not wholly so. Their strength: all know of the greater heaviness Eamn holds. And their weapon, stunning the mind through sight and hearing, is unknown here."

"Yeah." Understanding local and talking it were two different things; he spoke through young Marthe. "The Yainans: they didn't stay around after the raid, at all?"

"No. Two were seen taken; the rest retreated into their ship. Before the weapon's effects fully dissipated, that ship glowed at the bottom and lifted away. And when we make appeal," Staon added, "toward mutual aid against those of Eamn who have trespassed here, their greater ship does not respond."

Sam nodded. "Okay, Marthe. Tell 'em forget the Yainans, for now. We and the Maghrens, we'll do this together."

Hell; his DV outpushed anything the Yainans had, let alone chemical drives. "Say now that we're going to Eamn; they should think what they might bring along, that we have room for.''

It was time to call *Roamer* to come help put the lid on. Sam only hoped their mission could be rescue, not revenge.

Sydnie had the watch alone when Gowdy called. ''We lift in about ten hours,'' he said. ''We can't spot the Eamn ships just now; Magh's facing the wrong way. But coasting most of the time, they'll be a while en route.''

Sydnie munched a cracker. Sam's voice came urgent. ''Get loose there, Simone, as soon as Velucci can possibly spare you. We can't barge down on Eamn and spring our people by force; we need a good bluff. And *Roamer* making a pass, down low at the high scream, could clear up constipation all over the planet.''

Someone laughed, before he said, ''So get here quick and let me know soonest. You're shorthanded, but no help for that and it's not for long.'' A pause. ''Hey, tell Mose hello; I'm looking forward to seeing you guys. Gowdy out.''

And not a word to Sydnie! Brows creased, she considered her reply, and with a forceful nod flipped the send switch. ''Watch officer Lightner acknowledging. You go to hell, too.''

Then she wiped his message off the log.

Signing off, Gowdy looked outside the comm tent to growing darkness. Besides twenty minutes of signal lag, Simone wouldn't have a solid answer yet, anyway. He might as well tackle a job he dreaded: getting some cooperation out of Barry Krsnch.

While most of the exploration team lived in tents and much equipment still sheltered under tarps, Barry had moved himself into the Habgate pre-fab. Inside and down the hall, alongside the Gate room Sam read ''Barry Krsnch, Coordinator.''

Behind a large desk Krsnch leaned back, hands clasped at his nape. At Gowdy's entrance the man sat up and placed his hands on the desk. ''What's on your mind? I'm rather busy just now.''

And just what *would* be on his mind? Easy, though; maybe he should give Krsnch a chance to strut a little. The Earthgate assembly should be nearly finished. Gowdy asked, "How are the Gates coming? Pretty well, I expect."

"The Tush is up, but nothing's come through yet; Glen Springs may not have a test packet on the grid. To be safe, though, the night crew's running start-up again."

No complaint to that. "And the Mouth?"

Krsnch checked his chrono. "On line soon; I expect word any time now. And we'll put ours to test right away; you can be sure we won't be wasting time."

"That's good." Sam ignored Krsnch's patented air of smugness. "Oh yeh, while I'm here; how many people can you spare me for the DV, going to Eamn?" Even with leaving the comm tent unattended, five men and four women just wouldn't cut it.

"I've thought about that, Gowdy. The boat bunks twenty; right? Plus crew seating. Well, I'll tell you." Krsnch grinned. "Dealing with hostiles isn't in your workup. So why don't three of you in those control couches just provide transportation, and I'll bring the landing force. Twenty of us: automatic rifles, shoulder rockets, the lot. Upstairs you're in charge; once we hit ground, I am."

He spread his hands. "What do you say?"

Gowdy could only stare. "One tin can and twenty men, you want to take on a whole *world*? Krsnch, what do you—"

"How many do you suppose came from Eamn? And they got away with it, didn't they?"

What to say? Try reason. "They'll be braced for us, Barry; they have to know we'll try something."

Krsnch shrugged. "That's my offer. Take it, or run your own show. With your own people. And mine are out of it."

A voice behind Gowdy said, "Maybe not. You're the boss, Barry, but I doubt you could prevent anyone from volunteering for this effort. Not and look good in the records."

Sam turned to face Libby Verdoorn. He hardly knew Krsnch's tall, slender deputy, but in their few contacts he'd found the brown-eyed blond woman easy to work with. Now her dark straight eyebrows slanted and her lips set stiff with disapproval.

He started to say something appreciative but Krsnch cut in. "You don't get volunteers without asking. Gowdy, I forbid you—and you too, Libby—to air this discussion beyond these doors.''

Walking out, Sam made a very unoriginal suggestion. He wasn't proud of it, but it suited.

Halfway back to the comm tent, Verdoorn overtook him. ''Wait up, skipper,'' and she caught his arm. ''You haven't figured Barry out yet, have you?'' Shaking her head, she gave a brief laugh. ''Not that I handled it well, in there. But I do *know* better.''

Now he appreciated the company, too. ''I purely don't. What does make that bastard tick?''

''I wish I knew.'' She paused. ''All right; Barry thinks the way to be strong and independent is to refuse anyone else's suggestions out of hand and do just the opposite.''

Gowdy shook his head. ''How did he ever get a job in Coordination, let alone work up to colony level?''

''Barry's not stupid, just fixated. I suspect he only used his gimmick when it was safe: his superiors would never see it.''

''So how *should* I have put the problem?''

''Maybe like, I don't suppose you'd want to risk any of your people, or maybe, I know you're having trouble keeping sked, so you probably can't spare anyone . . .'' Verdoorn shrugged. ''Well, something on that order.''

Sam had to laugh. ''Y'know, that kind of pitch might've worked. Too late now, though. I—''

From over by the DV came shouts; he turned to see figures flee a growing, sputtering flare of light. Under the Vehicle, too low to involve the Traction nodes. ''What the—!''

Near as he could tell, the moving shapes looked more native than human. That wasn't important; running toward the DV he saw people slide down its ladder and sprint to get clear as the Vehicle itself tilted. Its drive nodes flared, but before thrust could build he saw it topple, a landing leg buckling at the white hot glow near its foot, and crash full length to ground.

Drive burst plowed the ship across yards of topsoil, then flickered and died. Slowly the Vehicle rolled almost half a turn, then came shuddering to rest.

As tight end for Mayfield High, Sam had caught more than one smash to the solar plexus. This time he didn't fall over.

Someone moved toward him; recognizing Marthe Vinler

he got some breath back and yelled. "Everybody out okay?"

"Milo is, and Jules. Feodor wouldn't leave watch and Dan thought he could lift. But there wasn't *time*."

So now, how did Sam Gowdy get to Eamn?

Later. First he had to get to Dan and Feodor.

IX

Sick with anger and frustration, Gowdy ran to the toppled Vehicle. The landing leg's crumpled tip had cooled to orange. Something like thermite had done this—but whose?

Skirting the heat, Sam looked up. With the DV lying flat, its central stern hatch sat thirty feet up.

"*Sonofabitch*!" Squinting in dimness he saw the access ladder hanging slaunchwise, its lower end maybe twelve feet off the ground. How much sidewise pull could its pivot mountings take? If he got a hook on it, would it bend down or break loose?

"Captain?" Libby Verdoorn came forward. "Can I help?"

"I could use a ladder." He gestured. "But I'd settle for a rope with a hook on one end."

"Hang on a minute, sir." It was Milo Vitale, the supply man. "I'll see what I can find."

Sam glared up at the ladder's end, well beyond his best vertical jump. What he needed was a seven-foot slam-dunker.

Suddenly Vitale reappeared with a coil of line. "Couldn't find any kind of grapnel. Maybe there's something lying around."

But handlights revealed nothing useful. "Thanks anyway." Sam assessed the possibilities. No, Vitale wasn't tall enough.

Verdoorn was, maybe. "Libby?"

She came over to him. "Yes?"

"If you stood on my shoulders, could you reach that ladder?'' He gestured upward. ''Tie this line on, or pull the thing down?'' Second thought took over. ''No. It might break, and . . .''

She hung the coil of line over one shoulder and shook loose an end. ''Stay back, out from under me; I know how to fall.''

''What about landing?'' But he moved to stand, feet spread, butt braced against the ship, and cupped his hands to stirrup. And where the hell was Jules Perrone, to add some muscle?

Never mind. ''Okay—alley *oop*!'' One burst of strain and Verdoorn was up; how she got faced forward he wasn't sure. In Magh's gravity she wasn't all that heavy; still he was glad she'd shucked down barefoot.

Her feet shifted; he heard a gasp, and then, ''Here goes!''

The downward thrust staggered him. The leap got her a hand on the ladder and her grip held; with a brittle snap the ladder swung down, bringing Verdoorn considerably nearer to ground.

She let go and landed crouched, touching one hand down for balance. ''Sorry; best I could do.''

''It's great, Libby. Give me the line.'' He could make the jump now, but one of the mounting hinges had torn free. Would the remaining pivot, bent around as it was, hold his weight?

Only one way to find out.

Looping the coil over his neck, Gowdy looked up; he'd need to take a run at it. Letting out a whoop he charged, lifting on the third stride and catching the bottom rung with both hands.

His legs swung out nearly flat; if the remaining joint gave, he was soup stock—but screeching protest, the sumbidge held. Like a ten-year-old he ''pumped'' the impromptu pendulum until he could throw his legs up and hook on.

From there, climbing was no problem. At the hatch he used some line to lash both pivots to their mounting bitts, then called down, ''It's solid now, but we're going to want better access. Inside, I expect I'll need some help.''

Pushing past the airlock hatches as they hung aslant, he entered the Vehicle's central shaft, careful not to trip over the inset climbing rungs.

The walk seemed long until he reached the control deck,

now vertical. Standing on the safety rail he got himself oriented: main screen to one side and the control positions opposite.

Screen and consoles seemed undamaged, but Glinka and Quillan hung, bloodied and silent, in their safety harnesses. From the debris scattered below, Sam couldn't make out just what the crashing impact, greatest here at the DV's tip, had thrown free to smash against their accel couches.

Glinka moaned, but Quillan gave no sign of life. Either way, Gowdy by himself couldn't do much in the way of rescue. Time to get help. Carefully he made his way back out.

Peering down from the hatch rim Sam saw a ladder being raised, long enough to slant out well and with the heft to support considerable load.

Leaning out he saw near its foot a woman holding two unfolded stretchers upright. Gowdy squinted. "Verdoorn?"

She looked up. "Captain. Will you need these?"

"You're reading my mind."

Not so much later, probably, as it felt like, Sam walked beside the stretcher that held Dan Quillan, still unconscious.

Glinka had come to and was "all right," his fractured clavicle and humerus notwithstanding. Dan was another matter: paramedic Heller Aalstrom said Quillan's smashed ribs might not have punctured a lung, and the great bloody bash on his forehead could be only a concussion—but he wouldn't bet any real money.

The only safe answer was: Gate both men back to Earth, right now. Assuming the Mouth had indeed come up operational . . .

Ahead of the rest, Sam barged into the Habgate pre-fab. At the far end Barry Krsnch emerged from the Gates room, pausing in the doorway. Sam asked, "Is the Mouth on line?"

Krsnch nodded. "Yes. Just a few minutes ago we found the test objects gone. There's still some tuning needed; meanwhile I'll prepare my formal inaugural packet. And then . . ."

"I need to use it right now."

The groundside chief drew himself up. "We will open this facility in proper fashion. I cannot permit—"

"We have two casualties, emergency cases." And what was keeping the stretcher bearers?

Krsnch neither moved nor spoke. Sam heard his own voice say, "I'd rather not smash your nose, Barry; I don't have time for the paperwork. So please get out of my way."

Once he did, the arriving stretchers went onto the send grid. At the Gate controls, Gowdy punched Transmit. Nothing happened. He looked around. "Who knows how to work this model?"

"I do." Libby Verdoorn stepped forward, punched Enable which was new to Sam, and *then* Transmit. Within the Mouth air opaqued, iridescing; when it cleared, the grid was empty.

"Should've sent a note," Sam commented. "So they'd know what happened." But Verdoorn wasn't listening; something within the Mouth held her attention.

She pointed. "What is that, down between the nodes? Bright, looks like gold or something. Is it yours, Barry?"

Krsnch shouldered forward. "Let me see." As he moved into the oval booth, Libby reached again for Transmit.

Alarmed, Sam pulled her arm away as Krsnch shook his head and stepped back. "Nothing there, Libby. Just a reflection or something." He turned to Sam. "I'm filing a complaint, you know, concerning your high-handed overriding of proper procedure." And he left the Gates room.

Hardly noting the man's words, Gowdy looked at Verdoorn. "What was that little stunt all about?"

She giggled. "Why not let him file his complaint directly? Not have to wait four years for a response. Though *we* wouldn't hear about it until at least that long."

"Meanwhile you'd be in charge here, groundside?"

"Not me, captain. You. Look it up."

Oh bloody hell! Sam felt his eyebrows take an attitude. "Is that your idea of doing me a favor?"

"Doing myself one, actually."

Well. Gating someone without consent was a chargeable offense, but by the grace of Sam Gowdy she hadn't done it.

He owed her a stern lecture. Didn't he? Clearing his throat he said, "I don't ever want to *catch* you trying that again." And trusted that she took his point.

"Captain?" He turned to face Jinx Lanihan; tears streaked her cheeks. "Feodor—they just told me—what happened to him?"

Oh hell. "He'll be all right. Banged up too bad to fix here, but no worry back at Glen Springs; we Gated him right out."

If he expected to see relief he guessed wrong; her face, usually cheerful, twisted with pain. "But I have to be with him! Captain—please."

Everybody had a "have to." Gowdy said, "All right, Jinx; we'll send the papers along later." He scribbled a note and handed it to her. She needed something more; a hug, maybe? He gave it, then gently led her to the Mouth. "Hit it, Libby." She did; the flaring came and died. "Thanks."

He'd spent enough time here. "See you later," and he left for the comm tent, finding Marthe Vinler at the main console.

She looked up. "*Roamer*'s gone below the horizon. I tried to reach them; didn't get on it soon enough."

Sam patted her shoulder. "No harm; they can't do anything until they get here. If at all; without the DV, where are we?"

"Two Yainans were lost on that raid, besides the colonist bearer. Maybe we should keep trying with their ship."

The idea didn't satisfy Gowdy's need for action, but he couldn't think of a better one.

Knowing nothing of what to expect in this metal cage, Irtuk assumed the hideous noise and shaking to be normal. If transport offworld required such discomfort, Irtuk-saa could endure with any Eamnet. So thinking, she negated fear.

Anger at her predicament, Irtuk could not quell. She watched as the cocksure Nsil talked with one prisoner and another, and in her turn behaved to him as to any seeder overly taken with petty authority yet not under her jurisdiction: with quiet and confident disapproval.

Nsil did not provoke easily. That quality tempered Irtuk's distaste—but left unquenched her thirst for his undoing. Nor her resentment that only she and Bretl from Shtai were restricted to their bedplaces, unable to speak together. Irtuk longed to know of Eamn's lost colony, and among those from it only Bretl was of her kind; Irtuk could give the enigmatic Yainans no trust.

Until Eamn was attained, should that event occur, Irtuk-saa would wait. Over cycles, as she rose to become senior bearer of the Nearer Archipelago, she had learned that vital skill.

* * *

With leisure to address his involuntary guests, Nsil found much of interest. Both Yainans seemed willing to speak freely—though the obvious subordinate referred all matters of import to the other. Neither showed sign of hostility or resentment, nor temperament to hold such feelings. He did not understand their passive reaction, but pitied their world its doom.

The yumins gave courtesy, yet Nsil could sense a will to oppose: just so would he behave in like case. While their custody required due caution, it caused Nsil no unease.

The Maghren Duant-tsi disgraced all seeders. Questioned, ever he peered sideward toward the bearer Irtuk-saa, disclaiming cognizance of matters Nsil would learn. In disgust, Nsil moved to the source of Duant's seeming fear.

The demeanor of Irtuk-saa was unlike that of any bearer Nsil had known. While he gave Scayna great privilege as such things went, a basic deference underlay the assertiveness he permitted her, as both knew without saying. However Scayna might think, she rarely spoke contrary to Eamnet custom.

Irtuk's saying respected no bounds at all. Courtesy shown her own seeder companion held condescension so ready as to be unthought. To Nsil she responded in like fashion, failing to treat him as superior or even equal. And seemed not to realize the incongruity.

His annoyance was mixed with a warmth that puzzled him, a feeling normally associated with sharing of some sort. Yet save the conflict between their worlds, what could he and Irtuk share?

Bretl from Shtai made a simpler problem, neither giving deference nor seeming to expect it. Her behavior, Nsil decided, might be typical of primitive groupings, in which no true social structure was evident or needed.

Over several speakings Nsil elaborated on his initial views. But as the joined ships neared rendezvous where Two circled Eamn, those elaborations constituted no meaningful changes.

To Kayo, Nsil the head pirate didn't seem all that hostile. When he got around to questioning her, the Eamnet seeder spoke with courtesy; all down the line he showed as much consideration as the setup permitted. After this ship met and joined another, he interviewed everyone separately. Later each prisoner was allowed to meet with one other. Except that both bearers stayed put.

Kayo used her one visit on Skeeter Cole, who affected a rosy but unrealistic view of their prospects. Later she realized she really should have given Irtuk-saa some company.

Now at Kayo's own bunk, Nsil had more questions. "The yumin Cole confirms that you have come many times the distance of Diell the Companion. He also disclaims knowledge of the mechanisms making this possible. Since Eamn lacks means to build such devices, that matter is of no present consequence."

Crouching in habitual fashion, Nsil leaned forward. "Other facts, we must know. You each say you came to learn and explore, perhaps find place where some may settle—though to relocate any significant number in mere ships . . ." And again Kayo saw no point in explaining Habgate logistics.

"But how could you know this star bore worlds, let alone that they support life? Our finest instruments fail to detect even the Yainan homeworld."

"So would most of ours." But—she told of Earth's far-flung web of space receptors feeding signals to form composite images of previously unimagined detail. "We can find worlds, yes. But until we arrive, we can't know if they're fit to live on."

He moved his head slightly; what the gesture meant, Kayo had no idea. "When you stationed your ship near Magh, we feared you came to join with their forces, against us."

"Was that why you came there, and . . . ?"

"Once Magh drove us near extinction—and, by irony, itself also. That they might try again—even the possibility forced us to take measures, to learn the truth and defend our existence."

"Well, now you won't need to."

"It is not so simple. Even without surety I tend to believe you. Yet there is still the Overgrouping to convince."

There were further talks, before Nsil's ships met with another. Kayo found all too much time to get tired of brackish water and pablum from a squeeze tube, much less diapers on demand in lieu of a decent pottie. Eventually their own ship separated; its engines kicked up a lengthy racket and then went silent.

Falling, Kayo knew, to attempt landing on Nsil's world. Aside from the reception they might receive, she wasn't sure whether to fret more about grounding safely or getting a bath. Given her druthers, she'd take both.

Having enself raised lander-carriers from Shtai to *Tayr* and returned safely, T'phee recognizes the maneuvers as this Emman ship drops free, makes corrective thrust, then drops further. Crude, this vessel, but the same principles govern.

Watching the Emman pilot at es controls, T'phee knows both curiosity and admiration. To do this thing by mere chemical means! Yet er finds no fear of the result. Feln has brought this device from Eamn to Magh without mishap; T'phee chooses to believe er can accomplish the reverse as well.

Near to Eamn, but no knowing *how* near, T'phee finds es belief tested; the din, the pummeling, the uncertainty above all, draws es neckskin taut and muscles rigid. But after a great jar comes quiet of movement and then, gradually, of bone-shaking sound.

What may occur next, T'phee cannot know. But now, waiting release from es restraints, er allows enself serenity.

Did all intelligent life suffer the disease of bureaucracy, or was Sam Gowdy just having a run of bad luck? When Nahei of the ship at L-2 finally responded, the Yainan disclaimed any authority to act. "I act only as preceptor in T'phee's stead," was his first line of obstruction. Next came, "I have signaled to Cejha who holds for T'phee on Yamar." Without a pink slip from one or the other, Nahei wasn't saying what time it was.

"Tell that furry pissant we'll start without him." Sam's voice came heavy on growl. "Tell him nice, though; someday we'll want to get along with those people."

The circuit cleared; Marthe said, "I think the problem is, he wants to *talk* things right. Action isn't in his book."

"You're probably right. Well, let's try *Roamer* again."

She nodded. "Yes, it should be time. Go ahead."

He opened the circuit. "Gowdy calling. Simone, we're in deeper shit than ever." He told it, then added, "If my last call doesn't have you on your way already, cut it short and make it march. From now on I don't want to hear any feet dragging!''

Checking for recorded messages he flipped the switch and heard Sydnie tell him to go to hell. ''*What* . . . ?'' Was she just blowing smoke, venting pique, or was this something serious?

Twenty-two-plus minutes later, Leopold's voice came. ''My God, Sam! This is terrible. Look—there's still about two days work here, but I'll scrape bone and move us out by, say, twenty hours. We'll lock down the belt and push a full gee.'' She paused. ''Without the DV I'm not sure what we can do; we'll have to think of something.'' Then, ''You say you called before and asked for a hurry up? I don't find that call. Or anything logged from you in the past forty hours.'' Meaning, the day before his call answered so ill-temperedly by Sydnie.

As Leopold signed off, Gowdy thought hard. He had trouble on *Roamer*, all right, and its name was Sydnie Lightner.

His first impulse was to order her Gated home. But if she were on watch when the order arrived, she'd be tipped off and nobody else would, and God only knew what she might do.

He couldn't risk it. Nor wait any longer, either, to get something moving. Even pushing a full standard gee, *Roamer* wouldn't be here for another four days, a little over.

So when he called back, he said, ''Try to leave by that twenty-hour estimate, Simone. I'll be thinking, too, how we work it when you get here. And,'' just in case, ''please acknowledge this in person. Gowdy out.''

All right; he stood. ''Marthe, I'll be back in twenty minutes. Meanwhile, record all incoming. Okay?''

''Sure, captain; anything wrong? Anything more, I mean?''

''Nothing you need to bother with.''

His mind churned. *Roamer* or no, there were things he could do. The question was, which ones gave him the best chance?

He wished he could think of one that needed no help or cooperation from Barry Krsnch.

Standing below the Eamnet ship, ears still ringing with the thunder of descent and hurting from abrupt exposure to

Eamn's greater air pressure, Kayo moved docilely as Feln the pilot herded the prisoners a distance away and instructed them to wait. First off the ship, Nsil was nowhere to be seen. Uneasy, Kayo resigned herself to waiting.

Trying to unpop her ears, she kept swallowing; Irtuk hadn't been kidding about the air here. It smelled good, though, with spicy scents from plant growth out at the edge of the spacefield, too far to make out details.

Eamn's gravity pulled more than Magh's, too. But still less than Earth's. And after Nsil's ship, mostly at zero gee but sometimes pushing fiercely, Kayo couldn't really gauge it.

Even so, after confinement and no exercise she had no wish to walk hellan'gone to the distant buildings; the approach of a vehicle raised her hopes. Looking homemade and sounding like imminent breakdown, it still beat walking.

As it stopped, Nsil opened its boxy cab and motioned the group inside. First in, Kayo found seating on a sort of beanbag at the rear. Her fellow prisoners followed, and finally Nsil, who sat forward and and faced the rest. "Forgive this primitive transport. Our request for newer equipment lies unfilled."

Surrounded by captives, two of them big enough to smash him like a bug, Nsil showed total confidence. Kayo had to admire his nerve. Now the driver, his only possible ally, moved levers and a steering crank; an engine racketed and movement began.

It wasn't steam because it didn't blow any, but internal combustion can't pull without revving up first. This one gave a jerk at initial turnover and built from there. Hot air, maybe? External combustion, anyway. The driving mechanism acted on the pivoting front wheel, with rods and tubing back to a sinister grunting piece of gear alongside the Eamnet who drove.

It all moved at a fair clip. Windows were poorly placed and currently unwashed, but Kayo could see buildings ahead. The vehicle stopped near one, and Nsil signaled everybody out.

The structure was bigger than anything at Denaize Shore, and studded with ornate domes. Inside, though, they entered a largish foyer. From there, one of several corridors led to a plain room furnished with several cots, two tables, and the odd chairs that suited Nsil's species but not humans.

Gesturing, the seeder said, "Until arrangements are made, you must wait here. I regret. Food and water will arrive."

He left. The door locked behind him; Skeeter checked it.

Curious, Kayo investigated an adjoining room and reported. "There's a tub, and hot water—*and I get first dibs!*" She headed for it. Not only her person needed scrubbing; her clothes were also pretty ripe.

There was a john, too, not built for humans but usable. That, she had dibsed before reporting.

Food could wait; she was still digesting shipboard pablum.

Vanity was the key to the seeder Gvan. By merely implying that in an intimate situation she might consider him desirable, Scayna gained his consent to await ship One and greet Nsil.

She had no fear that Gvan would presume on the compliment; the maneuver was a familiar courtesy, and he would never risk offending Nsil. No doubt Gvan derived more enjoyment from the pretense than he might have done had reality fulfilled it.

So, leaving her offspring with their longtime trusted attendants, Scayna took escort to the skyship base. There the confinement quarterings utilized by leading Overgrouping members gave distant view of the spacefield, and Scayna had monitor access as word came of ship One's safe arrival, and then of Three's. Uncrewed for the nonce, Two would circle above, where its remaining fuel might well find use later.

She had heard, by signals from Three in transit, of Nsil's raids and captures; since his landing she had waited, hoping he would come to her. Now as Nsil entered the richly draped dome, Scayna went to him and made embrace.

"Your safe return brings me joy." She stroked his head, behind an ear and then below it. "You have achieved much; I must hear every detail. But first . . . ?"

"Yes. We have been too long apart."

From her silence on the matter he would know that their intimacy last previous had not fruited. Taking his own for acceptance, Scayna abandoned herself to pursuit of joy.

Only for a time, however, could she abjure thought. Resting as she and Nsil sampled delicacies, she asked of the creatures he had brought from Magh, and hearkened to his answers.

At the end she said, "A very odd assortment." Her tongue worried the central toothgap. "The Yainans from Diell lie beyond my understanding; perhaps the yumins also."

She had not finished. "Even so, I may be of help." She flexed two digits of a forelimb. "In comprehension of the Maghren bearer, and of our lost sister from Shtai the Forerunner. Quarter these with me. I will question, and share with you what I learn." Studying his reaction, she added, "Do you agree?"

Yes, his headmove signified. "And more." A tilt of ear betrayed his amusement. "The strangeness of yumins defies mere telling, but of the two now present here, one serves its species as bearer. Unmistakably. Should you find the suggestion acceptable, I would quarter that one with you also."

Scayna's tilt of head and tapping of foredigits only feigned indecision. The opportunity to question one whose origin lay outside all Eamnet knowledge? "Yes, Nsil. I do accept."

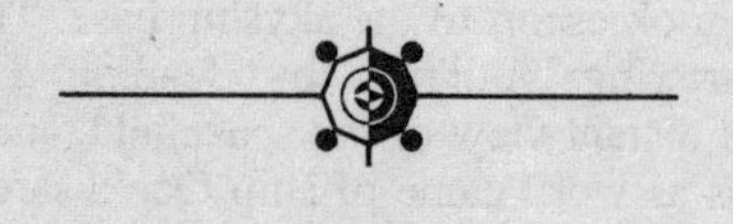

X

To begin with, Gowdy hoped to get the DV back up right away, but none of the colony gear could handle anything so heavy.

He had the landing leg fixed anyway. Barry Krsnch raised a snitfit when he caught a pair of his team's welders helping, but Sam kept him busy arguing until they were finished. And decided he was done wasting time keeping that sonofabitch off his back.

He tried Aalstrom the paramedic. "I'm not sleeping so good; do you have something for it? Liquid; I hate swallowing pills." Sam left with a vial of clear fluid, lifted a bottle of Skeeter Cole's Scotch, and headed for Barry's office.

To share a nice friendly drink. "Hi. I brought a peace offering. But I don't suppose you have time to talk, just now."

Libby's advice worked; Krsnch said, "Of course I do."

He produced glasses; Sam poured. "Cheers." The Scotch had a good strong bite. He gave Barry one more chance. "I know you have tough skeds, but isn't the DV important enough that we could put a rehab team together and—"

"Out of the question! Wait for the macroGate to start delivering; then you'll have all the people you need. And one of their cargo shuttles can do anything your DV could."

"When? A day? A week? *A month*?"

"Not that long, I wouldn't think. Just be patient."

"With two of my people taken?" Not to mention a pair of Yainans and a top banana from the Maghren bearers' council . . .

Rising, Krsnch turned to a cabinet behind him. "Let me show you our schedule." Sitting again, he spread papers on the desk. With his back turned, he hadn't seen a thing.

As Gowdy waited, he talked at random; when Barry's forward slump came, it barely missed knocking over his half-full glass.

Sam's call caught Libby Verdoorn in quarters. When she arrived he shushed her long enough to show her the missive he'd clunked out at a desk terminal:

> Colony Coordinator Barry Krsnch has developed some kind of automatic negative reaction that destroys his usefulness and threatens the success of this mission, which has enough trouble without his adding to it. Report follows when I have time. Accordingly I have relieved him of duty as you will notice, and appoint Deputy Coordinator Lisbet Taine Verdoorn to his place.
>
> Samuel Hall Gowdy, Captain, *Roamer*

Wide-eyed, shaking her head, Libby handed the paper back. "What does this mean? What do you expect me to do?"

Folding the message, Sam tucked it into Barry's shirt pocket. "For starters, help me carry Sleeping Beauty down the pike and Gate him the hell home. You were right the first time."

There were ways to tip the DV upright, but not soon enough for Gowdy's needs; Libby's crew chief's best guess was on the order of well sir about a month give or take a bunch. So there was no point in trying to clean up the control deck mess just yet, either. Meanwhile, armed Maghrens posted by Menig-dre guarded against further sabotage.

Gowdy needed another plan. What he settled on looked so improbable that at first he dismissed it without thinking. It began with a typical slur from the always-impeccable Jules Perrone—who, it turned out, had been romantically detained when everything hit the fan, and was terribly terribly sorry.

Yeh sure, Mike, wipe the canary feathers off your mouth.

A Maghren airfoil lifted, frail-seeming wings effective in the light atmosphere. Perrone said, "Why don't you put Traction Drive on one of those things and give Eamn a real surprise?"

Someday, Sam promised himself, he'd paste this guy one he'd feel through Christmas. But hold it—maybe for once the stube had a real idea! "Excuse me; I got a date with a junkyard."

He knew passenger transports were too flimsy. But off to one end of the warehouse area sat the hulk of an old freight carrier. From a brief look not long ago, he remembered it as sturdier than not.

Gowdy walked there, climbed a dusty ladder and entered. Inside he eyed the exposed ribs and stringers, rapped knuckles against the hull, and squinted at the heavy plastic windows. Then he nodded.

Bingo.

Kayo was asleep when Nsil came ramping in. "You three!" To Kayo and Irtuk and Bretl, he gestured. "Come with me."

"What the hell?" Skeeter Cole protested. "Where d'you think you're taking Kayo?" Then he said it in the right language.

"You have no cause for concern." Nsil sounded hurried but sincere. "These are granted hospitality by a valued member of my householding.'' He paused. ''Your own guesting I arrange soon.''

Cole gave a reluctant nod. ''You look after yourself, Kayo.''

''Sure. You too.''

She followed as Nsil led back to the entrance area, then along a more elegant corridor to an impressively paneled door. ''The confinement dome granted to my householding's use is now yours.'' At the door he gestured for the three to enter first.

Inside, in a spacious domed chamber hung with patterned tapestries, a bearer awaited. ''Nsil! You have brought them.''

''Yes, Scayna.'' Pointing to each in turn he said, ''I present you Irtuk-saa, Bretl-kai, Kaow-merll.'' Kaow? Oh well.

Midway between Irtuk and Bretl in size and proportions, Scayna displayed a somewhat different presence. With no trace of formality she said, ''I will show you to your quarterings. When you are refreshed we can feed and speak together.'' Then to Nsil, ''Do you choose to remain for that time?''

''No. But until then, I will hold company with you.''

No one else spoke up so Kayo said, ''We have had opportunity to refresh. Feeding would be most welcome.'' Hoping her accent wasn't too impenetrable . . .

Scayna looked to Nsil; he said, ''I will see to the others. Gvan, I surmise, can accommodate them.'' And with that, he left.

Farther back lay a large alcove, where Scayna led her guests—somehow Kayo couldn't feel like a prisoner here—to a food-laden table set for six. So the bearer had been prepared for Nsil to stay. . . .

Steaming cuts of meat seemed familiar: domestic animals, originally from Magh? Vegetation, cooked and uncooked, made an iffier proposition. Some Maghren plants were human-friendly and some weren't; here were specimens Kayo hadn't seen before. By now, though, she knew to judge by color and by subtle clues of scent. So she picked and chose, then ate without qualms.

Not until an adaptive served a hot liquid, smelling like freshly sawed lumber yet tasting rather pleasant, did conversation begin. Turning abruptly to Scayna, Irtuk said, ''They do see to your comfort, the upstarts who control here."

At a corner of Scayna's mouth her tonguetip flickered. "Does it surprise you? A tether has two ends."

For the first time, Kayo saw Irtuk-saa stumped for a reply. Instead the Maghren asked of Scayna's next birthings, their expectance in terms of time and of genitive type, and soon all three bearers were exchanging comparable personal information.

Bored, Kayo lost the thread. Then Bretl's words caught her ear. ". . . in one ship only, heritage enough that our species could live . . ."

Kayo began paying attention. The exact numbers weren't clear; base twelve didn't help. But two-thirds of Eamn's colonizing expedition to Shtai the Forerunner had been young bearers, each with all six wombs "in process." Of the remainder, two-thirds were also young, evenly divided between seeders and adaptives. And none of these had direct ancestors in common for three generations past. Quite the way to stock a gene pool!

The remaining ninth, officers and crew, were mature seeders and adaptives, charged with getting a colony into operation.

Again Kayo's mind wandered. With none of the younger colonists closer than third cousins or so, how many generations before some degree of inbreeding became inevitable?

She shook her head. Even human cousinships confused her; the sheer logistics of a third gender left her in the dust.

To hear Bretl-kai tell it, matings were carefully monitored until the original genetic endowment was pretty well spread around. Then traditional limits on consanguination took over.

Irtuk cut in on Scayna's attempted comment. "And who held responsibility to oversee these matters?" Then with a rare hesitancy, "Forgive my interruption. You would ask . . . ?"

Unfazed, Scayna inclined her head. "The same question."

"While they lived," Bretl replied, "the elders. And then, I suppose, much as now. All who are concerned hold voice."

The concept pleased Irtuk-saa not at all. Scayna, on the other hand, wore a look of considerable satisfaction.

Two sexes or three, politics didn't seem to change much.

* * *

To Irtuk-saa the Eamnet bearer Scayna defied comprehension. Despicable, at first seeming, by Maghren standards, but after some days it came to Irtuk that Scayna's ostensible subservience might cloak a subliminal and complex way of exerting power. Without overt acknowledgment, on either side, of its existence.

For while Scayna took pains to lay all matters of decision before the seeder Nsil, in general his decisions favored the bearer's own wishes. Or so it would appear.

Irtuk could not conceive of herself dealing in that fashion; in Maghren councils she exercised authority naturally and directly as befitted a bearer. Yet here Scayna achieved much the same ends by wholly different means, subverting the infamous and barbaric social order imposed by the usurping lesser genders. Almost, Irtuk could admire the Eamnet's devious actings. After so many subjugated generations, still to seek what rightful dominion might be had: this was cause for noting.

By contrast, the exiled colony's Bretl-kai—and why was Scayna's house of origin omitted from her greeting-name?—revealed no primacy indices high or low; those of others, including Irtuk's, she seemed to ignore. The surviving Eamnets on Shtai, thought Irtuk, must constitute a sorry lot indeed.

The yumins were different; among them gender and status held no apparent relation. Among the several on Magh, and later between Kayo and Skeeter in the Eamnet skyship, ordering and obedience relied not at all on the cruciality of bearing. But the concept of balance between only two genders? Irtuk could only construct guessworks, knowing they would fail of truth.

The thought came, that given the conditions facing small numbers isolated on strange and unknown ground, such absence of gender dominance may have resulted among Bretl's folk also.

More vital was a new sensing. Taken to this strange world, Irtuk had no intent of staying. How her return might be managed, she did not know—only that her endeavor to see it done would not cease. But until brought here, Irtuk had thought the seeder Nsil to be her chiefest foe, the major obstacle against the best good of Magh. Now she saw with more clarity: the hidden power of the bearer Scayna, the skills that bent confident Nsil without his knowing, these might well prove the greater threat.

She'd really screwed up this time, Sydnie had, and she knew it. Not for years had she let temper betray her aims, let alone her very security. *Damn* Sam Gowdy! How she'd let him goad her into such a ghastly fuckup, she wasn't sure.

The doctored reports to Earth, making him look bad and her good, those were no problem for at least four years. If then. But Sam knew she'd axed his first SOS—and been stupid enough to roger for it in her own name.

She wasn't quite certain why she'd done it: resentment that he'd short-circuited her ploy with Jules, hurt feelings that he didn't care what she thought or felt, not even enough to send her a greeting?

Sexual frustration? Sydnie could do without, so long as she kept the man squirming too. But here she was odd lech out; there was nobody aboard worth seducing. And down on Magh, Sam had the whole damn colony to pick from. It wasn't *fair*.

Simone hadn't let on yet; maybe Sam hadn't told her. Or did Simone dislike her so much already, that this made no difference?

The hell with Simone. Sam was the one; until she figured how to turn things around, Sydnie had no wish to face him.

How about Barry Krsnch? An ego freak, but Gowdy had no handle on him. Make a deal there, and Sydnie could start fresh.

One problem: with the DV down, how could she get to Magh?

By the same lights, though, Sam couldn't get to *her*.

Or could he? She had the nagging worry that if he really wanted to, he'd find a way.

For the moment, at least, she had room to think. Any time she couldn't outfinesse a plodder like Sam Gowdy . . . !

Gowdy climbed down from the Doodlebug. Of all the haywire rigs he'd ever met, this one took the prize. The kicker was, it was largely his very own invention.

For all the thought and work involved, the 'bug didn't look like much. But it just might do what Sam needed.

He wasn't sure how long the job took; he'd done his sleeping in short bursts and odd moments. The old transport hull was sound; now shortened and wingless it resembled an oversized torpedo: about sixty feet long, twelve wide and a little higher, rounded at the front where it still had viewports. At the rear, beefed-up landing wheels supported the newly installed Traction Drive units; the front landing gear passed muster as was.

What made it all work was standard parts. Traction thrustors came in only a few sizes and most fit several usages: class A for ship drives, B for ship yaw or DV main, C for DV yaw and ships' trimmers, and so on down. The C unit that couldn't tip up the Vehicle was good for maybe three gees here as main drive—if this can could take that much without coming apart. And the glory was that the DV carried spares for everything.

The Vehicle's spare generator-exciter powered the 'bug: main thrustor, lifters under the stabilizer fins for atmosphere work, vertical and horizontal steering, midship tangentials if Gowdy ever needed to roll the rig, and reverse thrust up front.

"Twelve units," he said. "That's not too many."

Major gear including fuel tanks and life support filled the 'bug's rear half, but Sam didn't need much passenger space. The pilot positions were a prime example of good ad-libbing; the principles of 3-D maneuvering had dictated the original layout, and switches don't care what circuits they control. Rigging those positions to pivot ninety degrees cost a lot of sweat, but it beat lying on your back with your feet up, in drive mode.

Aft of those positions a thick tubular cross held the vertical and horizontal steering units and braced the hull against their compression thrust. Behind that hung sleeping hammocks. And from the rear bulkhead, to sit upright in drive mode, projected what was supposed to be a zero-gee toilet; Gowdy hoped they'd got the fabricated parts more right than not.

The outside mounting cleats and air and fuel valves were just in case. Gowdy might not need to lash gear to the hull or take on fuel or air in space, but given the chance he'd be ready.

When installation was complete and the hull sealed, he pumped in air at four atmospheres and checked for leaks.

Tracer gas showed several, but nothing hard to fix. And to be on the safe side, each of the few remaining windows got a thick extra layer of tough clear plastic. He lacked the sensor gear for flying blind, so vision forward was a must.

What he did have were radars for distance and velocity readings, including rear sensors for dropping through atmosphere tail first. And the transport's original forward lights, to give him half a chance if he did have to land at night.

Plus, of course, comm gear; somewhere along the route he'd want to speak with *Roamer*. It wouldn't hurt, either, to hail Eamn going in, let them know he was a talker and not a fighter.

From down here, though, that equipment wouldn't reach much of anybody. Time to call *Roamer*; Sam headed for the comm tent.

Always delays; at the end of Leopold's reply, Gowdy swallowed disappointment. "Okay, you leave there at oh eight hundred. We'll rendezvous near Eamn," wherever that world might be by then. "Meet and talk, I mean; we don't have an airlock." Well, except the flusher for the biffy. They'd take suits, of course, but only for a chance at survival if the 'bug lost air. Plus two extra for Skeeter and Kayo, on return. He hoped.

An idea came. "Wait a minute. Say I bring the 'bug into the DV berth and you deploy the inflatable cover; we'd have access to the ship."

Tension hurt his neck; he tried to shrug it free. "We may not need it; I just want the option open." Anything else? "We take off here when everything's loaded." *Except for whatever I forget until too late*. "I'll call when we get topside, but our rig may not reach until you're in closer."

One more thing. "Oh yes, tell Sydnie I've missed her. I really look forward to seeing her again." *Oh, yes . . . !*

Gowdy cut the circuit. "Okay, Maril; your job here is relay. Does Jules know how to set up voice-operate recording, for when you're off duty and he has to go out for something?"

Yes, Maril Jencik assured him, so with a pat to her shoulder Sam left the tent. Squinting into late slanted sunlight, he took deliberate stride toward the Doodlebug. To join his crew.

He'd had to decline Libby Verdoorn's offer of volunteers from her team. "Thanks, but all we can manage in this can is six, and we need space for Kayo and Skeets on the way back. So I'm leaving Maril on comm here. And Jules."

"Sure," Libby said. "That's nice of you."

Jules and Maril were paired, yes. But Perrone was staying so that Gowdy wouldn't have to depend on him in a tight spot.

At any rate, the only ones waiting at the 'bug were Alix Dorais and Milo Vitale and Marthe Vinler.

Either the four of them could do it or they couldn't.

Sam had pulled some hairy stunts in his time, but getting the Doodlebug aloft ranked with the shaggiest. Strapped in and suited but with vision hoods open, everyone sat quiet as he eased the power on. First he ran the underfin lifters up until the 'bug began to tilt, so he could equalize them. That was all he could balance sitting still. With wheels locked he eased his main drive up to shuddering and added nominal upthrust at the front.

Taking a deep breath he slipped the brakes. The taxi part was short because the field was; he was running out so he hit drive heavy and fin lift nearly as hard, then for his life fiddled vertical and horizontal yaw until the 'bug quit trying to screw itself left-handed into the ground below.

Drive alignment was badly off; it took considerable port yaw and a good bit of noselift to keep the 'bug on a straight course. But with those defaults set into his thrustors, steering became normal. If that word applied to anything about this bucket.

Once he had his controls in shape, Gowdy pointed steeply up and rammed for topside. Then he had time to swing the seats and console to lean him at a comfortable angle instead of positioned for a pelvic exam. When the sky turned black he kept watch on the cabin pressure gauge, set for high sensitivity. "Everybody hold still; this goojie wiggles if you *breathe* at it."

At rest the hull held fine against three atmospheres of pressure differential. But hammering up through bumpy air and shaking with vibration from unsynchronized thrustors, that hull took a lot of punishment.

The gauge merely fluctuatied, with no incremental drop. "Okay gang; it's holding. Shuck the suits if you want to."

He kept his on until he had taken sightings and set course, based on data from the DV's computer. Working it while sideways to gravity had been a literal pain, but he didn't have an extra tin brain aboard here; he had to figure ahead and hope nothing happened to invalidate those numbers.

Oh, once he was near Eamn he could set down all right. Getting there was the hard part.

Even in es captive state, T'phee avoids fret. Since es forced and unpleasant journey to the Eamnet ship er has experienced no punitive treatment; er has ridden the sky in a primitive construct and been brought safely to this unfamiliar world. Es sojourn in the barely furnished room holds little of interest—but this, Nsil has pronounced, is not to endure long.

For the time, T'phee observes es companions; when Bretl and the Maghren bearer and the communicative yumin K'yo are taken to a place other, er is disappointed. But holds no fear for them.

Only es aide V'naet is of concern. Withdrawn and silent, necktrunk contracted, er shows no heed for es surroundings. The time since capture has allowed scant occasion for heartening, but now T'phee goes to en. "V'naet, does this place trouble you?" Silence remains. "It need not. The Emman Nsil harbors us no ill aim; with these others, we are taken as holders of knowledge, which Nsil feels paramount to Emman safebeing."

The necktrunk rises. "And when Nsil has satisfied enself, you credit that er returns us? That outcome occupies the least of probability. No, T'phee. We are not to end our time midst get and other kin, but held here with none else of Yain."

T'phee searches for modes of comfort. Were others not present, the boon of genitive sharing could well suffice.

Entrance of Nsil interrupts es thought. "By grace of my colleague Gvan I offer you quartering of greater ease. You may without delay follow me to that location."

Livened by conversing, V'naet needs no urging to secure es accessories and walk with T'phee, pursuant to Nsil and the yumin but preceding Duant the silent Maggen through one and other passageways to a colorful decorated space. Within, Nsil motions toward a second of es kind. "Gvan, who nobly consents to guest you." And speaks to Gvan the names of those er brings.

"Honor accrues," Gvan responds, "that you guest here." Es saying is to all in presence. Having spoken, er makes a dip of es head in direction of Nsil, then removes enself herefrom.

Nsil assumes direction. "To the rear lie a number of compartments; you may reside singly or some together. To this side," gesturing, "exists the dining space. Smallfoods are provided at all times, and beverage selections." He lays foredigits to a gleaming panel. "Through this speaking device you may order meals and other amenities."

Er pauses. "Do any queries arise?" When none speak, er concludes, "Then I leave you to rest and contemplation. Upon my next return we will confer at greater length."

Abruptly, er turns and goes. Stepping quickly, the yumin Cole tests the door latch. "Locked." To either side of es neck the bases of es forelimbs rise, then fall. "Hell; how else?"

Here is T'phee's first opportunity to speak with Cole and thus learn more of yumins. Unlike K'yo, this one is not skilled in Maggen or Emman speech; T'phee will muster patience.

The plight of V'naet, however, must first be assuaged. With sequesterment at hand, T'phee leads en to a residence space. There, since genitive activity has not occurred since capture, embrace endures far longer than would in usual be considered seemly. But circumstance justifies excess; at ending, anxieties of V'naet are well spent, and T'phee feels great benefit as well.

Reentering the major space, T'phee finds the yumin Cole still present, toying with small levers of the speaking device. T'phee approaches. "May I acquire information from you?"

"Sure. What would you like to know?"

Emerging unexpected from the speaking unit, Cole's voice drew Nsil's attention. ". . . can't put a colony here. Magh and Eamn are both settled, and you need Shtai—you and the lost Eamnets. We'll have an embassy: research groups, trade missions, that kind of thing. But we won't be coming in any numbers.''

''So great your venture, to end in failure.'' Even through the timbre-deadening circuit the Yainan's speaking carried disappointment. Nsil brooded; what motives lay here?

Cole made protest. ''Failure? No such thing. You see, we have another mode of transport. But to use it, first a ship must come, to set up a—a destination mechanism.''

The Yainan's next query escaped Nsil, but the yumin answered, ''The macroGate's a big ring, assembled in space. In orbit behind Chorm the same way Shtai rides ahead.'' Again the Yainan spoke too faintly for understanding; Cole responded, ''So ships get here in one jump, then go on in normal fashion to some more distant star. So as to give further exploration a head start.'' He paused before saying, ''Other things will come through, too: big supply pods, and cargo shuttles to land them.''

Louder now, the Yainan said, ''Do you then build another such device, that persons and materials might return to your origin?''

''No, that's not necessary. The one ring holds a matched pair of Gate terminals, one for each direction.''

Considering these new wonders, Nsil missed T'phee's reply. Absorbed in thought, he disengaged the vocal reproducer.

Fortuitous unsuspected listening, he decided, could at times be most rewarding.

XI

On *Roamer*'s log, Sam's latest had Sydnie shaking her head. A native airplane, wings replaced by fins, paste on a few peewee Traction units and go out where you had to carry your own air?

His actual numbers weren't too bad. Hull and all, weight came close to two hundred tons, with a displacement volume slightly over that in fresh water. Rule of thumb said a spaceship should float but not ride high, so maybe Sam did have it right. Not much room left for crew, but a DV yaw unit should give the rig more gees than anyone would care to ride very long.

And he wasn't taking many troops along. Alix on drive, Marthe on comm, Milo for general handy. Leaving on Magh only Jules Perrone and Maril Jencik. Not exactly ambassador material.

Could be, thought Sydnie, she could quit worrying about what Sam Gowdy might feel. If he did reach Eamn in that crackerbox with only three backers, they'd be lawn mulch. Well, judging by what a few Eamnets had managed on a strange and hostile world.

Which would leave Sydnie third in command behind Simone and Mose, and no surrogate clout whatsoever to boost her stock. A situation that suited her wishes not at all. It was time, she felt, to see what she could wangle out of Barry Krsnch.

In person is best but voice had to do. *Roamer* was nearing Chorm; when Sydnie came on watch and found that talk delay from Magh was down to half a minute, she took comm and made the call.

Perrone answered; Sydnie ignored his soft soap. "That's

nice, Jules. But right now I need to talk with Barry."

His laugh, following signal lag, surprised her. "That would be quite a trick, Sydnie. He's gone home. To Glen Springs. Libby Verdoorn's in charge now. Want to speak with her?"

Not in the slightest. "What the hell happened?"

After the delay, "The way Sam and Libby told it, Barry said he couldn't take the pressure any more, so they let him Gate back. But he didn't take his things with him; Libby had it all sent on later." Perrone cleared his throat. "Ah—anything else?"

"Nothing urgent. Thanks, Jules. Lightner out."

She hadn't thought to need a backup plan, and was puzzling at the rudiments of one when Molly Abele brought the mail from Earthtush. Setting command items aside for Simone Leopold, she scanned a routine flimsy. An inspection team was coming, and . . .

A name caught her attention; boredom vanished as never was. *Jorge Aroka?* How in God's name . . . ? With sudden conscious effort she stopped her hand from trembling.

She should have known better than to assume the Spider Prince was really dead. Sydnie never had that grade of luck.

Creaks and rattles aside, Sam congratulated himself, the 'bug rode like a jewel. It didn't belong out here and might prove that point at any moment, but somehow he liked the odds.

He hadn't expected much comfort so he wasn't disappointed. Eating was cold rations, sleeping more Spartan than not; the techniques of voiding required care and patience. The air smelled of stale old airplane and recycling didn't help. Add monotony and apprehension, and Gowdy felt blessed by the lack of serious bitching. Thanks be, Jules Perrone wasn't aboard.

Or Sydnie. Now wouldn't *that* have been a picnic!

The 'bug would be within reach of Eamn well before *Roamer* could arrive. So, well supplied for either option, did he want to take low orbit and wait for rendezvous, or just go on in?

He put the question. "How does everybody feel about it?"

Looking uneasy, Milo Vitale said, "We're a pretty small landing party. I wouldn't mind picking up some help from the ship, and maybe get some more input on our planning.''

''What planning?'' Alix Dorais was behind with her touch-ups; her short red hair overlay lengthening brown roots. ''We hail Eamn, we find where to land, we pick up our people. Skeeter's down there, damn it; I want to get to him.'' She scowled. ''And he'd better be all right!''

Vinler's usual eagerness showed wear. She'd worked hard, this trip, coaching the rest in speaking passable Maghren. Now she shook her head. ''I can't help but see it both ways. I'm not voting; you'll have to decide for yourself.''

He would have anyway; he always did. Advice, he'd asked for, not a vote to bind him. But let it stand. After a long moment's thought he said, ''I'll talk with *Roamer* first.''

Because just maybe, someone aboard might have an idea he'd overlooked.

A day came—another strange Eamnet day with Chorm itself crossing the sky—when Irtuk found insight. The dissemblings of Scayna with the seeder Nsil had counterpart in and about Magh's bearers' councils: the use of innuendo and finesse by lesser persons to influence the greater. The novelty here, realized Irtuk, lay only in altered conduct of the respective genders.

In example, both Waij and later Duant-tsi were wont to cozen Irtuk-saa herself, to gain their own views credence. Amused, she *snff'd* and moved thought to matters of more nascent import.

A casual reference by Scayna implied that Nsil held custody of records that might derive from prior to the Great Dying, texted in the long-lost Archival Mode. In these possibilities, Scayna appeared to put little or no significance.

Not so Irtuk-saa. In youthful times, Archival Mode had been one of her prime scholastic achievements. Were these Eamnet annals opened to her seeing, what secrets might emerge?

Herself adept at behavioral maneuverings, Irtuk recognized those same skills in Scayna. Thus she revealed no wish to study the rumored antiquities, but offered only respectful comment.

''Decipherable or no,'' she said as Scayna offered smallfoods, ''such artifacts merit veneration.'' She paused. ''You,

I would assume, have viewed them at considerable length?''

"In brief, only.'' Scayna *snff'd.* "Their foremost interest lies among ones adept in communicative mode transform; I hold no claim to such skills. But perhaps those have place with you?''

Too near, that venture! Irtuk turned to the human. "Would you find interest in seeing objects of ancient maufacture?''

Fervently, Irtuk-saa impleaded affirmative reply.

"Yes. Yes I would.'' Whatever Irtuk had in mind, Kayo could tell it carried an urgent load. So play along; it couldn't hurt. "I can't possibly understand any of it, of course, but really ancient things always interest me.''

She turned to Scayna. "Might we see them, do you suppose?''

Tongue tip worried the gap at Scayna's lower teeth. Irtuk did that sometimes; what could it mean? Finally, "I adduce no harm,'' Scayna answered. "Nsil approving, I will take you to those relics, at our householding. Or they may be brought here. Eitherly, in only a day, perhaps another, you may inspect them.''

"You are most accommodating,'' Irtuk began, but an adaptive entered. "Scayna! Nsil would see you at soonest possibility. A strange skyship calls by farvoice.'' Seeming uneasy, the Eamnet added, "Nsil identifies the speaker as a yumin.''

To Kayo, Scayna said, "Then you must accompany me.''

"May I, also?'' Irtuk. "And perhaps Bretl?''

"I see no adverse consequence. Come.''

Scayna led, past the entrance hall and up four levels to a spacious, windowed tower room where Nsil stood before a comm console, surrounded by other Eamnets as well as his "guests.''

"Hi, Kayo.'' Skeeter seemed cheerful enough. "You're looking good; how's it going?''

She looked awful and knew it: hair straggling, jumpsuit stained past remedy by Eamnet soap. But she said, "Not bad. For prisoners we've had it pretty cushy.''

A move of Nsil's head acknowledged her presence. "A yumin ship comes; one aboard it wishes speech with yourself and with Cole. I have said you would be brought; we now await his reply.''

Sam? It had sure's hell taken him a while! "Which ship is it? Our starship *Roamer*, or the one we landed on Magh?"

"A thing of much lesser size." He held out a picture. "By a device for distance seeing, this image was made."

Kayo peered. Whatever it might be, the vessel wasn't anything she'd seen before. Beside her, Irtuk *snff'd.* "This is no skyship! An air transport machine with liftfoils removed and, it would seem, subjected to other changes not clear to me. And it now approaches Eamn?"

From the console came a voice, distorted and noise-ridden but recognizable. "Kayo? Skeeter? Gowdy here. Is this Nsil character telling the truth—are you really all right?" All things considered, he sounded calmer than seemed reasonable.

Nsil pointed to an oval protrusion on the console. Leaning toward it, Kayo said—loudly in case the signal needed it, "Hi, Sam. Kayo Marlin. Skeeter and I are fine. Could use some fresh laundry, but otherwise shipshape." What else? "We're all here: Irtuk and Duant, the Yainans, Bretl from the lost Shtai colony."

She paused. "Did you come to get us?" Dumb question, maybe. But, "Where's the DV? What are you doing in *that* thing?"

The wait wasn't long, so Sam had to be fairly near. "The Vehicle? It's not available just now, so we slapped this rig together. And yes, your return is Priority One. So let me speak to Nsil again. He seems to be the one with the say-so."

And not only in charge, thought Gowdy, but making no bones about having led the raid on Magh. Sam had to watch what he said. He'd almost let slip that Nsil's guerrillas had scragged the DV. And he didn't really want to admit, just yet, that this bucket wouldn't hold all the captives even if Nsil agreed. For a haul of any length, two at most—or one bearer.

First priority had to be his shipmates. But come right down to it, could he walk out on Irtuk? Or even the Yainans?

Again Nsil came on the circuit. "Gowdy. You have not yet stated the assumptions under which you come here."

Damn right. *Imply* your own givens, until the other guy's talking on your terms without realizing it. So, "Before our needful time for departure,'' hoping he was getting the lingo right, "I would hope to see and experience some part of Eamn. Also to share discussion with you and others, to add to the exchange of knowledge you have begun with my colleagues.''

Chew on that, you blowtorch cowboy! In truth, Sam Gowdy sincerely admired the Eamnet's sheer guts—raiding across space on chemical thrust and getting away with it free and clear.

Still, it didn't hurt to define a few parameters. Lay down some guidelines.

And never let facts get in the way of a good story.

Done with farspeaking, Nsil turned to Kaow. "The person Gowdy seems to hold no rancor; I would have anticipated otherly. From your knowledge, is his pacific demeanor credible?''

"Sam is always full of surprises.''

"Mmm.'' Nsil thought. "Among all the number who arrived aboard your greater ship, what status does he maintain?''

"He is our ship's captain. Our unquestioned leader.''

"Then were I to take him also to be held here, I might gain much advantage in furtherance of Eamnet goals.''

The yumin bearer's eyes narrowed their exposure. "Knowing Sam, I would not advise such an attempt.''

She spoke further. "Your people on Magh someway disabled our smaller ship.'' He began to speak but she ignored the courtesy of listening in turn. "If they had not, Sam Gowdy would be in it now. Instead he has built something never seen before, and flown it here.''

Her feeding orifice took on a taut and unfamiliar aspect. "Before you undertake any action against Captain Gowdy, look long at that image, the ship he has built. And contemplate what might he do, should you indeed arouse his rancor.''

Asking no leave, Kaow turned to depart. With urgent seeming the bearer Irtuk spoke. "Your permission?'' At Nsil's gesture she followed, and also went Bretl from Shtai.

At this moment the Yainan would speak, but Nsil preempted. "Hold; I will hear you shortly.''

Conceptual change required all Nsil's heeding. Direct challenge of this yumin leader might well constitute grave error. Yet what better course offered?

Ah. The seeder's view of opportunity greatened. Boldness and ingenuity of Gowdy had given Nsil pause. Yet did not the deeds of Nsil also demonstrate such qualities?

In his thought grew a new venture. Not to challenge the yumin but to transcend his limited sovereignty. But for detail, the scheme bloomed complete. And certain preparations, already near entirety, sufficed also for this more ambitious dare.

No immediate need for haste. Now let the Yainan speak.

Earnestly T'phee beseeches. "What further would you learn of us? All knowledge in my capability to impart awaits only your request. Might you not do so with alacrity, and permit departure of V'naet and myself with this yumin Gowdy, to rejoin my ship *Tayr* and return to Yamar?"

T'phee explicates. The Stewardship of that world lies rightfully upon es own necktrunk. Cejha the former Steward, now surrogate for T'phee, is aged beyond the vigor requisite to such burden. And Nahei, preceptor of the new-come ship *L'lit*, lacks experience of Yamar.

"It is not," er continues, "that our continued presence could benefit you in any wise. Thus, I again—"

The Emman's forelimb makes abrupt movement. "Yainan, I do not wish you harm. But saying you cannot be of aid is to speak in error. Supposing I could be made free of a small vessel, one of the three you have said your larger ship contains?"

T'phee asserts fact. At Magh such possibility might exist, but not from Eamn. "You must accept, our lander-carriers have not the versatility of the yumins' lesser ship, moving from world to world. We utilize the vessels only between a world and circling ship, or on the world itself. The possibility of transits from Eamn to Magh is beyond my ability to evaluate."

The Emman moves es strange head. "This information is appreciated. I must think further, as to how it may best assuage our needs. In the interim I excuse you; feel free to eat, rest, or indulge in whatever diversions you choose."

Returning to es assigned compartment, T'phee seeks within enself for encouragement, but finds little.

* * *

Sometimes Sydnie got so involved with people that she forgot she was pretty damn good with things, too. Now, in urgent need of a Plan B, she put some heavy thinking in that direction. With *Roamer* half a day from Eamn while Sam in his Pipercub spacecan wondered out loud whether to orbit or head groundside, Sydnie listened. "... any bright ideas, let me hear 'em. Gowdy out."

Having blown every alternative, Sydnie knew her only hope was getting back into Sam Gowdy's good books. As she searched for an angle, Tuiasso said to Leopold, "I hate to see the four of them go down to Eamn in a peanut butter jar. There must be some way we can help their odds a little."

Neither seemed in a hurry to answer the captain. Leopold said, "But *how?* With the DV down, what else is there?"

Sydnie's mind filled an inside straight. She brought Inventory onscreen, got lucky, and pulled up the specs.

Maybe. Eamn's gravs were less than Earth's but not by much. Still, from low orbit—she ran the functions—it could work.

Then she noticed: Eamn had more atmosphere than a fashion show. Getting down slow enough to keep friction heating within limits would take more extra fuel tanks than Inventory showed.

Wait a minute, though! Suppose . . .

"Simone? I have an idea—maybe it's silly, but I'd like to check it with Sam. Okay?"

Leopold had ridden Sydnie's back rather hard for a time, but lately she'd eased off. Now she nodded.

"Thanks." Sydnie made sure she had the right figures on screen, then she spoke.

"Sam? It's Sydnie. I'm sorry about the misunderstanding and I want to help. I was upset, yes—but I didn't lose your message on purpose. Must have been a Sleudian Frip."

Chuckle now; sound like you mean it. "Anyway, here's my idea. We meet in your orbit and . . ."

Because with an extra fuel tank or two, each, the little space sleds would make very gung ho air transport. On Eamn, or wherever else. The trick was to get them there.

And in case some of Sam's planning could use this particular form of backup, Sydnie wouldn't mind a little appreciation.

Over and above getting the hell off here and staying alive.

Whatever had swung Sydnie's attitudes head for tail, Sam was all for it. And although her idea needed more work, it did have possibilities. He said, "I like it; thanks, Sydnie. But it'll take more than fuel tanks. Those gidgets have the gliding angle of a brick."

But so had the Doodlebug. "Look, here's what you do . . ." For lift, a triangle of minor Traction thrustors, one up front and the others back under most of the weight. "Differential joystick and a power control pedal, separate from normal thrust and steering. From the specs you quoted, a sled's power pack can handle the extras."

And what else? The sleds were just that: powered platforms. Eamn's heavy air would buffet a pilot or rider something fierce. Bubble canopies—or at least windshields, good sturdy ones.

Thinking aloud saved time. "Note all this for Neville and Jethro. And mainly, tell 'em we need it done fast."

Now, let's see. . . . "We'll take a two-hour orbit, about eight hundred fifty miles up. Forget the docking thing; it'd take too long. I need volunteers to bring the sleds out and secure them to my hull. Topside; this thing lands flat, on wheels. Anyone who wants to, strap in and come with us—we'll drop slow, no friction heating. But that means bring extra air."

He cleared his throat. "I can't order anyone to take that kind of hayride; if nobody likes the idea, I understand, and thanks for the sleds. But I'm not turning away hitchhikers."

Quit while you're ahead. "All right. Thanks again, Sydnie; fast independent transport could make a big difference, downside."

Anything else? No. "Gowdy out."

Suddenly it struck him that he had more than he'd realized, to thank Sydnie for. If people could ride down to Eamn outside the bug, they could come back the same way. Up to *Roamer* in low orbit, at least, with the DV berth on airlock duty.

And on a short haul like that he could jam more beings

inside. Extra couches . . . if *all* his own people rode piggyback, he might be able to pack in both sets of aliens. The five would be equivalent to seven humans; he'd have to run the Doodlebug all by himself. But it could be done.

Now, though: given the 'bug's limited instrumentation, how long would it take to achieve a good stable orbit?

Might as well start trying.

Not the greatest he'd ever set, Sam had to admit. Not that he'd had to do many. He wasn't messing with it, though; he only needed it until *Roamer* got here. Then with a little help from his radar he could match vee and make rendezvous well enough.

He had air and water, and more packaged rations than he ever wanted to see again. His main shortage was patience; the mission seemed endless. Sam was tired, hungry for something with taste to it, and getting pretty ripe; sponge baths simply didn't do it. Especially for a guy who had modesty problems in mixed company.

Eventually *Roamer* came into eyeball range and inched closer; under Gowdy's hands the 'bug moved to hover near the rear loading hatch, centered between the main drive nodes.

"Do you need any refills?" Simone Leopold's voice. "Air, water, fuel? We can run feed tubes out to you."

Eamn held air and water; as for fuel, Sam was well fixed to land, lift again, and return to Magh. But with outside passengers he couldn't make that run anyway. "No thanks; I'll settle for just the sleds."

"Agreed. And captain—right now, if you have to correct position, stay with the light touch. People coming out."

Sure enough, suited figures wrestled three sleds out the gaping hatch and moved them back past the limits of Sam's view. Soon he heard muffled thumps and scrapes as the makeshift flyers were secured to the hull. Via relay he could also hear Leopold's dialogue with the outship workers; his best move, he decided, was to shut up and stay out of their way.

After a time he saw the lock hatch close. No one had gone back inside. "Simone? Are they all three crazy enough to ride down piggyback?"

"That's the scenario, Sam. They're ready when you are."

"I see. You know, on the suits-to-ship I couldn't recognize voices. Who do I have the honor to thank?"

"We had volunteers up the wazoo—everyone who'd flown the sleds during macroGate assembly. To keep a balance of skills for your team and on here too, I made the picks: Fontaine to shoot trouble, Wang as drive tech backup, and officer Lightner."

Alix Dorais didn't need backup; Charlotte Wang was along to be with Neville Fontaine. And was it such a good idea to risk their only Gate specialist on this wingding?

There wasn't time to argue. But *Sydnie*?

"Relay thanks for me, will you? And to strap in tight."

He waited long enough to give them time for it. Then Gowdy turned his 'bug and began the long downward slide to Eamn.

Supporting only one mature bearer, with seeders and adaptives in due proportion, Nsil's householding covered much less area than that of Irtuk-saa on Magh. Nor did its trappings match her own. The confinement dome housing Scayna, however, held space and luxury enough for any bearer's taste. Another example, mused Irtuk, of the ambiguity of gender dominance here.

Begun after midday, the journey here had been brief; Eamnet airflyers, designed for denser air, carried stubby airfoils and produced rates of motion well beyond Irtuk's prior experience.

The difference was not all benefit: passengers endured considerable buffeting. Now, enjoying the relief of solid, unmoving floor, Irtuk was amused by the antics of two of the native animals kept by Eamnets. Smofs, they were called—small nonsapient caricatures of Eamnet or Maghren, lacking manes but flaunting puffy topknots and bushy furred tails. At home Irtuk had seen specimens stuffed and mounted; in the days of interworld venturing some had been brought from Eamn and bred, but none survived the plague years. In any case those immobile figures gave no hint of the species' native vivacity; Irtuk recognized their appeal and understood their value to Scayna.

She found herself intrigued by the young bearer who greeted their arrival—the barely matured Ilrin, borne by

Scayna almost ten Chormyears past and soon to go to the holding of the seeder Arnt. "I am not to be laden immediately with all a bearer's chargings," Ilrin confided, as she and Irtuk dined side by side at the large table. "Ymaat, herself beyond bearing, is to guide me in becoming bearer of the holding. That I may be worthy."

And for this, the young one felt gratitude! By dint of will, Irtuk suppressed her true reaction. "It is well, Ilrin, that you find such favor."

In Irtuk-saa's life experience, particularly as her station rose, extreme tact or patience had seldom been required. Trapped here and seeing no means of possible escape, she found those disciplines difficult indeed. Yet by showing outer calm where inner turmoil existed, Irtuk endured, now and then relieving strain by crunching a bulb from something called a splaybush, and inhaling its mildly euphoric gases.

This diversion sufficed until dining ended, and Scayna spoke. "After sleep and morning repast, we will view the antiquities."

The compartment to which Irtuk was shown had no great size, but was more than adequately equipped.

She had come to the place she wished to be; next day she might be privy to revelations undreamed of.

Why did rest and content elude her?

Kayo Marlin had seen Maghren writing. In no way did it resemble what she was shown now: silver webbings etched into thin sheets of translucent onyx. How anyone could make sense of the irregularly spaced patterns, Kayo had no idea.

Irtuk gave no sign of understanding the ornate markings, but Kayo had a strong hunch the bearer wasn't studying the symbols as artwork; five got you ten she was *reading* them.

And didn't want anyone to know it. Well, if Kayo had one friend on this world aside from Skeeter Cole, it was Irtuk-saa. So, stifling her own avid curiosity, Kayo did her best to keep Scayna's attention away from the Maghren.

Not that she had anything against Scayna personally; the Eamnet bearer was as gracious and hospitable as they come. She wore the wrong colors, was all.

With a sort of staccato groan, Irtuk rubbed primary knuckles against her eyelids, and stood. "Losing my sense of place in appreciation of these artifacts, I have allowed my energies to deplete. Scayna—with gratitude, I would end studies this day."

Irtuk sounded about as sincere as a cola commercial, but while Scayna led the way upramp to the quarters level, Kayo held her peace and kept a straight face. Alone with Irtuk and Bretl in the pleasantly draped common area by their sleeping rooms, she said, "All right, Irtuk; what have you found?"

Almost imperceptively the Maghren tilted her head toward Bretl. "The artisanship is of great merit," she declaimed, "and its techniques could give rise to much discussion. However . . ."

Her great jaws gaped, then closed; a Maghren bearer's yawn was impressive. "I must repose, prior to this day's next meal."

With that, Irtuk retired to her own room. After a moment, Bretl followed suit. What the hell; Kayo shrugged. A nap wasn't the worst idea she could think of.

She was halfway to having one when Irtuk tapped her shoulder. "There is that which you must know, Kayo. But which Bretl, still Eamnet even though generations exiled, must not."

"You learned something off those plates?"

"Indeed. They are not mere legibilities. The glyphic patterns only summarize in Archival Mode the true content, stored in magnetopolar fashion within the pane itself."

"Like one of our computer caps?" Irtuk knew of those.

"In function, likely so. On Magh we have long known of these devices, but only of late succeeded in partial revealment of that which is stored therein."

At Kayo's arm the bearer's grip tightened. "I must convey a sampling of the panes to Magh. These Eamnets have forgotten what exists here; they see only what is to see. But even that tells much, to one who can interpret. The ancient plague, Kayo Marlin. What I have learned . . ."

Unannounced, an adaptive entered. "Nsil summons; all must gather belongings and come." Seeming somehow apologetic, the creature added, "Direct me and I shall aid in the bringing."

As it moved out of hearing, Irtuk stuffed a cloth bundle into Kayo's bag. ". . . may it serve you well." Before Kayo could ask anything, they were escorted away from there.

At the entrance hall they found Scayna in no compliant mood. "First we shall feed," and the communications attendant now speaking for Nsil had no choice but to go report her stand.

Dining was hardly in relaxed mode; then immediately the four were hustled to an Eamnet plane. It looked like the same one, but in growing dark Kayo couldn't be sure either way.

The good side of this flight was that after dark the air smoothed out a lot. The bad was that with Scayna sitting between, Kayo had no chance to query Irtuk.

Hell with it. Most of the way, Kayo spent in nervous doze. On arrival, only half-waking as Irtuk helped her to a boxy vehicle and then, back in the dome, to her previous quarters, she stripped only to underwear before bedding down in earnest.

Until she had her sleep out, everybody's problems could wait their turn.

XII

Sweet Jesus; how had Sydnie ever got herself into *this*? As Sam's spacegoing airplane began to jitter in atmospheric resistance and her sled's bubble canopy rattled through several successive vibration modes, she gripped the armrests of her seat.

He'd said they'd be going down too slow for any real friction problems; she'd have to trust him on that. Probably it was the landing wheels and sleds sticking out, not the hull itself, causing all this irregular drag. Whatever, she'd just as soon he took it a little easier. She had enough air aboard to support more patience than usual.

She was just about getting used to the rough ride when

Eamn up ahead took a dive out of sight and the star Whitey swung to glare in at her. Sydnie had totally lost track of position with regard to Whitey and Chorm and Magh; the blinding light didn't help. But now again she heard or maybe felt the characteristic hum of Traction Drive, as decel pushed at the back of her seat.

At the same time the atmospheric jarring eased. Okay, Sam Gowdy did know what he was doing.

Since it wasn't her problem now, Sydnie lay back and relaxed.

At least she was well away from *Roamer*. And maybe by the time she went aboard again, Jorge Aroka would have come and gone.

Her name on the roster would mean nothing to him; so far as she knew, he'd never heard it. But if he'd seen her picture in the personnel files . . . and why else would he come here? How the Spider Prince had made the leap from a singularly dirty line of business to heading a ship inspection team, she couldn't imagine.

But here he was, or soon would be.

La Hoja Rubia had been considerably younger and wore a short haircut. But since her face had not, after all, been the last sight Aroka ever beheld, he'd have good reason to remember it.

Next time the sled bucked, the onetime Blonde Blade hardly noticed.

Waking once again in the compartment first allotted to her by Nsil, Irtuk paid heed to certain phenomena of her body and felt relief. Her restless discomfort of recent days no longer perplexed; simply, her dexter anterior womb readied to bear.

Now which . . . ? Those cherished intimacies back at her own holding now seemed so far past . . . who had conjoined with her, and to what issue? At last she recalled; this womb, earliest quickened of those in process, bore a seeder of Waij's giving.

Scayna must be advised, and proper facility arranged. Or in the deranged Eamnet view, would Nsil be charged with such doings? To Irtuk the question held little consequence;

she would speak with Scayna and tolerate whatever might result.

Thoughts cleared of the matter, Irtuk considered what she had done before leaving Nsil's holding. The summoning adaptive's presence had precluded detailed communication, yet perhaps the yumin understood. Aiding in assemblage of Kayo's possessions, Irtuk took opportunity to secrete three of the ancient record panes, wrapped within a thick drying-cloth, at the bottom of one of Kayo's containers. Partially but not entirely duplicating others hidden among Irtuk's own possession, the three roughly summarized the startling information the bearer had deciphered.

Making certain that Kayo observed her action, Irtuk said only, "May all that you keep with you, serve you well."

Before lifting the container, the yumin moved her head in its gesture of assent. Thus, Irtuk held hope that her intent was understood—that if Kayo were returned to Magh, there the panes could be more fully deciphered.

But from that moment, circumstance had debarred private speech with Kayo. On next meeting, perhaps . . .

The unannounced entrance of Nsil ended her musing. "Irtuk-saa, I have made decision that again you have passage within my skyship. You will collect that which you choose to bring."

What brash scheme was this? "You return us to Magh? What has changed your intent?"

"To Magh, no. To a new place; you will see."

A new place? No; not in her present circumstance. Head angled aside, Irtuk spoke. "If not to Magh, then nowhere off Eamn do I accompany you." And within herself admitted that even to regain her homeworld, subjecting her body now to the stresses of Nsil's skyship could be less than wise.

Shifting into warier stance, still the seeder gave voice with confidence. "Yet I venture you held similar view before; notwithstanding, I brought you here. What has been done . . ."

"Any new and clever ruse merits one success," came Irtuk's reply. "I was caught surprised, in passive observance, all ways unready to resist onslaught, and thus undone. Once aboard your ship, it seemed best gainful to indulge curiosity and defer confrontation."

Her massive shoulders hunched, then eased. "Do not mistake yourself, Nsil; repetition could not achieve that same result.'' To one forewarned, Irtuk reasoned, the sense-stunning device would prove resistible. And within a ship, Nsil must realize, its activation would incapacitate all, without partiality.

He did not appear to comprehend that Irtuk, subject to the agitations of imminent bearing, was in all ways capable of dealing him grievous hurt if aggravated much further.

As though both minds harked to one voice, Nsil drew back. ''My means vary; my success does not. Yet your recalcitrance may forfeit more than you know.''

His exit came even more abruptly than his entrance.

''. . . what you must do, Gvan,'' said Nsil. ''Do not resist the yumin leader directly, but implement compliance with all least possible haste. He must not know of my aim until its impediment is beyond his grasp. Do you understand in fullness?''

Most disturbing, this visit to the Maghren Irtuk; recalling it, Nsil felt his mane stir. Peril had companioned him there; in hap, the bearer's presence on his mission might prove adverse. No matter; now Nsil strove for serene thought—and to frame most concisely his intructions to Gvan who must act in his stead.

''In less than fullness, I regret,'' that one conceded. ''And you have not stated, Nsil—when does your venture commence?''

''The yumin Gowdy comes to ground earlier than I had hoped. My householding was advised; Scayna has brought Kaow and the two bearers. My choosing is complete, Gvan.'' Excepting—would he muster force to take the Maghren bearer unwilling, or leave her here, cast aloose from the sweep of great destiny?

But these concerns were not Gvan's. Nsil said, ''I will take those selected and leave the rest to your caregiving. Throughout this period and considerable ensuance the yumin Gowdy must be kept attentive to proceedings at this place, to forestall any farspeaking he might undertake, adverse to my actions.'' He paused. ''My departure awaits only the assemblage of those who will accompany me, and the necessaries for their well-being.''

"And you anticipate, Nsil, that the Overgathering will accept my direction as your appointed surrogate?"

"I shall so provide."

Yet such provision might not prove sufficient. There was a lack to Gvan, a need for support from others to validate his authority. With at the same time a tending toward unconsidered action. And Nsil would not be present to bolster—or to curb, as might elsewise be needful.

Therefore, "One further advisory. Well as not, Scayna of my householding can remain here during my absence. She is privy to my aims and will be instructed to aid you in all respects. As indeed her counsel has often aided my own plannings."

With a forelimb Nsil made the gesture of dismissal. "My station here now passes to you, Gvan."

"Then I go to renew acquaintance with your agenda charts, that I may assume your duties capably."

With Gvan's needings satisfied, Nsil opened farvoice to Tasr on ship Three. A difficult choice, Tasr or Feln—but although Feln had safely grounded ship One twice on Eamn and once on Magh, and possessed skill at bringing it to rendezvous, Tasr it was who on larger scale best performed vital calculations: the timings of ships' paths, the most favorable utilization of fuelings.

So, once more aloft and almost fully refueled from the last of Two's reserves, Three waited with Tasr directing its prime operating position, for Feln to bring ship One to meeting.

Now Tasr confirmed all a-ready. "As I knew confidence that you would have it," Nsil replied. "Here occurs a brief but unavoidable delay. Therefollowing, Feln will notify you of our readiness, that you may calculate and impart to him the moment at which our departure best facilitates meeting with you."

All the while riding in orbit, Sam hadn't seen anything lift off Eamn. But on straight eyeball he probably wouldn't. Not at any distance. Or the launch site could have been turned away at the time. Now, though, as he dropped bassackwards and slowing, there went *two* spacecans side by side, near and maybe a little above the orbit he'd left not so long ago. Riding along smug as you please, and how they'd got there he had no clue at all.

Why hadn't anyone on *Roamer* noticed? He thought of calling, but even on slow drop the interaction of air and Traction Drive field would swamp his weak rig. For the umptieth time he wished he had the DV here! Nothing against this good ol' Doodlebug which was by God crossyerfingers making it, but still and all . . .

Going tail first, the misalignment of his main thrustor made steering even trickier. The zero-bias fins helped, but still he needed a quick eye to the haywired rearview screen and a delicate hand at yaw and pitch. And he was in for a long haul, relatively speaking; by the time the sleds had been secured, his homing beacon on Eamn had moved out of quick'n'easy drop range.

Having figured his overall decel need beforehand, Sam knew he had plenty of slack if he stuck to his game plan: balancing vee and gravs and drive thrust to keep the ride slow enough for hitchhiker safety and low-gee enough for relative comfort, with little or no radial vee left over when the ground arrived.

All in all, things were working out pretty well. So far. Except that basically he was having to make more than half an extra turn around Eamn before he'd be in shape to set down. And playing it cautious, a lot of that distance was at the slow end of his descent.

He wouldn't be running his sled riders short of air, but he might very well stretch their patience farther than he'd like.

Behind him he could hear Marthe and Milo chatting—low-toned so as not to distract him. Well, he'd set the rule: in a hands-on piloting situation, don't talk to the pilot unless necessary.

Sometimes one person's necessity was another's nagging fret. Again Alix Dorais piped up "How much longer before we're down?"

Before she found out if Skeeter was really okay, she meant, so Gowdy couldn't be too harsh. "Well, the radar says . . ." He cited current height and drop rate; tangential vee wouldn't matter to her, though it did govern their sitting down at the right place or not. "Not long, Alix; hang tough some more."

He was searching his mind for something more encouraging when two things happened. First, from sideways came a layer of turbulent jet stream. As the 'bug fought Sam's effort to straighten out, off to his right a way rose a pillar of flame.

"*Shit*!" Gowdy's fist slammed against the console panel's cowling. "There goes another goddam blowtorch."

And this time headed where? To Magh again? Or, most likely, out to noodle with the two in orbit?

But until Sam landed, he couldn't get in touch with *Roamer*. Not that there was much the ship could do about anything.

At least now he was getting close to that landing.

Urgency notwithstanding, in Scayna's conduct of her farewell to Nsil their intimacy proceeded without haste, all aspects being developed well and thoroughly. Only with afterhuddling under way did Nsil alter behavior mode to speak of importances.

As befit, Scayna gave full heed. "Gvan has much capability," Nsil began, "yet in the extremes of this situation his holding to purpose may require reinforcement, or perhaps a restraining limb. To either need I could recommend none more highly than yourself. Scayna, I ask you to keep him in your charge, for me. Until I return."

Unspeaking, she stroked his neck in assent; he continued, "Where I go, none of our kind has ventured; what is to be found, none can guess. But for Eamn, I dare it."

Of a sudden she *knew* his aim. But how . . . ?

She asked. Once past his startlement at her perceptiveness Nsil said, "Here and at Erdth the yumins build great portals; ships leap between them as though the two were one. And what they can do, also can Nsil." He clutched her forelimb. "None here but yourself must know this plan. You will safeguard it?"

Without hesitance she so assured him; then for long moments they held each other against the time of separation.

When he had left, Scayna felt no urge to find company with her guests from Magh; her thought had not yet encompassed all ramifications of Nsil's planning. Nor of Irtuk's tidings—which, to all apparence, had not been vouchsafed to Nsil. Instead she ordered a small repast brought to her chamber. Done with eating, she sent request to Gvan, asking that he join her. Then, lying aslant on her comfortable, precisely tilted lounge, she waited.

And soon Gvan arrived. Dispensing with servitry, Scayna herself poured cupfuls of light euphoric for them both. "Gvan?" In unison each touched tongue to the brimming liquid, inhaled the vapor above its surface, then supped a portion.

Denoting appreciation, the seeder's head moved. "Nsil gave me assurance of your aid. My gratitude, Scayna."

"We both aid his foresighted planning, you and I. It is he who should properly be grateful."

Gvan supped more, brandished his cup. "And to give him just cause, I must exceed his expectations. With your help, Scayna, I shall do as much. So that he has pride of my doing."

With his departure, Scayna settled to rest. Yet her thought troubled her: why should Gvan's assurances rouse new fret?

Oh bloody hell, here we go again. Hauled off from her digs again with no warning and half her stuff straggling out the top of the bag she carried, Kayo fumed her way to the large room where Nsil was holding forth.

She wasn't the only one; Taffy the Yainan could hardly be said to have a face as such, but his sensory cluster and four little arms were working up a storm not exactly consonant with his mildly voiced protests. "It is that I deserve explanation, Nsil. To what place do you now conduct us, and for what reason? In fairness, Nsil . . ."

No fuggin' avail. Right now the Eamnet seeder was the straw boss, the ringmaster, the cop directing traffic. Looking around, Kayo saw no sign of Skeeter; of the seven captives from Magh, only she and Taffy were here. And why? What was going on?

When in doubt, create a disturbance. "*Nsil!*"

It took twice before he powered down and looked toward her. "Kaow? Does some aspect distress you?"

"You might say that." She paused to rethink the syntax. "Taffy implies that we now go to another place. He is correct that you should explain to us. And . . ." Oh yes. "Where is Skeeter Cole? I have need to speak with him before any other event occurs."

Visibly Nsil shifted down a gear or two. "Your request, Kaow, is within reason; he shall be summoned."

It took maybe seven–eight minutes, while Kayo found herself unable to follow the proceedings; she was too busy glowering. Then, like a cork out of a bottle, here the man was. Rumpled, looking sunburned although he probably hadn't been outdoors in a week, Skeeter edged over to her. "Kayo? What the hell's up?"

"I don't know." She told him what she did know, what she guessed, and for whatever it was worth, the things Irtuk had hinted. "So if Nsil's hauling us off to hide us from Sam for some reason . . ."

"But Sam should be landing any time now," Cole protested. "Why would Nsil wait until the last minute to get fancy?"

They hadn't come even close to an answer before Nsil got his circus moving again. Taffy must have made his point after all, or partially; in place of the Yainan leader, his subordinate—Vannet, or something like that—now marched in the convoy.

So that after a lot of confused hustling, once again Kayo found herself in a bunk on the smaller Eamnet space can, with Vannet alongside in the next couch. And the seeder Duant, looking both scared and despondent, across the way. That was it, though: no Skeeter, no Irtuk. No other captives at all.

On the plus side, nobody was being kept under restraint—except for strapping down as directed, in preparation for lift.

Kayo brooded. The crate had got her here in one piece. Was twice in a row too much to expect from the law of averages?

Someone speaking for Nsil talked Gowdy in toward where they wanted him to land, describing the site well enough that he recognized it onscreen by way of his rear sensor eye. Distance was trickier, but his radar told him when to flip out of the tail first approach—and at this point he was thoroughly fed up with steering by a streaky screen doubling for a rear-view mirror!—and go into lift-assisted glide mode.

Eamn's heavier air blanket gave him a lot more leeway than Magh's had done; his side fins needed less help from their jury-rigged Traction units. Almost like bringing in a regular plane he slowed by holding a near stall and gradually cut Traction lift. When his wheels jounced, he activated his reverse thrustor.

Well past the cluster of Eamnets grouped at one side of the open area, Sam brought the Doodlebug close to stopping, turned it, then used minimal forward thrust to taxi back. Squinting through the dust his landing had raised, he saw things he didn't care for.

He turned to Alix and Marthe and Milo. "Folks? Anybody recognize the gadgets some of our welcoming committee are toting?" Nobody did; Milo wanted to know why he asked. "Because that's not how I'd hold a camera; it's how I might hold a gun."

"Back on Magh they didn't use guns," said Marthe Vinler. "It was all sensory disruption, light and sound." He didn't have to ask out loud. "We never got a good look at what they used, but it could very well be what this bunch is carrying, too."

"Wha'd you want to do, Sam?" Alix Dorais. "We brought the general purpose big game rifles, didn't we?"

Gowdy thought about it. "Yes. All two. But we won't be carrying them. Even for show, and definitely not to plonk any Eamnets. We're going out there peaceably, because we have to."

He waited through the flurry of protest. "We're in suits. Ratchet your sun visors down into position and turn off your outside mikes. So if they do have a light show with the *1812 Overture*, not much crap gets in at us."

He paused; yes, they were catching on. "Keep in mind, last time you were caught by surprise in pitch-dark, out in the open, no suits no nothing. This time we go out, they give it their best shot, and it only hurts when we laugh."

Of all the wringers Sydnie Lightner had been put through during her varied careers, this one came close to the lifetime achievement award. It wasn't just being stuck outside a spacegoing tomato can and turned every way but front, time without end and nobody saying how much longer. She had also stewed in a spacesuit, uncomfortably tube-connected to all its conveniences, for more hours than any one should have to be.

In more than one sense of the word she was thoroughly pissed.

So when Sam's tin can bounced on the deck and finally stopped with a bunch of whatever-they-weres that lived here crowding around, Sydnie unbuckled and moved to unlash her space sled from its berth first in line atop the can's hull. She was loosing the final tie when her suit speakers blared such a cacophony of blasting sound that before she could turn them off she staggered and nearly fell away to the ground. Looking down after she caught a handhold, she couldn't stave off a shudder; a fall like that could solve a person's problems for keeps.

In peripheral vision she caught painful bursts of glare; these Eamnsiders were pulling the same crap Marthe Vinler had reported from when the bastards raided Magh.

Well chuck you Farley. . . .

With her outside mikes off, what came in through the suit wasn't worth bothering about. Realizing that her sled now merely balanced on the larger hull, gingerly Sydnie climbed across and strapped into the control seat.

Again with caution, she eased up power on her triangle of Traction lift units: don't hammer Sam's hull too hard. When a subliminal twitch told her the sled was free, she punched the bejeezus out of forward thrust and held on tight.

As the sled accelerated to flash past all her first view into new terrain, Sydnie fought to regain control and finally managed. Now then; what to do?

Turning, tilting into a bank and then having to nose up to hold altitude, she headed back. Approaching Gowdy's grounded vehicle and the group milling around it, she peered to see what the hell was happening, but couldn't discern much. All right; let's show these locals how it's done in the big city!

After all, she'd once got Aroka's jet up and away, largely unholed including themselves and cargo, by scything a path across a field full of tall grass and armed militia. Overhearing what that cargo really was had forced the realization that she had to get out, the hard way. And until a day or so ago, she thought she'd made a clean job of it. That she had, for once, lived up to her manufactured reputation. The Blonde Blade . . .

But compared to that patched-up jet with its homemade gun ports, this haywire raft was safer than baby's crib.

When she swung back after the low screaming pass, not a soul of any species stood upright. "And stay there!" she yelled, not that anyone would be hearing her.

Her outside mikes were off, but the suit-to-suit wasn't. Gowdy's voice came. "Sydnie, will you for Chris'sakes please come set that thing down before somebody gets hurt?"

Until Gowdy slowly let in the heavy native air and then led Marthe and Milo and Alix down and out from the Doodlebug a few yards, the welcome wagon was all smiles. So to speak: Sam had never had much luck interpreting Maghren faces and these were no easier reading. All he noticed for sure was that this crowd included no bearers, only the two smaller types.

Though these seemed a little shorter and considerably stockier than the Maghren versions. Hand to hand if it ever came to that, Gowdy was pretty sure he could take one of those seeders or adaptives; with this Eamnet bunch he wasn't so sure. At any rate the leader here kept on making greeting-type noises until blooey!—the light show and party bangers cut loose.

No surprise there. Sam's guesses paid off; closed suits and the shutdown of outside mikes cut the blast effect down to mildly annoying, and the visors made the pulsing glare tolerable.

Without breaking stride he cranked his own external sound output to max. "Greeting, our friends. We rejoice to meet you here on Eamn. We . . ." Wincing at the fierce rattle of his speakers' overload distortions, he felt moderate glee at seeing Eamnets cover their ears. Welcome to reciprocity. . . .

Their leader gestured; the light-and-sound barrage dwindled and ceased. Sam cut his outgoing audio gain and gave himself a mental pat on the back. Until he saw Eamnets dropping without cause and off to one side glimpsed some kind of big flat thing swooping to take his head off. With reflexes he hadn't even stretched lately he went for prone and made it; pushing up again he turned and recognized the space sled's shape.

Immediately came Sydnie's ultimatum. Before going on band to say knock off and sit down, Sam gave her a moment to enjoy it.

When the sled crunched to ground and slid in on its improvised skids, a new development had his attention. Between the Doodlebug and its disembarked complement, a sullen-looking lot of Eamnets now stood foursquare, parting only to allow Fontaine and Wang, leaving their sleds and clambering down the 'bug's side, to join their crewmates.

All right; ask the boss. Sam walked over to him. "You are Nsil?" And without waiting, "What do these want with my ship?"

"Nsil regrets he cannot meet with you. I am Gvan, acting for Nsil in welcome of you to Eamn. All will accompany me now. Those servitors ensure that your ship finds no harm here."

Maybe so, maybe not. "I am Sam Gowdy. Not only this ship, but also the great one in which we came to this star, is in my charge. Before I accompany you to any place whatsoever, I will see Kayo Marlin and Skeeter Cole whom Nsil took from Magh, along with three of your own species and two from your companion star." No comment from Gvan. "I will see these immediately."

Gvan's small movements of uncertainty and discomfort transcended species differences. "I regret that compliance with your desire is not possible until subsequent time. In alleviation we offer hospitality and comfort. If we may . . ."

Air whistled thinly as Sydnie, equalizing her suit pressure, approached. Gesturing the Eamnet to silence, Sam turned to her. "Nice barnstorming; you tilted the playing field our way in a hurry." Overkill maybe, but it hadn't hurt. "You ever dust crops for a living?"

Instead of answering, she bobbed her head toward the natives cordoning off the Doodlebug. "Maybe I should have given this bunch another round. Too late now, d'you think?"

"Mmmm. I think I'll try something a little different." Back to Gvan. "Hospitality, you mention. Are your people, over there, skilled and dependable at handling valuable equipment? Even though it may be of considerable weight?"

Obviously relieved at Gowdy's tone, Gvan overflowed with affirmatives. "Whatever such need you may have, it shall be fulfilled."

So while the Eamnet guards, under direction of Marthe Vinler, muscled and pulleyed the other two sleds down off the 'bug, Sam encountered no interference as he had his people gather any belongings they wished to take along. Meanwhile he programmed the 'bug's rudimentary computer facility to run the pumps, refilling his air tanks to specified pressure; Eamn's heavier atmosphere gave the operation a good head start.

He checked the time. Near as he could recall, *Roamer* would have gone below his horizon only a few minutes earlier. Assuming he'd kept track of position better than he probably had. At any rate, right now he couldn't afford to stall long enough to figure it out and wait for his next signal window. So be it.

Outside again, Gowdy looked around. When you're on a roll . . . "Before we go from this spot, Gvan, let us arrange replenishment of necessities on my ship." That would be water, mostly, but it couldn't hurt to sound a little more picky.

He turned to his supply man Milo Vitale. "Can you handle the lingo okay?" Vitale nodded. "Gvan, be acquainted with Milo. It is he who will describe to you our needs."

Gvan made a gesture of acknowledgment. "There will be those assigned to procure what is necessary. But to so choose, I must consult my listings which are kept in the structure to which we invite you. And in no wise can assignments be made effective until next day." The seeder blinked. "Will this suffice?"

Needs must, as they say. "At next day's beginning, then." All right; what else for now? Reentering the Doodlebug briefly, Sam activated the screecher alarm he'd haywired back on Magh to deter curious observatory students, then came out to rejoin Gvan. With a straight face he explained how dangerous the interior could be to anyone not knowledgeable of the vehicle's workings. Gvan's earnest delivery, relaying that warning to the guards' leader, made Sam happy all over again.

Not happy enough, though, to ease up a whole lot.

After all, hospitality was a two-way street.

* * *

Right off the bat Kayo saw that Nsil's ship Three had cards and spades over the smaller one. A lot more room, even for the considerably larger crew, plus a better grade of furnishings, notably including zero-gee toilets intended to fit Kayo and the Yainan. Maybe they would, too; Kayo was in no hurry to find out.

Eamnets seemed to have a knack for improving their designs. Even the decks and bulkheads were done in brighter, pleasant colors—and food came in more and tastier varieties. Also, Kayo gathered from Nsil's genteel boastings, this ship was much lighter, for its size, than either predecessor—and thus more fuel-efficient.

Transferring between ships, up in what Earth spacers referred to as low orbit, was a scary thing. Nsil said he had suits which had been fabricated for her and the Yainan, but no time to check them out just now; what they wore for the EVA were heavy plastic bags with air tanks attached and no outside view at all. The whole process probably took only about fifteen or twenty minutes but seemed to last for hours.

Once aboard, she found that ship Three offered bunks—single and bearer-sized both—in curtained cubbies, surrounding an open area that sported actual chairs and tables firmly affixed to the deck. Eamnet chairs mostly, not especially suited to humans, never mind Yainans who didn't need them anyway—but at the larger table stood one seat obviously intended for Kayo herself. It wasn't the most comfortable she'd ever tried but she thanked Nsil anyway. *It's the thought that counts. . . .*

Which also held true for the biffy.

Previous experience led her to expect a relatively short period of racketing acceleration and then a long time of merely coasting. But this ship, she learned, was carrying outboard fuel tanks as well as the rather sizable trio included in its original design. Noise and thrust and vibration continued for hours, far longer than she'd thought possible to Eamnet technology. And unless her somatic recalls were totally off, Nsil was pushing at considerably more than one Earth gee, let alone Eamn's.

Combined with the temperature—this ship, for some reason, ran a hotter cabin than One had—the excess definitely cut her comfort and energy levels.

Where in blazes could they be *going*? And she had to fight a sneaking anxiety that Nsil might be spending fuel he was going to need for decel at the far end.

But either the audacious raider knew what he was doing or he didn't. The matter was out of Kayo's hands—so she did her best to drop it out of her mind, too. Until he offered her a look through a forward viewing tube: there was *Chorm*—Big Red, no less!—covering a large part of what she saw. Only when the huge world's gradual inching toward that view's center slowed and reversed did her pulse and breathing slow also.

Nsil touched her shoulder. "If you would now secure yourself . . ." So she went to her bunk and strapped in.

Apparently Tasr had built vee to Nsil's satisfaction; within a few minutes the ship's drive died to silence. And not long after, Nsil gave her the all clear to come out again.

Once up and around, Kayo found that readjustment to zero gee came quick and easy. She ate, drank, tried to talk with Vannet and with Duant though neither seemed to rouse much enthusiasm for chat, and slept well.

The toilet worked as intended. They'd built it by guess, not measurement, but holding a wad of diapering material to the forward gap where some Eamnet's guess had been totally wrong, she managed her business neatly as could be.

Other business transpired, she noticed, that had been absent on the smaller ship. One bearer-sized cubby seemed to have no permanent occupant; rather, now and then a seeder and adaptive would enter, remain for a time, and emerge again. With Nsil it was usually but not inevitably the one named Tirys. So, the crew here enjoyed love lives. And why not? Certainly no one had to worry about getting pregnant.

Several mealtimes into the zero-gee period, with Nsil's permission Kayo squinted out through the ship's viewtubes—but couldn't make head or tail of what she saw. Eamn was back there, Magh over *there*, Chorm drifting rearward. And the star Whitey . . . Where in the name of common sense could the ship be heading?

When Nsil took a break from his duty station, Kayo tackled the question. "To what place, Nsil, do you take us now?"

By now she recognized the slight dropping of jaw and lip, exposing lower teeth with their central V-shaped gap, as the Eamnet equivalent of a grin. "To your home, Kaow. To Erdth."

XIII

Trying without success to control the tremblings of his rearlimbs, Gvan gripped the stanchion before him and made an attempt to hold his eyes open the bare slit required to see against the painful buffeting of air.

How had he so lost control of circumstance? When the yumin Gowdy agreed to accompany Gvan to the Overgrouping compound, he then pleaded fatigue on behalf of self and coterie. "Rather than walking such distance, we can ride. And of course yourself also, Gvan. It will be my honor to transport you."

Clearly the wheeled oblongate ground transport provided by Gvan was disdained. So, onto the construct so lately careened about the sky by the unmistakably disordered yumin bearer, Gvan and two of his aides were given escort. Soon, laden with yumins and the entire Eamnet presence except a minimal guard party for the yumin ship, all three frightful instruments of terror screamed jerkingly through what had been peaceful air.

And not in simple nor direct line to the compound. No; the yumin Gowdy said, "On our way, let us digress and view more of your countryside." At speeds too great for ease of breath, let alone vision, the three platforms veered and darted across field and hill, plantgrove and waterway, by some marvel keeping their relative positions fixed as though mounted to a framework.

"Formation flying," came the yumin's cryptic remark.

And now, as Gvan silently impleaded an end to this ordeal, Gowdy spoke into a farvoicer at his throat and the combined course swung toward the compound. Moments later the group landed at the site Gvan, on request, pointed out to Gowdy.

Now, perhaps, Gvan could resume position ascendant in this situation. As he led the yumins in through the great entrance hall and back toward the living compartments intended for them, his thought ranged futureward. Though he dared not cause any to enter and disable this Gowdy's skyship, he could yet bar the yumins from it. And once his dominance was thus established, negotiation and agreement could proceed as Nsil desired, on Eamnet terms. To commence, Gvan would arrange that Scayna guest these new Erdthans at the day's latemeal. In such venue, given the bearer's assistance, he could preside assuredly. With regained confidence he issued the invitation in Scayna's name.

The next moment saw his plans dashed to dust. From a side corrider emerged the yumin Skeeta. First, one of the yumin bearers voiced a shrill mating call and ran to Skeeta's embrace but did not, after all, consummate in any fashion recognizable to Gvan. Next Skeeta and Gowdy greeted loudly, smiting each other's dorsal areas and speaking without cease. All in Erdth speech; meanings eluded Gvan. But from the vehemence of it, these two might be deemed fiercely opposed.

Uncertain, Gvan waited for speakings he might understand.

Quieter now, Gowdy got to business. "So that was Nsil, was it, blasting off to upstairs?"

With one arm settled around Alix Dorais and her head tucked against his chin, Skeeter Cole nodded. "He took Kayo along, and Vannet the number two Yainan. Irtuk's pet seeder, too." And no, Skeeter had no idea where.

Scheist oh bloody fornicating hell forever! Whoever said a little internal cussing didn't help, never had to ease a head of steam; Sam felt a distinct measure of relief.

He turned to Gvan. Short on knowledge of Maghren or Eamnet body language, still Gowdy sensed a mixture of complacent triumph and nagging apprehension.

This species couldn't stand up straight. Sam did, glowering at Gvan eye to eye and downhill. "Your Nsil has taken action adverse to us, absconding with my valued colleague. We now return to my ship and depart your world. You will not interfere."

He had to hand it to Gvan; the seeder barely flinched before retorting, "Of a surety, you may depart at any time of your choosings. But as you have stated, ships impose their own imperatives. Maintainings and refurbishments: foods, water, the necessities of propulsion and of respiration. Have I not agreed to oblige you in such matters as meet our capabilities, prior to your leaving?"

And the hell of it was, the guy was right. Equipment and fuel and food and air were okay, but water definitely wasn't. And Sam had already admitted as much. Well, if Gvan paid his bills, the 'bug was in clover. If not, back to tile one.

Still a bone to pick, though. More of the parade ground glare might help. "You also, Gvan, have deceived me. Not until our landing did you divulge that Nsil was gone, nor that with him he has taken my colleague again captive."

An inch or so, the seeder's head thrust forward. "Not captive, but valued associate to Nsil as envoy." *Envoy*? Gvan wasn't done, though. ". . . and in all candor, I hold liege to Nsil only. To no other am I accountable."

Sam's push wasn't working; Gvan had backed down as far as his own rules would let him. So drop it. Cold. "Then we would now view our quarterings and enjoy their comfort." Afterthought: "You spoke of latemeal plannings. We will consider these."

"Yes. Auspiced by the bearer Scayna, privy to the goals of Nsil, and influential far beyond her gender's limitations. You will wish to speak long with Scayna; apparent contradictions can be resolved. Also present will be others brought from Magh: Irtuk of that world, Bretl from Shtai the Forerunner, T'phee the Yainan, of Companion Star, and this yumin Skeeta."

"Who has now joined my group here." Gvan tensed up but didn't argue. Shortly all eight from *Roamer* looked over their new quarters: several smallish bedchambers, a common area well supplied with refreshments, and behind large double doors a bath alcove holding a tub big enough for at least three bearers.

No secret who wanted firsts on that tub: everybody. "We

could go in shifts,'' Fontaine said. ''It's big enough.''

''. . . for a lifeboat,'' said Marthe Vinler. ''Which means, I guess you know, women and children first.''

''None of that!'' Milo Vitale protested. ''We'll flip a coin.''

It took some pockets-searching to find one, and Marthe won anyway.

Despite Gvan's urgency, Scayna demurred at guesting the new yumin arrivals for this day's latemeal. ''We must have Nsil's thought first, then refine it to our needs before this meeting.'' To do otherwise seemed to her unthinkable—and not until Jemra came near rising would Eamn's turning bring the course of ship Three into farspeaking capability from this place.

''We shall go,'' she insisted, ''and explicate matters to him together, by farvoice. He must know what transpires here, how it aids or imperils his planning.''

Obdurate, Gvan persisted. ''Given the meeting I require, more will transpire which Nsil can then be told. At this moment, what is to relate? That the yumins hold predictable anger? That we delay them with assurances slowly fulfilled? Nsil will know of these measures; he advised them.''

First hesitating, then Scayna held ground. ''The nature of this yumin ship, the types and numbers of yumins it brought, the audacious yumin bearer putting all at dire risk with her flying pallet, the speakings during and since first meeting—all these constitute information which might alter Nsil's view of how discussion should next proceed.''

Agendum coalesced. First would come speakings with Nsil; only then, at midmeal, would Gvan have meeting with the yumins. And Scayna, more familiar with the details of Nsil's venture, would maintain primary sourcehood for all information given them.

For of a surety, Scayna reflected, she was less apt than Gvan to reveal that which Nsil wished untold.

What Gvan now agreed to would therefore be done. And, could Irtuk-saa but hold from requiring the trappings and accouterments of her bearing until well after rise of Jemra, done with some heed to Scayna's need of repose.

* * *

The big tub, when the four women finally left it free, turned out to be quite something. So were the controls. Over the years Gowdy had puzzled out many variations ingeniously designed to frustrate hotel guests; in this case he was glad Sydnie and Marthe and Alix and Charlotte had pioneered that chore and were generous enough to share their solution.

But hey! An abundance of gloriously steaming water, a row of Jacuzzi-like burbling outlets along one end, and above the seething middle, a kind of kingsized shower head capable of veritable downpour. After a couple of minutes Gowdy saw why the floor outside the tub ran wet for several feet all around; in a place like this, who could resist starting a water fight?

And what better way to blow off accumulated tension?

Huge Eamnet towels felt like normal cloth but bulked several times thicker than anything Sam knew. Coming out to the common area he hung one around his waist; it felt more like wearing a heavy rug but kept his modesty intact.

Not for long. From a doorway Sydnie called to him. "Sam? I moved our things in here. If that's all right."

Before he could decide whether it was or not, Marthe said, "The big dinner confab's off for tonight. A seeder—not Gvan—came by a few minutes ago with the word. They'll bring us a meal here, though I'm not sure why." She waved a hand toward the table loaded with smallfoods. "Enough for a week, right there."

Bare feet not quite comfortable on the chilly tile floor, Gowdy halted and stood. "Why the delay? Any reason given?"

Marthe and Alix both shook their heads. "Something about Scayna needing more time to prepare," Alix said. "So now we're scheduled for midmeal tomorrow."

After a moment Sam reminded himself that Eamn's days were less than half the length of Magh's. "Okay; yeh." A thought. "How do we reach Gvan if we want to? Somehow he got out of here before we established communications protocol."

Skeeter Cole gestured. "Over there, one of their phones. Or intercom, more likely. Voicespeaker, they call it. Uh—you want to give him a holler now?"

The soles of Gowdy's feet decided. "Not just yet; I'll get

dressed first, have a nibble. Then maybe we should talk some.''

Silence gives consent. Not at all certain why Sydnie had moved the two of them in together, Sam entered that room and closed the door.

She was sitting on the bed; now she stood, her light, turqoise-tinted robe swirling with the movement. Eagerness dominated her face; when she didn't run to him he wasn't sure whether to feel disappointed or relieved. ''Sam? It really distresses me, that we still haven't worked things out.''

He thought he knew the game; whatever he said, he was wrong. But if he played it straight he wouldn't have to keep track; he'd always run his personal life that way and why change now? ''All right. I'm willing. You first.''

Graceful as always she came to him, took his hands, held them together with hers, leaned against him, kissed him gently on the cheek, then disengaged to back away and sit again. ''You may find this hard to understand. . . .''

I wouldn't be surprised. But he only nodded.

''All my life I've searched for perfection. I can't help it; it's just the way I am.''

''And?'' The less he said, the better. Keep the ball in her court.

''And every time I think I've found it, it goes wrong. I don't know why. And I suppose I react badly.''

Supposition valid. ''So?''

''What I've realized, Sam, is that I need to allow more leeway. When people aren't what I've been led to expect, I should give them more time.'' Her long eyes flickered. ''Do you see what I'm saying?''

It seemed obvious enough: although Sydnie was always and inevitably right, she was now willing to extend him the temporary privilege of being wrong without jumping down his throat for it. He said, ''I'd probably need more time than you have to spare.''

''No, Sam!'' Standing again, now she came up against him like a coat of paint. He'd forgotten what she could do with her tongue. When she pulled back, he strove for breath as she said, ''All right, what happens later can wait. Right now, though—Captain Gowdy, sir, it's been entirely too long.''

Not all his misgivings, dire though they might be, could resist the moment.

The depth and intensity of Sydnie's enjoyment astonished her. The first time went fast, but she didn't mind—or even try to slow it. For one thing it proved without words that if Sam had been getting any on the side it hadn't been lately. And her unexpected excitement brought her so near climax that in their second round, after a suitable but not overly long wait, she came up multiples. All in all, better luck than she'd had in years.

On plea of sore muscles she fobbed off his gallant offer of further encore; she couldn't think unless she cooled down, and right now the one thing Sydnie needed to do was think.

Sam might not be all the way back on her side yet, but she was getting him there. The sleds idea, then volunteering to ride one down—never mind her real reason for that—and now back in the saddle again.

So far so good, but she couldn't ease back and coast. Not yet, and maybe not for a long long while. All she usually needed from a man, but never quite managed, was free rein to her own will, whims, and tastes. What she needed from Sam Gowdy was to protect her life and physical integrity from the deadliest man she'd ever met. Just having Sam in her arsenal of weapons wasn't enough; he would also have to be loaded, aimed, and primed.

How could she warn him of what Aroka was, let alone the man's intentions? For that matter, how to explain her even knowing him—or vice versa, since whatever the Spider's plans, he would at first meeting make obvious their prior acquaintance.

The best lies contain a kernel of truth; here there was none that could bear usage. "Well, you see I'd gone to his suite, he insisted on party girl Numero Uno and seemed rich enough to warrant my personal attention—this was in Bangkok, you understand, the lower Peninsula having become a bit too hot . . ."

And in that life she was called Charel Secour. . . .

Throughout Charel's relatively few years at the game, almost never had she actually needed to perform; sweet words, skillful timing and buffered sedatives usually did the trick for her. This time, too, her choreography was on track; obviously taken with her, Aroka was making a preparatory bathroom visit when she laced a final "before" drink to derail his choo-choo.

The sudden burst of gunfire in some not too distant room made her jerk and slop the drink. Wondering whether to wipe up the minor spill or just run like hell, she gasped as he came out, teeth bared and one fist holding a flat ugly automatic.

He didn't seem to notice that his robe hung open. "Stay here! I'll take care of it." Behind him the door slammed.

Instinct said run but greed prevailed. She frisked Aroka's discarded clothes and explored the possible caches she'd noted earlier. The safe was really locked, not just dialed slightly off-center for easy opening, so she left it alone.

When she had all she could stuff into a satchel in under two minutes, she peeked out into the corridor and found it empty. Around one corner and to the end of that branch lay the freight elevator. It took forever to arrive but no one came along to see her; getting in, she punched for the basement garage.

And when the door opened again, found that this hard beautiful sonofabitch had somehow faked her out, caught up, and stood before her with his free hand held out for the satchel. Taking it, he removed the little tracker from under its flap.

Neither tall nor heavily muscled, with androgynously beautiful Latino features, at first look Jorge Aroka didn't seem dangerous. But the gleam under his distinctive eyelids, the only visible signs of the ancestor whose surname he bore, told Charel she was in deeper than even this offense seemed to warrant.

Their subsequent conversation brought color to her cheeks in slim palm-shaped patterns; its upshot was that they went back to his suite together.

They no longer had the place to themselves; bickering in low tones were two men, one holding a bloody towel to a shoulder but seemingly in no hurry to seek medical attention. "It's all taken care of," he said, and Aroka nodded.

Near the middle of the room lay the main attraction: a slim woman, pale hair almost crew-cut, heavy slanting eyebrows accented by deep blue eye shadow, and equally heavy pouting lips—or so painted. Against the dark red dress the blood didn't show very distinctly—but for someone dead of a bullet near the navel, this woman looked unsuitably peaceful.

"Who . . . ?" As if it made any difference.

Voice as quiet as though giving the time of day, Aroka answered. "La Hoja Rubia—the Blonde Blade. Marlene Klieng was with me a long time. I will miss her."

"What did she do?" God! Couldn't she make herself shut up?

"Oh, many things. Among other duties, La Hoja served as my primary disposal expert."

This time Charel managed not to ask. Aroka told her anyway.

"She disposed of persons I came to deem superfluous."

"Earth?" Stunned, Kayo stared at Nsil.

"Yes, Kaow. Are you not pleased?"

"But how?"

"The great outspacing portal you have created. Skeeta told the chief Yainan of it; I overheard. And that the mechanism heeds not what it transports; is my information not correct?"

"Yes, but . . ." The concept staggered her; go clear out to the macroGate on chemical engines? No wonder he'd been blowing fuel as if it might turn sour any minute; this jaunt was going to need a lot of vee. Built up and then eased back, both.

This was crazy. Up to now, thinking his aims limited to local space, she hadn't really tried to talk him out of his mission. Now she said, "None of this is truly necessary, Nsil. You should have waited for Sam Gowdy, and . . ."

"No, Kaow. You told me, and I saw, what his capabilities encompass. I dared not chance his wrath. Instead we go to those of greater authority, whose ire has not been raised. I will speak with them, and they will apply restraint to Gowdy."

She'd only tried to scare Nsil off from trying to capture Sam; now it seemed she'd made her pitch entirely too convincing. She said, "Gowdy came to recover Skeeter and myself—and the others you took from Magh. Had you agreed, you and he could then have discussed larger issues amicably."

"The risk was too great. I must do what I have determined."

Still puzzled, she shook her head. "What happens when you go through? You will not know where you are in relation to anything; there will be no fuel this ship can use." He wouldn't have enough left to land, either—but likely he already knew that. Rash this fledgling pirate might be, but not stupid.

Nsil showed no reaction; she tried again. "You cannot communicate with anyone there; you do not know our speech."

"The interpretative function will be yours, Kaow."

So *that* was why he'd brought her along. Oh, never mind. . . . "Even so, Nsil, in all other ways you will find yourself totally dependent on a species that never heard of you. Are you sure you want that kind of situation?"

At the tooth gap his tongue tip flickered. "It is precisely my desire. To demonstrate that Eamnets come to offer and negotiate aid and friendship, not in search of conquest."

Conquest? Kayo allowed herself no laughter. "So you just want to pop through, introduce yourself, and sign some treaties?"

"No lengthy process need be required. Those who govern Erdth will know of Eamn and of our difficulties. Gowdy has consorted only with Maghrens; he will have related the situation as biased by the Maghren view. It will be my privilege to redress the imbalance and achieve fairness for all."

This boy certainly didn't sell himself short. But skip that; it wouldn't get her anywhere. "And then what?"

"Then we return. Should understanding grow apace, terms may be reached within quite modest duration."

He smoothed his mane at the neck. "I would offer this ship to your Overgrouping as a memento of our first encounters, asking only return passage on one of their own. Expressly so as to be at hand on the occasion of Scayna's imminent bearing."

"Scayna's next . . . ?" But that was less than a month from now; in talk with Irtuk and Bretl, the timing had been mentioned.

OhferChris'sakes! Nsil didn't know about Habegger Gatelag!

* * *

For a long moment, looking down at the dead woman, Aroka seemed to lose interest in Charel. Then abruptly he stared at her, reached to turn her face one way and another, then pushed her hair back and away from it. "Yes. It could work. Sit!"

At this time Charel's hair fell a little past her shoulders but not much. A few minutes later the most of it was all the way to the floor by way of Aroka's clippers, and she was trying not to breathe the peroxide fumes. "With the warpaint and clothes, you'll be close enough. I can't let those *calebras* know they did for La Hoja Rubia. So from now, Charel, you are she."

"But I couldn't possibly . . . !"

"You cannot possibly do otherwise." He gestured toward her laden satchel. "I do not bother to threaten you with theft charges. It is your life we speak of. And only her death allows you the opportunity to speak at all."

That was the way Charel Secour found employment with Jorge Aroka, known in some circles as the Spider Prince. She didn't dare try to call Angelica, her deputy; Angie would just have to pick up the pieces on her own and take it from there. And trying to impersonate someone she'd never even met, living, gave Charel enough to worry about on her own account.

Next day Aroka's jet lifted his entire retinue across the equator. Since no one at their destination knew the real Marlene Klieng, the impersonation worked: La Hoja Rubia lived.

Island-hopping all the way, Aroka flew his weathered plane to the Western Hemisphere. Rather, he sat back and told his pilot where to go, and when. On arrival he did not, as Charel first feared, set her to whoring. Sex as such, in fact, was never her assignment. Sex as bait, with no delivery intended, was another matter entirely. No one, Aroka included, could teach Charel much along those lines; instead, at his behest she instructed new protégés. The Prince was no pimp, but rather a coordinator of con artists, smugglers and other purveyors of expensive illegalities, and experts in various methods of clandestine and/or coercive property transfer: in short, the Web.

Although Charel herself had never taken life, the omission was more a matter of circumstance than principle. On several occasions of necessity, her trademark weapon drew blood. Her skill lent versimilitude to the considerable number of deaths credited to the account of her *personna*. So any time she came in, according to Aroka's prior instruction, to stand at one side and a little behind his chair during tense and delicate negotiations, the presence of La Hoja Rubia tended to distract other parties sufficiently for Aroka's purposes. The basic ploy had many variations.

That was the role he paid her for, so like it or not, she did it. It beat the hell out of looking up at grass roots.

And not even seeing them.

Also she learned new skills. She'd never had occasion to drive a car at circumstantial max, shoot a gun at anything and especially if it might shoot back, pilot any kind of air transport, or throw a knife: overhand, underhand, and sidearm. Things like that; Aroka's teachings tended toward adrenal excess.

Not necessarily in bed, though. There he could show a kind of gentleness that never appeared at any other time.

Feeling at once pooped and exhilarated, Gowdy took a brief torrential shower to clear his thinking. Whatever had turned Sydnie around, Sam was all for it; still he couldn't quite accept the change at face value. Mixing metaphors he decided to ride the wave and let the other shoe drop where'er it might.

When he came back to dress he found her lounging in a light robe, listening to an abstract musical composition with eyes half-closed, obviously not in discussion mode. Well, he had things to do anyway. "I'll be back in a while." She nodded, so he went out to the common area, loaded himself a snack plate, and moved to tackle the Eamnet voicespeaker.

About forty minutes later, Gvan escorted him and Skeeter to the tower and up to what seemed to be their comm room, where he led Sam to a console. "This speaks to our skyships, and listens also. But those in circuit above do not pass for a time yet."

Wrong frequencies anyway; could this gear match *Roamer*'s? To Gowdy the calibration markings meant nothing, so when Gvan at his request cranked up a receiver array, Sam began slowly turning the dial the Eamnet indicated, end to end of its scale; then with coaching he flipped to the next band and started over.

Midway of his third try he recognized the pattern of his ship's beacon frequency. "Gvan? Set our speaking to this same wave rate." If he had that term right.

Then he called. Prepared for a long and frustrating wait, Gowdy was as much startled as pleased when almost immediately a voice superseded the beacon pattern. "Mose here, captain. I gather you got down okay? Right. So, any new orders?"

The man didn't dally. In kind, Sam replied, "Mainly, do you know where the Eamnet ship went, that lifted while we were coming down? Nsil took it up—the guy who raided on Magh—and he took Kayo with him! So, what can you tell me?"

This had to go fast; the ship was too low to offer much of a comm window. Of course it gave a good signal while it lasted.

Now Tuiasso said, "That last one's still up here. Look; let me tell it. They have three; at least that's all they've lifted. Okay; we didn't actually see all this—parts of it happened behind Eamn from our viewpoint—but here's our best guess. First Papa Bear came up to mate with Mama Bear who was already in orbit. Then you and Baby Bear passed each other in atmo, sort of. Mama and Papa had cooled off by then; Baby hooked up to Papa for a time, then separated and tied to Mama. But it's Papa Bear, the big one, that's hightailed it out of here."

"And going *where*, dammit Mose?"

"Well, that's the tough part. We don't know. It took off in a direction we didn't expect, and had to be pulling at least a gee and a quarter. What we got plotted of its course showed a curve that kept changing. And before we had enough points to approximate an equation for it, Big Red got in the way."

"It went behind Chorm?"

"Yep. Maybe Nsil knows about sling turns, using a world's gravs to pick yourself up some free vee. But the frustrating thing about 'em, right now, is that seeing somebody go into one gives absolutely no clue where he intends to come out."

"You've been scanning for it on the long range; right?" Of course they would; these were conscientious people.

"Oh sure. An Eamn ship on the loose, we knew you'd want us to keep track. But if his engines were still firing when he came out from behind the big one, we missed it. And by now he can't still be burning fuel. Papa Bear carried outside tanks, but nonetheless there's only so much you can do with chemicals."

Gowdy sighed. "You're right. Keep somebody on it, though. No matter where he's going, he has to use decel sometime."

"We hope," Mose responded. "Well, with Kayo aboard, finding that ship just became a priority. Any idea why he took her? I mean, is it some kind of hostage thing?"

Out of habit Sam shook his head, then answered, "Not according to Gvan. He says he's Nsil's *secundo*. I haven't figured out the setup here, but those two guys seem to be in charge of offworld dealings. Anyway, Gvan used the term 'valued associate to Nsil as envoy' if I got that right. So Kayo shouldn't come to harm unless the ship does. And on Gvan's testimony, I'm not even considering the possibility that Nsil left her with either ship still in orbit."

"Yes; I agree with that estimate. All right, captain; we'll do our best. If this team of wonks from the inspectors' branch leaves us any time for it."

"What team? First I've heard of it."

Slowly, Mose said, "Sydnie didn't tell you? The message arrived around the time we talked, when she got the idea for the sleds. Maybe before, maybe after; I don't remember. Anyway there's five of them: three men, two women, giving the ship a real once-over for their report. And this bird Aroka, heading the group . . ." In the pause, Gowdy could visualize his officer looking around to make sure no one was listening. ". . . the worst kind of upstage brasshat prick. Well, that's our problem; with any luck they'll Gate home before you get back up here."

"Yeah. Okay, Mose. Keep that lookout scan for Nsil's ship, though, when Eamn's not in the way of it. And I'll try to catch you again on the next pass. Or the one after."

Thanking Gvan, Gowdy went back to quarters. Thinking, was there any point in asking Sydnie if she'd heard about this team?

* * *

Sooner than she expected, Charel Secour got used to playing La Hoja; over months and years as confidence built, she came to enjoy the role. What with the geographical range of Aroka's operations, a previously unsuspected flair for languages helped her performance a lot. And with those operations going smoothly, mostly Charel forgot the terms of her employment. Until the time the old jet took them back to the Malay Peninsula on what Aroka said was a refugee run.

How all those scrawny, dirty little girls could be from rich families who would pay a bundle for their rescue, Charel couldn't imagine. But no time for questions. Aroka and his squad were getting the kids aboard under fire and not all of it missed; among those sprawled on the hard dirt runway and going nowhere at all was Miklos the pilot.

Flying was something Jorge did in a pinch; even he admitted he wasn't good at it. Especially at either end. "Charel!" To use what he thought was her real name, here on a mission with grunts listening, he had to be rattled. "Get us up!"

She scrambled to the seat. No time for preflight check even if she could find the list, just wind the fans up to top scream, cut the brakes and hang on. With entirely too many riflemen trying to punch her number. The jet sat at the intersection of two overgrown landing strips and the machine guns where they were being brought up could reach only the left-hand one, so first she held brakes on one side to pivot a ninety to the safer runway, overgrown or not and piss on the crosswind.

Trying to keep her head down and still see out had her neck in a knot. When she hadn't heard any *ping-zing*s for a while she straightened up and stretched.

That takeoff was the one she remembered, that made her recent game of chicken with the space sled look like a ride in the park. But she did get the sucker up and out of there.

Aroka took over for the easy part because he knew where they were going; when they got there, Charel brought the jet down through rain squalls to landing. Then they all waited while the Prince dealt with back-country Customs and Immigration using the universal passports with numbers in the corners.

By this time she'd lost track of what country they were in and was too pooped to care. She had no idea where or how

Jorge found the limo with the swamp buggy tires, but once his people had all the kids—snifflers and quiet ones both—herded into the big van and driven away, Aroka chivvied her and flamer Maxl Schläd and the local Web boss Arman Lioso, a sinister stick figure who limped on braces, into the long vehicle. "I'll drive." Sure: with everyone else beat out flat, Aroka was hot wired on his own adrenals. "In town I know a great hotel."

The big turbine whined up; as the limo plunged through slanting rain, water rooster-tailed behind each front wheel. Charel lay back, wanting to doze but still too tense. She heard Maxl say, "Hot time, would you say, in the old house tonight?"

Lioso sniggered. Zorba the Geek, Miklos had called this man—safely behind his back, of course. Charel was going to miss Miklos. "Not with green kids," said the Geek. "Give it a month, training, they'll be the best little hookers you'd ever want."

"Well yes, I remember one time . . ." Listening, Charel felt her insides cringe. So this was what the "rescue" was about.

Too muckin' futch, Charlie. Not a damn thing she could do for this batch, but from now on, first chance, she was out. It wouldn't be easy; she held her peace a good part of the way around the world, until she and Aroka were alone in a suite and no one else expected until morning. Then she said all of it.

He smiled. "Yes; I'd suspected. So I've sold you to a business associate. Akhiel the Mussulman: a fundamentalist, I'm afraid. I expect he'll do the circumcision himself, before . . ."

In a pig's ass he would! Up to now, even Charel's most ferocious deeds were basically softball; naturally the Spider Prince felt safe enough. But comes a time you have to learn. . . .

Sidearm, she interrupted him; his neck where the knife hilt lodged didn't bleed much, but he went limp. Seeing up close what killing really looked and felt like, she retched briefly but fought and barely held her dinner.

Relying on peremptory behavior as she'd seen Aroka use it, Charel reached the jet with all the marketable assets she'd managed to bag in a hurry, and took off after saying "Roger; clearance confirmed" when it hadn't been but her screen showed a possibly safe margin so the hell with it.

Once up, on course and on autopilot, she scrounged through the tail section and found the parachutes Aroka carried for last resort. She needed only one. At a time and place of her choosing the chute got her down safely, loot and all, a couple of hilly miles from a northern African dirt road. Autopilot guided Aroka's jet to the frontier of a country with little patience for unidentified aircraft. No survivors would be expected, or found.

Charel Secour died as discarded papers burning in a trash can. A bus took Sydnie to a local airport. From there she crossed the Mediterranian, first leg on her return home. Her ID was one of several Aroka had arranged for her early on; this one hadn't seen much wear. And the picture could be reconciled with the brown wig she wore when she was supposed to be inconspicuous.

At a Copenhagen hotel she accessed Omnet and entered an outline, detailed to the best of her recollection, of operations conducted by the Spider Prince, along with a listing of major subordinates who might expect to succeed him. His mysterious superior, the Connection, she mentioned but could not name.

The Prince himself she specified as rumored killed in Algiers, Marlene Klieng aka Charel Secour as presumed shot down over the Libyan border, and various others deceased, including the late pilot Miklos. After reviewing her entry and adding a few touches, she addressed it to major police organizations in nearly twenty countries. As an afterthought and just for luck, she entered a copy into Omnet under a password: her own initials and birthdate. The night before her transAtlantic scramjet flight, she slept the sleep of one absolved and ready to live anew.

Less than a month after her rebellion, Sydnie Lightner was relaxing in the midwestern United States, enjoying the luxury of a well-laundered official history in her own true name, a history kept sparse and simple. It was almost two years later, following a series of frustrating liaisons in the basic pattern of Oreadna her mother, that Sydnie realized she needed to try something entirely different.

So she studied up on math and space physics, well enough to get into Gayle Tech. By keeping her curriculum narrowly focused on her chief and only goal, she managed a rather impressive grade average and was graduated with honors. And from there, events followed a more or less straight path to here.

One hell of a long time ago, all that had been.

But not long enough that Jorge Aroka couldn't use it to bury her. Unless she buried him first—and this time, did it right.

Or maybe got Sam Gowdy to do it for her.

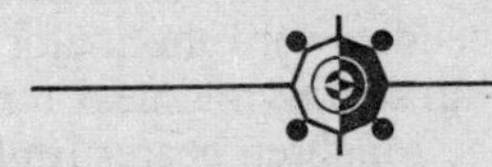

XIV

Dawning found Scayna and Gvan in the farspeaker area, high atop the tower. While a pair of knowledgeable adaptives made adjustments to their incomprehensible devices, Scayna stood, serene to all outward seeming yet inwardly aboil. When finally told she could speak, she found the wait to be only the first of many; Nsil had achieved such farness that signal radiation itself required agonizing lengths of time to arrive and return, and each time Nsil spoke, his voice came weaker.

Scayna persevered; after her first brief essay she included much in each message exchange, ending with, "I have related all happenings of conceivable importance, that memory retains. Your narration of events is valuable and noted; if necessary I can placate Gowdy with knowledge of the well-being of Kaow. It now becomes your place to delineate our procedures for further dealing with the yumins, and to do so without hesitance. For I misdoubt we speak again before you return, may that be soon."

For long, she feared him gone beyond farspeaking. Then his answer came. "Obstruct the yumins another daycycle, two perhaps; that time passed, their leaving cannot imperil my venture. Be as friends to them in all other ways; their ill will is to be avoided. And as yet they offer us no overt harm.''

It seemed he had concluded, but after a time he spoke again. ''Scayna, you have my gratitude; I honor you, and share your hope that our rejoining comes soon. I go to accomplish for Eamn our world, and for our own householding which you grace. And—Gvan, if you also attend, my thanks as well, and my reliance.'' Yet it was the possibility of Gvan's presence which prevented Nsil from any mention of his true plan.

Clearly his speaking was ended; Scayna said to Gvan, ''Nsil honors us both, may we merit the boon.'' They left the place and began to descend toward the major level. ''I will instruct my servitors in arranging midmeal for meeting with the yumins. Meantime the Maghren bearer Irtuk needs seeing to; she is very near to bearing, and as surrogate to Nsil who brought her here, I owe amends that she must bear in a strange holding, and without the comfort of the new one's cogenitor.'' Or would there be two who had contributed? Irtuk had not stated what she bore. . . .

''I understand.'' First escorting Scayna to the confinement dome, Gvan went to tend his and Nsil's own concerns.

Inside, Scayna sought Irtuk. She found the Maghren fretting over the choice of trappings in her compartment, its degree of warmth, and the lack of attendants trained to her needs.

Far from unmoved by Irtuk's unreasoned scoldings, Scayna essayed amelioration. ''Yes, Irtuk. To reach bearing while far from the familiar holding—more than one time have I experienced that malaise. Yet with aid from those who heed your distress . . . Irtuk, advise what may best provide comfort to you, and I will see to as much as can be managed.''

Generations without converse between worlds had brought no great divergence in the rituals of bearing; Irtuk's needs or wants or whims differed from Scayna's own, at such case, in no truly significant aspect.

As best she might, Scayna set to satisfying them.

All Skeeter Cole's descriptive talent hadn't quite prepared Gowdy for the Yainan. The substantial torso on four short legs, the tapering neck that could extend to reach nearly human height, the thick heavy fur petering out toward the tip of that neck where four slim and flexible manipulative limbs emerged—all right, that much he was braced for.

But the conglomeration of detail at the tip—the sensory cluster, Skeeter called it—that part floored him. Eyes and mouth and hearing organs and breathing orifices, Sam thought he had pegged; what confused him were various projections and recesses and color patterns and tufts, all arranged in bilateral symmetry but with no other guiding principle. *Like trying to talk with a crawdad.* At least a crawdad carried what brain it did have in the normal location, not down between its shoulders.

Still and all, Gowdy reminded himself, this furry dachshund giraffe was the emissary of another species, and stargoers at that. So as he and the other humans waited, along with the Yainan and Gvan, for Scayna to come and preside over lunch, Sam spoke to the creature. "I am Sam Gowdy, captain of our starship. You are Taffy, from the world called Yain?"

"Taffy is K'yo's approximation; it suffices." One of the wiry neck tendrils fluttered. "You have had speech with K'yo? Taken by the Emman Nsil in such fashion, what might transpire? Her circumstance is greatly uncertain."

At least that's what Gowdy thought the Yainan meant. What with it translating its thoughts from its own language, and Sam working from his own limited Maghren/Eamnet vocabulary, the stocky little guy might be saying something considerably different. But in context it all seemed to fit.

Taffy wasn't done. "Of deeper concern is V'naet, taken alone. Apart from our own kind a Yainan cannot thrive. Even I feel the impact of loss and foresee a worsening. And I embody strengths lacking in V'naet."

"Maybe the need will bring them to him." Stuck for any further comment, Gowdy poured himself a cup of the tangy, slightly hard juice of some unknown fruit; it wasn't wine but it was working on it. In afterthought he poured one for Taffy, too.

Cheers. It looked as if they might be in for quite a wait.

All through Irtuk's being raged tides of coming fulfillment. Fret and anxiety, products of earlier stages of imminent bearing, now transformed to anticipation and excitement: her fixated concern for detail turned to delighted appreciation of the bower Scayna had wrought.

Now all others, those who had labored at Scayna's behest, could take leave. Irtuk and Scayna, genetrix and protectrix—they alone would see to the bearing.

Exultation! It would not do for Irtuk's mind to lose itself in sensation; with rigor she strove to contain feeling within thought. No fear; this she had done, this she could do. But to hold, to wait for final delight—always a strenuous difficulty.

The great secret: once again Irtuk-saa approached that which seeders and adaptives could not know and must not be told. The lesser genders thought bearing an ordeal, and this belief the bearers fostered.

In truth it was during and culminating the final genetric process that bearers' lives reached peak. The limits set on womb activation arose from no aversion to bearing itself; quite the contrary. Simply put, even a bearer's sturdy body succumbs to malaise and fatigue and painful awkwardness if laden with an excess of wombs in process. It was that condition, to be suffered over long durations, which bearers determined to avoid.

And in another view, to seek and incur supreme delight too frequently and without restraint would bespeak a lack of discipline, unbefitting to ones who would lead a holding.

Now, lying back aslant among softly colored ornamentation, Irtuk released control and allowed pulsings to begin. At the lounge's farther end, her lower extremities quivered in Scayna's secure grasp. Now and soon, pulsing grew near to spasm; Irtuk's mouth fell slack, the croon of dispossession rose, ecstasies of tension alternating with momentary bliss of pause, soon overtaken by a next and greater wave.

A moment came when the sensing and knowing of Irtuk-saa spread all through her and seemed to fill the room; at its core a radiant-seeming band grew and shrank, repeating, until of a great sudden it flew wide—and with delicious graduality the young of Irtuk slid to and through and past.

Not until much time later, or so Irtuk knew it, did the tides of delight ebb, so that she came to see and comprehend Scayna holding the newly borne seeder.

Scayna gestured. "Food is here," so Irtuk took a mouthful

of the mix—bits of fruit and grains and meat and plant fibers—to chew into a moistened pulp.

Then, lying against Irtuk's chest, the new one extended a small muzzle to its bearer's mouth and began to lick the pulp, moistened with the flavor her mouthfluids derived at this time, as it extruded through the central gap between her lower teeth.

"If you need nothing further now," said Scayna, "perhaps I have caused the yumins to wait midmeal, and our proposed meeting, longer than would suit them."

When Scayna finally arrived, Gowdy felt the ambience change. Until her advent the seeder Gvan had showed edgy and ill at ease, more like a substitute teacher in a tough school than the supposed honcho of this bailiwick. But now Gvan's manner eased. "The bearer Scayna joins us; we shall proceed."

Around the large oval table someone had been busy; at eight seating positions the odd slanting chairs of this species were replaced by a motley assortment of padded shapes that made reasonably good stools for humans to sit on, and at one place stood a rectangular platform a little over a foot high. Sure enough, it was big enough for Taffy to stand on comfortably, and it brought his "head" and tendrils up to a good height for eating and conversation both.

From one end Scayna presided, or perhaps Gvan from the other. Gowdy was beginning to think he understood the setup; as a seeder Gvan was nominally in charge, but Scayna being closer to Nsil who really ran the railroad, she carried a lot of weight and not merely in the physical sense. All right, let's boogie. . . .

Seating began: Sam to Scayna's left and Taffy to her other side. From Gvan's end, assorted Eamnets of the lesser physical persuasions. In between, the other humans—arranged, by Gowdy's prior instruction, so that Neville Fontaine and Charlotte Wang and Sydnie each sat between two who did know the local lingo to some extent. Sydnie at his own left because when it came to loose cannons he'd still back her for first prize every time.

Milo Vitale looked a little mussed; he'd been back at the Doodlebug earlier, seeing to its resupplying according to

Sam's list, and got back barely in time to bathe and change clothes.

Food came steaming hot and tantalizingly aromatic. From what his group had been served in their quarters, guest or detention he wasn't sure yet, Sam felt no need for caution. Well, according to Skeeter Cole the Eamnets had paid heed to his and Kayo's tentative verdicts on what humans could eat and what they couldn't; now came the benefit from that groundwork.

Before taking even a first bite, Scayna announced, "I have pleasure to relate that Irtuk from Magh has borne a seeder. I myself stood protectrix for her and can affirm her well being and gladment." With that, she fell silent and set to eating.

Enjoying the meal, Gowdy almost forgot its purpose—until Scayna spoke again. "Nsil and I have farspoken, before he passed beyond the reach of our devices. I am to assure you, Sam Gowdy, that K'yo enjoys admirable function and ease of being. And to you, T'phee of Yain, that although your follower irks at this separation from his kind, he too functions adequately and ingests his quota of nutriment with apparent savor."

T'phee, huh? Not Taffy. Sam made a mental note; maybe this was only another approximation. He'd try it and see.

And so far, V'naet hadn't folded. Gowdy said, "I would still know, where does Nsil take them? And for what purpose?"

Scayna's great head tilted. "Those matters lie not within my competence; I relate his speaking to you only as I have been instructed. And is there more that you would know?"

There was plenty, but likely no use asking. "When we finish here I would speak with my own ship again."

Her stare came close to unnerving him. "Of a certainty, you may do so." She nudged a vegetable tray toward him; it was good stuff so he took a little extra. "There is this that I may say. Nsil seeks only to protect our world. You come to our system and reach to our ancient enemy, not to ourselves. Nsil fears your aid of Magh in attack on Eamn—and whatever deed may be required to prevent such outcome, Nsil will perform."

Her slow, deliberate blink punctuated an end to her statement. Voice tone changed as she said, "Do you understand my speaking? And have you a response?"

Oh hell yes, lady! What first, though? All right; coming in, seeing ships traveling between the moons, he'd assumed they were on trading terms. Contact either one, all the same thing—and only the velocity vectors chose Magh for him, over Eamn.

"We had no idea of your history," he continued. "That there had even been a war, let alone that hostility might still exist. As for how things are now: our only aim would be to help *avoid* another conflict, not take sides in it."

He leaned toward her. "Scayna, this is truth. Nsil is on a . . ." No, not a fool's mission; the guy who pulled off that raid and now this wild goose chase might be a lot of things, but fool wasn't one of them. "Whatever this venture of his may be, it is not necessary; his aims are assured without it."

What Scayna's blink meant this time, Gowdy had no idea. "Most unfortunate, then, that it has progressed beyond recall."

Navigation being one of Kayo's lesser fortes even in less enervating temperatures, it took longer than pleased her ego before she realized that Tasr was making a sling turn around Chorm, that the ship was accumulating a load of vee its rockets couldn't have produced in anywhere near the same short period. And for free, too.

The realization wasn't all good. If Sam was to have any chance of heading off this crazy scheme, he'd have to get to it. And there was much less time to spare than Kayo had thought.

She still couldn't figure how Tasr's course was going to work. Ship Three was moving both back along Chorm's orbit and at the same time outward from the star Jemra; how this was going to get them to the macroGate, Kayo had no clue at all.

But over days and hours as their course continued to alter, now wholly by natural forces, she began to get a glimmer or two. And when Tasr eventually pointed the ship at Jemra and, with all nonessential personnel strapped in once more, fired up his racketing drive again, Kayo knew what he had to be doing.

Above and behind the macroGate they'd be, now; going "down" was building their forward orbital speed.

Nsil and Tasr planned to hit the Gate too fast for any possible interception.

Too bad Skeeter seemed to have let it slip that the Gate passed traffic in only one direction. Without that bit of data, the ship would have gone hellbent the wrong way, been fended off by the Habegger fields, and never in this universe still retained fuel enough to slow and return. *Roamer* could have picked them all up at leisure.

But "if" never won a ball game. Not even in the minors.

Beyond recall: no sooner were the words spoken than Scayna realized her error. With sudden purpose she leaned toward the yumin Gowdy. "I mean only that—in light of the limitations of his ship—decisions must be made at certain crucial times, and these will now have been made . . ." She spoke falsehood; by Nsil's own speaking, the time of safety for his mission was not yet. But she *must* retrieve that which she had, unthinking, given away.

The yumin's stare, the set of his mouth at one corner, told the futility of her attempt; she had breached her own deception, and now there was no restoring it. In a level tone that somehow carried undefined menace, Gowdy said, "You have known all along; deliberately you have misled me." The bare skin of his features darkened. "You will tell me that which you have withheld and I shall inform my ship."

"Let me remind you," spoke Gvan, "that your access to farspeaking depends upon my willingness to allow it."

With swiftness Gowdy turned on Gvan. "Do you think I fail to realize our situation? That I have not provided against any action you might take? Be informed, Gvan! You have observed the power and capabilities of my ship. If its officers receive no word from me at times I have specified in my latest farspeaking, they will assume me victim of Eamnet treachery."

Now, swinging his head back and forth, the yumin spoke to Gvan and Scayna alike. "The consequence to this world and you who inhabit it will be beyond your imagining."

* * *

All Eamn at risk? Even for Nsil, Scayna could not hold against such threat. Abruptly she spoke. "Vow me no harm to Nsil; without that I can tell you nothing more."

"You have it. Speak."

"He goes to Erdth; by use of your great portal he seeks to plead for Eamn. Only to speak, not to harm. Presence of your bearer is required, that she may make his speaking known to those he meets with, there. And very soon they will return."

In his own speech the yumin spoke briefly but with great feeling; he did not rephrase it for Eamnet comprehension. Then, as though nothing had happened, he sat again and resumed eating. "When we are finished here, I will farspeak my ship."

Gvan did not demur, nor did Scayna.

Sam wouldn't have time or attention to spare for her, so Sydnie had Milo Vitale at her other side giving her the gist of what went on. Dealing with Maghrens with regard to the DV repairs, he had to be pretty well up on the lingo. "Word for word as near as you can, huh?" Because if she were going to be any use here, she had to be a fast study. And now more than ever before in her life, usefulness was the key to survival.

She wasn't sure just what brick this oversized Eamnet dropped, but where it landed was obvious: right on Sam Gowdy's toes. His unhesitating response, menace-laden and seemingly assured, truly shocked her.

And then, when he'd dragged some kind of answer out of Big Mama, he cut loose with a string of really inspired cussing.

This was the easygoing man she'd thought to manipulate? Once again Sydnie rethought her options. She turned to Sam. "Did Milo get that right? This Nsil's taking Kayo through the macroGate?" He nodded. "Then why are we sitting here?"

"Scayna had it wrong, because Nsil did; they think we can move ship faster than we really can, that he needed another day's head start. He doesn't. But at this point he's still a day or so from the Gate itself. The only people who can stop him would be mining ships or cargo shuttles that may have come through by now. I don't know just how they'd do it; let's hope somebody has a good idea. But another hour or two getting word out there won't make any difference. Especially when it'll be that long before *Roamer* hits our signal window again, anyway."

"Then you're not in any rush to get back to the ship?"

"Not immediately. Mose can Gate word home, so our people there could spot Nsil coming through and rescue the crazy pirate. Before somebody gets hurt in that tin can of his." Surprisingly, Gowdy chuckled. "Something I haven't told Scayna yet. And I kind of hate to have to do it."

"Oh?" Was he showing softhearted again?

"She and Nsil think he can just pop through, talk, and Gate home in time for the weekend. So to speak."

The idea took a minute to percolate; then, "Jeeeez . . ."

"Yeah. And as such things go on this world, I get the idea those two are pretty close."

"Mmm. Tough tiddlies, huh?"

"Maybe not." But he wouldn't say what he meant by that.

Eamnet psychology, Sam reflected, was something else again. They and Maghrens held the same old grudges but from different slants: the persecuted and harassed adolescent versus the outraged, betrayed parent, you might say. But while the folks on Magh tended to watch and wait and take precautions, the Eamn crowd seemed more inclined to go all out.

Take Nsil. Except on a voice circuit, Gowdy hadn't ever met him—but even knocking off some points for hair-trigger judgment, he couldn't help half liking and admiring the gutsy seeder.

Or Scayna. Supposedly subservient in this rebel society, still the bearer carried a lot of depth and savvy. Gowdy found a lot to like about Scayna, and felt a little bad at having to rattle his high-tech thunderbolts, real and imagined, to shake some truth loose from her. But you do what you have to.

Gvan he didn't much care for : a type all too common in Sam's own species, the Eager Achiever who doesn't quite have what it takes, and generally goes for broke on the wrong odds.

But here Gvan was only Nsil's figurehead; near as Gowdy could tell, it was Scayna who knew the ropes and kept balance. So as the lot of them climbed to the comm tower, Sam ranged himself alongside her.

He wasn't exactly sure what he wanted to say, but a little reconciliation couldn't hurt. So, "I regret the necessity of threat. But without it you would not reveal Nsil's intention toward my friend and colleague. I ask, Scayna: had I thus taken Nsil, would you not on his behalf threaten whatever need be?"

Her great head tilted. "Threaten? I misdoubt that especial approach would suggest itself. I would . . ." Scayna's eyelids drooped, then lifted. "More to be expected is that I would search my thought for something to be offered in exchange for your compassion. Did nothing of this sort come to your mind?"

Almost a stopper but not quite: *be honest now*! "No more so, I fear, than to Nsil's—when instead of remaining to parley he absconded, taking Kayo against her will and mine."

Scayna's mouth opened slightly; at the gap between her lower teeth he saw the tongue tip flicker. Now what had Skeeter said that expression meant? "You seeders! Three genders or two, your temper varies little. I posit that were you in Kayo's place and she in yours, matters would proceed differently."

Yeh, maybe. "We are not likely to know, are we, Scayna?"

Talking, they had climbed to the comm room. Without asking, Gowdy went to the same console he'd used before.

The settings were changed, but he'd watched closely the first time; juggling around, he caught *Roamer*'s beacon, then simply set the transmit side to a rough match and called. At least he'd kept the signal window timing reasonably straight!

Again more quickly than expected, "Leopold here, captain. First item, we did spot the Eamn ship—a long way back-orbit and up the star's gravity well from us, when it fired its burners and showed on the screen. It aimed nearly straight down—which gave it a good boost in forward-orbit speed, too. But Sam—as near as we can tell, it's heading for the macroGate."

"Yeah, I know. I wrung that info out of them here. Now the question is, has anything Gated through yet that might head this privateer off before he can inGate?"

"Not sure, skipper." That was Tuiasso. "What with us going behind Eamn half the time, and one blackout when

Chorm was in the way, we've missed a lot of signal window with the big Gate. And when we do get 'em, half the time Velucci's busy and nobody else knows anything." Abruptly his tone changed; Mose was done with making excuses. "We've passed the word; she's to be available next window, period. The question is, what do we want done?"

Gowdy could see his point. A mining ship's lasers and assorted torpedoes were fine for destruction but nothing more. Cargo shuttles didn't even have those. So how do you stop or divert a mass-ejecting can without breaking something?

He thought about it: if he had the DV out there and in position, could he match vees and somehow grapple on and pull the ship off course, run a transfer tube to Papa Bear's airlock and get his people out? Assuming the Yainan and Irtuk's seeder *were* his people, and in this case maybe that assumption was justified.

It didn't matter; he couldn't ask someone else to try such a harebrained scheme. So his answer was, "Somebody to play a little spaceside chicken with Nsil but not push it to real risk."

Reflexively he shook his head. "If he can be scared off, fine. He can't have much fuel left; once he missed the Gate he'd be falling free pretty soon and could be met and tied to." That part he didn't have to spell out. "But from what this bird's pulled off so far, I doubt he scares easy."

There wasn't a lot more to say. "All right," Simone came in. "We'll find out what Pia has, if anything, and pass along your orders. Emphasizing that the Eamnet ship's safety overrides our other concerns. Anything else, captain?"

"Nope. Call me when you get word. I'll have someone on duty here if I'm busy elsewhere. Thanks; Gowdy out."

Only after he'd shut down did Sam realize he'd totally forgotten to ask about the inspection team and its arrogant brasshat chief. Well, another time would have to do.

Now, what to tell Scayna? He turned to her. "If other ships have come through our Gate, they will intervene to deter Nsil from entering it. Should he refuse to turn aside, he will not be otherwise impeded. We hope the threat will suffice."

At her tooth gap the tongue tip flirted. "In like case, would you be deterred?"

She knew the answer as well as he did.

* * *

Just when Sydnie thought she finally had Sam Gowdy figured out, he crossed her up. His sudden fire, laying down the law to the big Eamnet sow, put him in a new light; now with regard to the wildcat raider he'd gone back to cautious. And obviously he'd been smoothing this Scayna's ruffled feathers, on the way up the tower and then after talking with *Roamer*.

Coming down, he walked alongside Scayna but without much talk, parting with her at the main floor where he led his troops back to quarters. Once inside he headed for the bedroom he and Sydnie shared, calling over his shoulder, "First dibs on the tub!" And then, more quietly to her alone, "Want to join me?"

As the door closed behind her, Skeeter Cole was saying, "A little rub-a-dub-dub there, skipper?"

If Gowdy heard, he didn't let on. Stripping quickly and hanging a thick Eamnet towel around his waist, he stood waiting.

"I'll be a moment." Sydnie ducked into the bathroom long enough to attend some needs and change to the turquoise robe.

As an obvious afterthought Sam made a pit stop of his own, before they went through the common area to the big tub. If Skeeter had more comic relief to add, he kept it to himself. Until the door closed, at least.

"Bloody hell!" Jumping back from a scalding stream, Gowdy fiddled at the controls. "Hey—I can't seem to make this thing work right. You want to try?"

She thought she remembered the tricks of it and she was right. It wasn't long before they lay side by side on the shallow sloping side, only their faces above water in the slanting downpour from the tilted overhead fixture, steaming away all tensions.

Well, maybe not all. When a new issue arose, she moved quickly and competently to cover it. Sam lay passive; squinting down through the soaked hair plastered across her forehead, she saw pure enjoyment. Only when she herself moaned in the beginnings of release did he grapple her fiercely, turn the two of them over on their sides, and charge the cavalry up the hill.

All the way to the top and back again. When he released

her they both lay breathless, laughing for no particular reason.

After a time the mainsprings ran down. As she pushed sopping wet hair back from her face, she saw his expression change. "Sam? Wasn't it all right?"

"Terrific; never better. Something else came to mind, is all. I forgot to ask, earlier: on the ship, did you know about that inspection team coming?"

"I saw the flimsy, yes." *What is this*?

"You didn't say anything."

Oh, was that all? "The whole time I was getting my sled out and secured, you had contact with control. I assumed someone else told you what was in the mail." She shook her head, spraying water. "Considering everything else that was going on, it didn't strike me as terribly important."

"No, I guess not." Then, as if changing the subject, "Mose says the guy in charge, this Jorge Aroka, is a—how did he put it?—a real brassbound prick. You know anything about him?"

Reflex brought a hand to her mouth; she sucked in a deep, noisy breath. This moment was crucial; whatever she said now, she was stuck with. "What did you say that name was?"

He repeated it.

"But that's impossible! He's supposed to be dead."

"Apparently not. And didn't you *see* the name?"

Sydnie shook her head. "I only skimmed the message, must have skipped right past. A bunch of civilians, naturally I wouldn't expect any of the names to register."

"His does, though. Obviously." When she didn't answer, he said, "Maybe you'd better tell me."

She laid a hand on one of his and chose her words carefully. "I'll have to preface this, Sam. Space wasn't my first career—and even now there are things I'm not authorized to talk about, so please don't ask me."

He nodded; so far, so good. "It's been so long; even if I *had* glanced at the name, it might not have clicked. Partly because in this context it simply didn't—doesn't—fit. Sam, this really jars me. I'm not sure what to say. What I *can* say."

"I don't understand."

I should hope not! She leaned toward him. "Neither do I, and that's my problem. Sam, this man was a major criminal.

The Spider Prince, he was called, and his organization the Web. When I knew of him I was, I guess I can say this much, I was operating what they call undercover . . ." She gave it her best can-you-imagine-such-a-thing? smile. ". . . and so far as I know, the man never saw through that cover."

Now she clutched Gowdy's wrist. "But if he were to see and recognize me, here . . ." She didn't have to fake the shudder. "He couldn't help but know. He's a killer, Sam. A killer and worse. How he ever got himself whitewashed onto an agency team . . . !"

"Well, I guess we can take care of that, can't we? With what you know about him."

Oh shit! "It's what we don't know that's dangerous. How he got here, what's his backing, what are his resources—all that and more. No, if he's still aboard when we reach the ship, we have to play it very very cagey. And until we're sure we have him cold, he mustn't see me at all."

He let out a kind of snort. "Hold on. This is Sam Gowdy you're talking to, not Sam Spade; that kind of game's way out of my league. I . . ."

"It's in mine, though. Or used to be. We need to *watch* the snake, see what he does, how he acts—and how he screws up. He doesn't know space, or ships, or how ships' people look out for each other. These things are out of *his* league. And so are you. As long as you never let him get behind you. Because that's where he's dangerous."

Had Gowdy bought it? His scowl gave no hint at all. Finally he nodded. "If major crime types are infiltrating the starship program, we're all in deep. Politicians being a rather ethically diverse bunch, who can we trust? All right; back onship I give this Aroka the full deadpan once-over. If something smells bad he Gates home, feet first if need be, and four years later Glen Springs can hassle me about it."

He shrugged. "Well, it worked with Barry Krsnch."

The new subject came as a lifeline; she grabbed it. "I never did understand what happened there. Tell me?"

Rising and stepping out of the tub, Gowdy wrapped himself in the bulky towel. "Back in digs. We've monopolized this place too long already."

Sydnie didn't mind the glares they caught while walking through the common area; the unwarranted time in the tub had been worth this resentment. Because from nothing, *less* than nothing, she had built a frame to position Sam Gowdy right where she needed him. And it looked to be holding.

Despite repeated pleas the Emman Gvan gives T'phee no satisfaction. Nor, so seems it, to the yumin Gowdy. Yet at the assemblage where speakings and food intake both occur, Scayna it is who in appearance holds the role of decision. For when Gowdy succumbs to disturbance of feeling, er primarily addresses Scayna, dismissing Gvan as little more than servitor. And to minor yet noticeable extent, the yumin achieves acquiescence.

If so for Gowdy, mayhap also for T'phee. Although er has no great ship nearby, as does Gowdy, still in this star system lie not one but two Yainan ships. Given effective statement of their potentialities, their existence may gain T'phee some trace of advantage—so vital now, for the sakes of Yamar and of Yain.

But Scayna, not Gvan, seems best to approach. In T'phee's estimate the seeder lacks both sensibility to discern true need and decisiveness to ameliorate it. Thusly it is Scayna with whom T'phee requests, and is granted, audience.

If only by sheer bulking as er lies aslant against a padded restframe, this Emman emanates overness; by effort, T'phee resists the concordant urge to cede or appease. Er opens converse, acknowledging Scayna's title and function as best er comprehends them, then saying, "Nsil has assured that once we shared knowledge I might return to Magh—and thus to Yamar, where I serve as Steward to all from Yain and am sorely needed."

Silent, Scayna gestures; the forelimb movement can only mean continuance. "Gvan who now speaks for Nsil does not honor Nsil's assurance to myself." Still Scayna withholds response. "It is of note that Scayna, though not named surrogate to Nsil, holds greater accord with Nsil's ventured aims."

"That is your own view, Yainan; I may not affirm it." Shifting es huge form to greater ease, the Emman speaks no further.

"Yet will you affirm Nsil's pledge? That when the yumin

Gowdy is allowed return to Magh, I am to be of his company?'' It is not that Nsil has granted those specific terms. T'phee assuages es compulsion to truth: given more time to consider, surely the Emman's logic and compassion would prevail.

At now, all is of Scayna's choosing. With trepidation, T'phee awaits. The Emman's head moves; er speaks. ''Gvan does not understand Nsil well enough to act without Nsil's expressed sanction. I do not suffer that lack. When Gowdy departs you are free to join him.''

Gratitude, T'phee finds, is difficult to convey in Emman.

Nsil's touch woke Kayo. ''A new yumin ship. It appeared from your portal, paused a time, and now approaches at speed.''

She rubbed her eyes and sat up. Coming out of her cubby she heard a man's tones, not quite clearly, from the farvoicer. ''You must tell me what it is he speaks.'' Nsil sounded anxious.

And with good cause. Gently twiddling the tuning knob, Kayo brought the voice in better. ''. . . say again: you must turn aside from the macroGate. And soon; you're getting too close. If you don't, I have orders to destroy you.''

What . . . ? ''Ahoy whoever the hell you are; this is Kayo Marlin, off *Roamer*. Are you crazy or something? This ship is from Eamn, the outer moon. It carries a major council chief of that world, the aide to one from the inner moon, a person from this system's companion star, not to mention my personal self whose side you're supposed to be on, dammit! Now what's this about destroying? And just how do you expect to go about it, anyway?''

''Laser or torpedoes, take your choice. This is Travis Yates, commanding the prospector ship *Golconda*. And all I know is, we outGated here and not ten minutes later I was given my orders. Which I've already explained.''

''Orders? Sam Gowdy wouldn't give an order like that—and neither would Pia Velucci.''

''She relayed it. Under protest, she said. From Commodore Aroka, on *Roamer*. So you'd better get that bucket turned, fast.''

XV

By evening Milo said the Doodlebug was ready, but still Gvan wouldn't give Sam clearance to leave. So he decided to play his ace. As soon as he entered Scayna's rather impressive "confinement dome" and made greeting, he dropped the other shoe.

Her reaction didn't disappoint him. "Three Chormcycles? Or very near to, before Nsil could return? Why have you withheld such dire fact?"

"Until Nsil made it so, it was not of your concern." And she'd taken her own sweet time telling him *that* item. "I have initiated what action I could, to divert him from the Gate."

"Has *he* been told?"

Gowdy didn't answer directly. "Would the telling stop him?"

"No. But—on your ship you have lesser portals; is this not true?" Reaching, she grasped his arm, not hard. "Gowdy—when you leave here, I must go with you. So that if . . ."

Her quick understanding and decision impressed him. "I know, Scayna. That's why I've told you now."

There was more to it, mostly hows and whens. Leaving Scayna to manage her end of the arrangements, Gowdy first returned to quarters and alerted the troops. "Get packed and ready. We'll have a night's sleep, and hope to lift sometime in the morning."

He checked the time and got lucky; in a few more minutes, *Roamer* would break the horizon. As he left quarters and went toward the tower, both Skeeter and Sydnie followed. He didn't especially want company for this chore, but couldn't spare any concentration for mere argument; let them come.

At the foot of the tower, two of Gvan's sidemen came from a side corridor and moved to intercept. Not breaking stride, Gowdy said, "I go to report to my ship. That my officers may know Gvan keeps faith. It is important to Gvan that this be known." In most satisfactory fashion the two got the hell out of his way.

Topside, breathing a little hard but not seriously, he cranked up Gvan's farvoice gear. This time no one had futzed with the tuning; he called *Roamer* and waited. SuZanne Craig answered. ". . . get Simone or Mose for you if you want, but I can tell you what's happened." And she did: a prospecting ship that had just outGated was ordered to divert the Eamnet ship from the Gate, and failing that, to destroy it.

Damn all; "*Who gave that order*?"

"Commodore Aroka; he wouldn't listen . . ."

Commodore, f'Chris'sakes? "Does that sonofabitch know we have a *crew member* on that ship? Put me through to him."

For the first time ever, Suzanne Craig sounded uncertain. "It won't . . . he told the miner to cut comm from here until the job was done. And if you do reach him—well, he outranks you."

Think fast. From here there was nothing, absolutely nothing, he could do for Kayo; that realization knotted his gut. What he would do *about* her was another story—and one that would not profit from undue haste. He said, "One of you call me during the window when this place first hits daylight. To arrange rendezvous. And let's don't tell the commodore." *Commodore*?

"Right, captain." Her voice tone changed. "Oh—we're losing signal now. Sorry, commodore; you just missed him."

At least fifteen minutes short of the window's end, her carrier wave chopped off. Well, nobody ever said Craig was dumb.

Gowdy turned to meet Sydnie's gaze. Ignoring Skeeter Cole's questioning look he said, "So far you seem to be calling it right down the line. Except, how come the guy's a commodore now?"

She frowned. "I can't imagine. And on the flimsy, I think I'd have noticed a listing like that." Her mouth twisted. "I guess it might have paid to look closer."

"So we could do what?" And so much for hindsight. "Let's go get some sleep."

"Now just hang on there!" Kayo pushed damp hair out of her eyes; she'd adjusted pretty well to the heat, but adrenal reaction had her pouring sweat. "I never heard of this commodore before, but it's not like you're cut off from the macroGate—or even from *Roamer*. Before you murder us all and checkmark your tidy little job sheet, don't you think you'd better ask somebody and be sure what you're doing?"

"Tell your pilot to turn aside; otherwise there's no time for asking."

She turned to Nsil. "They demand we turn away from the portal; if we do not, that ship will—will explode ours."

Moveless, he made no sign.

"He's going to kill us!"

Slowly the tongue tip peeked from behind his teeth. "Eamn has long lacked a name to follow; it is generations since one became of merit. Time arrives, mayhap, for another to emerge."

Even if she could have coined a fitting expletive, it probably wouldn't translate. Now from the farvoicer she heard talk, Yates and someone else, away from the mike a little. ". . . can't do that, Travis! Orders or no orders."

"Now you listen to me; I'm in command. When I say fire, you fire."

In a killing rage herself, Kayo yelled, "Don't you even want a casualty list, you tin soldier? Mustn't have any messy blank spaces in your report. All right, first entry is Nsil, an Eamnet seeder, head of a major householding and recently in charge of all offworld dealings for his planet. Or moon, if you want to be picky. Next—"

The other voice answered, the sane one. "Kayo? Kayo Marlin? Is that really you?"

"For the next minute or so, yes. Who the hell's that?"

"Larry. Larry Corcoran. Remember me?"

Considering that they'd been married for nearly three years, it took her an unflattering long time to place the name. "Larry! What're you doing out here?"

"The same as you, probably. Earth didn't quite fit any more. But listen, Kayo . . ."

"No. To *me*, you listen." Yates again. "You turn that can or we shoot."

"Yeah sure, Travis," Corcoran said. "Too bad I'm such a lousy shot."

"I'm doing the aiming." Right; a prospector's main laser, the only one good for much distance, pointed straight ahead. "You just push the button."

"Well, if you say so." Corcoran's voice held a mocking edge. Then, "Oops; we just lost our drive. Sorry." And Kayo saw the other ship's Traction field waver and fade to nothing.

As the prospector went into free-fall drift, no longer on intercept and pointing several degrees away, Kayo gathered from Yates's cursing that Larry had shut down the base generator, exciters, and main thrustor power stages. Total wipe-out; retuning alone would need over half an hour.

"You cretin! Aroka will have your balls on toast—and mine too, dammit! How am I going to . . ."

The macroGate loomed; not much time now. Kayo said, "Why don't you just chase us on through and report later?" And added, "Thanks, Larry. I mean, *thanks*."

As they entered the big ring, Nsil's viewtubes dazzled with the iridescent opaquing of surrounding space. The farvoicer conveyed "That's not such a bad . . ." and then went silent.

Suddenly the clearing viewtubes showed Earth, the moon, and a bewildering display of spaceborne constructs in apparent random motion. Eyes astare, Nsil stood unmoving as the engines died.

Kayo touched his forelimb. "Well, you got us here. Now what do you have in mind for an encore?"

First thing in the morning, Gowdy called *Roamer*. He had barely begun getting rendezvous timing straight with Simone Leopold when she said, sharply, "Well, if you can't finish moving the equipment before thirteen hundred hours, Technician Samuels, I suppose I'll have to settle for that. You *can* meet that deadline, can't you?"

So Aroka had entered control and was listening. Sam punched for ship's time on his chrono: yes, thirteen hundred gave him plenty of leeway. He said so, and Leopold replied, "You understand, don't you, that we'll have to cut the rear sensor feed at twelve hundred, and restore it after your own work is complete?''

''That won't cause any problems, Exec.'' *Bless you, Simone*! She'd just told him what he needed to know—how to sneak the sleds in without being spotted. Not to mention Sydnie, though Leopold couldn't know of that problem.

''Very well, Samuels. I'll expect you to deliver on time.''

''Yes, ma'am. Samuels out.''

And now he knew something more about Commodore Jorge Aroka: the man couldn't tell the difference between an offship call and the intercom.

Utter startlement held Nsil rigid. His viewtubes showed a multitude of ships and other objects, moving in various directions at quite disconsonant rates.

Reeling, he clutched at Kaow's arm. ''A bare instant ago,'' he gasped, ''we entered your portal. And now . . . !''

Her features took on a strange look. ''That instant, Nsil, was not as it seemed. But I believe you have more than enough adaptation to achieve, here; I will hold my saying for a time of greater ease.''

He gestured at the nearest viewtube. ''All of those vessels—what it is that we should do now?''

From the farvoicer sounded distorted speakings; Tasr made adjustment until they came more clearly. Kaow bent to listen; when the voice paused, she answered at length in her own speech, then said, ''That is one charged with control of ships' movements in this vicinity. He required that we name ourselves, and asserts that we intrude without permission on established lift and transfer lanes. Our conformance with mandated procedures is demanded.''

''And your response, Kaow?''

''I informed him of our identity. Although he did not credit my statement, I related also that this ship is near to exhaustion of its fuels, and retains little capability of maneuver.''

The bases of her forelimbs rose and fell. ''If someone out there does not believe *that* truth and act upon it . . .'' Peering toward the image from the forward viewtube, suddenly her voice pitch rose. ''We will end, Nsil, as an unsightly crater on my homeworld!''

"But why should such dire consequence result?"
"Because that is where our present course concludes."

The 'bug had plenty of power to lift the extra weight; what it lacked, Gowdy had to admit, was room inside.

For the most part his impromptu planning came off well. He didn't ask how Scayna wangled the release of all Nsil's captives; so long as he could get everybody and his suitcase on the sleds, plus a trio of escorts including Gvan, he was ahead of the game.

He had no idea how Scayna got herself included in the bon voyage party, either. But whatever worked . . .

On Sam's own sled he'd had Milo adjust the control circuits to training-wheels level; low sensitivity and limited response, for a smooth and uneventful ride. So all in all it was safe enough to show Gvan how they worked, then encourage the seeder to have a try on his own account. His grounding, when they reached the 'bug, was about as bad as the gentled circuits would allow, but nobody got hurt.

While everyone else piled off and began loading the 'bug, Sam held Gvan's attention. "This flying device I give you, in the name of friendship between ourselves and with Nsil." As Gvan struggled to digest the concept, Gowdy pointed out the spare fuel tank he was leaving—well, *Roamer* wasn't all that far up. "Your assistants are informed as to refueling. This indicator . . ." He pointed. ". . . warns you of that need. And before this auxiliary container can be exhausted," he added, "by all probabilities we shall have returned to replenish it."

Well, it *could* happen. "Be free, Gvan, to direct this vehicle as you choose; I will await and observe."

Gowdy stepped off. And lo and behold, all by himself the seeder gingerly lifted the sled for a trial run.

Sam looked around. The other two sleds and their extra passengers were already lashed on topside; a quick scan showed nobody lagging AWOL, and it looked as though Gowdy's distraction of Gvan had given Scayna her chance to board.

All rightie. Locals safely inside, humans suited up and riding on or alongside the sleds. Sam went up the ladder and in, dogged the hatch, scrambled into the pilot seat. First looking around to see that everyone clung or huddled somewhere safe, he warmed up Traction Drive and initiated takeoff.

Heavy air and all, the Doodlebug did itself proud.

Braced against improvised cushioning at the rear of the crowded compartment, Irtuk-saa cradled young Tuik between her forelimbs as pressure held her to wall and floor. Marveling at this small skyship, she observed differences from Nsil's vessel: this one first moved flatly ahead, then turned upward. And without the clamor of the Eamnet ship; only a strongly vibrating hum accompanied attainment of speed and height.

Forward, beyond the heavy cross-bracing that blocked much of her view, she glimpsed first normal sky and then a darkening, spangled with stars. For a moment great Chorm came into sight, then passed across and vanished.

What carried her now, she knew, was not originally of yumin forming. Utilizing a Maghren airfoil transport hull, Gowdy had emplaced yumin devices to produce this semblance of a skyship. As she had done before, Irtuk chose to believe his working would prove adequate and grant safety.

Tuik gave voice, no longer mewling as at the first but making protest with vigor. At the side of his carrying hamper a pouch held food; chewing and moistening the mixture, Irtuk carefully brought the young seeder up to feeding position.

They had given him his name, she and Waij, upon her body's confirmation of his growing existence. A sadness, that Waij could not be present when Tuik was formally displayed to all who had aided in preparation for her bearing. But soon, perhaps . . .

To one side, Scayna of Eamn gently touched the eagerly feeding head. "He will be strong, Irtuk."

"Events willing." Speaking, now, was not Irtuk's desire.

Rebuffed, Scayna turned away—toward T'phee, crouched not far from her other side. For all the strangeness of this enclosure, its cramped state and unforeseen lurchings, Scayna found no fear. From others she had learned of the difficulties and discomfitures on Nsil's ship One; to the best of her evaluation, Gowdy's smaller vessel gave a smoother passage. To question its reliability did not occur to her.

Still, confirmation always reassures. To the Yainan she said, "Of this skyship and Nsil's, which do you favor?"

''That one tore me from my duties; this returns me.''

''Granted. Yet putting that factor beside, which offers greater ease, least stressings?''

''When matters cannot be altered, I make effort to allow them no concern. But giving consideration to your request, it must be stated that vessels of Nsil are further proven than this which carries us. Elseway, however, yumins hold greater experience of movement between worlds. And of certainty their devices produce less din and shakings.''

That certainty itself was shaken, as the engines' hum became almost a roar and the entire ship received buffets as though by a great forelimb. From the front came Gowdy's voice, first in his own speech to those outside the vessel, and then in Scayna's. ''At this height we pass through a layer of agitated air and must expend greater power. The disturbance will be short-lived.''

''Such reassurance,'' said T'phee, ''is a service Nsil did not find necessary. I must bestow my favor on this ship.''

Comforted, Scayna lay back and waited easement.

Either Kayo's inquisitor decided to believe her or someone with more imagination overruled him. The class C cargo shuttle that came alongside, allowing suited figures to attach towing lines, was a bit smaller than ship Three itself. ''Just stay put and don't fire up anything,'' a new voice said. ''When you're docked they'll put a tube to your airlock and bang on the hatch to let you know you can open up.''

Something else had changed too, though. The speaker added, ''They will not, repeat not, want to see any weapons whatsoever.''

''Weapons? We don't have any.'' Unless Nsil had brought one of his sound-and-light blasters—but she hadn't seen any. Either way, Kayo's disclaimer brought no reply.

Traction Drive gave the shuttle cards and spades in power and maneuverability. The nearly one-eighty U-turn had Nsil's crew and passengers hanging on tight to whatever lay in reach, but the tow to one of nearly a dozen macroGates, joined rim to rim like the facets of a giant insect eye, went gently.

In the spaces between the tangentially abutting rims lay docking facilities: hollow tubes large enough to accommodate cargo shuttles, with necessary fittings including personnel and cargo access tubes deployed neatly around their perimeters.

Having caught ship Three heading down, the tug had an easy chore in killing excess vee: first the one-eighty to dump the rather moderate forward orbit speed, then a slowing lift against Earth's attenuated gravs, to reach the big Gates. Belatedly, Kayo reminded Nsil to bleed air into space, slowly, so as to avoid abrupt decompression when docking was achieved.

The class C chose a docking cylinder at least one size larger than itself. As it eased through the tube at less than walking pace, Three's hull shuddered and motion ceased. Right: magnetic braking; Kayo had heard of it. On a side viewtube she saw people in suits making mooring lines secure, and heard thumps and scrapings from the airlock hatch. Then, after a longer wait than she somehow expected, came a knock.

Kayo turned to Nsil. "You wished to speak with humans in our own system. It is your place to allow them access here."

Nsil opened the inner hatch, then the outer one; his pressure matching hadn't been too bad a guess. The look on the humans' faces, then, behind the isolation masks of their quarantine suits, was definitely worth the price of admission.

Even with the guns. Both stayed aimed, but neither wielder looked much like shooting anyone.

Simone Leopold's time estimate had been a good one; climbing to meet *Roamer* in orbit, Gowdy needed only to ease thrust a bit now and then. If she'd misguessed the other way, he'd have to pour on extra coal, and regardless of pride in design and workmanship, he'd just as soon not.

Someone, probably Ol' Man Mose, had tilted *Roamer*'s stance; on this pass the ship pointed outward and about thirty degrees forward, perfect for Gowdy to sneak up behind. Matching vee he hovered only a few meters from the ship's stern docking facility and listened to hull noises topside, indicating that someone was unlashing the sleds. Hoping the outriders had remembered to bleed their suit pressures ahead of time—here in the 'bug he'd lowered it early—he waited.

When he saw both vehicles and the suited outside passengers enter the opened cargo hatch, he didn't wait to see its closure. Now he inched the 'bug aside, forward alongside *Roamer*'s greater hull, and finally stern first into the DV berth at the ship's nose. Some residual drift was inevitable; as three suited figures deployed the inflatable cover up forward, the 'bug gently touched the well's side and made a slow rebound. But then the expanding plastic membrane swelled to reach the 'bug's nose and pin its stern, slightly askew, against the berth's rear bulkhead.

Near as Gowdy could tell, his passengers seemed reasonably calm: Irtuk protectively holding her young one, Scayna looking around with obvious interest, Bretl and T'phee their usual inscrutable selves. When a series of raps sounded at the entrance hatch, Sam nodded; there was air outside now. "We are being told that we may leave here and enter my ship. If you will gather your belongings?"

He went to help Scayna; the others had lived and moved in zero gee, but not the Eamnet bearer. "Do you have difficulty?"

The flesh around her jaws seemed taut, but she said, "Not greatly. Irtuk-saa had spoken of this condition. I find it strange and surprising in its sensations, but acclimature proceeds well."

So he quit worrying. About that, anyway. Undogging the hatch he opened it to face Mose and SuZanne Craig and Molly Abele, all suits' slanting viewplates now opened to hang behind, the lot of them grinning welcome.

"Hey, gang!" Shaking hands and giving bear hugs didn't work too well with suits, but everyone tried anyway. Sam motioned back to where T'phee and the three bearers were emerging. "None of these folks talk our lingo, so I'll introduce you later. Right now I think I need to see what's what on my ship."

"Problem, Sam," said Tuiasso. "It hasn't come to shove yet, but Commodore Aroka's saying it's *his* ship now."

Gowdy felt tension grip him. "No shit."

"Not to mention," said Molly Abele, "his colony, too."

"There never was any plague on that ship." Still riled from the unceremonious testings she'd been put through, Kayo wasted no thought on polites. "I don't care who told you; there wasn't. I've been aboard for . . ." Jeez, how long *had* it been? "Over a week, anyway. Nobody's sick and nobody was. Even in zero gee, which we had a lot of."

Someone coming into the centrifugally gee'd conference room, moving up through the group either standing guard or just curious, tried to say something; Kayo overrode. "What's the matter with you people? Here you have the first interstellar neighbors you've ever met face-to-face . . ." The Liij didn't count; neither species could breathe the other's air. "From three different worlds and two star systems."

Four worlds really, if you counted Yamar.

"So what do you do? You stand around quoting garbage from someone you haven't even named yet, and where does that one get off calling us a plague ship, anyway? You . . ."

"Young woman!" The recent entrant, now in the front row, stood straight and slim. Her pale vivid hair color looked younger than her face; Kayo guessed mid-fifties but maybe older with good genes. "I'm Jocelyn Waymire, chairing the Senate Space Committee, and I've just ridden at a gee and a half to get here. In case you haven't noticed, no one's wearing isolation suits now. So why don't you simmer down and answer a few questions?"

About to do so, Kayo saw something else she didn't like. Brought here with her because no one else could communicate with them, Nsil and his crew and passengers were being served food and drink. "What the hell are you people doing? We don't know what they can eat safely, of ours. A lot of theirs is poison to us, and probably it works both ways. You send somebody to Nsil's ship and bring some of *their* rations. Then you can run chemical analyses on theirs and ours both, and make reasonable guesses."

To Nsil she made quick explanation, then turned back to the senator. Waymire sat; Kayo took a chair facing her. "Sorry, but that wouldn't wait. My name's Kayo Marlin, by the way. Now could you tell me, just a little bit, what's going on here?"

The woman sighed. "Our information came from Commodore Jorge Aroka, who was sent a little over two years ago to evaluate conditions aboard your ship and at the developing nucleus of your proposed colony." Briefly frowning, she added, "Originally, I believe, it was to be a purely civilian assignment. Where the military ranks came from, I haven't been able to trace."

She shrugged away annoyance. "Your ship, though. Until quite recently, of course, we had no idea what the situation was, there. Then our supporting action began to seem very prudent indeed. Errors appeared in Captain Gowdy's reports. In several cases follow-up corrections were sent by one of his officers, a Sydnie Lightner."

Kayo tried to speak but Waymire gave her no opening. "Also we became concerned about the colony administrator, Barry Krsnch, when discrepancies were uncovered in reports from his previous assignment. Of course we could do nothing directly. But not long ago Krsnch outGated groundside, claiming that Gowdy had Gated him by trickery. So you can see why we became concerned. And why we are relying on Commodore Aroka to set matters right."

"By telling a mining ship to blow us out of space? That's exactly what the bastard did, when we approached the macroGate."

"Plague is nothing to fool with." She stared at Kayo. "Oh, we know now, you're healthy enough. Although you do look . . ."

Unkempt, uncombed, and unwashed; right.

Waymire shook her head. "Nonetheless, Aroka reported a dangerous situation. Suspected plague wasn't his only reason for recommending that we ourselves destroy your ship."

"*He said that*? On what possible grounds?"

"The war, of course. Eamn, the outer moon, destroyed both civilizations a long time ago by means of plague, and Aroka learned they were beginning hostile operations again."

"It wasn't like that. Nsil only—"

"Raided Magh, kidnapped you and others, and crippled your ship's Deployment Vehicle. Isn't that all true?"

"In a way it is, yes. But . . ."

"And when Gowdy somehow went to rescue you, this Nsil—and which one is he, by the way?—abducted you *again*, and aimed ship for the macroGate. The commodore had no more idea than we did, what this loose cannon might be capable of. So he advised us to cut our losses." The senator's brows rose. "You're lucky, you know. Your ship was intercepted and boarded before that recommendation got through channels and up to Operations.''

''I guess red tape *is* good for something. This once.''

''Yes. Well, struggling with difficulties on so many fronts at the same time, it's understandable that the commodore might make the occasional error. Don't you agree?''

''Easy for you,'' said Kayo. ''It's not your ass he tried to get shot off. And what other fronts do you mean?''

''The attacks on Magh, by Eamn. Aroka's determined not to let history repeat itself; he's giving the Maghrens means to fight back.''

Bloody hell. ''Such as what?''

''Ships. The prospector, with tools that can be used as defensive or preemptive armament, and a class B cargo shuttle, for troop transport. We'll have to send more now, in case the Eamnets have more firepower than we think, but . . .''

Shaking, Kayo stood; then without warning her laughter erupted. At Waymire's puzzled frown, she said, ''Hell, you're as bad as Nsil. He still doesn't know about Gatelag, and now you're acting as if you don't.''

The senator's face showed blank. Kayo said, ''Until this Aroka stuck his oar in, there was no real war and wasn't going to be. By now, either Sam Gowdy has matters under control, or else you and your commodore have started your own war and the whole lot of you should be shot. But whatever you do here, makes no difference there. Not for four years after what you know now.''

And not a damn thing Kayo herself could do about it, either. Taking no pity on Waymire's stricken expression, she plopped back down in her chair. ''For a high-level reception, it sure takes forever to get a drink around here.''

To tell Nsil's story and get it right, she was going to need one.

''I still don't see why it's important that nobody else knows you're aboard, Sydnie.'' Puzzlement showed on Skeeter Cole's face. ''But if you and Sam say so . . .'' He looked around the cargo bay, where other outside riders were still unsuiting. ''So let's everybody keep the story straight: watch officer Lightner stayed on Eamn, as liaison. Can we do that?'' Several nods said yes.

"But where will you sleep and eat?" Marthe Vinler looked concerned. "You can't sneak on and off the belt, surely."

"A week or two of zero gee won't kill me." Though Sydnie wasn't looking forward to the lesser evil. "All right, people; you'd better go have your reunion before the commodore gets curious." And then, "Don't forget, Skeeter. Plug a recording cap into the intercom unit in cargo hold Two; that's where I'll pick up word from Sam. And what I need to hear first is which stations are safe for me to call him back."

"You've got it."

As they all left the cargo bay, Skeeter sealed its hatch. Standing, Sydnie felt shaken; how totally her concerns had changed since she was last on this ship—actually, since she saw the flimsy with Aroka's name on it. Well, it wasn't the first time her world had flipped poles on her.

Nor even the first time she had no one to blame it on. Even if she did, now, what good would it do her? Blame had always been one of her best tools, a way to make people atone to her for offenses only she understood. Not this time, though.

She watched the others, Alix and Milo who had Velcro helping Skeeter, who didn't, start forward to meet with Gowdy before leaving the central cylinder for outship. Not until they reached the far end of the corridor and turned out of sight did she pick up her rations knapsack and set off for her own destination.

So long as nobody knew where she was holing up, nobody could give her to Aroka by mistake.

Coming out the DV airlock hatch onto the curving ramp, Gowdy took a deep breath; it seemed years since he'd last been here, boarding the Vehicle for return to Magh. And he'd almost forgotten the nonsmell of filtered, recycled shipside air; the 'bug's had more bite to it.

Lacking Velcro, Sam's passengers made do with handholds, plus some steadying by their three greeters. Looking ahead, Gowdy saw his outside riders emerging from the corridor leading to the ship's stern. Except Sydnie, of course, and for now he wouldn't think about her role.

"A little help here, gang? Our friends don't have the right shoes." Awkwardly the three bearers and T'phee were convoyed through hatches and down ramps all the way to the control deck. As Gowdy started toward the final ramp, leading to the transfer ring, somebody yelled, "Hey you! Hold it right there."

Gowdy didn't know the voice. Nor, as he looked back along the corridor to control, the man holding the gun.

Guns? Aboard ship? At parade ground pitch he shouted back, "I am Captain Gowdy. Put that thing away. Right now, before it gets you in trouble." And to his followers, "Keep moving."

He couldn't do anything about the gun; his only choice was to pretend it didn't matter and hope to be convincing. Facing the downramp and trying to ignore the warning itch at the back of his neck as unsteady-sounding footsteps approached from behind, he stood until the others passed.

As he started to follow, a bullet spanged off the bulkhead beside him and splattered against the forward wall. Sam moved fast. At the ramp's lower end the transfer ring doors stood open; he helped jostle everyone inside, then hit the button.

The doors closed in the outraged face of the man who hadn't obeyed orders. As the transfer car accelerated and Irtuk braced to protect her child, her sidewise lurch briefly pinned Gowdy against the end bulkhead. Centrifugal force built, the ring locked to the residential belt, and the doors reopened.

"Everybody out." Last to leave, Sam paused. The doors were closing; all too soon Hopalong Cassidy could be stepping out here.

No. Gowdy remembered how Old Iron Tits was trapped on *Starfinder*'s belt while Rance Collier and Su Teng Gated off that ship. Unsnapping a belt pouch of powdered rations, he jammed it between the closing segments; pressure squinched its thickness down to about an inch, but that inch held.

Standing over him, Marthe Vinler looked puzzled. Sam grinned. "The safety interlocks. With the doors blocked from closing all the way, the transfer ring won't budge."

He stood. "Okay, folks. Whatever we're up against, let's see if we can get this part of the ship to make sense. And then maybe figure how to handle that cowboy up in zero gee."

There'd be more than one, but why rain on the picnic?

* * *

It didn't take long for the basically hospitable attitude of this macroGate operation to overcome Kayo Marlin's initial bias. As soon as ship Three's complement was delivered to a rotating point-four-gee residence module and installed in roomier digs than she expected, a cheerful technician reported that comparative food analyses were complete; from now on, Earth's visitors could be guaranteed safe meals.

The door chime brought Kayo robed but still damp from the shower she'd dreamed of since leaving Eamn; entering, Jocelyn Waymire looked contrite. "One shipment of lasers had already been Gated. But consequent to your translation of Nsil's case, further weapons procurements for the Triad Worlds are canceled. And as you've said, Marlin, by the time those lasers arrive, the situation that seemed to require them will be four years past."

She frowned. "We *know* that—intellectually, at least. But we legislators aren't scientists. Under pressure, people urging the Committee to action, sometimes we forget."

Sure. But, "Isn't that what staff's for? To catch the bosses' mistakes before they get loose and have kittens?"

The senator chuckled. "Bill Flynn would love you."

Before Kayo could place the name, the chime sounded again.

"Excuse me."

At the door stood Vannet; in some indefinable way the Yainan's every aspect implied despond. "K'yo, I have great need. To one here of decision power will you transpose my speaking?"

"Senator Waymire attends; does her authority suffice?"

Vannet stumped in; after a quick rundown the senator said, "If I can help, let's get on with it."

"We of Yain," Vannet began at Kayo's prompting, "grow and flourish in congress with others of our kind. Aloneness is not to be suffered; solitary we diminish and fail."

All four grasping appendages writhed, then sagged limp. "T'phee instructed me, for this time we must bear absence of communion. Time too long endures; all effort wastes itself. Failing resumption of Yainan lifehelp, soon my being ends."

Jeez, even his syntax was downhilling. After Kayo's translation Waymire asked, "Have you known about this before?"

"No. But I believe it. Just *look* at him."

"I'm hardly qualified to judge. Well, we can Gate him back, of course. But there'll be a lot of specialists wanting to study him first, learn not only about him but about his world. I'm not at all clear on how it relates to . . ."

"Didn't you hear what I told you? He's going to *die*, dammitall." Kayo shook her head. "All right; take pictures, tissue samples, whatever makes you happy—but do it fast and get him out of here. I can tell you the major facts about his world; surely the details aren't urgent enough to risk killing him."

After a moment Waymire nodded. "Very well; I'll take the responsibility for clearing him to leave—and most likely catch a lot of flak for it, too. He can Gate in a few hours. But to where? *Roamer*? The colony base on Magh? Marlin, how can we know what this being's best chance is?"

And how could such a smart woman think so dumb? Kayo said, "Magh isn't going anyplace, but God only knows where *Roamer* could be in four years. What's the nearest Gate we can use?"

And to the Yainan, "Hold strength; aloneness will end."

Leading the way, Gowdy looked first into the lounge—empty—and then the galley, where Owen Tanacross was concluding a snack.

The man came to his feet. "Captain! You're all right? The commodore's people . . ."

"Yeh, I know. We met one; he took a shot at me."

"Case Beringer," Molly Abele put in. "Aroka's deputy."

"Whoever. So before we try to establish diplomatic relations, I think we'd better secure our perimeter. So to speak. How many of them are there—and where, right now? I've got the transfer ring blocked, if that helps."

"Five. Aroka's up in control, along with Beringer and the woman Estilete. Silva and Atwell came past here a few minutes ago; I think they're in his digs having themselves a matinee."

Sam grinned. First indicating who, including his nonhuman guests, should remain here, he picked up a couple of galley utensils and said, "I hope nobody has anything against a little harmless voyeurism. Let's go see the lovebirds."

XVI

In all seen since entering this ship, T'phee finds great interest. Comparable of size to *Tayr* or *L'lit*, Gowdy's vessel differs in many fashions. This portion where T'phee now stands, feigning a light worldpull by circular movement—why have not Yainan builders entertained such novel conception?

Yet to observe the result tells en nought of how such a construct could be made to function with safety. The rubbings, between still and moving portions—the balance, so delicate to avoid destructive vibration—T'phee can but marvel.

The yumin bearer Vinler speaks. "Do any thirst or hunger? We stand in the feeding place. On Magh I learned to judge which yumin foods may and may not be ingested by Maghrens—and would anticipate applicability also to you of Eamn and Yamar."

Er turns to T'phee. "I regret, my knowings fail with regard to persons from Yain. In some or any manner may I aid?"

Appreciative, T'phee strokes the tips of Vinler's extended manipular with one of es own. "Your concern is valued—yet not in this circumstance required. To a Yainan the suitability of any foodthing comes apparent. By our feeling of . . ." and finds no term the Maghren tongue can convey.

The yumin patpats es neckskin below es manipulars. "If you are certain, then feeding may commence."

Choosing and ensampling, T'phee assuages hunger. In es mind, burdens move and shift importance. T'phee enself as yet finds little decline from lack of lifehelp; firm purpose guides and shields en. But what of V'naet?

Had not V'naet volitioned to accompany T'phee, the other would now be among support, not cloven away bereft. In hap it may be T'phee's duty to reclaim es follower.

The great portal still exists; Gowdy could convey en to it.

But painful as that burden lies, primary grievement resurges to overlie. Though deeply valued, V'naet is but one; on Yain, *all* will die. And at Yamar, all weight falls to feeble Cejha.

Unforewarned, need of lifehelp aches throughout T'phee.

As the compartment door opened quietly to Sam's key, it was no scene of passion he faced; obviously warned by intercom, the pair was up and priming for action. The man's shirt wasn't tucked in, nor his fly closed, but neither lack would have handicapped him much if he'd reached his gun in time. But being relatively new to point-three gee and Coriolis forces, he misgauged his lunge by at least a foot.

Gowdy didn't. The stocky, balding man caught the broad side of the steak tenderizing mallet just under his right ear. Twisting away to one side just in case, Sam turned to see the skinny woman, bright frizzy hair aflop, being shaken like a rug by SuZanne Craig while Skeeter Cole grabbed for the gun in her wildly flailing hand and finally got it.

"You can hang her up now, SuZanne." Red-faced with exertion, Craig sputtered; it came out a laugh, as Skeeter went on, "What do we do with them, captain?"

If only all his choices could be so simple! "Search the place for weapons, disable the intercom, and lock 'em in."

None of it took long. Out in the corridor again, Gowdy said, "Now then; who else might be here on the belt?"

Eyes squinting as she counted off names, SuZanne said, "None of theirs. Simone's on watch, with the commodore and his other two goons looking down her neck. Jethro's in drive."

She frowned. "You know, captain; maybe we jumped too fast. Aroka may be blocked from the belt, but he has the control room—and Simone and Jethro as potential hostages."

"Beringer's the one, jumped too fast," Sam protested. "Once he pulled that trigger, school was out. All right; let's extend our weapons search—to all areas occupied or used by those people. Right now I need to get on my terminal, in quarters."

Mose cleared his throat. "Aroka took those; moved in last week, with his rather sinister woman. So if you don't mind I'll come with you, do that search while you . . . well, whatever . . ."

They walked fast. Opening the door, Gowdy was shocked to see no possessions he recognized. The place was cluttered with gaudy yet obviously expensive stuff: furniture, clothing, ornamental objects. "Sonofabitch . . . !"

His computer terminal still sat where it belonged. On his intercom station, sitting alongside, he punched for the pilot's console.

"First Officer Leopold." She sounded calm enough.

"Gowdy here. Give me Configuration B."

Within seconds his indicator lights showed that Simone had transferred all major operating command functions, from the control room to the augmented terminal before him.

The trick was, only from here could they be switched back again.

Restless, Sydnie decided to prowl farther outship. The hatches up forward by no means constituted her only access. Near the cargo hold entrance lay a tunnel leading aft along the inner cylinder's boundary; partway back she clambered "down" through a hatchway into the first of the middle cylinder's three decks.

The circuit equipment racks and their indicator displays were outside Sydnie's fields of knowledge or interest; she opened another hatch and descended one more level, to where the drive mode quarters had been. One or two of those, she seemed to remember, had been left in place, their shapes and locations rendering the space not especially useful for other purposes.

But the main point was, nobody ever went there.

Actually, at the deck's rear she found three intact units; wryly she chose the one she and Johnnie Rio had used, shortly before he left. Even the hammock nets were still in place.

On a hunch she checked a water tap, clipping her canteen to its spigot and hearing the rush of fluid. Good; now she wasn't tied to the supply at the cargo hold. But on this deck the nearest zero-gee toilet would be forward, near Ship's Supplies reserve storage. And now seemed a good time to check it out.

Partway there, Sydnie gave a silent laugh. Almost directly under her Velcro'd feet lay the control room. With biffies right across the corridor. Too bad she couldn't just drop by. . . .

She couldn't, of course, but maybe she could *see* into control. After the business at hand, she began checking. . . .

In drive mode configuration there'd been equipment mounted to the control room's inner bulkhead, more or less directly under where she now stood. A major structural feature, the bulkhead's hollow and intricately braced shell provided a crawl space of nearly eighteen inches. With entrance hatches at either side.

Recessed tethered wing bolts are neat, easy to remove without tools, and not easily lost. Sydnie pivoted the hatch cover, still loosely secured at one corner, out of the way, and took a deep breath; narrow confined spaces tended to jitter her.

The other side's corresponding hatch wasn't directly in line, but light through a section of ventilating screen helped her find one. Whatever its wall-mounting function might have been, not that she even tried to remember, now it held a ceiling light panel with vent screen segments at either end.

Sydnie found herself looking down at control from near an aft corner of the room, with the watch positions facing away. The screen impeded vision. Squinting, she located and unscrewed another wing bolt, then gently swung the screen up far enough to peek past it; so near the ceiling light, against its glare no upward glance was apt to note the slight discrepancy.

All right, look it over. Simone sat pilot; that was normal. A man Sydnie had never seen stood a few feet to one side, apparently studying some flimsies. A tall woman sat nearer Simone, sidewise and facing her. If Sydnie had ever seen that one before, she'd have remembered: strong features, almost harsh, below black hair clipped to little more than stubble. Sydnie didn't have to guess; she knew. Whatever this one's *nom de guerre*, here was the latest successor to Marlene Klieng.

But where . . . ? The door opened and a man entered. Thin, white-haired and slightly limping, wearing a pale yellow scarf in ascot fashion with his tailored jumpsuit, his gaunt, deeply lined face struck no chord of familiarity.

The intercom sounded. Sydnie heard Simone's voice, then from the box Sam Gowdy's—but not their words. As the exec operated switches at her console, the newcomer's voice crackled.

"What did you do?" And with one smooth movement, the man took the seat next to Simone's.

Aroka hadn't changed much, after all. Only on the outside.

Fingers trembling, Sydnie refastened the screen. Tempering hurry with need for quiet she retreated to sanctuary and put the hatch back to normal.

For a long moment she stood, thinking. Somewhere, in all the areas of *Roamer* that were free to her, there must be a thing she could use to kill the Spider Prince.

"Gowdy? What's going on?"

From the intercom, a brand-new voice. Sam hit the talk switch. "You have to ask? On my own ship, a man I never saw before fires a gun at me. For starters, guns aboard ship are a major violation. Next, who authorized that sonofabitch to potshoot anybody? So that's two asses I mean to have on toast."

"This is Commodore Jorge Aroka. Do you know who I am?"

"Somewhat." Who he was now, yes; who he used to be, maybe. How he got here in a commodore suit, not a clue. "But rank's no excuse for some idiot spanging lead around a starship."

"The guns are aboard on my authority, for security purposes. Commander Beringer reported to me that he apprehended unannounced intruders who refused to halt when hailed. He . . ."

"I told him who I was; he fired anyway."

"And he's supposed to believe a fleeing man?"

Damn; not a bad point. But, "Nonetheless, he and the rest of you will deliver all firearms to Earthmouth, where Executive Officer Leopold will inGate the lot. Is that clear?"

"What's clear," in the most arrogant tone yet, "is that

you're no longer in command here. On this ship, and by proxy at the colony, I have assumed that position. Second to me is Commander Beringer, next is Lieutenant Commander Silva. That puts you—let me see—fourth in the chain of command. *And* unarmed, I gather. So I suggest you reconsider."

Cutting that circuit, Gowdy punched for the main drive room. "Jethro? Sam here. I'm in quarters."

"When'd you get back? Look, captain, you have to watch out; this commodore's taken over, and I don't trust him."

"Two of us. Listen . . ." Quickly he told it: who was where, the blockage of the transfer ring, the present impasse. Sydnie, he left out. "Jeth, why don't you secure the drive room from intrusion and then give us a nice sharp nudge? Not enough to cause real damage, but spill everybody's milk. It'll make a mess, sure—but it may prevent a much worse one."

"You've got it. In ten."

Seconds, that would be. Switching back to control, Sam waited. The momentary surge of Traction Drive made quite a satisfactory impact; over the intercom came "What did you *do*?"

Sam chuckled. "The point is, I did it; you didn't. And you can't stop its happening again, if I want it to."

Aroka's voice steadied. "So you sloshed coffee all over my scarf. Is that supposed to scare me?"

"I could just as easy lay on two gees. And keep it on."

"But that would . . ." Heavy breathing; maybe even some heavy thinking. "You're saying you'd wreck your own ship?"

"Course not. But I just might bust the shit out of yours. And then leave the way I got here."

Which ought to shake him up. If it didn't . . . Frantically, Sam made mental search for a Plan B.

"All right." Aroka's voice. "We can come to terms. But I need some assurances. You've brought alien beings onto this ship. We know nothing about them; you have to allow us some defense against possible aggression. I suggest—"

"I give you my personal guarantee. No more, no less. The guns go. Or the gees come." A thought came. "And if your boy Beringer's up there banging on the drive room door,

Jethro might be of a mood to hammer in a few gravs on his own initiative."

Right: we're all loose cannons here, so watch your head.

Silence lengthened before Aroka answered. Light-toned as if in casual greeting, the man said, "Competent negotiators are rare; my congratulations, captain. You will next hear from your officer, reporting that weapons have been Gated as you request."

Yah sure you betcha. Sam didn't need Sydnie to nudge his worry button. He'd won a skirmish; the war was still to come.

And Aroka had yet to answer for Kayo Marlin.

Watching Earth, blue and white, grow in the cargo shuttle's forward screens, gave Kayo a thrill she hadn't expected. The macroGate cluster rode lead-Trojan to the moon, so the ride down took a fair time. Especially keeping it gentle because no seats fit any of the visitors, who had to make do with floor pads and handholds.

Not Nsil, though. The Eamnet stood, forelimbs gripping the backs of two adjacent seats, and watched the approaching planet. Mostly silent, at one point he turned, saying, "This is your homeworld, Kaow? Coursing alone, lacking any primary but its star? With only a barren rock nearby, how did your species find cause and reason to build skyships?"

"Actually we almost didn't." But that stagnation, born of political pressures and relieved only by the fortuitous discovery of Traction Drive, was past and gone. "Then we had fortune."

Massing twice the DV, the shuttle came to ground at Glen Springs every bit as gently. Waymire, who now bustled out to confer with a clipboard-carrying man, must have been busy talking space-to-ground; of the overgrown vans lined up outside the landing circle's safety perimeter, several had most of their normal seating removed. Quietly, with Nsil's help Kayo assigned and herded the Eamnet contingent into three of these; with Duant and V'naet she and the senator entered a fourth, and the convoy proceeded to the station's quarters area.

Once there, seeing the alien visitors peering about in confusion and agency employees looking more scared to death of them than not, she began to realize just what she was in for.

In a way, it was what she had signed up to do. Because right now, Kayo Marlin was the only person in forty-odd light-years who could talk with the outworlders.

Gowdy wouldn't bet any real money on a clean sweep, but all the guns he and his could find were off the ship. One each from Aroka and Beringer and Estilete plus two more from a control room cabinet, inGated by Simone. Then the pair from Silva and Atwell, and two Mose found in the quarters that would be Sam's again when he had time. The old logs said Compartment Seven had once housed senators; it should do just fine for a commodore.

Resisting the temptation to stash a piece for himself just in case, Gowdy consigned the lot to Earth which didn't need them either. Riding the transfer ring, then bypassing control to lead Mose and Skeeter and Milo back to Earthmouth, he felt more than a fair share of misgivings. But sure things are as rare as free lunches; Sam had to play this the way it fell.

So he laid the last four handguns on the Gate's floor grid and Mosu Tuiasso brought up the flaring colors; when they died, the Mouth sat empty. Now it was time to visit control.

Standing in the doorway, Gowdy paused. At pilot and not looking happy about it, Simone Leopold had her abundant hair nominally tamed in a thick, springy braid. Sam gave her a quick nod, then scanned the room in appraisal.

From the brief glimpse he'd had earlier, he recognized the man sitting at an aux position as Case Beringer—medium size, ruddy complexion, and a trait not so obvious now that he sat quiet: poor judgment.

The tall, dark-complexioned woman with the five o'clock shadow on top would be the one mentioned by Owen Tanacross: Estilete. Spanish for stiletto; some kind of macabre nickname? From the air and stance of her, it could fit.

Never mind. The meat in the sandwich was the guy at the comm position, wearing the expensively tailored jumpsuit with the fancy trim. Sam took a good long look at him. Lean, not terribly tall, gaunt-faced with cheeks hollowing below strong cheekbones, a slim nose and controlled lips, black brows contrasting with neatly brushed white hair. An ascot-type scarf, now coffee-stained, hid neck and throat. All in all, the man had the look of someone who might have survived serious illness.

The eyes gave a different impression. Sunken under lids that hinted of Asian genes without quite saying so out loud, they glinted in a basilisk stare that didn't move from Sam as the man asked, "You would be Gowdy?"

"Captain Samuel Hall Gowdy, commanding *Roamer.*"

"Commodore Jorge Aroka. Captain, I regret our misunderstanding. But you boarded unannounced, like a raiding party—and rather than reporting in to me you ignored Commander Beringer's challenge and blocked all access to the residential belt. You can hardly blame me for taking exception."

With a thin-lipped smile he added, "I confess, however, that in the heat of argument I overstated the scope of changes to our mutual command structure."

A lifted hand stopped Sam's protest. "You must understand. My authority and qualifications do not stem from space agency training. Command is my specialty, not ship operations. You will continue to run the ship; I will direct its doings, and those of the colony, in furthering the policies of our mission."

Maybe so, maybe not. "What policies?"

"Why, to colonize and assimilate this system, with due regard for the welfare of its present inhabitants. We will stop the developing war and then enforce the peace."

Passing the point that you don't colonize inhabited systems, Sam retorted, "What war? All I've seen here is skirmishing."

"Eamn has attacked Magh, which had no means of defense. I intend giving the Maghrens that means, but should they use it for aggressive purposes, we will suppress that aggression also." He smiled. "We'll need to establish a protectorate, you see. A protectorate with sweeping powers. But I can handle those."

From history classes Gowdy recognized the classic contrived justification for takeover. But although he wanted to know just what Aroka planned to give the Maghrens and what the hell for, this wasn't the best time to argue. "And the colony?"

"It was necessary to replace the Verdoorn woman as administrator. I've given the position to one of your own, captain. Mr. Jules Perrone.''

''Jules couldn't administer Lost and Found at a picnic.''

''He follows orders. Verdoorn had difficulty with that concept.''

What orders? Sam decided not to ask. He had a better idea. ''The welfare of the natives, you mentioned. Have you met any of them yet?''

Aroka shrugged. ''With your landing craft disabled, under your very nose as I understand it, I've had no way to do so.''

''You do now. I brought an assortment with me; they're down on the belt.''

Without waiting for response Gowdy stepped forward and leaned across to the intercom. ''SuZanne? The alert's over; we're coming down. And you may as well open the bird cage.'' Aroka looked puzzled, but Sam didn't explain.

Another thought. ''It would be nice if *everybody* showed up to greet the commodore.''

Even if Sydnie could have made a throw, downward and slanting in zero gee, from a cramped crawl space with no room to swing her arm, the only knives she could locate weren't balanced right for it. Not to mention her sore elbow, from some idiot hitting the drive when she wasn't holding onto anything.

She might makc a slingshot powerful enough to dent a skull properly—but would she have the leverage to pull it? Not cramped inside that damn bulkhead. The self-powered laser tools lacked range by an order of magnitude; the cord-fed models bulked too large to horse around in that limited space, and she didn't have tools to splice power leads into a junction box, anyway.

She'd checked the phone at hold Two; no recording cap unit on it yet. Now, back above control for a second look, watching as Simone Leopold collected everybody's guns for some reason, Sydnie chewed her sleeve to keep from screaming at the exec to *shoot* the murdering sonofabitch and get it over with.

She didn't, though. It wouldn't work. Simone would be calm and logical and want to know for sure what was going on, and Aroka like lightning would seize a gun back and

Sydnie would be up here a sitting duck by virtue of her own big mouth and why the hell couldn't anything work out *right*?

Five handguns Simone carried out the control room door, and all Sydnie needed was one. Well, there had to be another way. She looked at the overall assembly that replaced the old hatch.

It was big enough, and held in place only by wing bolts. But since the knives were no good for throwing any distance, she hadn't brought them. Rethinking, she went to retrieve a couple.

When she returned, Sam was down there talking to Aroka! But then he moved so close to the man that if she did burst through and down, Gowdy's reflexes would trigger against the new unidentified threat; before he got matters sorted out, Aroka would have Sydnie dead and maybe Sam too.

For now, the hell with it. Not waiting to see and maybe hear what happened between the two men, Sydnie crawled back out.

In relief of Simone on watch, Mose stayed behind when the group left. Mumbling something about an errand, Skeeter Cole dropped back as Gowdy led the party downramp to the transfer ring. The doors stood open; they entered, and in less than a minute the rear pair slid aside, opening onto the rotating belt.

Even with T'phee absent, the reception committee outdid Sam's expectations: the look on Aroka's face at sight of Irtuk and Bretl, barely a pace away and looming, was well worth the price of admission.

Almost too late Gowdy caught the woman's motion. Unable to see what she reached for, he lunged and clamped his hold around her waist, pinning her arms at the elbows. Surprisingly limber as her breath hissed, she twisted to snake gaping jaws at his throat. He froze—no way to fend her off and no room to duck—but suddenly her head jerked back, the digits of one of Irtuk's great forelimbs splayed across the forehead.

"Estilete! Enough." At Aroka's words, the woman's struggle ceased.

Keeping his voice steadier than he felt, Gowdy said, "You may release her, Irtuk. My thanks to you."

"Yes. I end restraint, yet still maintain scrutiny."

Estilete's eyes slitted. "Not to touch me again." But only to Sam did she make the flat command; toward Irtuk she did not look at all.

Still at the car's doorway, Gowdy faced Aroka. "The weapon. What she was reaching for. Tell her to hand it over."

In another tongue the white-haired man addressed her. Not Spanish, something Asian-sounding. Her scowl made her usual glower look like Mary Sunshine; fast as magic, from somewhere near her waistband flashed a long, thin, ivory-handled blade. For a moment Gowdy tensed, but inclining her head slightly she presented the weapon hilt first. "Keep it in good care."

"I will." Then, for no good reason, "Thank you."

So much for the knife act and cat tamer; time to start action in the center ring. As a beginning Gowdy made complete introductions, in both systems' languages and sparing no one. Gauging Aroka's impatience quotient at close to offscale, he escorted the parade to the rec lounge, asked Owen Tanacross to scrounge up a few snack trays, and offered drinks all around. Including the bearers; both Magh and Eamn produced alcohol in forms approximating beers and wines. T'phee's people preferred something entirely different, which the Yainan could not specify in recognizable terms. But he wasn't here anyway . . .

Thc recent losing team was, though, and Aroka beckoned the two over. "Captain Gowdy—Lieutenant Commander Rocco Silva and Lieutenant Vivian Atwell."

"We've met." The man's tough guy face looked about as sullen as he had reason to be, but Vivian Atwell's thin plain features showed an odd, eager interest. Her raggedly riotous mop of orange-blond hair would have looked more at home in a Vegas strip act; Sam reminded himself not to judge by appearances and expressed regrets for the "misunderstanding." Atwell smiled; Silva did an "aw shucks 'warn't nothin' " number; neither was any great shakes as a liar but Gowdy spread a grin in return.

As Aroka's sipping of neat schnapps noticeably eased the man's barely concealed ire, Sam off the top of his head helpfully filled him in on various local data he couldn't possibly care about. "Surprisingly efficient, the Maghren social organization, considering the hierarchal levels involved . . ." and so on.

When he guessed the commodore had half his mind elsewhere in sheer self-defense, Gowdy shifted gears. "I'm having your things moved to Seven, the senators' suite. Bill Flynn stayed there, you know. And before him, old Methuselah Wallin himself." The Methuselah part came from Wallin's use of Gatelag to extend his last two decades of life over several of most people's.

Before Aroka could refocus: "Understand, there's no rank or ego thing involved." Oh, perish the thought! "The fact is, my quarters are equipped with circuits that are essential to normal control of operational functions, and it would take at least a month at Earth macroGate refitting facilities—where we're not—to relocate them. So can we consider the matter settled?" Since Milo and Alix and Charlotte Wang were already moving Aroka's belongings and returning Sam's from storage, they'd better!

Out of his element but obviously determined to master the situation, Aroka hesitated. And then, bless happenstance, in through the door waddled T'phee. The gaunt man stared. Well, at first sight of a Yainan, who didn't? "What . . . ?"

"Ah," said Gowdy. "Allow me to present T'phee, who represents the inhabitants of this system's companion star system and its colony on the world Yamar." Again introductions, with T'phee in all innocence speaking at considerable length which Sam scrupulously refrained from abridging in translation. "And now . . ." He looked across the room. "Marthe? Could you come handle the language situation for a while?"

As Vinler approached, he stood. "Some things I need to do."

The first one was, talk with Simone Leopold in private.

Although only faded freckles testified to the gray-haired man's original coloring, Bill Flynn certainly didn't look his true age; a few spells of Gatelag can do that for you. By now Kayo remembered who he was: Jocelyn Waymire's predecessor as head of the space committee, and protégé of the legendary Senator Wallin who first recognized the potential of Traction Drive and went on to ramrod *Starfinder* through the legislative process.

In Waymire's temporary Glen Springs office the stocky Flynn greeted the senator and Kayo with a friendly grin, asked for coffee, and sat down. "Well, Jocelyn, what's it about?" And when Waymire gestured to Kayo, "Yes, first-hand's best. All right, young woman, what's the situation at the Triad Worlds? And isn't that a marvel for you—three livable mudballs in one star system? Well, never mind; let's hear the story."

As quickly as she could, Kayo told it: how *Roamer*'s advent, along with the exploring ships from the system's companion star, had inadvertently triggered a flare-up of old hostilities. "But it wouldn't have amounted to much," she insisted. "You've seen Nsil's ship—on Tri-V at least. Chemical propulsion. Even in their glory days those people got only one ship out as far as Yamar. That's the Trojan world—leading, if it matters—at roughly a hundred and a quarter megamiles distance."

"Still," Flynn said, "your Nsil managed to raid the sister world. Or you wouldn't be here. And the macroGate, if I understand correctly, is as far from home one way as Yamar the other. Glory days, it seems, are here again. And trouble."

Shaking her head, Kayo protested. "We weren't going to let it happen. We were talking with the Maghrens; then I tried with Nsil. Just a little more time—but things went too fast. Or too slow: if Nsil's guerrilla squad hadn't snockered the DV, *or* if Sam hadn't put the Doodlebug together so soon—and arrived while Nsil was still deciding whether to believe me. Because he hadn't quite got past the idea that Sam came to attack."

A deep breath. "But there was still a good chance; the lid hadn't blown. And then this idiot commodore! Orders us blasted out of space and intends to give Earth weapons to the Maghrens. How did he ever get into the program, anyway?"

"Er—let's say he had a sponsor with leverage," said Flynn. "I looked it up. But not long after the commodore and his team Gated, the lever broke. Well, partly. Aroka's still out there, with all the authority of his mission orders and four years head start on any countermove we might make. But the support corps that was supposed to follow, never got funded."

"Well, that's a break. So how many does he have with him?"

"Umm, let's see. He left with only a few aides; Commander Lioso and the rest of his staff didn't follow for maybe a month."

Waymire's brows converged. "Lioso. Is that the baleful little mummy with the powered prosthetic braces?"

"That's right," Flynn said. "And how Aroka greased him past the physical I'll never know. But just guessing, I'd put his total cadre at somewhere between fifteen and twenty. Not counting any sleepers he may have slipped into the colony quotas." He paused. "I could check it out."

Kayo shrugged. "No offense, but what for? What's sent is sent. Including hardware. How many mining ships have gone, with lasers and all?"

"Only the one, I believe; according to reports, your planet Big Red has pretty well swept out most asteroid groupings near enough to be mined economically without macroGates. We concentrated on cargo shuttles and colonists. And a couple of exploration ships, leapfrog type—but those went later."

"I don't suppose the miner followed us back here, did it? Or we'd have heard. After what Larry did, I was hoping . . ."

Flynn's brows raised, but Kayo didn't elaborate. Instead, "Well, it looks as if all we can do from here is hope Sam Gowdy pulled a miracle, and stopped the hassle before things got completely out of hand."

"Miracle's the word," said Jocelyn Waymire. "To buck the kind of rank and official backing Aroka has, your Captain Gowdy would have to be a real maverick. And a lucky one."

Flynn's expression lit with a smile. "As a matter of fact he's a bit of both. I don't suppose either of you ever heard of Ironhead Kennealy and the *Tarpon*. Well, young Gowdy bent some regulations into a figure eight for his old friend; touch-and-go whether he'd get a medal or a court-martial."

He reached for more coffee. "I think we've pretty well summed up the basic situation. Thank you, Kayo, for confirming my opinion. Now, Jocelyn mentioned some difficulty with this other species, from the twin star. Care to fill me in?''

Having been viewed, goggled at, poked, probed, sampled, and interviewed at length in translation, Vannet had finally Gated to the colony base on Magh. Four years after his departure he would either find a Yainan presence on that world or he wouldn't, but that chance was all anyone could give him.

So what Bill Flynn referred to was the greater peril faced by Vannet's species. Kayo didn't even like to think of Yain's tragedy, but she gave a sigh and told about it, anyway.

". . . in hell has he been doing? What else, I mean?''

Gowdy read Simone's gesture as, where do I start? They were in his reclaimed quarters, with Aroka's gear removed and his own slopping out of boxes scattered around the deck. "Besides taking over here?'' she said. "And giving the colony to Jules Perrone of all people, and planning to turn the mining ship and a cargo shuttle over to the Maghrens? Well, of course he did send the miner to interdict the Eamnet ship or kill it, and . . .''

Sam felt his face tighten. "I haven't forgotten that. Believe me; once I find the handle, the man's compost.''

"You mustn't underestimate him. He—''

"He doesn't know the first thing about this ship.''

"Don't be so sure.'' Now Leopold looked worried. "The tech side, no; he doesn't seem to think he needs that, and maybe he's right. But other things . . . Aroka adapted to zero gee as if he was born in it. He's done vacuum suit drill in the DV well, taking Owen along to teach him, with Estilete at the airlock controls to make sure he came back in or nobody did. When he enters a room he sees all of it. Sam, I've seen some hard cases; this one could walk into any back alley in the world without a care.''

Pausing only a moment, she added, "And that woman. You got very lucky there, you know.''

He must have looked skeptical; Simone's voice rose. "There were two of them. A redhead about a quarter inch less butch in the haircut department. They started having words in the lounge and Estilete put her down, gut-stabbed.''

"Is she dead?''

"Who knows? Aroka went furious in that cold way of his, cursing through his teeth in God only knows what language, and we had to carry the redhead up to Earthmouth. And when Mose wasn't fast enough to suit her, setting up, Estilete gave him a jab in the ribs. To the bone; he took some antibiotic just in case. So you see . . ."

Gowdy felt himself coming down with a bad case of the stubborns. "Doesn't matter. Not any damn bit of it. After what that mining ship did . . ."

"But it didn't! I shut down the offship speakers when Aroka's people visit control, so he doesn't know, but Velucci called and it's recorded. Kayo got away through the macroGate."

All at once Sam was glad he hadn't yet worked up to brace the commodore on that count; the whole situation could have blown wide-open, over something that hadn't actually happened.

Now he grinned. "If I could find any of my booze in this mess we'd drink to that." He reached to squeeze her hand. With Kayo's doom repealed and off his soul, other issues surfaced. "Look; at first, here, on the intercom I put you in a bad spot, getting hardnose with Aroka. All the while I was scared stiff he'd try to use you as a hostage. Still not sure why he didn't."

Simone's expression went grim. "I know why. You see, the woman suggested just that tactic. He said, no man who'd beat his way to ship command would give it up for a mere hostage, any more than he would himself, so why irritate you and achieve nothing?"

Her expression sobered. "That was scary. If he hadn't assumed you were as callous as he is, he might have done *any* damn thing. And without batting those weird eyes of his."

She clutched his wrist, squeezing. "We're all supposed to be *civilized*, here in the starship program. How did people like that . . . ?"

". . . get into the system? And him so high up in it?" Gowdy shook his head. "Political, it has to be. Whose clout he rode, I have no idea—and with a four-year comm lag, no way to undercut it now when we need to. We're on our own, and regardless of Aroka's character, our actions have to look justified on the record. In the long haul, that is. For now, he and I have established our relationship on a firm basis.''

''Oh? What's that?''

''Mutual hypocrisy.'' His quick grin vanished. ''Trouble is, he caved in too easy; it feels wrong. Of course, right now there's only the five of them. And why? He's been here—what?—two–three weeks? So how come more muscle hasn't come through Earthtush? Or political backup, at least.''

Leopold shrugged. ''You want us to plug it?'' Because a Habegger transmitter won't send if a previous load still fills the receiver. ''A few empty crates should do the trick.''

''We'd need to post a guard.'' Then he thought harder. ''Wait a minute. The Mouth knows the Tush is full *two years later?* That implies faster than light communication.''

''Nope.'' Looking smug, Simone went on, ''That's been tried; it didn't work. Top Hush, but somebody left a classified report open on a desk and I sneaked a peek.''

''Then just how . . . ?'' Puzzled, Gowdy shook his head.

''Well, Habegger's math needs extra dimensions; maybe that's where the feedback signal goes.'' She frowned. ''Look—haven't you ever been driving behind one of those damned big vans, and something's blocking traffic but all you know is, the van won't move. You're not getting any message from up ahead, just from right where you are. Same here, only time instead of distance.''

He nodded. ''Okay, I'll think about plugging the Tush.''

''Before or after a new bunch of armed thugs comes through?''

''All right; I'll *see* about it.'' He began thinking out loud: he didn't want to block all news from Earth, so periodically the Gate would need to be reopened. But without guns, how do you put the stopper to an emerging goon squad? Post someone as guard at either side, ready to cut loose with . . . with what?

''How about liquid air?'' Leopold suggested. ''That should stop somebody. Bring out a couple of the extended-outing size suit tanks, fitted with Venturi nozzels. Put 'em back in chill between times.'' Her brows raised. ''You like it?''

He gave one grunting chuckle. ''Just so the guard folks remember to wear their insulating gloves.''

XVII

"Yain's star," said Kayo, "lies roughly three-point-seven light-years from the Triad system, about ninety degrees from our own line of approach. So from here, travel time's the same."

"If we sent a ship right now," Jocelyn Waymire said, "it might arrive in time to see the comet swarm's effect at its worst, before the dust settled. Assuming we had a ship ready, which we don't."

"We have one," said Bill Flynn. "*Roamer*. Our problem is, the two years before they could get the word. When that time comes, who's in charge and will he obey orders?"

"Not to mention," Kayo put in, "what does the ship do when it gets there?"

Waymire tapped fingers against her coffee cup. "I'll staff that problem. My own aides are generally good at coming up with suggestions, and if that fails I'm sure that with input from a panel of expert consultants we can frame an agenda that will . . ."

Kayo quit listening. With the situation already four years beyond what was known in this room, obviously a few expert studies were just what the doctor ordered. To put off the evil day of admitting there *was* no solution.

A beep at Sam's remote operating panel interrupted. "Uh-oh—offship message, Simone." He brought the circuit up on speaker. "Gowdy here," but someone kept talking. So the call was either from Magh or the macroGate; he had to allow for signal lag.

A little finer tuning brought Maril Jencik's voice in recognizable and clear. Magh, then. After a moment, she paused. "Yes, captain. To repeat, the Deployment Vehicle is now up and operational. Libby Verdoorn's had ship training, you know; she switched to colony work later. Since Jules got appointed over her head and bumped her out of HQ, she's been spelling me here at the comm tent."

So Maril hadn't moved into Administrator's quarters with Jules? Do tell . . . He waited, and Jencik continued: "Anyway, she ran instrument tests and checked the drive on Virtual Thrust, and says it's all on the money. Now she has a question for you."

"Go ahead." What were their relative positions? He began counting seconds.

A little mumbling in the background, then Verdoorn came in. On a fourteen count: Eamn and Magh were roughly in quadrature. She said, "I had some DV work, Sam, several years ago. I'd be a little rusty now, but I can guarantee to lift or land the Vehicle safely, and get it where it's supposed to go. Not so quickly or efficiently as SuZanne, probably. Or poor young Quillan. But I'm here and they're not. You might have to talk me in for the docking, but if you want the Vehicle out there, I can bring it."

"Docking wouldn't be necessary; we'd use mooring lines at the stern cargo hatch, and run a transfer tube." But his mind was on larger issues.

At a purely gut level, Gowdy trusted Libby Verdoorn. If she said she could do it, she could. So his answer was not in doubt.

Except, this plan had to be waterproof the first time.

"Are you two alone there?" he asked. And waited for her reply.

"Yes, we are. Why?"

He cleared his throat. "I'd need the Vehicle here before Aroka knows you're coming. Never mind why, just now; it's too long a story. But when you call in, you can't know if this end's free of eavesdropping. So unless I—or Simone, or someone else you know speaks for me—clear you to speak openly, never mention you're even on the DV, let alone where it is."

The pause gave him time for qualms, before Verdoorn said, "All right; I have that. What else?"

"Dammit, I forgot. Too intent on my own problems. But you can't possibly do this, all by yourself."

The next voice was Maril Jencik's. "She won't be. I'm going, too; for that time and distance we can alternate watches one-and-one." Her voice sharpened. "And we'll see how Jules likes managing his own comm for a change!"

Too savvy to comment on domestic friction, Gowdy said, "Welcome aboard. Now then; how soon would you plan to lift?"

In time Libby answered. "Any favorable vee-differential window, beginning with one late tonight—it's about midafternoon here now. So it depends on whether you need me to bring along anything special that's not already on board."

"Tonight sounds fine. Except for maybe one thing: if I start moving *Roamer* toward Magh—gently again, so's we don't have to stop the rotating belt and lock it in place—is your visual and radar navigation good enough to meet us somewhere along the way and match vee okay? Or would you feel safer waiting until we're in position at that end?"

Her silence went longer than signal lag. "Sorry. Uh, I can match you en route all right. But I was wondering—I expect our watch officers can stifle the usual sensor indications, but could my ranging radar set off any bells and nail the DV's approach?"

The hell of it was, Gowdy had no idea. He said so, then added, "The way you beat that is, be all set up to get your reading, and then fire only short bursts. Giving nobody time to get a fix on you."

Eventually, "Sure; I can do that. Anything more?"

Pause. "No, I guess that's about all. Oops, wait a minute; is the Yainan ship still at L-two?"

"No; it left for Yamar. And I gather the Yainans won't talk to us again until we put T'phee on the comm."

Well, who could blame them? "Okay; thanks, Libby. And one more thing: you two are the best news I've had in a long time."

In comparative regard to those smaller skyships of prior experience, Irtuk-saa granted this yumin vessel due awe. Yet here she acclimed with ease unachievable when first taken from Magh. That ordeal struck heavily to her mindview; all since came more easily. As, or so it appeared, to Bretl from Shtai the Forerunner and to T'phee the Yainan.

Scayna, though, would seem to fare less well. And why so, when earlier in Gowdy's bold improvisation of a ship the bearer had displayed admirable balance? Whatever the cause, to Irtuk's perceiving the Eamnet at present held only outward calm, revealing inner stressings by occasional random tics and lapses of heeding.

Eamnet or no, her distress called to Irtuk. It was not only Scayna's nurturing aid at Irtuk's time of bearing; over and beyond those ritual doings, somehow a feel of kinship had eventuated. In the room's corner, away from the speakings of the yumin group, Irtuk moved to Scayna's side.

"Have you found their foods satisfactory? By my samplings it appears the yumin bearer Vinler shows reliability in her discriminations. In particular I find the soft paste, amply provided in yon larger bowl, to be well flavored."

Scayna gripped Irtuk's forelimb. "Of such matters I have no unease, only of a promise I deemed made to me by Gowdy but no longer mentioned. On this huge ship, Irtuk, where do they destine us? And what of the discord between Gowdy who brought us here and those who dispute his legitimacy of primature?"

"That is the contested issue? To me the rancor has seemed obvious but its source a mystery."

"Vinler also accommodates well in matters of information. Though lacking knowledge of the basis for this conflict, she gave me comprehension of its subject. Aroka claims Gowdy's ship."

Irtuk touched the digits held against her forelimb. "Gowdy possesses much goodwill, and steadfastness toward all who follow him. In Aroka I sense little of either quality."

Scayna's head bobbed slightly. "We are agreed. If occasion requires, we must act to Gowdy's advantage."

"Might Bretl be persuaded to the same end?"

"Let us essay that persuasion." Together, the two moved toward the exile.

Accepting his own inadvertent causation of V'naet's urgent distress, Nsil held patience until the Yainan's plight came to solution. But subsequent to the creature's vanishment into a portal, these Erdthans yet maintained heeding on other concerns with no apparent thought to those of Nsil—or of Eamn.

Even with the knowing, belatedly given him by Kaow, of the Chormyears lost to him by his unadvised venture through the great portal, Nsil held to purpose. If the power of Erdth could not be swayed to Eamn's cause, neither must it accrue to Magh's.

It was not that the Eamnets, nor Duant the Maghren who was become to Nsil more colleague than erstwhile captive, fell victim to neglect. Erdthans in plenty tended their usual needs, came here to study them both directly and by means of unfamiliar devices, and struggled to acquire a rudiment of Eamnet speaking.

But from none of these proceedings derived converse of true meaning. That goal of Nsil's required Erdthans of decision-determinant status, and at now he had observed only two such: the bearer Wamir and seeder Flin, who with Kaow largely occupied their time elsewhere than in Nsil's presence.

Was it for this stagnation that Nsil had taken ship Three far beyond its designed capabilities of distance, then through the great Erdthan portal to a place not yet reached by the radiance Jemra shed upon the season of Nsil's own bearing?

Brooding thusly in his assigned resting space, its door left less than fully closed now that he and Tirys had completed intimacy and the adaptive departed to pursue other pastimes, Nsil roused as Kaow rapped curled forelimb digits beside that door.

At his gesture she entered. "Kaow. Be welcome here."

She nodded. "And is the day well with you, Nsil?"

"Idle without redress, I suffer unrest. Kaow, I inquire: now after great awaitment will Erdthans of primacy hear the plea of Eamn?"

"Nsil, I regret the delays. Yes; I come to escort you to a place of speakings. Wamir and Flin will accompany. Though not in full presence, others will commune through viewscreens."

Kaow appeared uncertain as to Nsil's comprehension; offering assurance, he said, "We have all observed the screens, though it seemed that those appearing had no cognizance of ourselves."

"At the assemblage we go to join, that lack is remedied."

It developed that Tasr and Duant became included in the entourage led by Kaow to a seating area faced by numerous viewing screens. Centered nearest these stood Erdthmade versions of Eamnet reclining pieces; at Kaow's bidding, Nsil and Tasr and Duant took position on three of those.

One by one the screens lit from dullness to portray Erdthans all looking out toward this place.

Kaow spoke. "Nsil, now you tell of Eamn's need and hope. Speak without hurry—and when I motion, halt while I repeat your speaking to all, in our own tongue."

Thereupon Nsil, with studied care selecting what to expound from what would not avail, related in utmost brief the grim olden happening, and then Eamn's alarm that again disaster might come. "We had in our ships only observed, with neither move nor intent to ground on Magh. There had been strange ships—from Diell the Companion, we now know—venturing in similar, coming near both Magh and ourselves. Then ensued arrival of your yumin ship, of vaster force than any known, taking station near Magh our enemy, even sending a smaller craft to its very surface."

At Kaow's nod he waited while she spoke in Erdthan; on two screens yumins lifted forelimbs and spoke, but Kaow motioned waiting. And then for Nsil to continue.

Now no need for earlier caution; from this juncture, surely all should understand! ". . . first only to reconnoiter on Magh, to obtain proof of aggressive intent. Then the opportunity, to gather and transport to Eamn for study and acquaintance . . ." Not only Maghrens but also two from Companion Star and two from this Erdth so far distant from Jemra as to be unimagined.

As Kaow transposed speech, screen communants gestured; she twisted her head in reciprocal rotation. "Speak more, Nsil."

On the skyship and on Eamn, Nsil now told, he had grown to know Kaow; entrustment grew. But then had come Gowdy who might with apparent cause feel need of violent retaliation. And having been in converse only with Maghrens, the yumin would be disposed toward the falsities embodied in Maghren views.

Thus had it come about that Nsil brought in his ship a number of his Eamnet supporters, and Duant the seeder from

Magh, and Kaow who now in friendship rendered his speaking into Erdthan understanding, through the great portal and here to Erdth.

Nsil waited. At length, after much speech between herself and several on viewscreens, Kaow spoke to him.

"All appreciate your narration. And in consideration of your state of knowledge before coming here, no offense is felt at the more assertive actions you have taken."

Of a briefness only, her lower mouth membrane hid between gapless teeth. "One inquiry persists. It is that now, with regard to your knowing of the Chormyears that pass outside our portals the while we enter and emerge the same moment, what action on Eamn's behalf would you have of these who hear?"

"Only to refrain from common cause with Magh against us."

"But, Nsil—Wamir and Flin have given that pledge!"

Nsil's head bobbed. "Yet is it they who make ultimate decision? Only from those who do may I derive assurance that my world lies safe from devastation."

Toward the viewscreens Kaow waved a pointing digit. "These persons hold power to so assure." Quickly she spoke in Erdthan; one by one the images responded, and she turned again to Nsil.

"It is done."

So simply, and dealing only with depictions on viewscreens? Yet Kaow of all Erdthans would not mislead him. "To each of these," spoke Nsil, "convey the gratitude of Eamn."

And now he must petition for return. To face Scayna, left abandoned for near onto three Chormcycles.

He had not so intended, but she could not know. And after so long a wait, in what manner would she greet him?

Turning back to Simone, Gowdy said, "Well, that's a start." He would have said more, but the intercom sounded. "Skeeter Cole calling—uh, command quarters."

"Gowdy. And Simone's here."

In re Sydnie the exec had no "need to know," so she didn't. Cole spoke in cryptic terms; when he signed off, Sam said to her, "You want to head back and keep an eye on things for me? I have a couple more calls to make."

When she had left he called hold Two. "Gowdy here. Alone." No answer, so he began the same cautionary instructions he'd given Libby Verdoorn.

Sydnie's voice cut in. "I'm here. Just came in, saw the incoming light blink."

"In from where?"

"The north pole and I'm Santa Claus. Look, Sam; just because you got rid of some guns, don't let your guard down. The woman with the sandpaper haircut . . ."

"Estilete." And how did Sydnie know about the guns?

"Stiletto." Her brief harsh laugh startled him. "La Sombria, maybe? It fits the pattern; she'll have a knife."

"She did. I took it." Well, in a way . . .

Given pause for once, after a moment Sydnie answered, "There'll be other weapons."

"I suppose there will. Sydnie, what's on your mind?"

"Getting the Spider Prince off this ship. Dead or alive."

"Preferably alive." And to forestall any protest he added, "Less paperwork that way."

"Dead's safer; I don't mind paperwork."

Since when? Oh well . . . "Are you planning anything?"

"There aren't many options. Except . . . Sam, if something pops down into control through a ceiling hatch, it's me. So if you're there and not in position to help, just stay back. Okay?"

Not okay. "I'd have to clue all our own folks, and several don't even know you're here." Leaks happen, and ". . . how many do you think could keep from sneaking a look up every so often, just out of nervousness and not meaning to?"

Reluctantly, "Oh. Well then; any suggestions?"

"Not what you want, not just now. But hey, up forward in the DV well, could you unship the hose and refuel the Doodlebug? Just in case we need it? The fittings will match."

Not sounding happy, Lightner agreed to give it a try. With a nagging unease, Gowdy wondered what needed doing next.

Scayna. He'd promised her she could rejoin Nsil, but he couldn't just Gate her to a bunch of unprepared humans and no way to communicate. Send a message first?

Better idea. He rummaged out a small audiocap set, inserted a fresh cap unit, and began speaking. When after several tries and a few revisions he felt he had it right, he reset it to the start and stuffed the unit into a pocket. As he left for the lounge he felt a little better, but not much.

There were just too damn many loose ends here, and on most he had no grasp at all. Tying this one up would help some.

Staunchly though T'phee resists lonelorn decline, still the malady encroaches. In present er partakes nutriment both fluid and solid, exchanges speech with Bretl and with Vinler, but aims concern toward framing converse with Gowdy.

On watch at the gathering room's entrance for that one's return, T'phee at first sighting ventures to es adjacency and opens discourse. "You have made a speaking that I may return to Yamar. In reiterancy, such return lies primely essential to my continuance. To what further duration must I await it?"

After holding silence, Gowdy grants response. "Fact exists, T'phee, that speech with Magh toward that aim occurred not long past. Our smaller ship, with ability to reach Yamar, has been made whole and comes to meet with ourselves. At that juncture, your need stands early among those to be assuaged."

"T'phee of Yamar acknowledges debt." The yumin will not understand the movements conveying T'phee's greatestly profound thankment; nonetheless er performs them.

Entering the lounge again, Gowdy saw Aroka apparently laying down the law to Silva and Atwell. Beringer and Estilete weren't present; well, presumably the commodore's people didn't spend *all* their time comforting themselves with snacks and chat.

Avoiding Aroka's stare, Sam walked over to Simone. "Anything new?"

"Milo and Neville are constipating the Tush. Using some half-empty crates, from ship's supplies down the corridor. Milo says they'll fit just fine."

"What's Aroka say? Or does he know yet?"

"A little collusion helps. SuZanne took Mose a snack on watch and came back with a message printout." She winked. "Seems some armed terrorists broke into Glen Springs and

Gated off Earth. The warning is that we should be on guard here in case we're the next target."

Sam grinned. "Which explains our liquid air deterrent."

Headshake. "Milo says that option's just too much work—having to lug it in and out of storage every time. But we have some old compressed-CO_2 fire extinguishers, the king-size model, up in the equipment rack area; they're still the simplest way to handle electrical fires. So he brought down a couple. And guarantees they'll do the trick."

"I'll take his word for it." Across the room he saw Irtuk and Scayna and Bretl talking together. "You want to come with me a few minutes? I need to keep a promise."

Approaching the three bearers he felt like a quarterback among nose tackles, though young Tuik was about four times too big to be the football. "Scayna? Do you wish to join Nsil now?"

All three spoke at once; Gowdy said, "Lacking requisite footwear it is best that Irtuk and Bretl speak farewells here. Simone and I will aid Scayna to the portal."

It wasn't easy, but shortly they stood before Earthmouth, Scayna burdened with her few belongings and holding uncomfortably tight to Gowdy's shoulder.

He took out the audio set and punched Play, letting his recorded voice sound for half a minute or so before stopping and resetting. "On Earth, Scayna, Kayo is the only human who speaks your tongue. I give you this device which carries my voice explaining who you are and asking that you be taken to the company of Kayo and Nsil. Here is how you use it. . . ."

When she had the procedure well in hand, he gripped her forelimb. "Scayna, I wish you well on Earth and in returning. Inform Nsil that when we next see one another it shall be in all friendship. Now here, let me help you. . . ."

When she was roughly centered on the grid, holding fast to handstraps and looking very tense, Simone activated the Gate. As usual, the cessation of color flare revealed an empty Mouth.

Nobody had explained to Sydnie how the damn fitting worked, but once she figured it out the refueling began without a hitch. Sam's sardine can lacked indicators to tell her when to stop, so she stayed by the valve and watched for the hose to buck or stiffen.

Lulled by boredom, she daydreamed. Suddenly in peripheral vision a moving figure impinged; she turned to see the woman Estilete, lips pursed, mincing carefully along one of the broad Velcro strips leading from the airlock hatch.

Before Sydnie could say anything the woman's gaze flashed up at her. The gesture that followed could easily have held a blade, but only a finger pointed. "You are who? Not listed. Not special mentioned; Aroka has not said."

Trying to be inconspicuous about it, Sydnie got herself turned from sideways to the makings of a good square push-off. "Well, he wouldn't, would he? You know how he is."

"What I know is, you spy. To take the Web from Jorge."

"Hey, no such thing, La Sombria." The name guess worked; Sydnie used the woman's involuntary pause to get her feet braced. "*I* don't want the damn thing."

Words weren't going to do it; almost too fast for seeing, a hand darted and a thin dagger emerged. First crouching, Estilete uncoiled into a leap, blade first.

You can't just sit there; instinct took Sydnie, adrenalized to the toenails, straight at her attacker.

Slowly turned the wheel of time as the blade *came* but her hand chopped across behind its thrust putting Estilete spread-eagled into rotation one way and Sydnie the other with her forearm spitting beads of blood from the incredible twisting flick of Estilete's knife hand. But Sydnie knew zero gee and moments of inertia so she pulled her arms in and legs together spinning faster and coming to face the back of Estilete's head and got a good grip on it with one hand, a fulcrum from which to deliver the granddaddy of all rabbit punches to daze the woman until the right moment of spin for Sydnie to push off to the airlock hatch and pull herself through and close it and dog it.

Then she hit the button and listened to the high whine as the pump drew air from the DV well. Once her racing heart and gasping breath flushed most of the panic juice from her bloodstream, she began to slow toward normal. When her hands steadied a little better, she managed to fold and tie a hand cloth around the forearm wound. It wasn't good first aid but it stopped the emission of more blood globules; there were too many floating around already and no way to clear them out. How long would they take to dry by evaporation? She didn't know. . . .

She waited five minutes before repressurizing and going back inside, but got the fuel line shut off before the bucking hose burst loose from the 'bug's filler vent. And before tackling anything else, carefully put the hose back in storage position.

Then she had to look at what she'd done. Death by anoxia made Estilete a mottle-faced gargoyle. Throwing up wasn't going to help, either. Knowing how the Spider Prince's aides had dealt with fresh corpses without messing up their car seats, Sydnie removed the dead woman's jumpsuit and emptied its pockets into her own beltbag; refolded and properly applied, the suit made a reasonably adequate outside diaper.

Almost ready to leave, Sydnie had another thought. She had to circle the Doodlebug to locate the floating knife, slim-bladed with a smooth black gemstone hilt. As she'd guessed, it was balanced for throwing. Estilete wore the sheath under her blouse, but Sydnie managed to undo the harness and bring the assembly out without actually removing the garment. Knife and sheath reunited, for the present she tucked the lot into a side pocket.

Estilete had carried some handy items: twine bound her wrists together and her ankles, so extremities wouldn't flop around loose. A shot-loaded cosh was there; no gun, though. Miscellaneous tools, nothing Sydnie needed at the moment.

And exactly what she did need: a hefty bar with chocolate-coated nuts around a crunchy filling. Right there in the DV well, one hand gripping a stanchion beside her unseeing victim, Sydnie corrected her low blood sugar.

The charge helped her thinking. Gauging her jump carefully she caught the 'bug's hatch lever, got braced, and pulled to open. If Estilete could have managed this in time . . . ! But she hadn't; maybe the idea didn't come to mind. Sydnie expropriated a blanket, made exit leaving the hatch ajar, and returned to wrap the dead woman well, using more twine to tie up the package. Now if someone saw her, the nature of her burden wouldn't be quite so immediately apparent.

Reentering the ship she dutifully secured both airlock hatches and headed aft, moving cautiously because zero gee has no respect for mass or inertia. As she progressed, thought kept rerunning the encounter, coming always to the same conclusion: in almost any other circumstance it would be Sydnie dead now. If La Sombria had any decent zero-gee training, if she'd managed to get hands on Sydnie, if she'd stayed with Velcro rather than jumping: given any one of these alternatives, her size and weight and freshly trained physical condition would have prevailed.

Two things came to Sydnie's mind: overconfidence never pays, and maybe her luck wasn't all bad, at that.

All the way back through the largely open areas and then the main sternward tunnel of this sector, her nape prickled against the threat of being seen; when she reached the stern cargo airlock hatch she jerked the handle awkwardly, and once inside, slammed it locked.

The suits, discarded when they had all entered the ship, lay undisturbed; hers would still have one air tank untapped and another only about half-used. Once she had it on and sealed she went to the small auxiliary personnel lock, towed Estilete in with her, and cycled the chamber to vacuum.

She had no intention of going outship; instead she doubled up against the inside hatch with her feet planted at the middle of her bundle as she steadied it by cords at each end, and with both legs gave a mighty propelling kick.

One or the other end of Estilete bumped the right side of the hatch opening on the way through; deflected in passing, the bundle spun to that side and out of view.

Close hatch, let in air, return to main chamber, unsuit, exit cargo airlock, go to hold Two. At Sam's quarters no one answered the intercom.

Sydnie really didn't feel up to leaving a message.

Kayo wasn't in the Habgate building at the time, but she saw the monitor video later, and in a way it was pretty funny. Not, though, to the horrified technicians who saw the Tush from *Roamer* flare and fade, leaving a great bulky creature half-crouched and lurching as if—they probably thought—to charge and rend.

The lurch, of course, would be the unexpected change from zero gee. But you couldn't expect groundsiders to know that.

The young fellow certainly squealed a lot. The older

woman, probably just as scared but maybe not, stood and tried to say something, but the looming apparition held up an incongruously small object and carefully did something to its controls.

It spoke. "This is Captain Samuel Hall Gowdy of *Roamer.* Let me introduce Scayna, a bearer from the world Eamn. Scayna doesn't know our language, and nobody at your end speaks hers except Katharine Olivia Marlin. She's my crew member who Gated through to you in a rocket-powered Eamnet ship, directed by the seeder Nsil. Scayna, you should know, is the adult bearer of Nsil's householding; her reasons for Gating to Glen Springs are largely personal. But not entirely; besides being reunited with Nsil she also wishes to help him establish friendly relations there. Her mission has my approval and best wishes, and any cooperation you can give her will have my deepest appreciation."

His tone changed. "Once the greetings are over with, get this to Senator Waymire. Some official stuff follows." And peremptorily, "Machine *off*!"

Kayo turned hers off, too. As the screen blanked, suddenly she was close to crying. She *missed* Sam Gowdy, and the ship, and everybody; even if she Gated back there right now she'd have been out of their lives for over four years.

On the other hand, things weren't exactly boring right here. By the time she'd been called in, not having the faintest idea what the flap was about, everyone was off the panic button; meanwhile, all the action had moved to the quarters of Nsil and his crew. From the door she saw Eamnets making much of someone hidden in their midst—as humans stood back, smiling nervously but obviously at a loss. A shift of movement cleared her line of sight; with a shock, Kayo recognized the central figure: Scayna.

How in the worlds . . .

As she entered, Nsil turned to meet her. "Kaow! Great fortune, out of all anticipation, is here occurred."

"So I observe. May I now have speech with Scayna?"

Then she'd listened to the bearer's-eye view of doings between human factions back in the Triad system. Much of Scayna's telling made no particular sense in Kayo's frame of reference; maybe it would mesh better when she knew more.

Her token stay at the party sufficed to reassure Nsil and Scayna of her aid and support; then she went hotfoot to Waymire's office-in-residence and viewed Scayna's advent and Sam's intro. Moments later, trying to wipe her eyes so no one would notice, she said, "The official stuff Sam mentioned. Can I hear that too, or is it out of my clearance range?"

Bill Flynn's laugh could blast you, but this time it came light and quiet. "Insiders don't need clearance; outsiders can't get it. The situation defines the labels. Sit down and see if you can shed any light."

All right; she listened. Aroka ordering Nsil's ship destroyed; well, these people already knew about that. And arming the Maghrens and, ". . . what he's trying to do," Sam went on, "is set up a phony conflict, suppress it, then use that as an excuse to make himself a little tin Napoleon over this whole system. And he sees the natives as the White Man's Burden."

The voice paused. "I'm telling you this now because I am damn well going to resist it all the way, and I want the facts on the record, down the line in case I live that long."

Now the tone changed. "This next is going to sound totally henshit, but I've been given to believe that Commodore Aroka's background, going back say ten–fifteen years, won't stand up under a good investigation. Extensive involvement in major crime is the way I heard it. You realize that right or wrong the truth of this won't do me one bit of good in dealing with what he's doing here; basically it's for the record, win or lose."

Kayo thought Sam had finished, but again the silence broke. "One more thing. If it turns out this guy is the copperhead I think he is, don't forget to go after the sonofabitch who turned him loose on us."

When only the subliminal hiss of background noise could be heard, Flynn pushed the button. "Gowdy hasn't changed much, since the *Tarpon* incident."

"How's that?" Oblique references always irked Kayo.

"If he thinks he's right, stay clear of his flight plan."

As Gowdy and Simone came past control, heading for the transfer ring ramp, SuZanne Craig called out. "Message from the macroGate." Sam turned and led the way in.

Sitting alongside Craig, Case Beringer gave a barely civil nod. "At ease," said Gowdy, then to SuZanne, "Printout?"

"No. I took it verbally. Before my assistant, here, arrived."

Her sidewise glance at Beringer clued Sam; he told the man, "Go have lunch."

"The commodore assigned me here."

"Go have lunch anyway." With a scowl, Aroka's man left; Gowdy nodded to Craig. "Something touchy?"

"Twelve of Aroka's people outGated there. All armed, of course. One of them, a man by the name of Driscoll, has taken command of the Gate away from Pia Velucci; he and two bodyguards are staying there. The other nine, headed by a Commander Lioso who sounds like the Mummy's Curse with power steering, intend to come here in that mining ship, *Golconda.* Whether they've left yet wasn't quite clear."

Bloody hell. "Where's my brains? Should've warned Pia to plug the personnel Tush there, too." Too late now . . .

She grinned. "You have them worried, anyway. It's when our regular Mouth wouldn't swallow, that they rerouted to the macro."

"Big win, yeah." Though come to think of it, having the new batch of goons here later did beat having them here now. "All right, nothing we can do about that part—and now I guess we know why Aroka's been playing possum. Just waiting for reinforcements he knew were on the way."

He shrugged. "Mistakes happen. Anyway, here's what comes next. Call Mose to figure optimum time to leave here, not sooner than maybe sixteen hours from now and at quarter gee, for least delta vee to resume lead Trojan at Magh."

What with relative positions of the two worlds plus *Roamer*'s own orbit, the problem could get furry. "Tell him I'll run one, too, and we can check each other. Then on all-ship here, advise everyone to start buttoning up again for low thrust, like on the macroGate trip. The belt bearings handled it okay then, so we'll stay with that same level."

Craig nodded. "I've got those. Any more?"

"Well, in spare moments you might keep an eye out for that prospector, keep tabs on how quick it could get to be a nuisance." And pass the word—but he didn't need to say that.

He and Simone went on their way. At the transfer ring

doors they met Beringer emerging. "The commodore wasn't pleased."

"If he wants me to know that, he'll tell me."

Inside, as the ring accelerated, Leopold said, "You make a point of not giving that man an inch. Any particular reason?"

"If I can keep his little mind busy trying to buy that inch, it's not so apt to get into other mischief."

She laughed, then said, "Is that an analytical judgment?"

"No. Just a hunch."

The doors opened; they walked out onto the belt and along the corridor. As they neared the lounge Gowdy said, "What the hell, let's mingle." And hadn't he earned a little bourbon?

At first glimpse the place seemed empty, but it wasn't. In one corner sat Skeeter Cole, determinedly ignoring Rocco Silva and Vivian Atwell who at the room's far side were doing their best to return the compliment. So "Well! How's everybody doing?" said the suddenly jovial Captain Gowdy. "Cheer up; it can't be that bad. Let's all have a drink."

Atwell's eyes popped wide. Silva, all suspicion now, yanked her upright by one thin arm as he stood, then moved them both to the door and out. "And a good day to you, too," Sam murmured.

He left Simone's puzzled stare unanswered until Cole sauntered over and said, "Now what was that in aid of?"

"It worked, didn't it? Come on; let's sit down. We need to talk.

"And I meant the part about the drink."

XVIII

When it dawned on Kayo that there wasn't much she could do here right now except sit around holding people's hands, another thought surfaced. All this time she'd been back and hadn't even *asked* about Dan Quillan: was he alive or dead, healed or maimed? Or with that head wound, maybe the question was: animal, vegetable, or mineral?

She called the on-base medical facility. No, Mr. Quillan had been discharged some time ago and posted home for outpatient therapy. Persisting, she got the where of it, called the transport office, and started packing. What little there was . . .

A sound behind her made her turn to see Nsil standing, in the hunched way of his species, looking at her. "Kaow? Do you depart this place?"

"Only for a time. There is one I must see; on our greater ship we shared living area and intimacy. And in the wrecking of Gowdy's smaller vessel he incurred grave injury."

Instantly she regretted her last comment; even across the barrier of species she recognized Nsil's remorse. Too late now, but she tried anyway. "You could not predict, Nsil."

"It was only the mechanism we sought to disable, not . . ."

"I am well aware." She patted the hunched, sloping shoulder. "Plague yourself not; I will relate to him your wish that he regain all soundness."

But when she finally came to meet with Quillan, after suffering three tranportation modes of which only the initial bullet train could make any real claim to humanitarian considerations, Nsil took a backseat in her thinking.

Small towns still had fenced front yards with lawn chairs under shade trees, and in one of those sat Dan, bathrobe and slippers and tall ice-tinkling glass which if it held booze she hoped it was okay with his doctor.

He was reading, looking intent, though the apparent frown came mostly from the livid slanting scar at the right of his forehead. Walking closer, she set down her bag. "Hi there, sailor. Buy me a drink?"

Before Gowdy had even sketched in the situation background, the little conference was interrupted. "There you are." Aroka's limp varied; now, apparently, he wasn't tired in the least.

"That I am. Something, commodore?"

"Information, captain." He sat. "The aliens aboard: Maghrens and Eamnets and so forth. Which are which?"

They were all getting along now, so what difference did it make? Nonetheless, "No Eamnets; Scayna wanted to join Nsil at Earth so I Gated her." Firsthand now, Gowdy saw Aroka suppress anger before giving a grudging nod of acceptance. "Irtuk-saa is high among the bearers' council on Magh, and—"

"That's the one with the pup?"

What the hell; Sam nodded. "Bretl and T'phee, now . . ."

Learning how those two came to be on Yamar in the first place, Aroka's obvious disdain for nonhumans cracked a little. "Traction Drive, you say? That furry dwarf giraffe?"

"But no Habgate refueling; they're forty years en route."

Aroka shrugged. "Not a factor, then. Gowdy, you should have asked before disposing of the Eamnet. But the Maghren will do. Her ordeal on Eamn, the mistreatment and so on. After all, it's the Maghrens who need to be prodded, and with a few other provocations we should have a disturbance worth suppressing. And since I have no pipeline into Eamn . . ."

Gowdy stared. "You're asking me to help you start a war?"

Aroka's face went stony. "I seem to have misjudged you. My intent was to make you somewhat of a partner in policy matters."

Right. And then, no doubt, Queen of the May.

"Nonetheless, as an employee you will *follow* policy. Is that understood?"

"Your meaning is clear." A true statement, that.

Either Aroka got the point or he didn't; in any case his expression eased. "Anything else, then?" Gowdy asked.

"The whereabouts of Estilete, my personal assistant. She is past due reporting to me."

Trying to project a facade of civility, Sam thought back. "Now that you mention it . . . After we all came in here the first time, I had business and left for a while. When I got back she was gone—and I haven't seen her since." Which was strange, at that; it had been quite some time now.

The strangely lidded eyes swiveled to Skeeter, then to Simone. "And you?"

"Not me." "I'm afraid not."

"I have had contact since then," said Aroka, "but not for a considerable period. She was tasked to a certain matter more central in this ship; apparently she has not returned." The man's stare probed each of the three in turn. "Never mind; when time allows, I will attend to the dereliction myself." Rising, he stalked away and out.

Sam stood. "Excuse me, folks; I need to make a phone call."

Skeeter and Simone stared, but even if he'd had the time to explain, Gowdy wasn't sure how to go about it.

At least a day since she'd spaced Aroka's latest blade artiste and still no sign that anybody noticed. First, unable to reach Sam, she'd left the cautious message, "This is Santa Claus; call back," giving no clue to any chance snooper. But when he did call, he'd made no mention of Estilete one way or the other—and somehow she didn't feel like opening the subject herself.

Ranging the generally deserted inship corridors, wriggling inside the bulkhead for another frustrating look down into control, brooding and planning in her improvised quarters, staying out of sight when Jethro Blaine came through the inner level corridor on his inspection tour following drive room watch, Sydnie worked up a fine head of nerves and irritation.

Sometimes she lay low when it wasn't necessary; she'd lose track of whose shift it was and find she'd hidden from Alix Dorais or Charlotte Wang who already knew she was aboard. She wasn't supposed to talk to them anyway; that was agreed, so as not to load them with anything more to keep shut about. It made sense, but sitting on the mess all by herself was no fun either.

Too restless to stay still, for want of anything better she decided to spy on control again. Entry to the bulkhead and maneuvering inside it had become routine to her. A quick peek below showed Aroka standing over SuZanne Craig, who had the watch, with the orange-haired floozie seated next to her. Sydnie tilted the side vent screen back for a better view.

A momentary pressure spike in ventilation rattled the loosened panel, but she had it steadied before Aroka jerked his head up for a sharp glance. So he couldn't have seen anything; it was only the sound that caught his attention.

But hold on! Now he pulled Craig out of her seat, leaned over, and spoke rapid-fire into the intercom. Turning, he motioned the mophead to the vacated position, then moved catlike to the door and out.

Maybe this was the wrong place to be. Rapidly, more than once banging knee or elbow, Sydnie crawled her way out. By habit she began replacing the hatch, then stopped. If Aroka knew enough to come here, why not let the sonofabitch wonder if she were still inside? His uncertainty might just give her an edge.

In a hurry, she went to gather other items she might need. When she checked at hold Two she heard Gowdy's message. Stretching caution, Sydnie left one of her own. "She tried to kill me, but it backfired." To his warning about Aroka she said only, "He may be heading this way, at that." Whatever Sam did was up to him.

Grudgingly she opted for the open hatch as her best bait.

Now Dan Quillan's frown was real, a grimace of puzzlement. Then it cleared. His eyes went wide, and he smiled. "Kayo. Kayo Marlin. Though something's different . . ."

Right. The hair growing out straggly-ended and needing a trim; she never seemed to find time for it.

But he was past that discrepancy. "Yes. I remember now; I wanted—" Predictably his cheeks began to redden. "On the ship I hoped we'd pair."

Before she could frame an answer he said, "I'm getting it all back, you know." Flexing the fingers of both hands, he bent and straightened his arms. "The control, see? And reflexes. Strength is going to take longer, of course. But I've walked, some. They said I couldn't, so soon, but I have."

"You don't remember . . ."

"Acey. I was looking forward to seeing that world, taking the Vehicle down and landing. They say I did, but you can't prove it by me. And it was the Vehicle falling over that hurt me and—and *Feodor*, that's it! The Vehicle, they said. So I must have really screwed up the landing."

"No. You landed just fine." Coming back from *Roamer*, from the macroGate assembly point, but no point in confusing him. "Didn't Feodor tell you?"

"They moved him, someplace else. Before I came back enough to make sense. He sat and talked to me first, but nothing registered. Not to remember, anyway."

Now the frown again, but less intense. "But you're here, you're home. Has it been that long? Your contract's finished? I didn't think it's been that long."

"It hasn't. Some stuff happened; quite a lot, in fact. I'll tell you about it later." Kayo paused. "The main thing, though: you're getting better now?"

"Oh sure. But . . ." Even redder, his cheeks went. "I really did hope we'd pair up."

"Dan . . ." Kayo stopped. She hadn't intended—what was she getting herself into, here? She said it anyway. "We did, Dan."

Reaching, she squeezed his hand. "We are."

Calling from quarters, to check on his earlier warning that Aroka might venture inship, Gowdy got a real shock. Sydnie had *killed* the Spider Prince's knifelady?

Sam no longer doubted Lightner's story. Not the part about Aroka, anyway; her own past might well be something else again and likely was.

It didn't matter; like it or not they were on the same side here. All right; what first? He called control. Something haywire there: delay before SuZanne Craig came on, and someone mumbling in the background. He said, "Who's there with you?"

More mumbles, before she said, "Vivian Atwell."

"Nobody else?" She said no. "Has Commodore Aroka

been through there recently? And did he say where he was going?''

This time he broke into the *sotto voce* coaching. ''Dammit Atwell, shut up and let her answer.'' No sooner said than regretted; remembering how SuZanne had handled the skinny woman in Silva's quarters, he realized there must be a weapon involved. Too late to back up, though. ''SuZanne?''

''About ten minutes ago. To talk with the mining ship—all in code words, though. And no, he didn't say.''

Which might even be true. ''Okay. Thanks. Gowdy out.''

What next? Take the census—well, humans, anyway. Calls to the galley, lounge, drive room and various quarters accounted for all his own people, some of whom weren't happy about being wakened. Nor was Case Beringer.

Not accounted for: Aroka and Rocco Silva.

Two on one made bad odds; Gowdy could even matters up. He debated taking more help along, decided not to. Stuffing a few selected objects into belt clips he prepared to head inship.

So long had Scayna been gone from Eamn that the source of her undue fatigue did not immediately become apparent. Upon mention, however, Nsil explained the greater weight experienced on Erdth. ''And here we breathe a lighter, thinner gas.'' Contrary to expectation, these knowings reduced her discomfort.

In most else of this new place, Scayna found pleasure: sky and clouds and plant growths, the bustle of yumins more friendly than not once their startlement at her was past, the unfamiliar foods and fluids Nsil assured her to be well selected for Eamnet suitability. Since he also assured that his mission had won success, then if not for one difficulty, Scayna might well have discarded care to savor full enjoyment.

Yet the one fact would not yield. Near to bearing, she had here no other bearers, none who could—as had she for Irtuk—stand protectrix to herself as genetrix.

To allow the presence of seeders or adaptives, even had any possessed the needed strength, lay beyond consideration. And Kaow, a time back when Scayna voiced concern, seemed to find little consequence to it, suggesting that yumins might aid!

Urgency grew with discomfort, restlessness routed serenity. As the time of fulfillment neared, her midsinistral womb came to throb in rhythm with her bloodbeat—not unpleasant in the sensing, yet always a reminder that bearing would not wait even for necessities, let alone proprieties.

Against the time Kaow should return, Scayna held control of outward mien. With Nsil, Kaow's absence freeing his days of preemption by yumins' curiosities, she indulged full intimacy to his very limits. The seeder did not protest; rather, he strove to outdo those bounds.

In aftermath she found periods of calm. At one time of excess-enforced resting, quietly stroking Nsil's mane at its forward peak, Scayna voiced her anxiety. "Only a brief time remains, Nsil—only a few of these daycycles—before I come to bearing." Erdthdays longer than Eamn's; two of these made three of the homeworld's. "Yet I lack what is needful."

She did not embellish her plaint; he knew as well as she what those lacks were. "Could we not, Nsil, now again traverse a portal and return to Eamn?"

"But, Scayna . . ." and he cited the obstacles she knew he would. The learning, on both sides, yet to be achieved. The exchangings between Eamn and Erdth, to the advantage of both and not yet delineated but in rough conjecture. And the granting of an Erdthan ship, much spoken on yet still unspecified, for Nsil's greatly successful return to Eamn. "These doings," he said now, "await deliberation."

Scayna drew hesitant breath, then spoke. "And my bearing cannot. So if it must be, Nsil, I beg leave to return alone."

"And I beg you, Scayna—hold yet a time. Until Kaow shall be returned, there is none here well cognizant of our speech. To arrange a matter of this sort requires such knowing."

Before she could marshal protest he added, "And assume you do return alone. To which destination? The great portal? The ship *Roamer*? Magh? For none opens onto Eamn. Beside lacking one to attend you, you would find yourself among strangers."

As often, Nsil's capability of assessment received less of Scayna's appreciation than mayhap it merited. Still she put good countenance to the situation. "Then shall we feed now?"

A gratifying number of the yumins hereabouts had mastered enough Eamnet speaking to converse regarding such matters as food, the locating of any Eamnet named in inquiry, and the imminence in Erdthan time of arranged meetings or the like. Nsil rose and left the chamber, soon returning. "There will in satisfactorily brief time be fruits and meats brought."

For that minor fulfillment, Scayna could wait well enough.

In the complexities of this ship's structure, Sydnie knew, she and Aroka could play cat and mouse forever without once meeting. In theory, at least. Practice was different. If he wanted to know about the spying in control, there was only one place to find out. But what level of guile would govern his approach?

Deliberately she'd left him time to find the open hatch. Now would he be inside the bulkhead, or lurking in ambush nearby? Always a man for maps and floor plans, and a quick study to boot, he'd know the terrain before invading it.

She chose a rearward entry, climbing out to the old drive mode quarters deck at a point behind her own temporary nest and looking forward along the corridor above control.

Nothing showed. All doors solidly closed, none cracked ajar. Right hand clenched on Estilete's dagger she took one slow Velcro'd step after another, peering all round and back and forth, until she neared the hatch. Its cover still lay turned aside. More to the point, from inside the bulkhead came sounds.

Lock him in! Anyone else, she'd have rushed to do it, but with Aroka there had to be a catch. Cautiously she backtracked, knife at the ready, and checked each door along the way. All locked, and the sound of unlocking one would give her warning.

So. With no traction except at shoe soles, Sydnie could hardly creep, but instinct crouched her as she moved again toward the hatch. She listened: yes, someone was in there, and the scuffing sounded near her vent screen spypoint.

All she had to do was pivot the hatch into position and

seat a couple of wing bolts; she reached to do it. But the hatch cover wouldn't move.

What . . . ? The remaining wing bolt was cinched down tight. Bending, she grasped and tried to turn it, but the pressure bruised her fingers painfully; she had to back off.

Mouthing silent curses she slid the knife through a belt loop and used both hands. Even so, it hurt like crazy. Gritting her teeth, finally she managed to break the bolt loose.

As she reached to pull the cover around, something snaked out and jerked her other wrist. Her footing gave, and in zero gee she sprawled floating. Aroka's head and shoulders emerged; scrambling to get out he levered at her arm, keeping her feet well away from the deck and any hope of traction.

His lips had been full and sensual; now tension tucked them into a thin line. Blindly reaching, she couldn't find the knife; with all her strength she flexed her right arm and got her jaws to the clutching hand. She caught the thumb at its base knuckle, forward molars finding purchase, and clamped hard. Something gave a little, but from Aroka came only a thin whuffling moan.

Then his other hand, fingertips braced behind her ear and thumb thrusting at her eye, began to clench.

Flashing pain ripped her vision. Purpose failed; instinct, need to survive, loosed her will and jaws. Too late she got her left hand up inside and pried the horrid grip away. He was clear of the bulkhead now—and unlike Estilete, in zero gee he knew to close and grapple, hampering motion to negate another's skill.

When he had both her hands pinned, Aroka turned back to the open hatch. "Enough sound effects, Rocco. We have our spy."

Then he looked at her. "Charel. Charel Secour!"

In another circumstance she might have enjoyed his shock.

Recovering, he shook his head. "You fooled me, sacrificing the plane. But now I know who put me to so much trouble, intercepting and clearing from Omnet the puzzlingly detailed report of my activities." He had the knife now; first checking to be sure she carried no other weapons, he released her.

"Clearing?" With a twist she got her feet to the deck and stood to face him, blinking as bright floating blotches faded gradually from her sight. "You simply got rid of it all?"

"Not precisely." From the hatch climbed a stocky, balding man; before continuing, Aroka gestured him forward to the next corridor junction. "Editing, was more to the point. To fit the picture I had so carefully cultivated in official circles, of Jorge Aroka the daring undercover agent. Who so often came so close to breaking apart the shadowy, largely unknown Web."

So that was how he'd whitewashed his record. Much the same as she'd done herself, to Sam, but with computer clout added.

He wouldn't have found her cached copy—but then, neither would anyone else. No matter now; briefly relaxed, again Aroka's face tautened. Below the jaw, where the ascot lay pulled aside to bare his throat, she saw the hideous scar she'd put there.

Returning her stare, he nodded. "Yes, you nearly did for me, La Hoja. A long time I lay ill. With spinal complications; by learning to walk again I outraged the medical profession."

The limp, yes. Pleading would be futile; still she said, "You didn't give me much choice. The Mussulman, Akhiel . . ."

His new, lipless smile. "An error. I should not have indulged my love of taunting. But you annoyed me."

No mercy here and never was. "I tried," remembering the sidearm throw she'd thought final.

His finger traced the discolored ridge. "And quite well for a first attempt. But there will be no second."

Feeling wooden and unreal, she squared her shoulders. "I suppose you want to get it over with."

What surprised her was, she couldn't find any fear. Just a dull ache of loss—and for what, she wasn't at all certain.

"Not so soon," he said, and as she stared, "I do not recall releasing you from my employ. When I do, we will talk again."

The call from Waymire's aide said Kayo was needed at Glen Springs. Some problem with the Eamnets, was all the man knew. Assuring Quillan that she'd be back—". . . or maybe you'll be down for a checkup first"—she packed to leave. Wiser now, with a little advice from the aide she rode taxibus to a nearby airbase and then deadhead to Glen Springs on an agency jet.

The young woman who met her couldn't have been past her teens, but cowboyed the little electric two-seater like a veteran. Grinning all the way. Declining her offer to help with the luggage, Kayo hauled it to quarters, dumped it, and went to the leisure lounge assigned to Eamnet use.

Apparently absorbed in a holovid soap ("So much uncertainty and turmoil, among only two genders!" without needing to understand a word of it), Nsil spotted her entry immediately. "Kaow! My gratitude for your coming."

The problem was Scayna: readying to bear, lacking another of her kind for that ritual, and no assurance that the far end of a return Gating would be any improvement or even safe.

"She has lost all composure, Kaow. Taken herself to her chamber, from which I am barred—I, and all others. She states, Kaow—she states she will end now, and our offspring with her."

"Destroy herself? How? Why?"

"Not by intent, but through lack of aid to focus, to maintain cohesion of thought and effort. This is the function of the protectrix. Only bearers know what is done then."

"Then it is time, Nsil, that others learn. Where is this chamber?"

Minutes later, Kayo pleaded at a closed door. Nothing barred her from the room except Scayna's edict and Nsil's acceptance of it; without Scayna's permission, he said, no one would enter. And Eamnet bearers were supposed to be slaves?

"Scayna." Nothing to do but keep trying. "I beg you, allow me to speak seeing you. I hold you in friendship. On Eamn you granted me hospitality to your best abilities. May I not attempt to offer you some return? Otherwise you spurn my good intent."

The voice came hoarsely. "Enter, Kaow. I will hear you."

She gave Nsil's forelimb a squeeze and went in, closing the door quickly; Scayna's order to do so faded in mid-syllable. Kayo looked; the bearer lay along a wide slanting Eamnet pallet, the whole of its surface adorned with swaths of brilliantly decorated cloths. At the lower end, her extremities were braced on a massive footstool; beside her sat a conical bowl filled with a mix of food bits ranging from grain to fruit wedges.

Inscrutable, Scayna gazed. "What would you speak?"

Approaching, hesitantly Kayo touched a great shoulder. "I would know what it is you need, that I might try to provide it."

"Your thought is good. Yet you are not a bearer."

"I am the nearest thing to one, this side of Eamn! Granted, we are not the same. Nor have I ever borne, as yet. But what is it which must be done, that is not possible for me to attempt?"

She couldn't have said just how the small movements at Scayna's mouth and eyes conveyed feelings, but Kayo sensed a change. "It is the protectrix' duty to restrain the genetrix in thought and body, to prevent a giving way to sensation before bearing is certain of success. Control may in part be maintained by reminder; this much lies within your capability. But the other . . ."

A bit of a stopper, the other: by main force and bulk to hold the bearer's rearlimb extremities as near to immobile as could be managed. Kayo mulled, then said, "Do you look to those parts during the time of bearing?" No. "Then what matters it, the precise fashion by which you are held?"

Dubious at first, in the face of oncoming bodily disturbance Scayna consented. Twisting spare lengths of the bright cloths into soft, smooth ropes, Kayo secured the extremities in question to either side of the footstool, then firmly sat astraddle and took a solid grip on each limb. Hoping she understood what she'd just been told, she began. "I stand protectrix, Scayna, to ward you from premature dispossession. You will hold you firm, as I do. Until the time of giving." Deep breath. "I stand . . ."

There were variations to the theme, but the gist stayed pretty much the same. Over the sounds Scayna began to make, Kayo kept the litany going.

Even hobbled, the limbs thrashed. Wondering if she'd bitten off too big a mouthful, Kayo Marlin looked to a long night.

This was crazy. Desperately Sydnie looked both ways along the corridor, but saw no one. Not even Aroka's stationed decoy; had she missed a signal he'd made, sending the man elsewhere?

"You want me to work for you again? You think I would?"

Almost lazily his hand swung, jolting her head to one side and leaving her cheek stinging. Just like that first night . . . ! "Moments ago I deduced it was you that happened to La Sombria, Estilete. You will tell me later how you did this and what disposition you made of her. More important, you have caused a gap in my working apparatus."

Those odd eyelids flickered. "Something you don't know. My training system; I needed you in a hurry and found no time for it later. Or you could never have risen against me."

"If you say so." Keep him talking; it can't hurt.

"There's no time now, either. Or facilities. Later perhaps, I'll put you back on my roster for good and all." His brows rose. "Possibly even into my bed."

Her shudder stifled an unwelcome pang of arousal as he added, "With a few minor changes you may prefer not to be told in advance."

"Or ever." Inside, she felt cold.

"Now, though, I demand much less. In fact, one thing only."

He waited, so she had to ask. "What thing?"

"Remove the major obstacle to my venture here. This ship's captain, Samuel Gowdy."

"Why?" Indefinite queries make the best stall.

"I mean to extend the Web to new star systems; to best do so, I must rule this one. Own it, actually—for the sake of the trade routes that will pass through its Gates. And the ships to be taken, the new Gates to be placed for my benefit, not that of the authorities. Smuggling is the lifeblood of trade, and new worlds provide products worth smuggling. New drugs, for example. Why, some of the things discovered at Tetzl's Planet . . ."

"What's all this have to do with—with Gowdy?"

"As an entrepeneur my natural enemy is the practitioner of governance, the bureaucrat. Face-to-face or knife to back, I can deal with those, even masquerade as one. This Gowdy, though—he defies category. Breaking their idiotic rules when it suits him, yet for the most part upholding them."

"Why should that be a problem to *you*?" Keep juggling; don't let anything hit the deck. "Can't you handle a mere ship's captain? Or am I missing something?"

One barb too many; at her throat the knifepoint touched very near her death. "You know enough; more would only confuse you. Come." The knife retreated as a hand on her arm impelled her forward, toward a major interdeck hatch.

Questions boiled within her, but asking wouldn't help. Lagging as much as she thought she could get away with, Sydnie let herself be taken to the inner cylinder, then aft.

He'd been quiet so long that his voice startled her. "You're not on the roster; when did you board? And how? Through earthGate, I suppose. So Gowdy and the rest have to know you're here. Yet none of them slipped up and gave you away. I see that this crew merits closer surveillance . . ."

He seemed to have answered his own question, so she went with it. "Who says they had to see me? Earthtush isn't under guard. And it's not far from an inship access hatch." Aroka didn't answer; maybe she'd made a point and maybe not.

They turned a corner; near the opened entrance to hold Two stood the stocky man, Rocco. "She's been in touch, sir. Audiocap on the intercom in here has messages from Gowdy."

Had he spoken her name? She couldn't remember. As they went inside, Aroka said, "Anything I should know?"

"Only that they're pretty much onto us." Sydnie tried not to look as relieved as she felt.

"That's to be expected." He looked to Sydnie. "Now here's the situation: I'd rather control Gowdy than kill him. You could get to him, Charel; if anyone can, it's you. His shipwife—Sydnie somebody, I forget—he's left her on Eamn, so they can't be too tight, and by now he has to be overdue for bedding. I'll give you a little something for his foreplay time drink—or afterplay, your choice. Then you call me."

As always, when the Spider Prince made a proposal he considered the matter settled. At the intercom he mumbled a bit and finally chose a switch. "Case? It's time we pressured the Maghren. The way I told you. Take someone along to interpret. For now, just do the first part; I'll get back to you."

Now he turned to Rocco. "Cobble the send-receive switch on this commbox; I want full feedback." The stocky man needed little over a minute for the task. Aroka hit the all-ship broadcast button and whistled; quickly surpassing the ambient drive hum, the resultant howl rose to deafening and didn't stop.

Outside the hold and with the hatch closed, Sydnie's ears still rang. "What was that for?"

Aroka grinned. "All over the ship, the intercom's useless. Until someone comes to turn this station off or disconnects the line at the central terminal board." And how would anyone know which line was gimmicked? He added, "Gowdy can't coordinate anything and I don't need to. So we're more even now."

For what? Again, no use asking. When they reached the nearest main corridor Sydnie began thinking of possible escape. But no, Aroka clutched her arm and again steered her aft. Toward the stern cargo bay. The knife had been put away, but she had no doubt he could reach it in a hurry. And then there was the other man. Pickstepping her way as if zero gee were new to her, she let herself be taken farther from any possible aid.

Because she had no other choice.

Ahead, Rocco opened the cargo bay's personnel hatch. But the voice came from behind. "Sydnie! Stand clear of him!"

Sam's voice. Oh bloody hell.

She might have known he'd bitch it up.

Always had Nsil suspected the apparent calm indifference of his fellow seeders at occasions of bearing; to himself these times grew filled by seeming endless anxious fret.

Now, with only the strengthless yumin Kaow to aid and guide Scayna, unsureness roiled his being. Tasr, Tirys, even Duant the Maghren attempted the comfort of comradeship—and in the case of Tirys, that of intimacy as well. Without avail: worry resisting all effort toward assuagement, Nsil toyed with food or drink and managed little response to attempted converse.

So it was not only Nsil himself who showed relief when the yumin Kaow spoke from the door of Scayna's chamber. "It is done. Scayna is dispossessed of the bearer child also parented by Nsil and Tirys—and now, as agreed, to be known as Nyrl. Although fatigued, Scayna experiences excellent vital condition and wishes to assure you that Nyrl feeds well.''

Less sanguine appeared Kaow herself: face and headmane alike ran damp with exuded moisture, and in the set of features Nsil recognized stress of unease as the yumin said, ''The protectrix gift, Nsil! Only now has Scayna informed me; I did not know. Go to my quartering and bring the Earthsky-colored bag to me, I plead you. Some object therein should suffice.''

''I make haste.'' The place was not far, and immediately he sighted the container. Inadequately closed, it fell agape when lifted, strewing its contents across the floor. As Nsil began to replace them he saw three objects that should not be there: old Eamnet record panes, ebon yet not wholly opaque, their anterior surfaces webbed with silvered etchings.

The implications slowed his return. When Kaow opened to his digitnail rapping he held the sheets to her gaze. ''I gave you and Irtuk-saa permission to visit my householding. To neither did I grant leave to take from there what is mine.''

Coming inship by way of the ramps and hatches debouching at the rear of the DV well, Gowdy saw no one, so he headed back along the corridor to hold Two, Sydnie's message drop. Nobody home there, either, and rechecking his census via intercom brought little new information. The miner *Golconda* was closing fast. And an elliptical reference, phrased to go over Atwell's head, told him that the DV wasn't far behind. Too far, though, to be counted on in any way for the time being.

Unsure of his next move, Sam left the hold and started forward, but almost immediately heard voices approaching. The minor echoes in corridors made mincemeat out of directional hearing, but whoever it was clearly had his forward progress blocked.

For the time being, then, he returned to the hold. Moments later he was thankful he'd been overcautious, taking cover behind a lashed-down stack of crates. Because the man who entered was Rocco Silva.

Making himself at home Silva went to the intercom, spotted the audiocap unit, and played off Sam's messages to Sydnie. Then he went to stand at the entrance. Well, that blew it; now they'd know she was aboard. And the next moment or so erased any doubts; propelled by Aroka, Sydnie herself entered.

As they came farther inside, Gowdy could hear voice tones well enough. But from where he stood, the usually unnoticed drive hum blanketed their words. What bothered Sam was how calm everyone seemed to be; from Sydnie's story, this didn't figure.

Then Silva fiddled with the comm unit and Aroka whistled: welcome to the earsplitting world of positive feedback! Fingers to his ears, Gowdy waited until the three departed and the hatch closed behind them, then another couple of minutes just for luck, before he moved to cut power to the terminal. He didn't know the circuits so he couldn't fix it, but now it was off-line, no longer disabling the whole system.

Outside, he reached the main corridor and saw the trio nearing the stern cargo bay. Shitohdear! Once they got in there he'd have no way at all to help Sydnie. Assuming she needed it, and he pretty much had to assume that.

All right, skip the Velcro; let's use the handholds and zoom. Bumming around the Oort Cloud, after *Starfinder*, he'd gotten pretty good at that sort of thing. So giving himself no time for sensible afterthoughts, Sam grabbed, pulled, missed one handhold but caught the next for a good corrective thrust.

He couldn't make any kind of throw on the fly, though, and Silva was opening the bay hatch. Gowdy caught a stanchion and yanked himself to a halt, planted both feet, then yelled.

"Sydnie! Stand clear of him!"

Fat chance. Before Sam could wind up to throw, Aroka had Lightner tightheld in shield mode.

Well, cut the odds. Gowdy sent the tenderizing mallet spinning; its heavy end caught Silva alongside his left eye. Shoe soles holding, the man swayed limp. Dead? Sam hoped not. All that paperwork. Though come to think of it, there was still Estilete to account for. . . .

Not now, though; Aroka brought out an automatic with a long, jutting clip. "Captain Gowdy. Come join us."

As though he had a choice, Sam paused. The gunhand beckoned. "I suppose you thought you eliminated all these."

"No. I only hoped so."

"And still you came to challenge me." As Gowdy stepped

forward, slowly and weighing his chances, Aroka shook his head. "I will never understand civilians."

"That works both ways." It didn't, but what the hell?

Ignoring the ploy, Aroka turned Sydnie to face him. "So, Charel; you are the elusive Sydnie Lightner. Not on Eamn after all. Now what was the point of that lie? And you two are pairmates. How interesting."

He shrugged. "It all evens out. You two have cost me Estilete and Rocco; you will now serve in their stead." Without so much as looking to see if Silva still lived, he motioned them into the cargo bay. "Come."

Sam didn't get it. "What for?"

Aroka scowled. "Later I will teach you not to question me. But now—here is where we find the vacuum suits. We are all going outside the ship. To meet with some friends of mine."

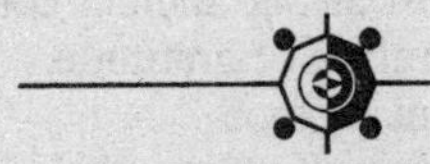

XIX

Sweating and bedraggled, Kayo stared at Nsil. Tired as she was, for more than moments the wrongness eluded her. But before her mouth could spout words while engulfing her foot, she recognized the jewellike Eamnet record sheets he held.

"Oh. Those."

"Yes, Kaow. For what purpose do you take and conceal them?"

Dilemma. Kayo herself hadn't swiped the plates, but would Nsil believe that? Even if he did, who likes a tattletale? On the other hand, Irtuk-saa was forty-two light-years out of Nsil's reach. And twice his bulk, to boot. But then again . . .

In case of doubt, try the truth; it's simpler.

". . . something of importance, Irtuk appeared to believe.

She did not have opportunity to share with me the foundation of that belief. But deeming you bound once more for Magh, Irtuk-saa consigned those panes thereto. In my custody."

If Nsil didn't understand a shrug by now, let him puzzle on it. "By what means Irtuk expected I should convey the archival sheets to Maghren decipherant scholars, I lack even conjecture."

Woops! Nsil wasn't supposed to know the true nature of the records. Now he blinked. "The communicant symbols should not have altered all so much, between Magh and Eamn." Briefly his jaw dropped to grin mode. "Ah. Kaow, you misspoke. Archival Mode scholar is the term you seek, not decipherant."

Right, boss; I sure do screw up a lot. Kayo suppressed her sigh of relief. "Whatever her aim," she said, "it has fallen far wide of accomplishment."

"And with no harm resulting." The seeder made his drop-jaw grin. "You may keep these, Kaow. In hap your own scholars may rouse interest at our ancient constructs."

Relief fueled her declaration of gratitude. "And now, Nsil, I must go. I am long scant of food."

But even ahead of hunger, Kayo needed a hot bath.

Aroka knew suits, all right; Simone had been right on that score. From the airlock, where the commodore had confined him and Sydnie ". . . to keep you out of mischief," Sam squinted through the window panel as the man shucked into the tight-fitting protective garment, somewhat awkwardly but without help.

First checking his air tanks and the reaction pistol used for free flight maneuvering, Aroka retrieved his automatic, then undogged the airlock hatch. "Out here now, and suit up."

In no hurry, Sam chose a suit and ran his own checklist. He didn't inspect the reaction unit because he didn't want Aroka to notice, and maybe make him leave it behind. But Sydnie was checking hers, and the commodore didn't react. Gowdy said, "You want to take a sled out? Or just lines, and hang in close?"

Until Aroka had his weapons belt adjusted, the gun and a knife each sheathed and tethered by three-foot cords, the man didn't answer. Then, "We'll be roped up. But not to the ship."

With about fifteen feet of line between him and Sydnie, it turned out, and roughly the same length from her on to Sam. In the airlock, faceplates closed now, Aroka cracked the outer hatch briefly, exhausting maybe half the air. "Anyone leaking?"

Nobody was, and the suit-to-suit comm units all worked, so whoosh and push clear, outside where *Roamer*'s stern first filled half the universe, then quickly shrank as they moved away.

Awesome, but Gowdy had been here before. On the off chance he checked suit-to-ship frequencies and heard Aroka saying ". . . soon will you arrive, Arman?" but couldn't find the other party's channel and missed the response. Scanning back, he caught Aroka's voice again. ". . . near this ship, so Mr. Yates can locate me easily. And I trust that by the time of your arrival I shall have settled these other concerns."

The commodore, Sam decided, had a really nasty chuckle.

Being shot at wasn't Skeeter Cole's idea of fun; ducking from the *wheee* of Case Beringer's spanging bullet fragments had rather prejudiced him against the ruddy-faced swaggerer. So when Beringer ordered him off watch, saying, "The commodore says I need an interpreter for this job, so come on," Skeeter wasn't in his most cooperative mood.

He called the lounge. "Cole, from watch, requesting relief out of sked. Orders from the commodore; I have to ride shotgun for Billy the Kid. Anyone available?"

Ignoring Beringer's scowl he waited until Marthe Vinler answered. "I'll take it, Skeet. In five; okay?"

"Blossings on thee." Irrelevant chat annoyed the bejeezus out of the commodore's people so he used it in due proportion. To Beringer he said, "What am I supposed to interpret?"

"Wait and see." Not until Skeeter was relieved and herded to the belt, then aft to the quarters area, did Beringer speak in more than grunts. "It's the one from Acey, we want."

Magh. Irtuk. "What for, Case?" Try sounding friendly. . . .

Stiff-fingered, Beringer poked his shoulder. Hard. "Anything you need to know, little man, I'll tell you. Now you find me the one from Acey."

Do tell. "That would be Irtuk-saa of Magh's council of bearers, second only to Paith the Elect." Or, don't fuck around with what you don't understand. But the guy wouldn't get it. Mentally shrugging, Cole gestured. "In there. And be careful."

Beringer made a snort. "Of Sloopy the Seagoing Sloth? You just watch your ownself," and pushed Skeeter inside ahead of him.

Sitting almost erect on two of the slanting recliners, Bretl and Irtuk looked up from young Tuik who tottered along the deck between them, mostly on hindlimbs but often propping a forelimb down for balance. Something like a bear cub, Skeeter thought. While to one side stood T'phee, immobile.

Irtuk spoke. "What would the clamorous one do here?"

"Wha'd she say?" Not *much*, Beringer wasn't worried. . . .

"She says hello; I'll tell her the same." But he said, "I am not informed as yet, Irtuk, of what Case intends. I recommend guardedness and caution; his weapon carries much danger."

"It propels metal, yes," Bretl said. "We have seen—but none were struck."

"Distance was greater, then. And all were moving." She wasn't getting it, and apparently neither was Irtuk. As a sop to Beringer's impatience Cole said, "Ritual greetings; they take a while."

"Yatata, sure. All right, now tell her . . ." Looking back and forth between the two bearers, Beringer seemed uncertain. "Whichever one it is, tell her I'm taking the whelp with me and don't even think about trying to stop me."

"You're *what*?" The bearers' stances showed concern; voice timbre was enough to alert them. No time now, to fill them in. "You can't do that. Case . . ."

"Famous last words. The commodore says do it. Tell her she gets it back when she makes a speech to Acey. Aroka wrote the script—and before we beam the recording we'll have several of you translate Sloopy's version for us. Separately, so nobody slips anything past us." The gun muzzle jerked. "Tell her."

No help for it; Cole began. At his first words Irtuk rose,

stood rigid, and gave forth a deep bass ululation. In moments Bretl followed suit, the two voices weaving in and out of eerie harmonics. Against the suddenly wavering gun, Skeeter gestured. "Don't get stupid; this is a small room and they're pretty big for that seven-mimi of yours. You can't . . ."

But moving the gun back and forth to cover both bearers, Case Beringer lunged with his free hand to grab young Tuik.

The action Skeeta announces is not to be considered. Peril to get impels even Yainans to deeds against normal temperament—and T'phee comprehends that among Irtuk's species the bond may drive even more fiercely.

Skeeta remonstrates; Case, the weaponed yumin, disregards. Foreign to Yain is physical contesting—yet of some act there is need. Against all es tendings, T'phee finds enself moving to place es body against the entrance panel; while er there remains, it cannot be made to open.

To T'phee, breathing constricted as duration elongates, es situation reeks of malchoice. The intonations of Irtuk and Bretl hold threat. The movements of Case carry more; as voices rise to bury meaning under clamor Case propels enself forward, es weapon extended toward Irtuk and es other forelimb toward Irtuk's get.

Now Irtuk and Bretl converge upon en. The weapon activates; painful reverberation overrides all sound except the sharpnesses as metal whines and rebounds. Irtuk's forelimb sprays lifefluid; er swings it at the attacker's head but strikes only a swiping blow. Moving with strength derived from habituation to Yamar's worldpull but lacking familiarity with kinetic vectors unique to this rotating place, Bretl reels sidelong into Irtuk's path.

Grasped and lifted, the Maghren get Tuik mounts high-pitched protest. Again the weapon points; then as the yumin Case shouts greatly, once more occurs sharp and painful outnoise.

T'phee stares. Young Tuik's jaws tightgrip Case's idle forelimb directly behind the digits. As the yumin raises es weapon to strike the get away, its arc meets the head of Skeeta, lunging to aid, and Skeeta falls aside.

Bending and bracing, Case sets to smash the get; none in view can halt es attack. Unbelieving es own doing, T'phee extends es necktrunk gape-mouthed, strikes, and clamps es jaws.

Shrieking, Case shakes the get free, tears enself loose, and still grasping es weapon, leaps spraddling from the room.

As Irtuk crouches to es get, Bretl of Yamar seeks to pursue. "Enough!" Skeeta's forepaw thrusts high in Bretl's course. "It is done; no need to do more."

Bretl halts. "The death would be not of your need, Skeeta, but of mine. And Irtuk's. As bearers we ask of you: for what purpose must this violator of nurture continue living?"

On Skeeta's newly damaged face, puzzled thought is evident. "Yumins in general punish evil done, not that attempted. Since I must with regret own Case as yumin, allow us to judge him by our ways. Though I grant much merit to your own."

Expelling flesh and fabric bitten from Case, none of it savory, T'phee inquires, "In this instance, to what severity do your penal measures extend?"

The yumin pauses. "The decision will be Captain Gowdy's." Then er adds, "What would be your recommendation?"

T'phee must ponder. "Es immediate acts caused less harm than es intent willed. Yet es unregarding view of beings other than enself bodes ill of es ensuing behavior." Er considers. "I would perforce ordain interdiction, utter separateness, and thus the doom of inevitable decline."

Skeeta's gaze lingers. "I will so inform the captain." Er goes from the compartment, leaving T'phee to the discomfort of Irtuk's unbounded thankings as evidenced by the forceful embrace of es dripping forelimb.

Perhaps a hundred yards off *Roamer*'s stern Gowdy watched Aroka use his reaction gun briefly, bringing the group nearly to a halt but slowly rotating in a V formation, tie lines tautening and going slack again at seeming random.

"Now we will talk."

Gas pistols being on the approved list, Sam used his to stop his own slow spin and face the commodore. No point in asking "Why here?" Obviously Aroka liked melodrama.

Time, maybe, to throw in a side issue. "Why did you order

the Eamnet ship destroyed? You couldn't have considered any serious threat at the Earth end."

"The threat of plague, I've told Glen Springs. But largely, I wished no report by that ship, of events here, reaching the authorities." The suit didn't disguise his shrug. "And I deemed it advantageous to set an example. May we now continue?"

"Go ahead; it's your program."

The commodore's voice settled to purpose. "Would you call yourself a man who keeps his promises?"

"If I can. If I can't, I don't make 'em." And how did Aroka know the unmoving keystone of his generally more adaptable ethics? "What are you getting at?"

"To you, what defines can and can't? For instance, when you proceeded to the rescue of Ira Kennealy, what factors governed?"

"How does that figure in? I never promised Ironhead anything. It was just—I wasn't going to let him and his crew die if I could help it. Which I nearly couldn't; my authority as acting first got stretched so thin you could see through it."

"And if you'd lacked that authority?"

Sam was getting tired of this. "I'd have bitched, moaned, argued, threatened, played guilt games, whatever. I probably wouldn't have mutinied, if that's what you're asking."

"Then can't is relative."

"Sometimes. But won't isn't." Let him try that for size.

"So we come to it." Gowdy deduced the nod hidden by glint off the slanting faceplate. "Very well. The matter is simple. Will you give promise to accept my authority and follow my orders so long as you serve on *Roamer*?"

"Or else what?"

The nasty chuckle. "Look around you." The object with which Aroka gestured wasn't the reaction pistol; it was the automatic, newly unsheathed, oversized clip and all.

And now, with temperature differential to the fourth power getting its licks in, it was time to stall a little, throw a curve. "Within what limits are we talking about?" Syntax poor, meaning clear.

"No limit. Unconditional allegiance."

Well, Sam hadn't expected much from that move. Try another sidetrack. "So what's *she* doing out here?"

"Your shipwife, Charel Secour my former lover and would-be killer, La Hoja Rubia here with a new name?" Laughter gurgled. "Two birds, captain. It remains to be seen how many, or which, return to the nest." A pull on the line sent Sydnie drifting toward him and lessened the slack between her and Sam.

Silent for a surprising long time, now her voice came shrill. "You're testing *me*? What could I do, here?"

"When your turn comes, I will tell you. Now, captain—what qualms hold you back from the promise I ask?"

"You want me to help you set Magh and Eamn at war?"

"Ah, the trogs. And the long-necked furry quadruped, no doubt. Once matters are settled, you may coddle them all you like. But until then . . ."

And how were things on the Kelvin scale, by now? Give it a little more. "You don't need a real war, you know. You can tell Earth anything you want, and no response can reach you for another four years. By then it won't matter."

"To me it will. I want my reports to hold up. And also a spot of war will provide some fun, some excitement. There hasn't been much of either, since the Peninsula."

"Was *that* what it was, for you?" Sydnie again.

Drift had brought her within Aroka's reach. By one arm he turned her facing toward Sam. "Wait, I told you. Now, Gowdy—enough talk. Yes or no?"

Feeling contrary, Sam made no answer at all. "Very well; it is your own choice. Now, La Hoja, comes time for your star turn." Putting one arm around her waist from behind, he handed her the gun, then quickly brought his knife up to nudge her side. "Must I state the obvious?"

Damn! This wasn't working right. "Sydnie! Don't!"

"You expect her to die in your stead?"

And ". . . he'll kill me! Sam—what can I do?"

Think fast! "You really think he's that stupid? He needs you; you heard him say so. What you don't need is me on your conscience. If you can't help, at least make him do it himself!"

No response. All right: twisting the line's slack around a forearm, with his other hand Gowdy fired the reaction pistol; the jolt pulled her free of Aroka, but not before the commodore got his gun back. "Very well, trog-lover!" and the barrel came up.

By now Kelvin had to be well below three figures; Sam watched as Aroka needed both hands for the trigger pull. Nothing happened. Gowdy began to haul in line.

Lacking stupidity, Aroka made do with ignorance. Slamming the heel of his left hand against the gun, he sure enough jarred its hammer loose from the film of frozen lube. Because the gun fired; supercooled and brittle it blew apart, so much silent shrapnel. Whatever hit the side of Gowdy's thigh hurt like hell and set him turning, but the skintight fabric held.

Over the suitphones someone kept screaming. Not Sydnie; directly ahead she spun, doubled over, arms wrapped around her head. From her side where the knife had touched came a thin, wavering plume: vapor that froze to a fine sprinkle of pinkness.

As Gowdy's drift brought him past her he put out a hand to swing himself facing Aroka. *Jeez!* No wonder the man screamed. His gun hand looked basically intact; its bleeding formed only small fragile patterns, freezing a few inches from its source. But the other, that had struck the firing chamber itself, spurted a series of crimson sculptures floating off beyond recall.

Damn all; making a desperate reach Gowdy threw a bight of line around the upper arm, hiked it up snug below the armpit, then cinched it tight. The knife still swung at Aroka's waist; Sam cut its securing cord and slipped the blade inside his own belt. Just in case.

Minor suit tears posed no immediate threat; the shredding at Aroka's wrist was something else. Gowdy didn't know how long it would take the semi-exposed hand to go icecube and didn't want to find out. But he had nothing he could use, to shield it from Kelvin's baseline.

The screams were getting on his nerves; reaching again he unplugged Aroka's suit batteries. Using his gas pistol he turned and headed for *Roamer*, the other two in tow. Sydnie had begun to sob, but it wasn't all that loud and who's perfect?

He was seconds from the airlock hatch when a voice boomed on the ship-to-suit. "Hold it right there. This is the mining ship *Golconda,* Travis Yates directing ship for Arman Lioso."

Gowdy looked around. It sure as hell was.

A little heavier bleeding on Beringer's part would have helped; the spots fell too widely scattered to give Skeeter a good trail. Back to the rear peripheral corridor and then turning left, he had no problem, but missed the next turn and had to backtrack before going forward again.

What he was doing in pursuit of an armed man, what he intended to do when he caught up—these questions took a time to surface in his mind. When they did, he slowed his pace.

This corridor passed both galley and lounge; at the first he peered in cautiously and saw pairmates Craig and Tuiasso sharing a snack. Which placed Simone Leopold on watch. "You see Beringer come by here?"

Mose gave a snort. "Like a bat out of."

"A gimpy bat," SuZanne added. "What bit *him*?"

No mention of the gun. Why?

"I always said he was a halfass piece of work," Mose put in. "Now I can prove it."

"All *right.*" Skeeter shook his head. "Where'd he go?" If they'd seen the gun they'd say so.

"On forward." SuZanne. "And I thought I heard the transfer ring doors clunk shut."

"Okay, thanks." And turning back, "The Yainan did it. Our ultimate pacifist. In defense of Irtuk's youngster."

At the lounge door he paused: Jethro sat dealing Seven-toed Pete to Milo and Marthe and Molly Abele. Beringer had looked in but gone right past; if he had a gun it was put away, and yes, he'd left the belt. "Or just worked the doors and then stayed," said Marthe Vinler. "But who's that supposed to fool?"

True. Push the button; if the doors open right now, nobody went anywhere. On a hunch, Cole moved to the intercom and called control. Simone answered; he said, "Who else is there with you?"

"Atwell." In the background he heard the other woman ask why Leopold refused to call her Vivian. No answer.

"Seen Case Beringer? In the past five minutes, say?"

He couldn't make out the words of Atwell's urgent whisper, but Simone blurted out, "The hell with your games!" Then she said, "Not you, Skeets. Yes, he was here. Bleeding at the left buttock; he said somebody bit him and he needed a rabies shot. The other way round, if you ask me!"

Deep breath. "He wanted me to Gate him home, but I'm not taking responsibility for sending off Aroka's chief deputy."

All well and good, and she needed to get some steam off, but, "Come on, Simone; what *did* happen?"

"He waved his gun; what else? So I told Alix in drive that if she heard a shot *or* the intercom here went off-line before I said so, we had a war and she could hit drive thrust bugger-all. Beringer backed off. He let Atwell fix him some first aid; then he went inship looking for the commodore."

"I see. Thanks." If chasing one armed man was crazy, what would you call going after two? Which brought to mind: "How about your monitor there? Atwell. What's she carrying?"

"Pretty much the usual. Smallish. Why?"

"I just like to keep posted. Thanks, Simone. Cole out."

The question was, how much deeper did he want to get in?

"Emergency!" Sam yelled into the suit-to-ship. Thinking fast: this was the dickhead who tried to kill Kayo. He liked to shoot people. He took orders from Aroka and knew the commodore was out here. By looking, he couldn't tell which suit was whose.

Fair enough. "Casualty!" Gowdy followed up. At the airlock he took a handhold and tugged the line to speed the other two.

But kept talking. ". . . get him inside, then I'll come talk with you."

"Hold it, I said! Or we'll fry you."

Golconda and its primary laser were pointing off several degrees; unless miners' sidelasers and their aiming had improved greatly, Sam at this distance put very little weight to the threat. Still, "You'd zitz the commodore? I hope you're prepared to swim home from the court-martial."

"Commodore Aroka? If he's there, why doesn't he answer me?" Because that's what Yates was expecting. Not an incommunicado boss with his batteries unplugged.

But Sydnie was past and inside, and now Aroka pinwheeled in where Gowdy could stuff him through the hatch, follow, and dog it closed. Yates out there could go fry a kite.

Air in, people exit. In the cargo bay, flipping open the slanting faceplates cut everyone's feed of suit air.

Sydnie showed signs of shock but she'd have to wait, because Aroka had somehow put his head together. Good hand gripping the shattered wrist, he turned a taut, drained face toward Gowdy. "How long to Magh?"

Somehow his meaning came clear. "For medical help? Too slow." In *Roamer*, anyway, at a quarter gee. The Doodlebug maybe, but damned if Sam Gowdy was going to take that little bucket on a haywire emergency run for this sonofabitch. And *Golconda* couldn't land anywhere at all. "You want to keep the hand, we Gate you home."

The hooded stare almost made Sam believe in mesmerism. "Then you will do that. And captain—report anything you wish. I will survive any investigation you may launch."

A sneering laugh. "Whether you survive *my* report is of course another matter."

Sydnie clutched at Sam's elbow. "Are you crazy?" Actually, Sam was beginning to wonder about that, himself. She went on, "Let him die! Why didn't you leave him out there, anyway?"

One hand gripping her jaw, Gowdy said, "Sydnie! I don't want to have to slap you. We'll talk later."

There really wasn't time to unsuit, but the backhanging faceplates made an awkward nuisance. "Here." He unhinged Sydnie's, then Aroka's as she got Sam's free. "Come on." With the two of them steadying the commodore, everybody moved out.

In the corridor outside the cargo bay, no sign of Rocco Silva. But moving forward and turning aside to hold Two, Gowdy found the man. Bloody temple contrasting with pale sallow skin, he slumped against the intercom station.

"Silva? Do you need help?"

The man looked up. "Gowdy? M'dizzy, try'n call somebody."

Concussion, maybe? "You gimmicked the intercom, remember? Feedback howl. So I unplugged the station. Can you put it back right? I'll help, if I can.''

Amazing, how simply a knowledgeable person could put a piece of electronic wizardry out of business. Rocco's coordination was shot but he tracked well enough to give directions. Sam got the switch housing loose and pulled away the strapping wire that didn't belong. Then he plugged the station in and tried it.

''Control? Gowdy, at hold Two.'' Simone responded. He said, ''Medical emergency; two to Gate home. We'll come outship via the rear interdeck hatches. And if you can send a couple of strong bodies to meet us, we could use some help with the lame ducks.''

Rocco Silva sagged headhammered–punchy and beyond pride, but Jorge Aroka straightened and glared. ''I don't want to hear it,'' said Gowdy. ''Come on; let's march. Tied off from blood supply, that arm of yours has a short shelf life.''

But before he could get anyone moving, Simone Leopold's voice came again. ''Captain! *Golconda*'s calling—a man named Arman Lioso. Demanding that you bring Aroka to that ship. Now. Or he'll order a Mr. Yates to melt down our drive nodes.''

And that, Gowdy realized, the sonofabitch could actually do. Because *Roamer* was the sittingest of ducks,

For quite some time Kayo couldn't shake loose to go visit Dan Quillan. As soon as Nsil and Scayna were willing to spare her, she was overwhelmed by teams of specialists back from studying Nsil's ship Three, variously described as unique, mystifyingly ingenious, differently conceptualized, and how did that can of spare parts ever get off the ground?

It had, though, and curious researchers wanted to know more about the how of things, so with Kayo as interpreter they interviewed Nsil and other Eamnets. To little avail: as Kayo said to Dr. Sara Lynesse, the most compatible and least arrogant of the team chiefs, ''Nsil's a political leader; Tasr's a pilot and navigator; Fogt and Siln and a number of others are skilled technical operators. But there isn't an Eamnet scientist or engineer or ship design expert this side of the macroGate.''

''I see what you mean,'' Lynesse said. ''Thanks. Now I

can quit wasting time here and concentrate on the ship itself.''

Well now. Kayo posted a meeting notice and read the other research team honchos that same pitch. As if by magic her calendar cleared. For half a day she reveled in unaccustomed leisure. Then, remembering, she called Dan. Only to learn that he was on his way to Glen Springs. For a recovery status checkup, as she'd halfway predicted he might.

He wasn't due for several hours; meanwhile she had a call from Bill Flynn, to meet with him and Jocelyn Waymire. As she entered, Flynn was saying ''. . . simply aggravate whatever situation may exist. What do you think, Kayo?''

About what? Giving Nsil a mining ship to take back, rather than a cargo shuttle. Kayo pulled a chair over near Waymire's desk. ''Aren't we being a little premature? Whatever's happened at the Triad Worlds, we should be getting word soon, one way or the other. Why not wait, see what may be needed, then decide?''

Pushing fingers through her bright hair, Waymire said, ''You're probably right. It's just that . . . there've been leaks, and the media are pushing for action.''

''In both directions,'' Flynn added. ''There's the indigenes' rights faction screaming for aid against the invading oppressor, and the alien peril lobby demanding protection for our colonists.'' He made a wry grin. ''So far, nothing from the proponents of if it ain't broke, don't fix it. The trouble is, how do we know if it's broke?''

''Assuming someone other than Nsil,'' Jocelyn put in, ''we might be inclined to give him the miner and trust to his discretion. But his performance to date . . .''

''Made sense according to what he knew.'' Kayo said it firmly. ''The people of Magh and of Eamn each think the other started the plague that nearly destroyed both cultures, and fear each other accordingly.'' Her listeners knew this, but a recap couldn't hurt. ''It was outsiders turning up—first the Yainans and then *Roamer*—that stirred the pot. Eamn reconnoitered and were reassured, until we parked near Magh and sent the DV in. Well, you know the rest.''

She leaned forward. ''He'd never met a Maghren before, Nsil hadn't—let alone a Yainan or one of us. When he took off for *here*, for heaven's sake, he'd only dealt with two of each—and even so, was beginning to turn his attitudes around. You underestimate the changes he's made since we got here.''

Flynn's scowl showed concern, not displeasure. ''This guy abducted you twice; his guerrillas wrecked the DV and almost killed your pairmate. And you're on his side?''

''I see his viewpoint. Then and now. Two different things. He saw the Vehicle as a major threat—and for what it's worth, he feels bad about the injuries.

''But the point is . . .'' If she hadn't lost track of it; oh yes: ''He understands now, Magh's no threat to him. Nor Earth, as such. But Aroka's something else. The point is, Nsil knows the difference.''

The meeting ended on tentative consensus: for now, wait for some decisive info to outGate. If the news were bad, give the Eamnets a souped-up mining vessel—but send along a helpful ''training cadre'' of human officers and crew; any combat-type operations would be conducted by the species most familiar with the tools of the trade.

Not a bad compromise, though it might need some sugar coating to go down easily with Nsil. Checking her chrono, Kayo made quick good-byes and walked briskly to the base clinic. As she approached the entrance, the doors parted and Dan Quillan strolled out.

He looked and moved so much better she could hardly believe it. ''Dan!'' Running, she threw a fervent hug and felt him stagger. ''Oops, sorry. I get carried away sometimes.''

''That's all right.'' *Now* why did his cheeks redden? ''My test results earn me a beer, the doc says.'' Join me? was implied so Kayo hooked an arm with his, noting with critical gaze that his stride was almost sure and certain but not quite. The Landing Circle was a good place and near; looking across the plates of complimentary pretzels and nachos the two clinked tall, cold-beaded glasses with not too much of a head, and sipped deep.

Quillan sighed deeper. ''If I wasn't getting well before, I am now. Right after you came up, actually, everything all of a sudden started improving lots faster. You're good for me, Kayo.''

Maybe so; certainly the tenuous cloud of dazed confusion was gone. Now he was off chasing another subject. ''. . . the odds, Kayo, that there at two stars not all that far apart there'd be *two* species enough like us to breathe the same air, eat the same foods, and even communicate?''

Forbearing to nitpick about the food, Kayo said, ''People used to wonder if we were all alone in the universe. I could never see that.'' She took a swallow and wiped foam from her lip. ''Look, I forget how many Carlsaganbillion stars in this galaxy or how many galaxies all told. But one thing we do know; if something works, the universe likes to do it a lot. That's just the way it *is*. So if it could produce life here, with a dubious claim to intelligence, why throw away the process pattern?''

He was grinning now, as in the best of their times before. ''Like parallel evolution. If the general design works for one kind of critter, try it on some others.'' Counting on fingers, ''Flying fish, flying frogs, pterodactyls, birds, bats, flying squirrels, flying lemurs, what have you; two designs there, but maybe one's the early stage of the other. Invertebrates only managed it with insects, but a whole lot of varieties.''

''Streamlined swimmers.'' Her turn. ''Fish, sharks not quite the same and maybe earlier, some amphibians, icthyosaurus, all kinds flightless seagoing birds, whales and seals and manatees and a whole batch of mammals only partially reverted.''

''Yes.'' He drained his glass. ''Your place? Since I don't have one down here?''

She already knew it was right, so her nod came immediately.

Damn all! Gowdy hesitated. ''Put *Golconda* through to here.'' He waited ten seconds, then said, ''Hold your fire. This is Gowdy. Commodore Aroka's going to lose part of an arm if I don't Gate him back to Earth; I can't possibly get him to Magh in time to help anything.''

''Not your problem.'' The voice was little more than a thin, dry whisper. Not Yates; this Lioso, maybe? ''Bring him.''

Shattered wrist, tourniquet, no blood supply to the hand: Sam spilled it all, fast. The brittle wisp of voice said, ''We have a reasonably competent paramedic aboard; she will improvise. I want to see you coming out that hatch.''

''His suit's breached. You have to give us time to haywire a protective covering.''

A pause, and then, "Very well. But be quick about it."

Ignoring Aroka's startled flinch, Gowdy reached to feel the maimed hand. Deathly cold, but not ice yet. "It might work."

He looked up as Milo Vitale entered. "Owen's on his way. What do you need first?"

"Change of plan," Gowdy said. "Go cut the sleeve off a suit—biggest one you can find. Right hand; take it off about the elbow. Roll the sleeve down as far as the wrist." He pointed to Aroka's gruesome injury. "We'll horse the glove part on, then roll the forearm section back up, for overlap."

Milo left; at the door Owen Tanacross appeared. Sam took Rocco Silva by the shoulder. "Escort this one down and have Simone Gate him the hell home." Tanacross nodded and left, with the wobbly Silva in tow. One nuisance, at least, out of the way.

Sydnie came over, close enough to talk quietly. "Sam—I didn't realize at the time. But when you told me not to shoot, it was *me* you were trying to protect."

"Which made two of us." He hadn't forgotten how close she'd come. . . .

"I didn't want—I asked you, remember? Asked you, what could I do? Because he had that knife on me, and . . ." She had tears, but didn't wipe at them. Just blinked. "You knew what would happen, though, didn't you? With the gun, I mean."

"Not exactly. Either it wouldn't shoot or it'd blow. I hadn't figured on anyone not settling for the first option."

"I wasn't going to shoot you, Sam, I swear. I could miss, empty the magazine—I put it on full auto, to make a lot of recoil so maybe I could twist loose before . . ."

Maybe so, maybe not. He plain wasn't interested, and she must have seen he wasn't because she shut up.

Which gave him a chance to plan. There wasn't much to go on, but he did have a few basic ideas. He saw Milo roll the cut sleeve up Aroka's arm; the fit seemed snug enough. Gowdy eyed the injured man. "You're sure this is what you want?"

"For your ship's sake, it had better be, hadn't it?" The commodore had made a rally; purpose burned in his gaze. "And in the past I have found Arman's assurances to be trustworthy."

"All right, let's go. Just the two of us, should do."

"No." Aroka stopped. "La Hoja, also. Arman would never forgive me. More to the point, he would not forgive you."

So the three of them, Milo following to help with minor chores, went to the cargo bay. When Gowdy and Sydnie had their suits sealed and before Sam plugged Aroka's batteries back in, he said on the suit-to-suit, "Listen, Sydnie. When we're over in there, watch me and take your cues. When I see my chance, there won't be time to say much." Because while he had little faith in her ability to maintain loyalty, he had no wish to see her dead, either. He even took the time to slap a temporary tape repair on her suit where Aroka's knife had pinked it.

Of course he had no firm idea how to get anybody out alive, either, and that scared him a lot. What he did know was, these bastards weren't taking his ship.

Now the three went out and across, and entered the miner at a midships airlock, its inner hatch opening directly into the main central area. Nearly a dozen and mostly armed, Aroka's reinforcements waited in greeting. Reluctantly Sam joined the commodore and Sydnie as they opened and folded back their suits' slanting faceplates.

The rawboned hulk with the insignia on his cap was probably Yates, but the wizened figure wearing the heavy, corsetlike torso sheath, its limbs cradled in powered prosthetic braces—the thin, crackling voice identified Arman Lioso. "Jorge! And Captain Gowdy. And after so long—La Hoja Rubia, my very dear."

Seeing Lightner cringe, Sam nudged her with an elbow. "Stay savvy, dammit!" His move put both her and Aroka in front of him as he came abreast the inner hatch's hinge pivots, and suddenly he knew what his move had to be. With one hand he depressed the interlock stud while the other slid Aroka's knife blade in beside it, pushing until both stuck solidly.

Having barely paused he moved ahead, saying, "Nice ship you've got here," not for content but only something to be listened to, to hold attention. "How's it for fuel economy?"

Lioso paid no heed; motioning a woman over to Aroka he watched as she peeled the severed sleeve free and with a scalpel began to dissect the suit's own glove. "Can you save it?"

She nodded. "Splice plastic into the artery to keep the hand alive until we rendezvous with a shuttle, to take him to the colony hospital. I can do it."

"Good." Lioso's head raised. "Now, captain, we will talk."

"I hope you make better sense than threatening to cripple my ship. Where did you think that would leave you?"

"With a fine pipeline refueling station, which is really all we need it for. Here or near Magh makes no real difference. Our long-term plans, you see, depend largely on bootleg Gates, and right aboard this ship we have a considerable number of the essential matrices. Pre-activated, and of the same capacity as those used in tandem by the macroGates."

Keep him talking; it can't hurt. "A Gate's only good with both ends in place."

If he'd thought the voice creepy, Lioso's laugh was worse. "Our Earth terminals, quite unknown to the authorities, were up and ready before we left. Also of course we've brought groups of paired units; we can establish links quite independently of Earth, wherever our vessels take us."

Bootleg Gates, huh? Somebody in this mob really had connections. Still, though: "*Roamer* aside," Gowdy argued, "nothing out here can take you much of anyplace, except local."

"Which is why we're pleased to avoid immobilizing that ship. But alternatives exist. The two Yainan starships would seem quite vulnerable to capture, and providing them fuel-Gates from your ship or from the macroGate . . ."

"You'd need more than that; how about food, water, air?"

Powered bracing moved the twiglike hand. "Surmountable obstacles. And of course we'll be ready, at the macroGate, to board and commandeer any leapfrog ships as they appear."

They could do it, too; suddenly Gowdy realized that the threat reached far beyond this one system. But despite all instincts screeching for action, Sam held silence.

Lioso looked over at his medic. "How does it go?"

"I'm getting there. But if he'd let me give him a shot, I wouldn't have to fight the reflex jerks when I touch a nerve."

"Our leader dislikes sedatives. Do your best."

With a twitch of his head toward Gowdy, the stick man said, "It would seem we have no further need of the captain.

La Hoja, however, awaits lengthy ministrations of my own devising. So gentlemen, if you will discriminate carefully with your weapons . . .''

''Hold!'' Wincing at some repercussion from his involuntary gesture, Aroka went on, ''You may not have use for the man, but I do. And while I am present, my wishes govern.''

With a skeletal smile Lioso said, ''Ordinarily true. But since you are incapacitated, I act in your stead.''

''You're taking over? Why not just kill me?''

''Jorge! Our friendship! Not to mention that due to my . . . singular attributes . . . I hardly project a leader's image. So you'll live, and remain here to see our success. But at a cost, Jorge—when you recover, we'll be equal partners.''

Furious yet helpless, Aroka spluttered. ''Arman . . . !''

They weren't going to get any more distracted than this.

''*Now*, Sydnie!''

It was all or nothing; Gowdy slammed his faceplate home and managed to clip one latch snug as he leaped for the outer hatch. Its handle came around at his first desperate pull, and with the interlock jammed, fourteen-point-seven pounds to the square inch threw the hatch door wide, jerking Sam out and around away from the stream of bullets that lasted considerably longer than one might expect, seeing as the shooters' lungs were running on empty. As he hung there, sprawled out of the line of fire, its sheer volume reflected fleeting streaks of sunlight against the black void.

A combination of luck and determination held his grip on the lock handle. When he was reasonably certain the barrage was over, but with due heed for anyone who might pop up suited, he swung around and climbed back inboard.

He'd seen prettier.

XX

Praisings of T'phee by Irtuk and Bretl flood en with inner discomfiture. For Yainans an act such as er has done to the yumin Beringa is cause for shame, not pride. Yet to their view, er realizes, er has acted most well; in consequence es soon ceases disclaimature of merit in their esteeming and directs converse to welfare of the get of Irtuk, now seemingly untroubled as it ends feeding and sets enself to drowse.

"Appearings and behavings of the get Tuik display no token of damage incurred," T'phee observes. Irtuk, es injury assessed as minor and now neatly covered, affirms T'phee's estimation, yet erself expresses no trace of satisfaction.

Instead, to Bretl the Maggen speaks. "While T'phee protected Tuik, and Skeeta has gone unweaponed to pursue the miscreant Case, why do we two bide like ungrown young?"

And to T'phee, "Tuik shall sleep in fullness now. Will you stand protector as Bretl and I go in aid of Skeeta?"

Er should risk being again provoked to unnatural contention? But such consequence need not eventuate; T'phee signs agreement. "I will secure the entrance latch. And release it to none, except that in my knowledge they merit trust."

Irtuk signifies affirmation. As er and Bretl make exit, T'phee calls after them, "Irtuk. Bretl. Be of all caution." Then er secures the latch and looks to the get.

Commencing sleep, Tuik essays to feed on one of es forelimb digits, though not with true intent.

Explosive decompression hadn't helped anyone's looks, especially Arman Lioso's. Aroka had brought his faceplate near to closing, but one-handed he hadn't managed to latch it against internal pressure; lack of firm closure had drained his air.

Sydnie didn't seem to be perforated anywhere, but two streams of vapor issued from the seal at one side of her faceplate. Maybe that was what she was yelling about on the suit-to-suit, but she wasn't coherent enough to tell for sure.

Gowdy looked closer; a thick strand of hair protruded to distort the sealing gasket. She was twisting her head around, trying to pull it free, but no luck. Then she changed tactics, leaned her face to that side and reached to yank hard on the dangling lock. "Get that knife over here!"

He saw what she wanted. Closing and dogging the outer hatch he unstuck the interlock, then shut the inner hatch also before going to hack off the eight inches or so she'd managed to bring out through the seal. With a jerk of her head she tore the shortened hair free inside; the vapor streams ceased.

"Thanks! Jeez, what a fix!" So she'd be all right.

Deliberately Gowdy looked around, seeing what he'd done. Of the dead strangers, Aroka's troops wore weapons belts; the few others might or might not be innocents caught in the gears. What especially hurt was seeing the dead paramedic—but there hadn't been a way he could save her. Not and still keep himself alive.

Now he pushed a switch and paused, waiting to see if the miner's air tanks held enough liquefied reserve to refill the ship. When he rapped at a console and heard the sound clearly on his suit mikes, he cracked his faceplate. Outrushing air popped his ears; pressurewise *Golconda* was at about nine thousand feet.

It would have to do. Again he looked at Sydnie, and gestured; reluctantly she opened her own suit, wincing at the sudden pressure drop. He asked, "You okay?"

"Now I am. My damn *hair* . . ."

"Yeah. It can happen when you're in a hurry. Now then—did anybody get away? Make it to a door and seal off?"

As she shook her head a voice sounded. This bucket's intercoms needed some tuning; distortion was bad. "Is anybody out there?" High-pitched, that voice. "We got our cubby closed off safe, Abe and I—but we lost a lot of pressure first." A pause, with only some thin gasping heard. "This is Larry Corcoran calling Mayday. We're low on air, and—"

At the box, Sam hit the talk switch. "Roger, Corcoran; I read you. This is—" Woops; whose side was this bird on? "I'm here from the big ship and there's been some changes made, so be prepared to accept them." Now let's see what he says. . . .

After a time Corcoran answered. "I can do that. The way it's been—I'm a Glen Springs graduate, but Commander Yates hasn't been operating a Glen Springs ship. If I hadn't disobeyed orders all to hell, he'd have blasted Kayo Marlin. So I'm not exactly in anyone's good books lately. Sir." Right; by now, Corcoran was wondering how deep he'd put his foot in his mouth.

This one saved Kayo's skin? Take him off the hook! "You are now. This is Captain Sam Gowdy, of *Roamer*. We're a mite short of air pressure out here, too, but it's okay to unzip." Second thoughts. "How about your buddy? Where's he from?"

"Abe Sheffield. He was with Velucci on the big Gate, but Lioso the Clockwork Assassin drafted him onto here. You don't remember Abe?"

"By sight, maybe. Anyway, come on out. Is anyone else holed up, that you know of?"

"We'll check along the way."

The offship circuit was still tuned to *Roamer*; Sam hit the switch. "Watch officer, come in. Gowdy here, from *Golconda*."

"Mose speaking. Captain, are you all right?"

Not really. But, "This ship's secured. How there?"

"Simone's Gated Silva home, if that's what you mean. We've lost track of Beringer. Atwell's sitting here wondering whether to shoot me or not. I keep telling her it's not a good idea."

"It isn't, Vivian." Sam put emphatic sincerity to his words. "Aroka's dead, and Lioso and all the gang he brought with him." *I hope*; he hadn't counted that closely. "So be nice."

"But, the commodore . . ." Her voice came thinly. "I only did what he told us." That tired old excuse. "Here's my gun, Mr. Tuiasso. I'm out of a job now. I request to be Gated home."

"I'll rule on that," Gowdy said, "when I have time for it." But aside from a little bullying, the woman hadn't done much worth filing charges on. "Oh hell; let her gather her stuff, then show her the pretty colors. Okay then; anything else?"

"The Vehicle's nearly in; I guess it's safe, now, to say so out loud. You want it where?"

Oh sheest. The DV well was occupied, and for the immediate future this floating morgue was going to preempt stern access to *Roamer*. Or maybe not. "Tell Libby to keep checking in; when she gets here I'll think of something." And he signed off.

Niggling clatter from an access ramp drew Sam's attention. He looked up to see not two but seven persons entering the open area. First tensing, he saw that none appeared to be armed, and eased again. "Corcoran?"

"Captain." A medium-built man, noticeable mostly for pale red hair and fair complexion, raised a hand but seemed somehow restrained. From behind him a larger fellow, holding him by one arm, produced a gun. "Sorry," Corcoran said. "Slade had that in my back; I guess I'm not much of a hero."

No time for handholding. And why hadn't he or Sydnie picked up a weapon while they had the chance? "What you want, Slade?"

Looking around, the burly man seemed hesitant. ". . . six, seven, eight . . . and Aroka himself f'godsakes! Besides me, that leaves just Case and Rocco and the two women, and then Driscoll and his two back at the 'gate." He spat, then realized his mistake in zero gee and made a futile grab at the floating globules, inadvertently freeing Corcoran in the process.

"Your count's off," Sam corrected him. "Rocco and Estilete aren't around any more, and Vivian's handed in her weapon so I'm Gating her home without filing any charges. Would you like the same deal?" When the adrenalin wore off, Gowdy realized, he was going to fold like a pair of deuces.

The man scowled. "Not exactly. I'd like to stay alive when I get there."

Sam reminded himself that heavy features and a low forehead didn't necessarily mean stupidity. "Explain."

"If I go home free and clear, not a scratch on me, it'll be thought I sold Aroka out. I *need* some charges filed—though I'd just as soon pass on the hard time categories." The gun wasn't pointing anywhere in particular; flipping it end for end, Slade caught it by the barrel and held it toward Gowdy. "And I'd smell better if I outGated there with a bullet needing dug out of me."

Sam shook his head. "I couldn't . . ."

"Civilians!" Reversing the gun again, Slade reached out to point it back toward his thigh. "Never mind," and he fired.

"You bloody fool!" The adjective suited. Only flowing, though, not spurting. "What if you hit the artery? There wouldn't be a damn thing we could do for you."

"I know where it is," but for all his bravado the man was paling. Aroka had no further use for a tourniquet; Gowdy freed the loop of line and started toward Slade.

He held it out. "Rather do this yourself, too?" But noting strain around the eyes he said, "Hold still," and saw to the task, then stood. "Someone bring this man's vac suit. And . . ."

From one side Sydnie spoke. "Maxl! Maxl Schläd. Calling ourselves Slade now, are we? Torched any good books lately?"

"Wasn't my fault the target holed up in his library; I ran out of time, was all. And that was a long time ago."

Then he looked closer. "Charel Secour! I was right; you did get away. Lioso owes me two thou on that bet." Limping, he moved across to rifle the stick man's pockets.

"What the hell are you doing?" Gowdy couldn't believe it.

"Collecting." Slade held up a handful of bills. "He's short, but it'll have to do." Then he held still while Corcoran and another man worked to get the suit onto him.

At the ragged edge of losing control, Sam knew he had to get out of here. "Corcoran. Move us in to *Roamer*'s stern hatch. You have enough people to deploy your ship-to-ship tube?" The man nodded, so Gowdy told the rest of it: run mooring lines, hook up air tanks resupply; when *Golconda*'s integrity was secured, bring the dead ones across and then outship, to Earthmouth. "We'll go on ahead; I'll meet you at the control deck."

Anything else? No. The wounded man's suit was on and sealed. "Come on, Sydnie; help me with Slade."

One more thing. "Corcoran, you work the airlock for us.

And you can't afford to lose any more air. So remember the old motto: pump, don't dump.''

Unsure what he meant to do if he did find Beringer, Skeeter was even less prepared for Beringer to find him; nobody wins 'em all. Figuring the stern for where the action was and cargo hold Two a good checkpoint, Cole ducked inside it, called control, and heard an earful: Aroka hurt, he and Lightner and the captain gone back to the mining ship. ''You sure, Mose?''

''Milo saw them off, then came back out here. How come you two missed passing each other?''

''Different routes, I guess. Look—I'm going back to the stern bay. Maybe suit up, in case I can do something.''

Signing off, Skeeter emerged into the corridor. Just in time to face Beringer, heading aft. ''Hold it, Cole. Have you seen the commodore? What's going on?''

''That's what I'm trying to find out.'' Don't tell this ape anything! Well, maybe a little . . . ''Aroka's gone offship.'' Further, though, Cole professed ignorance.

''Then I'd better go hold the fort in control until he gets back.'' Gingerly he rubbed his left buttock. ''Maybe I don't need a shot after all. Come on.'' He gestured: the gun, always the goddamned gun. So Skeeter led the way, down through the equipment and drive mode quarters levels to reach the control deck, clambering out not far from Earthmouth.

The surprise was when he turned to see the hulking shapes of Irtuk and Bretl, their lower extremities Velcro-swathed, moving none too steadily but with considerable determination.

The bearers turned, looked, and moved faster. Toward him and Beringer.

The first two yumins approached by Irtuk-saa lacked sufficient Maghren speech to be of avail; only when Vinler entered the place of feeding did progress result. Now in this inner shipspace where no force held beings or objects to a surface, with lower limb ends encapped by the same material yumins utilized here, Irtuk and Bretl sought to achieve skill in movement. Longwise of the ship they trudged, then around its arc to the next straight and parallel way. Effort brought strain to untaught muscles, but Irtuk persevered and Bretl with her.

At one turn hardly distinguishable from another in this place of monohue, Bretl spoke. ''Irtuk. If we are to seek the yumin Case, let it be quickly. Further repetition of these movements brings more fatigue than skill.''

''Our thought joins.'' Irtuk indicated a direction. ''There lies access toward the inner portions, where we are told Beringa has taken retreat.'' But after only a few pacements, passing the juncture of another passage Irtuk saw movement and turned to take cognizance: first came Skeeta, but under menace; behind skulked Beringa holding the weapon already used to Irtuk's harm.

A cold twitching betook Irtuk, yet she would not yield to past or future pain. Hindlimbs flexing, she bore down on the yumins, in full surety that Bretl followed.

''Hold, Irtuk!'' Skeeta thrust a fending forelimb. ''The weapon. You cannot hope to overcome it.''

The weapon of Case and the forelimb holding it held none so steady, yet short of reaching the yumin, Irtuk gave halt. And observed his activating digit lessen pressure at the mechanism; no act of decision was yet mandatory. Slowly, Irtuk again made approach, and now the yumin gave ground, making harsh sounds in his own speech. ''He warns you to cease advance,'' Skeeta spoke.

But Irtuk's next pace brought sight along the side passage; only a short way off stood this ship's portal to Erdth, and there one yumin bearer aided another in depositing bags and cases. Beringa had already seen; he scuttled to the device and stood just short of it, moving his weapon about and perhaps berating the two there as the smaller entered the portal's shell and the other manipulated levers at a nearby panel. Advantaging the seeder's lack of attention Irtuk came nearer, and behind heard Bretl follow, breathing at increased rate.

To one side Skeeta spoke. ''Allow his departure! He . . .'' But Case now raised the weapon toward Irtuk. ''Get away!'' The voice of Cole came thin and urgent. ''For your life, Irtuk!''

The weapon spat; Irtuk had barely time to sense the sting beside her jaw when Bretl's charge buffeted her forward and to the side. Again the weapon's sound; then, flinging the object at Bretl, Beringa turned and made a great leap into the portal. A multihued burst of light hid the device's interior, then died.

The yumin bearer who had waited inside it was gone, and with her almost the entirety of Beringa.

While Simone was deciding she didn't have to throw up, Skeeter inspected Beringer's left foot and lower shin. At the plane of shear a sort of shiny brownish film half-hid the exposed cross section. He didn't touch it; it looked fragile and who needs a mess?

"What are you going to do? *Frame* it?" Cole didn't think Simone was any more shaken than he was; she just let it show more freely.

"Send it after him; what else?" As Leopold reached again to the operating panel Skeeter added, "Give it a few minutes. Even if someone was right there, it'll take a little time to clear the Tush." *Was*? Will be, two years from now. Oh well . . .

"You think they can put it back on?" Simone looked dubious.

"Why not? Cleanest cut I ever saw, and not even burnt. I expect this film'll dissolve in saline solution okay."

She was setting up the transmit sequence, so he placed the severed member on the grid. "Has anything like this ever happened before?"

"I'd be surprised if it hasn't. I've never heard of such an instance, but it's the kind of goof that gets covered up."

Waiting, Cole finally noticed the nick at Irtuk's jaw; the bearer hadn't said anything, just stood in supportive embrace with Bretl. Looking now at that one, Skeeter saw no sign of any wound. He gestured. "How could he have missed?"

Simone paused at her chore "Bretl reared up, then bent again and charged; Beringer shot high. I expect he was pretty well rattled."

She flipped one more switch. "Okay. Let's try."

Two minutes and forty-seven seconds after she hit Activate, the foot followed Beringer to Glen Springs.

Sam looked like death warmed over and left to cool again, but he wasn't about to admit needing any help. Twice Sydnie had tried, and couldn't tell if she were rebuffed or merely ignored.

Without a flicker of expression he heard Simone tell what happened to Case Beringer, and said, "You'll write it up? This man," pointing to Maxl Schläd, "will give you the names of the dead ones Corcoran's bringing over. Before you Gate him."

Then, Sydnie following, he went to control and began his own report. After a few minutes at the keyboard his pace slowed and stopped; he leaned forward and rested his head on folded arms. When his shoulders began twitching she went to him. "Sam?"

His face when he raised it was tear-streaked. "How many dead? This isn't what I came here for. Why . . . ?"

She hugged his head against her. "To save your ship."

He raised his head again to look at her, and she knew that for once she'd come up with the right answer.

About yumins there was much Scayna failed to comprehend; sometimes even Kaow could not clear away the bearer's uncertainties. Why, when all agreed that Nsil would receive a yumin ship in which to return through the great portal, was no such ship forthcoming?

The delay, Scayna understood, came of caution. Some warning by Gowdy, carried on the speaking device he had given her, still continued to forestall decision. That warning's nature was not told her; inquiry brought only evasion. Not, Scayna thought, of Kaow's doing, but by those Kaow in turn queried.

Feeding and cosseting Nyrl, aiding the bearer-child to gain strength and control of its limbs, Scayna endured the elapsing daycycles—enriched at darktimes by intimacies with Nsil. So it was with eager expectance, not long after one earlylight, that she saw Nsil and Kaow enter her chamber with looks of purpose.

"Has decision ripened? Do we return to Eamn?"

"Soon," Nsil answered. "But allow Kaow to explain."

The narration confused Scayna; why should the sudden and unanticipated arrival here, at the portal fed by Gowdy's vessel, of numerous yumins and most no longer living—why should such disaster precipitate decision, allowing Nsil his ship at last?

"Because these," spoke Kaow, "posed danger. Among the dead is the one who would have destroyed Nsil's ship Three, and also the one who ordered that destruction. And although some of the dead fell as victims, most were of the same stripe as those two."

Nsil spoke. "Some living, also. There is one"—his jaw dropped in amusement—"one who arrived missing part of a hindlimb. The severed piece appeared shortly, and we are to believe that it has been restored to him and to normal function!"

"That much," spoke Kaow, "is true." Seeming impatient, she resumed speech. "The fact of note, however, is that your new ship is in preparation for assumption of Eamnet control. At the beginning there will be yumin skyship persons also, to teach and to maintain operations as Eamnets learn. Also, at Eamn to aid in construction of manufacturies for the fuel these ships require, that your use may be independent of our supply apparatus. If such has not been accomplished before your arrival."

"And what category of ship," Scayna inquired, "comes to Nsil's command? Is it of the kind that threatened all your lives when you approached the great portal?"

Kaow made the yumin headmove of negation. "Were these recent dead still alive and of menace in your home system, such would be the case. Even though a mining ship, being unable to ground on any world, would have been of greatly limited utility. But now, Gowdy assures, no need of weaponry exists."

Scayna would have spoken, but Nsil preempted. "Can we not put trust in Gowdy, then in no one. Scayna, I more than any have come near provoking great conflict. I do not recant my acts; they came of reasoned cause, yet from knowledge lacking fullness. Here at Erdth I have learned greatly, and no longer fear any deeds of Magh. And now with these ill-meaning yumins removed, the assurance of Gowdy suffices to me."

"Then to me also." To Kaow she spoke. "At what later time are we to expect embarkment and departure?"

"I will ascertain," spoke Kaow, "as soon as may be done."

Not sure just how far he should trust Sydnie, Sam let her bed him anyway. Tense to the edge of snapping and tired near collapse, he thrashed and rolled and thrust and clenched embrace to explosion. When he sagged free and lay panting, laughter broke loose and threatened not to stop. He knew better than to fight it. As Sydnie rose and left the room he let himself run down; when she returned he lay flat, looking up, his intermittent giggle disturbed only by the occasional hiccup.

Ice cubes barely dented the dark hue of bourbon in the glass she handed him. "Doctor's orders."

It wasn't filled too deep for this time of day. "Thanks." Her glass showed paler but not much. Clink, and sip.

A little later Gowdy edged toward sleep feeling more relaxed than he had any right to be. Next morning he woke to muscle soreness from tension and exertion, but limbered up before dressing and breakfasted in quarters with good appetite. Last night he'd needed Sydnie to banish the dead faces from his mind; this morning he managed it alone.

"Now you're aboard ship officially again," he told her, "go plug yourself back into the watch skeds."

"And just what are *you* going to be doing?"

"Sizing up Corcoran, and planning *Golconda*'s next move. There's still an Aroka toady bossing the macroGate. Question is, is Corcoran up to tackling the setup?"

"You mean you'd actually stand back and let someone else do it?" One last try at brushing the chopped-off strands of hair to blend in with the overall flow, and Sydnie left. Suddenly Gowdy realized something: before all the trouble, the Doodlebug and Eamn and after, he couldn't have talked to Sydnie like this. Not without offending her in some unknown way, throwing her into an upstage sulk and himself into the doghouse basement.

He still didn't know how far or how long he could trust the change, but he liked it. For now, at least, he wasn't going to push too hard for the real Sydnie Lightner to please stand up.

Time to move. Going inship he checked with SuZanne

Craig in control; the DV would be here very soon, and Larry Corcoran awaited Gowdy's visit. First things first; in to the stern bay and through the tube to *Golconda*, Sam found that ship cleaned up better than he expected. Corcoran offered welcome: "Coffee in a zeegee cup? Or we could sit in the exercise 'fuge."

"Zeegee's fine." What did this fellow think they used in *Roamer*'s control room? Accepting the container, Gowdy asked, "Do you have enough personnel left to operate this bucket properly? Or should I lend you a few?"

The younger man looked concerned. "It depends. Driscoll and Lioso bumped some of my original crew back at the macro, to make room for the muscle goons. We can get back there all right; the problem is whether Driscoll will release my people."

Go down, Moses . . . "Who says we need his consent? Look—out here it wasn't supposed to be weapons country; when I ran a bluff and got most of Aroka's guns we Gated them home. But then the fit purely hit the Shan; folks got killed and I can't guarantee you it's over. Right now we have handguns up the wazoo. The way I hear it, this Driscoll has just two sidekicks, plus maybe some recruits. If you don't want to go face him down, maybe I will."

"You want to walk into a shootout?"

"Not hardly. What I want is to hand Driscoll a can't-win situation." Sam paused. "Those killings on here were my first." Go away, faces. "If I have anything to say about it they're my last, too." Not easily, they went.

Corcoran leaned forward. "Do you have a plan?"

"Just the obvious. I'm working on something better." A vagrant memory tickled. "Corcoran." He wasn't addressing the man, just running the name past his recalls. "Kayo Marlin's mentioned you, I think. Did you know her before?"

The young man looked flustered. "Not much of a mention, I guess. We were married once. Out on Tetzl's Planet, where we met working the same project site. Larry and Kayo, a team for the ages. But our contracts wound up, and back on Earth it quit working." He shrugged. "Nobody's fault. And I was glad of the chance to save her cute butt, out by the macroGate."

"I'm glad you did, too. All right; I'm going to pick some

folks to ride with us, back out to the 'gate.'' Corcoran looked surprised at the ''us'' but didn't comment. ''Give it maybe a day, then we'll move.''

''Fine. Meanwhile I'd like to transship some cargo—most or all of those Gate matrices. The way things stand, you'll be the one deciding where they can be used best.''

''Fine.'' An idea showed a timid silhouette, then hid again. ''Coordinate with Milo Vitale; he handles supply for us.'' Gowdy stood. ''Welcome to the team, Larry. Good to have you aboard.''

A handy device, the ship-to-ship tube. Inside *Roamer* Sam got down to control in time to hear Libby Verdoorn telling SuZanne Craig, ''Since the stern tube fitting's occupied, we'll ease in alongside your visitor and suit up to connect resupply. Then . . .''

Gowdy cut in. ''Hi, Libby; Sam here. Sorry about the traffic jam. We've had a few problems. Look: you get moored and I'll assign people to top up your fuel and air. Soon as you're tied on, give a holler; I'm coming over. New mission.''

T'phee would be glad to hear it. But first Gowdy went back to quarters.

''You can't tackle him on the macroGate; he'd ambush you.'' Sydnie kept her voice patient. Coming in, Sam had started telling her his ideas for liberating the huge structure, and right off the mark she saw fallacies. Sam Gowdy simply didn't know the league he intended to play in.

''I don't know Driscoll personally but I've heard of him; the man outsnakes a cobra. Fangs at both ends, so to speak.''

''Now hold on; you haven't heard me out.'' Still patient, Gowdy didn't look to stay that way much longer. ''I can bring him out, him and his two goons. Tell him it's Aroka's orders and . . .''

''And he'll believe you, won't even ask for confirmation. Oh sure.'' Now her own scheme machine began cranking over.

Sam wasn't done, though. ''I'm sending this ship to Magh at slow pace, and taking *Golconda* to the 'gate. So we'll have the laser; I can threaten to hole the hull in enough places that they'd have to evacuate, all Gate home. With suitable warning, of course.'' His face twisted; whatever he saw wasn't nice. ''He'll have to come out.'' Gowdy's expression said he hoped so.

She seized the pause. ''He'd say the hell with you, suit up whoever he's managed to recruit, along with the pair he brought, and dare you to come in after him.''

Silenced, Sam waited. Then, ''You have a better idea?''

Just the outlines, so far. But, ''I go with you.''

''What could you do?''

''As Sydnie Lightner, nothing. I'm thinking of Charel Secour and one hell of a good cover story.''

A little later than he'd intended, Gowdy climbed into the Deployment Vehicle, cycled himself through its airlock, and propelled himself the length of its central tunnel. ''Hi, Libby, Maril. Any problems getting here?''

The two looked well; the activity of running the DV seemed to have the juices flowing. Each slender, Verdoorn considerably the taller, both would probably be termed blond, though blue-eyed pale-haired Maril Jencik didn't especially match coloring with Libby's brown eyes, honey-colored hair, and straight black brows.

Jencik had always seemed a bit fragile; now she moved with confidence. ''Not after I got my sighting coordinates straight. Then I could point and Libby pushed.''

Oddly, Verdoorn colored. Out of some perverse subconscious quirk Sam asked, ''How was Jules, the last you saw him?''

Primly, Libby pursed her lips. ''Mainly pissed off.''

''Even after Aroka handed him your colony? Which we'll be doing something about, I expect, before too long. Anyway, what does the man want? An egg in it?''

Jencik cleared her throat. ''I expect he wanted me to go be Missus Colony Pooh-bah. Instead of pairing with Libby.''

Speechless, Sam looked from one to the other. Shipboard liaisons in a small group got complicated enough with only one variety of each gender, which was why Glen Springs arbitrarily chose crews on that basis. So out here, away from Earth, Gowdy simply never gave a thought to the alternatives.

Feeling embarrassed he tried a recovery. ''Well, judging on performance, getting the DV here and all, you make a great team.'' And the Vehicle so neat and clean, and running so shorthanded . . . He shut up while maybe he was still ahead, and wondered at an unexpected pang. Had he, back where he didn't really notice it, been carrying some kind of a letch for Libby? Grow up, Gowdy.

Verdoorn grinned; openness had dispersed her high color. ''No bi bondings on ships; right? Well, it's new to us, too—and at this point we really don't know how permanent. But I hope you'll grant a waiver while we're aboard here. Unless you want to relieve us with your original DV people.''

He hadn't considered that option, and a moment's thought told him not to bother; SuZanne Craig was too essential to *Roamer*'s watch rotation. So first, ''Do you feel up to doing a run from Magh to Yamar and back?'' Oops: Forerunner, Scout. Libby nodded recognition; he continued, ''I can lend you a relief hand or two.''

''Yes. Over that kind of distance we could use the help.'' Her grin went impish. ''And a triad might be nice. Are you sure you wouldn't like to come along, yourself?''

The grin faded; she looked *serious*, f'Pete'sakes. And after an initial start, Jencik looked more expectant than otherwise. So say it straight: ''Captains can't indulge that kind of temptation, and I couldn't possibly get free right now. But you have no idea how much I appreciate the compliment.''

This time Verdoorn actually dimpled. ''It was overdue. For the present, though, just assign someone who can help navigate.''

''All right.'' Another thought. ''You speak some local, don't you, Maril?''

''Sure. Why?''

''Your passengers don't talk ours. Irtuk-saa and young Tuik to Magh. And for Yamar, the bearer Bretl and T'phee the Yainan.''

Unheralded revealment by Gowdy brings T'phee renewed vigor. ''To Yamar you transport me? Truly? At how near a time?''

''Not myself,'' the yumin speaks, ''but those whom I commend to do so. Maril and Libby, they are; also two not yet chosen. Upon them your reliance will be well placed. And departure eventuates before passing of another Yamar daycycle. Should there be any with whom you wish to exchange speech, before that time . . ."

T'phee considers, then speaks. "To seek out one and another presents me difficulty. Friend Gowdy, might you inform to all the fact that until your next group feeding occasion is passed, T'phee awaits converse with any who so desire, in that place?"

"As you request. And T'phee—our acquaintance is not concluded, yours and mine. I will later come to you on Yamar, and lend effort in aid of the greater Yainan peril."

So affirming, Gowdy enself departs. With unprecedented mixture of feelings, T'phee begins to assemble es few accessory belongings.

Between farewells to Vinler and Skeeta and others, Irtuk turns to Bretl. "I have not expressed my gratitude. For your aid in pursuing Beringa. Few would have risked so much."

"You feel so? Scayna, if present, would have rendered support equally. I have certainty."

Irtuk-saa pondered, then moved her head in assent. "But such assumption portends—I do not know. What of the ancient enmity?"

"What of Scayna standing protectrix for you?"

"As one bearer to another's need. Yes, Maghren or Eamnet notwithstanding. But the seeders. Nsil . . ."

"For the greater part, did not Nsil tender you both courtesy and forebearance? Irtuk, I have given ear to much that was spoken in my presence. Maghrens came to Eamn and were changed by Eamn; the change did not assimilate well. Old ways were uprooted; such disruptions are not easily accepted."

Reaching to snatch young Tuik from the path of an unwary yumin foot, Bretl spoke again. "Hap is that changed and olden ways may now find toleration, each of the other."

"Neither being your own."

"But not outside my understanding, nor ability to accept."

Speech suffered interruption as Alix Dorais gave greeting. Irtuk resolved to contemplate further the speaking of Bretl.

As often as she'd told herself she was ready for this, Sydnie really wasn't. Hovering with its midship airlock closely adjacent to one of the macroGate's, *Golconda* was meat on the hoof if Driscoll had any real armament installed. Not that he'd be on any kind of alert here; no one who wasn't on *Roamer* or *Golconda* or the DV knew of the recent deaths, and those who did also knew the importance of keeping matters that way. Standing alongside Gowdy in control, Sydnie watched as he opened an offship circuit. "Sam Gowdy here; I'd like to speak with your commandant."

It took a while; then a voice came. "Driscoll, commanding. Get off the line, Gowdy, and let me talk with Aroka."

Now was the time; Sydnie's breath shuddered. "Mr. Driscoll, surely you wouldn't want to disturb the commodore against his clearly expressed wishes. I am Charel Secour; for the moment you may speak with me instead."

"Secour?" A pause, then Driscoll's voice changed. "The *traitor*? She's dead, long since—what the hell is this?"

She forced a laugh. "Jorge didn't tell you? I'd have thought you knew about our plan. That traitor business; we needed some credentials to establish me as an agent, a role that led me into Glen Springs training and a commission on *Roamer*. Aroka was always a good long-term planner, wouldn't you agree?"

"I don't believe this. Let him tell me himself."

"Over a circuit? Don't be naive. You'll have to come here; in fact, those are the instructions I've been told to give you. You're welcome to bring your two aides, of course—but not more than four others, of any you may have recruited."

She overrode his reply. "You're expected at nine hundred hours. Aroka has always disliked tardiness. Secour out."

Switching off, she wiped sweat from her forehead. "Jeez! That was *work*." But she'd managed without having to brandish their hole card, the laser threat.

Sam's gaze held outright admiration. "And damn good. I paid attention; except for the agent thing, you hardly lied at all. That takes talent."

She couldn't help grinning. "You do it, too; I've watched."

He sighed. "Well, I guess we're ready for him. Though this plan doesn't take a whole lot of preparation."

It didn't. When seven suited figures entered the miner's airlock, Gowdy closed the outer hatch only enough to bar exit, leaving the chamber open to vacuum as Owen Tanacross and Molly Abele stood ready to cover the inner entrance. "It's still your play, Sydnie."

She used the ship-to-suits line. "Mr. Driscoll, I need to ask you about some disturbing rumors."

"Rumors? Who's saying things about me?"

"Does the name Arman Lioso ring a bell?"

"That poison little windup toy! What's he trying to pull?"

"I'd rather not be specific, just yet. But I'm instructed to tell you and all those with you to toss your weapons out the hatch."

"What kind of fool do you think I am?"

"No kind at all, we hope. Because until you comply, there you stay. And we're moving out from the macroGate. Think about it."

Another voice sounded. "Dammit, Driscoll, I want no part of this! I only signed on to wear a gun and back your play. Well, my contract just now lapsed. And there goes my gun, too."

Then he screamed, and Driscoll said, "I don't know if any of our outside suit mikes are on, so that you in *Golconda* could hear my shot. But that's also what'll happen to any other who tries to turn against me."

Some shouting for a time then, and the next voice was new. "Always did call us a bunch of amateurs; I guess he thought we'd just stand here and take it. Well, he shot Crawford, all right. And look what it got him."

Of the three living men, all unarmed, who were eventually brought inside, only one was Driscoll's.

And he wasn't saying much.

XXI

Entering yet a third yumin vessel, Irtuk-saa marveled; never did these beings achieve equivalent purpose by utilization of similar design. Or so the matter appeared. Whereas Gowdy's improvised construct had provided only minimal resting and sleeping facilities, his greater ship included the vast spinning area to simulate the effect of a small world's mass.

Here the residence area lay at cross direction to the Deevee's length; the weighting effect of its engines' forces would be directed toward the deck, not along it. Recalling the long weight-free time as Nsil's clamoring engines rested quiet, Irtuk misgave her plea for haste. Gowdy's small craft had maintained force throughout, but Shtai lay at far remove; might Gowdy needs do as had Nsil? And at Tuik's stage of learning, could such unnatural experience impair his fragile melding of instinct with slow growth of reason?

Yet soon after she and Tuik and Bretl and T'phee the Yainan followed the four yumins through the unsteady wrinkled cylinder that held air to breathe as they clambered between ships, Skeeta addressed her cares. ''These engines provide force throughout near all the voyage; only at the turning over must they cease.''

Although the term ''turning over'' held no meaning for Irtuk, his statement allayed her apprehensions.

''And here in the Deevee,'' remarked Skeeta's bearer Alix, ''you will find furnishings of greater comfort.''

Such was indeed the reality; sleeping platforms had been modified for Irtuk and for Bretl, and between the necessary arrangements lay opennesses where one might move with ease. Granting these amenities perhaps less appreciative attention than was deserved, Irtuk turned to Skeeta and raised question. "I would know of our designated routing from this point."

Directly to Magh, came his reply—and then, with Irtuk and Tuik returned home, on to Yamar with Bretl and T'phee. "After which," Skeeta added, "we shall confer with *Roamer* and most probably alight again on Magh."

"A wasteful plan." Signing negation, Irtuk explained. "To Yamar we should first go; it is T'phee who suffers when isolated from his own. And only then, bring Tuik and me to Magh."

"But do you not desire return to your home, your friends?"

"Of a surety. But more do I wish to see the third of Jemra's worlds on which my kind can exist. And my alternative eliminates one descent to a world and consequent arising from it; have you no wish to conserve that which powers your engines?"

Pushing forelimb digits through his patch of manegrowth, Skeeta replied. "The captain's deputy on *Roamer* must decide, but I am certain your preference can be accommodated."

And when Irtuk cushioned Tuik against the engines' force, she had Cole's assurance that her wish had prevailed.

Considering the havoc Driscoll's storm trooper tactics had wrought with macroGate morale, Pia Velucci got things shipshape again faster than Gowdy expected. She'd lost personnel, less by direct action of Aroka's minions than by desertion: "He and Lioso threw a scare into everybody the first week," Velucci said. "That little prosthetic monster had Driscoll space a young woman, a galley helper, for spilling soup on him." She shook her head. "After that, until Driscoll caught on and stationed guards at Earthmouth, quite a few just bailed out."

She didn't say how she'd felt about all this and Gowdy didn't ask. "So you're shorthanded."

"Not too bad. Most who got away were construction types, finished with their assignments here. Just doing odd jobs and waiting for cargo shuttles to take them to Magh. We'll manage."

Maybe so; Larry Corcoran had most of his crew back, the

ones Driscoll had pulled off *Golconda*. He and Pia would have to fill their respective vacancies from incoming shuttles—and maybe, when everyone had time to sort things out, from colonists who had Gated directly to Magh. Of the two shuttles already arrived in this system, one had gone to the inner moon and the other still lay alongside the macroGate, in process of lading.

The colony, now. Riding supercargo with Corcoran en route to rendezvous with *Roamer*—which should be on station near Magh by this time—Sam considered what to do about Jules Perrone.

Gowdy's descent to Magh needn't wait for the DV's return. Or for commandeering a cargo shuttle, either. The Doodlebug was a really handy item to have in reserve. The main question was: returning to the inner moon, who did he want to take along?

His choices were limited. With only eight of the original roster left on *Roamer*, shorthanded was an understatement; when *Golconda* reached the ship, Simone would definitely want Owen and Molly back to duty. Which left him Sydnie.

Still, how many would it take to deal with dandy Jules? Up to this point, what exactly had the man done? Ousted Libby Verdoorn at Aroka's orders; no more, no less. On the other hand, Sam had to wonder just what attributes, real or imagined, had brought him to the commodore's attention in the first place?

The best thing might be to get Perrone on the circuit and have a little talk, see how the land lay. Nothing heavy, just feel the situation out before choosing his own moves.

Maybe Sydnie would have some ideas.

Kayo couldn't believe it. "Don't these departments ever talk to each other?" Because the specialists who had pored over Nsil's ship Three could have told the procurement group that the cargo shuttle *Hermes* needed extensive modification for Eamnet use. Seating, controls, instruments: none were suited to the alien physique. "Didn't anyone think to check?"

On the vidphone screen, Jocelyn Waymire spread her hands. "Things fall through the cracks; you know that. We'll have a shuttle set Nsil's ship down alongside *Hermes*, run catwalks between for easy transshipment of fixtures, and you can interpret while he tells what he needs. If you're willing."

"Sure, all right. And thanks, senator."

After drawing blanks everywhere she had expected to find Nsil, Kayo found him in her own quarters, playing checkers with Dan Quillan. How he'd learned the rules she had no idea; maybe he hadn't and Dan was simply humoring him. With a certain reluctance she gave the bad news and waited for the eruption.

Nsil surprised her. "Yes, Kaow! A vessel like none other, we will take to Eamn." To Quillan he made a deferential gesture. "With thankings and regret I cede this pastime; I must inform Scayna." And with no other word, the seeder left.

Thirsty, Kayo made her homecoming embrace fervent but brief. At the fridge she found they'd bottomed out the iced tea pitcher, and opened a beer instead. "I didn't know you two were buddies."

"He likes to hear about Magh. And it helps me brush up on the language." As she sat, Dan leaned closer. "Kayo—we need to talk. About what we're going to do."

Bemused by Nsil's ready acceptance of further delay, she needed a moment to refocus. "Do? We're going back, aren't we?"

"That's what I thought. But I had another physical today."

She waited; he said, "I'm cleared to go, all right. But not as a pilot. They don't trust my reflexes to stay solid."

"But it's been . . ." Three months at least, she thought. Since the last spell when his reflex arcs cut out and he had to do everything by deliberate volition. It had been a little scary, she remembered; the groundcar at high speed and Dan suddenly overcontrolling. He'd slowed, compensating, and in a matter of seconds regained mastery. Still, in the DV . . .

"It's probably all right, they say. But probably isn't good enough. They okayed me for duty, but only on instruments and navigation. I'm not entirely sure I want to go that route."

So? Carefully she said, "What's your Plan B?"

Cautiously feeling out the Doodlebug's controls, Larry Corcoran broke into laughter. "I *love* this beast!" Somehow, Gowdy wasn't much surprised; Sydnie, given first dibs at learning the small ship's quirks, had seemed to enjoy it a lot also. "You really built it yourself?"

They were still a way out from Magh, Larry and Sam and Sydnie, having intercepted *Roamer* near that tide-locked moon before the greater ship again took leading Trojan position. Abele and Tanacross were back at regular duty, and *Golconda* for the time being ran escort to *Roamer*. So here, with quite a lot of room to make mistakes, was a good place for Larry to practice.

"It was my idea," Gowdy said now, "to build on the Maghren freight plane fuselage. But mostly I just supervised a lot."

"Uh-huh." Playing with yaw and pitch, upping and easing accel, the younger man couldn't get the grin off his face. "And it even lands like a plane?"

"Another time," and saw that Larry knew what he meant. "But you can take it down to the top fringe of air if you like."

Lacking map images or screens on which to project them, he pointed. "We want to cross the horizon right about there." A quick guess said they'd reach the currently visible rim shortly after the midday eclipse. "At the terminator I want us—oh, say ten miles up." Barely into atmosphere.

Sydnie looked over to Sam. "Coming in to the colony on the low and flat? Any special reason?"

"What with Jules dodging my calls on comm, we don't know what's going on down there. I'd rather see before being seen."

Of course when they got near, decelerating tail first toward the bottom of Magh's thinnish air blanket and squinting at a streaky screen view of Denaize Shore from the 'bug's rear and only video sensor pod, Sam couldn't really see a whole lot. Not until his vee and altitude figures shrank to where he could flip around and make like an airplane with vertical thrustors in lieu of wings. Then coming in toward colony HQ he dropped even lower and leveled off, passing alongside a cargo shuttle that sat alone, loading ramps extended, on the landing area.

Cutting down on forward thrust he turned and rode his verticals across to colony Admin, moving at slow pace and hardly any altitude. As the 'bug passed over the building itself, he jazzed the verts. *Hi, there, Jules*!

An explosive rise of dust confirmed that he'd given the roof of Perrone's HQ a good whomp, enough to tell the current administration that Sam Gowdy was here to talk business. Turning again, he landed and taxied near the main entrance, swung the 'bug to face an open lane for future reference, and cut power.

"Let's go in and say hello."

The pair of armed guards added a new and unwelcome touch. Keeping stride, Sam walked directly past a supply truck toward the man who stood not quite blocking entrance. "Gowdy. *Roamer*. To see Perrone. I'll announce myself."

Faced with obvious expectation of clear passage, the guard stepped aside. "Way to go," Sydnie murmured.

In the office that had housed Barry Krsnch, Jules Perrone sat looking across the desk at a large man with a red, sullen face and a holster-sized bulge below one shoulder. Not quite his old sleek self, Jules: hair mussed and expression strained, he began, "Sam! Was that you, rattling the building? What . . . ?"

The other tried to cut in; Gowdy beat him to it. "Just a cheery hello, Jules. Look—before getting into all the official stuff, what say we go have a drink someplace? Oh—I'd like you to meet Larry Corcoran; he runs the miner *Golconda*."

"Like hell he does." The big one wouldn't be left out. "Not unless I say so. Where's Commander Yates?"

"Earth. Well, in Gatelag toward there." True. And the man hadn't asked *how* Yates was.

"This is Mr. Ames Griswold," Jules put in. "Security." A nod toward Sam. "Captain Gowdy, of the ship *Roamer*."

Security. Of course; how else? Griswold didn't look as if he wanted to shake hands any more than Sam did, but what the hell; Gowdy went bland. "Everything under control?"

Griswold didn't answer; totally ignoring Larry Corcoran, the security man jerked his head in Sydnie's direction. "Who's this? Anyone we really need?"

She spoke before Sam could. "On the ship's roster I'm Third Officer Sydnie Lightner, under *Captain* Gowdy." She paused. "But in real life, whatever you have in mind to say to Jorge, you tell it to me."

She parked one buttock on a desk corner. "It works the other way, too. And the first thing you need to produce is an updated working roster of our people here."

"A list of colonists?" Griswold tried a sneer. "You don't need Security for that. Any clerk . . ."

"I said *our* people. Not the full dossier version, mind you, but I do intend to review the histories since they joined up with us. Dupe me a datacap; I'm sure you haven't left that kind of information loose in your main computer."

A *superior* sneer. "It's under password, Lightner."

Her brows rose. "Password? Any snoop with a terahertz random number generator—forty-five minutes, tops! You cut me a copy of that material, then wipe it out of there, clean."

Sam didn't know what was going on, but trying to butt in wouldn't speed the learning process. Unobtrusively he edged toward a better angle on Griswold, as the man said, "Do I have this straight? For your sake I'd better have; lying to me could get you shot, Lightner. Hell; without even giving your right name, you claim to stand surrogate for the commodore?"

She tilted her head, tossing back hair that hung forward on one side. "No. You said commodore; I didn't. And possibly you're not close enough to Jorge to know the difference. But in the Web I am Charel Secour, and I speak for the Spider Prince."

Yainans, Skeeter Cole decided, were good with ships. Their two big ones, roughly *Roamer*'s size but somewhat differently configured, rode around Yamar along orbits so near to circular as made no difference.

Cole would have liked a look inside one of those vessels. T'phee in fact suggested such a visit, but aside from Libby Verdoorn's concern about matching a transfer tube to alien and unfamiliar fittings, consensus favored landing first and planning from there.

It did make sense. T'phee and Bretl had waited long enough for homecoming; also, the locals here would need time to absorb the implications of recent events. So as Libby brought the DV down to flipover altitude and tail first descent, Cole put his mind to the instruments before him, giving her readoffs as needed. Maril Jencik had been kind enough to let him take her copilot seat for this drop; he purely didn't want to screw up!

Neither, he saw, did Libby; an unaccustomed scowl tautened her features as she swung ship and set thrust to slow their drop. Through air less turbulent than Magh's and lighter in resistance than Eamn's she brought the Vehicle down toward the Yainan settlement, near the noon of Yamar's day. Twenty-eight hours and a bit? Something like that.

The landing wasn't quite free of jar, but for a first effort Skeeter gave Libby good marks. She wasn't SuZanne Craig yet, but who else was?

As Cole stood, muscles protested. He'd hardly noticed the lightening of gravity on Magh or the slight increase on Eamn. This world, he knew, ran to one-point-two gee. But the way his legs felt, it could have been at least one and a half, easy.

Either it would work or it wouldn't; watching Sam angle for position Sydnie managed not to hold her breath—until slowly, reluctantly, Griswold nodded. "Yes. Not many here know that name. All right, then. For now, anyway. Come on, uh . . ."

"Let's stick with Lightner. Less confusing." As the Security honcho led the way out, Sydnie turned aside to Sam. "Why don't you and Jules go have that drink, get things straightened out?" Then she added, "When do you want to meet next? And where? Here, or back at the 'bug?"

"There's a vacant VIP suite you can use," Perrone said. He seemed apprehensive; well, he'd earned it.

"We'd have to go to the 'bug anyway," said Gowdy, "to get our stuff. So make it there."

"Right." Sydnie nodded. "This won't take over half an hour, I'd expect." And she followed Griswold out, along a corridor to an office two doors short of the Gates room.

Inserting a fresh datacap into the proper niche, the Security chief called up a file and made the proper moves, then removed the cap and handed it to her. "There you are. Now, since you insist, I'll wipe it off here. I have my own copy."

"Hold it; while it's up, I may as well have a look."

He stood and she sat. Well, well; forty-three names, including Griswold himself. And, out of sequence, obviously a late addition, Jules; did he know what company he was keeping?

She scanned more closely: only three other names she recognized, none she'd met personally. Small potatoes, likely—but in any hierarchy some rise fast, so don't prejudge.

Qualifications varied. Near as she could tell, less than a third served as out-and-out muscle; the rest seemed to be bona fide techs of one sort and another, and whether they knew what kind of outfit they'd signed on with, Sydnie couldn't guess. Probably some yes, some no.

Keep it moving. "The operations map, now."

"Didn't you see the one I screened out? Three days ago?"

"I haven't been on the ship much lately." Careful now . . . "Here and there on *Golconda*, mostly. We did touch base before coming in here, but not long enough to catch up."

The map read more cryptic than not. Remembering what Aroka had said about bootleg Gates, she took the group of Ms and Ts to symbolize those constructs: six Mouths, three Tushes. "And how far along do you have these?" As she pointed.

"Didn't you ask *any* questions aboard ship?" She held her stare until he told her: one Mouth and one Tush almost ready, the others in various stages of construction and assembly.

"And how long before you have weapons covering the landing area?" She wasn't especially interested in the answer, but it was something she'd be expected to ask. Field security was an Aroka trademark, when he could manage it—but no guns were in operation as yet, because the 'bug had come in unchallenged.

"We've got 'em up and mounted," Griswold said. "Lasers. But the power hookups are still in progress."

"All right. That's enough for now. Thank you, chief." As though the jockeying of two Aroka subordinates was settled into a good working relationship. "We can talk later."

"Right. After I've checked with Aroka. Which I intend to do immediately."

Think fast. "If you're going to the comm tent, it's on my way." If worse came to worst, this could be a job for La Hoja.

She purely hoped not. Griswold might be faster than he looked.

* * *

When the door closed, Sam put Sydnie's ploy out of mind. He'd seen her work this ballpark before. As to whether he could trust her, the fact was that he had no alternative.

Perrone said, "Where do you want to go? My quarters?"

"Here's okay." With Griswold gone. "And I don't really need a drink."

"I have some on hand. Bourbon's yours; right?"

"Fine." And Corcoran nodded agreement. As Jules did the honors, Gowdy said, "Tell it."

"I—none of this was my idea. Taking Libby Verdoorn's position, I mean. Aroka sent the order down."

"Why you?" Pretty good bourbon the man stocked.

"Based on my career profile, he said. But look—I'm not an administrator; I'm a drive tech. And a good one. I could be drive chief, too; I know when not to give orders. But this job, it's way beyond me." Taking a sip, Perrone said, "I didn't get a chance to learn, either. Griswold arrived and took over. I'm only a figurehead. Trying to cope with the routine stuff, the original colony agenda, while he bosses the real work."

"What real work?" Damn good stuff, in fact.

The setting up of unauthorized Gates, mostly. Big ones, ". . . that you could drive trucks through. Either way. Or march a regiment directly from Earth."

Sam considered. "By squads? A little time-consuming."

Headshake. "No. They've got adapter units. Like for the macroGates, the tapering asymptotic fields for continuous pass-through transmission. The same kind of unit fits either end; I don't know why." Perrone's grin came sheepish. "Actually I haven't a clue how they work; I've heard the jargon, is all."

Gowdy didn't know either—and didn't care. Pass-through transmission, though! Suddenly his earlier shadowy idea began to flesh out; he could use these gadgets. In fact, he'd need to.

Change the subject. "Is Griswold as tough as he comes on?"

"Tougher. His third day here he had two people executed. Since then, nobody says boo." Jules leaned forward. "Sam—if you could take me back to the ship . . ."

"Later, maybe." End of bourbon; at Perrone's gesture, Gowdy shook his head. "No, that's plenty."

"Please, Sam. As a favor. I know you don't owe me any, and I'm really sorry, but . . ."

"Sorry for what?"

Perrone shrugged. "Oh, you know; this and that. Being kind of a horse's ass sometimes. But look—I don't know what Sydnie's told you, but it was only that one time. And as much her idea as mine. I . . ."

Nothing Sydnie might do, nowadays, could much surprise Sam. But what a sorry sonofabitch this was! Blabbing his grotty little secret, and in front of a third party f'Chris'sakes. "Yeah," said Gowdy. "Now how about you show me a map of these Gate installations, and an estimate of how far along they are."

There were nine: six Mouths, three Tushes. One of each due up soon, the rest still somewhere in the construction stages. The matrices were of less capacity than the paired sets he'd transshipped from *Golconda* to *Roamer*, but unpaired single ends were no use to him anyway. It was the tapered-field gear he wanted, once he had this operation shut down and God only knew how he was going to manage that.

But his plan needed doing, and in case something happened to him personally, a few other folks should know about it. Sam stood. "If anybody asks, I have business at the comm tent. You want to come along, Larry?"

"About getting back to the ship," Perrone began again, but Gowdy shook his head. With Griswold he could use a buffer. Somebody had to be in the middle, and Jules would do as well as any.

Besides, he'd earned it.

Sydnie guessed the man on comm duty to be a colonist, not one of Aroka's people. She said, "Is *Roamer* on station yet?" He looked blank. "Call control for us, would you please?"

About three seconds after the call-in ended, a voice came; the ship was back to lead Trojan position, or nearly. "Watch Officer Tuiasso. Go ahead."

Good; Mose was always quick on the pickup. "Watch Officer Lightner here. I have Commodore Aroka's security chief, Mr. Ames Griswold. With a few questions."

"Sure. Fire away."

Pushing in, Griswold began, "I want to talk with Commodore Aroka. If he's not available I want to know why. And when he will be. I'm tired of being stalled."

Delay. Then, "Sir, I'm afraid the commodore hasn't authorized me to release that information. It's a matter of—"

Griswold's raised voice overrode the rest. "I'm ordering you! Whatever it is, spit it out. Or I'll have your ass."

Which way to take this scenario? Sydnie made her choice. "Under the circumstances, Mr. Tuiasso, I believe the chief is entitled to know the commodore's whereabouts." And nothing more; mentally, she crossed her fingers.

She could almost hear Mose sorting out his possible moves. Finally he said, "I don't like being put in the middle. The fact is, chief, the commodore has inGated for Earth."

Shock held Griswold silent long enough; Sydnie spoke first. "All right, Mr. Tuiasso; I'll fill in the rest. Lightner out."

By one arm she turned the chief to face her. Trying to keep her mind at least one sentence ahead of her mouth, she plunged ahead. "Yes, Jorge's been Gated home—along with Estilete, and Lioso, everyone important who was offworld."

"Why? And why leave me here, without a warning?"

"I *am* warning you. As Security chief, who else you tell is your pigeon." Time to embroider, now. "I'm not saying I have all the facts, but try this on for size. Say, Jorge gets a tip that we're pegged; he's not sure just what Glen Springs is sending against us, or when, but in close confines—like the ship or the macroGate—we wouldn't have a chance. Here on Magh, though, with all this space to maneuver . . ."

"Then why didn't Aroka come here himself?"

Here was good use for her mother's incredulous stare: how can you be so stupid? She shook her head. "You won't catch me saying Jorge lost his nerve. But if he couldn't estimate a safety margin, and transport here wasn't available in a hurry . . ." She shrugged. "Maybe he guessed wrong; it's not disloyal to say that much."

"And you, you're safe behind the Lightner cover. But what about *me*?" Among Griswold's worries, loyalty didn't seem to rate much of a priority.

"Would Jorge leave you to ambush a task force—probably not more than a battalion or so, and they'll have to come through in small groups—if he didn't feel the odds were with you?"

"I can get better odds than that." The security man grinned. "What if we simply block the official Tush?"

"And ambush the troop carrier they'd send instead, when it lands?" She pretended to give thought. "Wouldn't they expect to need one anyway, or another miner, just to retake the macroGate?"

She gestured. "You're the expert; it's your decision. But you'll want to consider your options carefully."

And as though in afterthought, "If you had that new Mouth working, just for fail-safe . . ."

She stared at his retreating back. *Damn; I'm good.*

Setting limbs again on Yamar, T'phee enfills with content; the sturdy pull of this world speaks to en of homeness. At the front of those gathering to greet en, er espies Nahei of *L'lit* and the Steward Cejha. Both speak welcome, and Nahei comes to exchange grasp of manipulars, promising intimacy in near time.

But first must occur presentation of Irtuk-saa and the yumins, and then explanation, the delineation of events experienced and others in prospect. Er begins, "I make known to you the yumin Skeeta who has best our speech and can transpose speakings of these others who are"—gesturing—"Maril, and Alik, and Libi," then explains that although origin of Irtuk-saa is the inner Get, no discord exists between en and Bretl. "All, you observe, require accommodations of greater height than our own usage."

After two sidehelpers are detailed to tend the visitors' needs, T'phee and Nahei follow Cejha, accompanied by a number of substewards and lesser aides, to the Steward's place of function. "Although Nahei has learned much of Stewardship," speaks the older Yainan, "and greatly eases my burdens, still it brings relief that you resume your duties here."

Forbearing to reveal that such relief may not be at all soon, T'phee with exacting care tells of es experiences, then of es evaluations. "The yumins traverse over ten times the span from origin as we,'' er states at one point, ''yet reach here in a tenth the duration we consume.''

Er adds es hope that yumin devices may be provided to Yainan vessels. ''Though even such a boon would multiply our capacity for rescue by only a petty factor.'' It is not fitting, er feels, to mention Gowdy's final speaking on the yumin ship, wherein might be implied greater promise.

Through a feeding at onset of dark and for much time after, T'phee narrates. At beginment, many of es hearers fail to hide evident disbelief. But as event after event undergoes explication, a grudging acceptance grows.

Throughout, the glorious sensing of reunion with es own kind holds T'phee above fatigue. So that when speaking ends and the lesser functionaries are gone to further disseminate what has been spoken, er gladly accepts invitation to Nahei's abode. Where without further readyings er and *L'lit*'s preceptor engage genitive interact in full, continuing for phenomenal duration.

Scent of *cruance* reminds T'phee, es matrix may now be of a ripeness sufficient to the engenderment of get. Should such result accrue, er reflects, er freely accepts consequence.

For by all truth, T'phee has merited enself the indulgence.

To ensure vigor of get, er realizes, er must insorb more and varied genitive endowment. But many yet ungreeted will pleasure in so welcoming es return to Yamar.

Outside the Admin Building, Gowdy felt his idea grow a new branch. ''Larry? What's Tetzl's Planet like? In terms of Earth standard.''

The digest version: air and gravs slightly lighter, climate a bit warmish, axial tilt inconsequential and orbital eccentricity not a factor, land area a third of the total, flourishing biota but nothing that could outthink a catfish. ''Very primitive, even the landgoers.''

Corcoran paused, then added, ''Why the sudden interest?''

''Maybe it sounds like a good place to settle down.''

As they came in sight of the comm tent Ames Griswold emerged, then took off at a jog-trot toward the nearest woods. Moments later, Sydnie also left the tent, clearly heading for the Doodlebug.

Leading the way in no hurry through sparse pedestrian traffic, Sam reached and entered the tent. He recognized the young man on duty by sight but the name eluded him. "Hi. Remember me? It's been a while. How's everything going?"

"Not bad, captain. Is it true the commodore's gone back to Earth?"

What the hell? "Unless you saw that on official paper, best not to pass it along." Solemnly the youngster nodded. All right. "I need to make some calls. First, *Roamer* and the DV."

Roamer, sure, any time. But signal windows to the Vehicle, on or near Scout/Shtai/Yamar, weren't all that long or frequent, and this wasn't one of them.

"Right. Let's have the ship, then."

Answering for *Roamer*, item by item Tuiasso acknowledged Gowdy's rather condensed list of instructions. ". . . and I tell Glen Springs you'll follow up with a detailed confirmation before we Gate the hardware?"

"Please do." Anything more? No. Because maybe this caper didn't need the Vehicle after all. "Thanks, Mose. Gowdy out."

He gave the young fellow on duty a good word, too, before stepping out to growing dimness. Chorm's daily eclipse had begun, and neither man carried a belt lamp. Still, the grounded cargo shuttle stood out pretty well in the twilight. Sam could even make out the name: *Totebag*.

So they hurried to it, then at an easier pace walked up the deserted ramp. Everybody taking a break during the midday dark spell, Gowdy thought, and sure enough found over a dozen people in the galley. "Hello!" As some looked around he said, "Captain Sam Gowdy, off *Roamer*. Would one of you be skipper here?"

The tall skinny man had baked under a lot of hot sun. Rising, he said, "Bart Cullan," and moved to shake hands.

"Mr. Cullan. What are your current orders?"

"After we finish unloading? Not sure. We expected another cargo run to the big Gate. But first Mr. Perrone took charge, for the commodore, and now this Security bonzo Griswold. I guess we're on hold."

"Are you fueled? Supplied? Life support, and all?"

Cullan nodded. "Ms. Verdoorn's people already had those facilities up and working. Why do you ask?"

"The commodore's gone home. How'd you like to make a run for me, move some cargo from *Roamer* out to the Trojan world? If I keep Griswold off your back?"

"Captain Gowdy, I'd like that a great deal."

"You've worked with Gowdy." Looking to Kayo, Jocelyn Waymire sounded worried. "What do you think he's up to?"

For Bill Flynn to interrupt his and his wife's vacation cruise, this had to be hotter than it first seemed. Kayo waited, but Flynn didn't add anything to the senator's query, so she said, "Could I see the message itself? I'm sure you've summarized it accurately, but still . . ."

"The insidious ubiquity of paraphrasing, yes. Here." And as Flynn mumbled something about swallowing a dictionary, Kayo reached to accept the message sheet. She skipped past the routing codes and lead-in remarks . . .

. . . most urgent that these four Tush and two Mouth matrices be Gated to Tetzl's Planet with specs as follows: Tushes A through C to be equipped with asymptotic field adapters for pass-through transmission. Gating field apertures no less than thirty feet wide and twenty high. Locate installations where large, repeat, large incoming staging areas can be provided. Abundant water supplies essential, and I recommend early start on cultivation of food crops for refugee influx.

I will arrange for similar facilities on Scout our local Trojan body, and my matrix allotment for Tetzl's includes two-way Gating between those worlds, also between Tetzl's and Yain. See invoice, attached.

As soon as I get things moving here, I'm taking *Roamer* to Yain. I hope to neutralize Aroka's Security pit bull first, but I'm in a hurry, so if I can't, it's your problem.

Kayo Marlin can tell you what mine is.

"Well?" Waymire and Flynn both stared at her, and the woman added, "It can't be what it sounds like. Can it?"

Kayo breathed a deep one. "He's out to evacuate the whole damn planet. I think you'd better plan to help push."

* * *

Groundside again, Sam found the eclipse ending. Mentally he went down his list: six pass-through adapters for Yain-mouths and three for Tushes on Yamar, with Glen Springs making up the difference at Tetzl's. Even leaving the non-urgent links unadapted, it wasn't enough; later he'd try for more units to be Gated from Earth. But not now, because calling changes before initial procurement went through was the sure way to screw up an operation.

Of course he didn't exactly have his adapters in hand yet.

As he and Corcoran walked toward the Doodlebug, from off to their left came smells of food. "Commissary," he said. "You hungry?"

"Well, as a matter of fact . . . how about you?"

"Later. But you go ahead."

As Larry peeled off toward the good aromas, Sam wasn't home free yet; approaching on intercept he saw Menig-dre.

"Gowdy. There has been an event."

Indeed there had. Foraging among resident holdings at the outskirts of Denaize Shore, three of Nsil's guerrillas had been apprehended; by backtracking over hills and to a canyon, another seven were located and taken. Gaunt and wearied, none had made resistance. "To our holdings, Gowdy," the bearer stated, "they did only trivial harm. But to your ship when agrounded, dire."

Her gaze did not move. "What punishment do you decree?"

This might be tricky. "You hold them confined?" Yes. "Do they feed well?"

"Why would they not? No punishment status is yet imposed."

"Then for the time, continue as at present. Later I will assume custody and make decision." Actually it made itself: come right down to it, Nsil's raiders were POWs of a sort; he might as well see them repatriated. "Meanwhile, my gratitude."

"It is sufficient recompense." She stayed, though. "On the matter of constructing ships to defend against Eamn, Paith the Elect seeks your counsel."

Oh hell. "My counsel is this: none are needed. Eamn cannot attack Magh, nor do its leaders wish to do so."

"But the sabotage . . . the abductions . . ."

"Past and done with. No more will ensue." But Paith, insisted Menig-dre, was determined. Gowdy sighed. "At earliest opportunity, I will speak with Paith."

So the bearer left him, and finally he climbed into the Doodlebug. "Sydnie?"

"Yes?" Coming past the heavy cross-bracing she carried two laden bags. "What's on your mind?"

With her, a plenty. But first, Griswold's rapid departure from the comm tent. "What got into Mr. Security, anyway?"

"I think he wants to go home." Sam felt his brows rise; she said, "I'd better tell you before I forget something important."

By the end of it he stared in frank awe. "He believed you?"

"Believe? I didn't tell him anything; I asked questions and posed hypotheses. Labeled as such. He picked his own answers."

"And you think he means to evacuate, goons and all?"

Sydnie shrugged. "How do I know? If he gets his panic button unstuck, he may try to rush the Tush on line and hope for reinforcements. But the way he cut out of the comm tent . . ."

"Yeah." Given the uncertainties of timing, would Aroka's Web operatives have a force assembled, waiting and ready to Gate? Gowdy shook his head; in the long run it wouldn't matter.

Just now, though . . . He said, "Whatever Griswold decides, *we* want that bootleg Mouth working."

"What for?"

Thinking out loud he said, "We'll need a truck. Wideband transmitter, burst mode, pre-recorded audio datacap. Shielding against small arms fire, long enough to give a location fix."

Sam grinned. "It could work."

She stared at him. "What if Griswold still has troops guarding this end?"

"Then we might have to change the plan a little." Which was an understatement if ever he'd made one.

XXII

Still near to height of strength, Irtuk-saa had well accommodated increased weightiness on Eamn. Shtai, however—or Yamar as T'phee's people called this world—taxed her muscles. Though its air, high in energizing component, aided endurance. But the accommodations provided by Yainan courtesy, however kindly meant, fell sadly short of comfort for one of her bulk, or Bretl's.

Following a night of less than restful recumbence, the two bearers found the yumins at morningmeal. Shortly after all were served, T'phee joined the gathering and fed also. "If you go now to Threewaters, Bretl, I can arrange transport and accompany you. There is much to tell your village, and each of us has seen and heard what others have not."

The groundcar, an unroofed cargo mover, served well for four-limbed Yainans. Skeeta sat, leaning back against a low siderail. Irtuk and Bretl stood crouching and gripped the rails for balance as the contrivance, only mildly jostling, conveyed itself and them across gentle swells and dips marked by clumps of darker growth amid generally pale ground cover.

Driven, according to T'phee, by means of electrochemical storage units, the car moved in silence; undistracted by sounds, Irtuk sampled strange but not unpleasant scents of this world's plant life. The route dipped into a shallow valley, traversed a makeshift-seeming structure that spanned a running stream, and ended in an open space among regularly placed dwellings.

Not large, but ample for small householdings centered on only one bearer each, for the most part these abodes utilized stone below and tight-woven thatch above. Now as Bretl gave a shrill whistling call, persons young and old emerged to join those already gathering near the vehicle.

Bretl spoke fact without embroidery. This was Skeeta, a yumin from Erdth, ten times more far than Diell the Companion. Yumins were friends. This was Irtuk, a Maghren bearer but no enemy. The ancient war was dead.

Eamn had not abandoned Shtai; Eamn and Magh had long lost means to move between worlds. Only now had Eamn, in slight measure, regained that power. But . . .

Bretl turned to Irtuk. "Better than I, you can describe."

These strong, stocky Shtai folk looked less friendly than Irtuk would have wished. She breathed deeply. "The new Eamnet ships could reach Magh and return, but never so far as Shtai." Not cogent to relate that Nsil had gone as great a distance but could not have grounded safely again. "One such took several of us from Magh to Eamn; we and Eamnets learned much from each other before a yumin ship came and brought us away."

From the grouping came protests; a seeder cried, "If you are not an enemy, tell why Magh inflicted plague upon Eamn!"

With care, Irtuk chose words. "Neither on Eamn nor on Magh do any know how or where that ancient plague came to be. As is natural in such case, each world has blamed the other. Through many lifetimes, hatred has endured. Now at last Maghren and Eamnet have met again and found each other not so monstrous."

Having achieved silence, Irtuk pressed advantage. "You on Shtai were spared that plague. In turn, spare us your hatred."

From one side, Bretl grasped a forelimb. "At this point, cease. We will take midmeal with others of the leaders here, and speak further. While you have them of a mind to hear you."

Though plain, the feeding held savor; refreshened, Irtuk prepared for renewed questioning. An elder adaptive, persistent in antagonism, demanded, "How can the bearer tyranny of Magh meet and deal fairly with the enlightened ways of Eamn?"

"Enlightenment is relative. And you yourselves follow not Eamn's ways. On Yamar are not all genders of equal voice?"

"Our circumstances . . . the need for compromise . . . we . . ."

"Exactly." Irtuk's head made emphatic move. "Compromise has been made, and still proceeds, on Eamn itself." And before the other could protest, "My own stay on Eamn, begun against my will and by force but leading to acquaintance and understanding, convinces me that Magh must change also."

"And who will change it? You?"

"As a beginning, yes. And also circumstance."

A time later, seeing Magh her homeworld grow on the Deevee's frontseeing picture screen as landing neared, Irtuk wondered what that beginning might encompass.

Urgency jabbed at Gowdy; whatever Ames Griswold did or didn't, Sam couldn't waste time waiting for it. He needed to get Mouth and Tush sites designated on Yamar, deliver the matrices, and make a start on power supplies and other hardware, all before he could begin preparing to leave for Yain. Because none of this was going to be fast or easy.

He couldn't plan the setup from here because he didn't know the logistic layout. For that information he needed T'phee, and T'phee was at the business end already. Talking on the circuit wouldn't help; for this sort of work you needed all parties looking at the same part of the same map.

So, thinking ahead: when Bart Cullan on *Totebag* took the Habegger gear to Yamar, Gowdy had to go along for the ride. But at the same time he'd need someone here to watch the henhouse, someone who could think like these weasels only better. The trouble was, he had only one candidate.

Sydnie Lightner. And he still didn't know what made her tick. She was good to work with now, ever since the massacre on *Golconda*, and any night they got to bed around the same time and him not totally pooped, he wished it could happen more often.

But there was, or had been, the other Sydnie. The one he couldn't trust, certainly not with a situation as antsy as this one. Gowdy had to know; more realistically, he had to try to find out.

It was mid-evening in their Admin Building quarters. Taking a deep breath Sam pushed away his stack of power estimate sheets. "Sydnie? I have to ask some questions."

She was still robed after a shower, her hair in a towel. "I

told you, there's a transmitter in the warehouse, and Kendall says we can have the construction explosives in a day or so." Frowning, she shook her head. "Or am I forgetting something?"

"This isn't about what we're doing now, exactly. It's about us, you, all along. I need to know where you really stand."

When Sydnie looked puzzled it could break your heart. Sam steeled his. "Jules is a blabbermouth."

Of all the reactions he might have expected, relief wasn't one of them. "Oh. That."

"Just the once, he said. Was that your only fling?" Yes, it sounded fatuous, what with shipside group marriage and all. But he *had* set criteria for a captain's lady. . . .

Her head came up. "No. Just before the sendoff for cadre 5-A. Johnnie Rio. In zero gee." Her eyes widened in the way that meant here come the thunderbolts, then relaxed. "You pissed me off. A lot. Not necessarily your fault. And—oh yes, I almost forgot—on *Roamer* I tried to undercut you with Glen Springs. Added glitches in your reports, corrections by me, all small shit, hell I'll send in a signed confession. *All right?*"

Incredible. Sam leaned forward. "How could you be like that? And then change the way you have lately? Who are you, anyway? Who will you turn into next?"

He shook his head. "What in God's name pulls your strings?"

Something hit a nerve; her face paled. Of a sudden she said, "God doesn't have a whole lot to do with it."

Struggling to breathe, Sydnie fought for coherence. Because she was beginning to see something that scared the crap out of her. "My mother. Eighteen years away from her, and still . . ."

He wasn't going to understand this. But maybe, saying it all out, *she* would. "A man's place is to know what a woman wants and get it for her. If he doesn't measure up, and they never do, you take it out on him." Sam stared. "That's the rule, what I grew up with. Then I ran off, never mind why."

"And?"

"That was Sydnie; Charel was different. I had a stable of

scam artists, sex for bait. Maybe not so different after all, just the flip side of the same disk.''

One side of her mouth smiled. ''Until Aroka, it worked. He bossed all kinds of operations, big scale stuff—I learned a lot, and believe me, I toed the line. What Jorge said, Charel did.''

In a quiet voice, Gowdy asked, ''Like trying to kill him?''

''I got his jet off the ground under fire, but those girls weren't refugees; he'd had them rounded up to be whores.'' This couldn't make sense to him, but keep going. ''When I wanted out, he was going to have me mutilated. So I threw the knife.''

Sam looked puzzled. ''And then went back under cover?''

Cover? Oh yes. Well, here goes. ''That was crap; sorry. I never was an agent. But this is truth.'' Now her grin came fully. ''There's a first time for everything.''

''Why?''

The question was clearer than it sounded. ''Because starting at Eamn, and then on *Roamer* and outship with Aroka and when we went into *Golconda*, you—'' She had to swallow. ''I'm not sure just how, but you taught me something.''

He didn't ask so she said it anyway. ''That all along, my mother was full of it.''

He reached to squeeze her hand. ''Let's sack out early.''

So maybe it was all right. It had better be—because the trouble with truth was, it left you without a hole card.

''Because that's my job, Dan, and Tetzl's is where I'll be most needed.'' And why, Kayo Marlin asked God or somebody, did she always get stuck with stubborn Irishmen?

Wearing only pajama bottoms at early morning, Quillan poured her coffee and then his own. ''There are hundreds of trained linguists, Kayo. I'm sure—''

''How many have worked with other species on their own turf? Damn zip, is what.'' Less angry than frustrated, from under lowered brows she glared at him and edited the sarcasm from what she needed to say. ''It's this simple. Every place needs pilots, and if heaven forbid you don't get recertified, instrument techs and navigators are always in demand, too. So what difference does it make to you, where we go?''

Rhetorical question; she kept pushing. ''The only question

is, maybe we shouldn't Gate directly to Tetzl's Planet.'' His face expressed a profane question, but he kept his mouth shut. ''I know Maghren or Eamnet, whatever, but I've never heard enough Yainan to make sense of it. T'phee, though; he'll be on *Roamer*, dead cert. So maybe we should Gate there, instead.''

She took advantage of Quillan's baffled silence to do some figuring. Using normal procedures, *Roamer* would go from Whitey to the Yain star in about sixty-two months real time or—let's see—two-point-two years ship's time, most of that under drive.

And how long, since the messages and Gate matrices were sent, before the ship departed? Not very, if she knew Sam Gowdy. So let's say he was now about two real years out, or—hmm!—a ship's month into free-fall time. Even if she Gated immediately, *Roamer* would be in one-gee decel when she got there.

Aside: with only about a hundred ship's days of free fall, would Sam even bother to reconfigure control and crank up the rotating belt? In his shoes, *she* certainly wouldn't.

''. . . either one,'' Dan was saying, ''I don't see the point. No fault of yours, but you're off that job.''

She really wanted to avoid a fight. ''Nobody fired me and I didn't quit; involuntary leave is how I see it. Same as you, except nobody dropped the Vehicle on me.''

That got a grin out of him, so, ''Let me put it to Jocelyn Waymire. Us to Tetzl's by way of *Roamer*, and a special endorsement on your pilot's certificate: until you medcheck a hundred percent, you don't operate without a backup.''

After a moment, his incipient flare-up died. ''It beats riding instruments. And hey—it gives me somebody to talk to.''

He said it deadpan, but his eyes crinkled at the corners.

''No need at all,'' Gowdy affirmed to the bearers' council, but in the mien of Paith the Elect, Irtuk-saa saw no acceptance. ''We of Erdth offer to provide ships for exploration and commerce, in exchange for your hospitality: that of granting access and living space to our study and trade missions.''

So that to develop and build chemical drives like those of Eamn, or even ion propulsors as before the Great Dying, would constitute grievous waste. ''Benefit from our learning,'' said Gowdy, ''as in other ways, I am certain, we shall from yours.''

Unmollified, Paith challenged him. ''You give ships to Eamn, also! So they can again attack us. Is this not true?''

''There will be no attacks.'' With patience greater than Irtuk's, Gowdy reiterated the causes of Eamnet fears and his efforts toward their alleviation. And to further questions: initially one ship to either world, convenient fueling availability to be arranged. ''The macroGate supply outlet offers the benefit of requiring no expenditure for landing and ascent.''

For the too-manyeth time, *no* weapons on any such vessel. Yes, one yumin ship here bore tools capable of destructive usage, but their application was the mining of distant worldlets. And ships of this type could neither land on a true world nor safely venture proximate to its surface. ''As is the case with my greater vessel,'' the yumin added.

Obdurate, Paith held firm. The offer of a yumin ship was welcome, yet Magh would build others to its own defending. And contacts between the worlds would be at Magh's terms only.

Irtuk raised to hindlimbs. ''I submit, Paith the Elect, that this sitting be adjourned. I plead necessity of conferring between you and myself, privately. From Eamn I have brought objects to which you as head of councils need give view.''

Gowdy gripped her forelimb. ''What do you do?''

''I seek establishment of peace and survival of Magh. The means does not concern yumins, only the result.''

''As you say.''

Reluctant, it seemed, he released her, as Paith put end to the gathering. Without further questioning the Elect accompanied Irtuk to a nearby study compartment, where Irtuk uncovered a long-unused interpretive device. She said, ''You have at an earlier time given study to Archival Mode recordances?''

''My facility of such comprehension has dried and withered,'' said Paith, but her gaze carried almost-physical pressure.

''I will attempt to supplement it.'' Slipping one of the silver-webbed onyx panes into a transverse slit, Irtuk activated the device. ''Now observe.''

* * *

Near onto three Chormyears, mused Scayna, she and Nsil would be absented from Eamn. Or as their stay extended, in hap more. Done feeding, small Nyrl slumped dozing against Scayna's thorax; the bearer laid the young one down for sleep and herself reclined to indulge in an overdue exercise of grooming procedures.

As Nsil entered, the briskness of his pacings told of cheer. "I have been to our ship," he began, "learning the manipulations of it as the yumins teach these to Tasr. I tell you, Scayna—I too can direct a ship such as this *Hermes*. Though I would never claim to equal Tasr's skill, much less belittle it."

"Of a certainty," she said, rising to embrace with him. "Nor would I."

"You?"

"I have also visited *Hermes*. At the time you were traveled to bespeak their great council, at the place Deeci." Her jaw dropped to show pleasure. "Nyrl, have assurement, takes well to sky travel." And to his question's intent, "For a time, in await of Tasr who yet slept, the yumin Fairl granted me teachings of the ship's directive devices."

Her embrace tightened. "Aside from bringing *Hermes* safe to ground, little of its direction would set me askance."

After a moment he spoke. "You please me, Scayna." Then without transition he commenced invitational rituals. For rea son unfathomable to Scayna, at this occasion he took upon himself an unusual proportion of decidings, among their ways of intimacy.

"This is true?" As the textual narration came to an end, the voice of Paith carried agony.

"Yes." Irtuk's tone held no comfort. "Always we have been told only one version of the ancient conflict. Here we view another. We—Maghren bearers of that time—enforced trade and supply domination over the Eamnet colony. The new world altered the workings of their bodies, and we neither allowed them to change their ways in adjustment nor to sustain their numbers by sky migration. So the seeders and adaptives rebelled. And when we could not otherwise prevail . . ."

"*We* sowed the Plague?"

"Against all will, I must deem the proof conclusive."

"And from what time period have you known this?"

"As certainty, only now. The metalweb symbols, scanned at Nsil's householding on Eamn, promised revelation but only hinted at its content." Her head moved to show regret. "I did not hope for this; rather, I feared it. But our necessities are clear."

To Paith's incomprehension Irtuk spoke. "Other such text-sheets must exist, and Eamnets will in time succeed in their interpretation. Including the vaster areas of recordage thereon, not consonant to our devices and therefore yet unknown to us. Before such a thing can occur we must make evident by speech and action that old enmity lies dead, that putting all past deed and blame behind, we now seek friendship."

"With those who enslave bearers?"

"In form, only. Scayna, whom I came to understand only with difficulty, holds voice of weight both in her householding and, through Nsil, in councils. Much more so than do our seeders and adaptives—a disparity I feel we need alleviate."

Paith drew back. "To what end? What can they offer?"

"If you had but known Nsil! The daring of him, the free use of imagination. Fearing the yumins here a danger to Eamn, he ventured out to learn. Then on Eamn, seeing threat from Gowdy, Nsil took his ship beyond its limits, through the yumin portal and lacking fuel for safe grounding beyond it, gambling survival on yumin aid at Erdth. Granted, he based decisions on faulty understanding. Yet who among *us* would have moved so boldly?"

"You approve direction by unrestrained seeders?"

"Not unrestrained. We bearers by nature conserve tradition, feeling that our other genders lack fixity. Yet that virtue taken to excess yields stagnation." Hesitant, she tongued her tooth gap. "With no advantage other than seeder direction, Eamn regained sky travel while we did not."

"In any case, then, you propose extending powers of decision to seeders and adaptives."

"I advocate their holding formal voice in councils here, and that such as Scayna be given the same right on Eamn. I feel we should urge these changes. But only when accord builds can we so speak, and be heard. So we must do as I have said."

"None of that which I propose," she added, "will derive easily. Neither here nor on Eamn. Still, we must make a beginning."

The Elect gestured. "Yet in light of this dread record, Eamn can say with truth that we act only from expedience."

Irtuk made a mouthsign of sly amusement. "If all our acts and speakings proceed in good faith toward future concord, who is to say we ever knew?"

After a moment, "Certainly not I," spoke Paith the Elect.

Sydnie letting it all hang out was a series of surprises; some jolted Gowdy more than a little, but for the most part he welcomed her new openness. When time came for him and *Totebag* to leave he made an excuse to hold lift, to stay over until the next morning. He pretty well knew what Bart Cullan's crew would be saying behind his back, but truth was, he didn't care.

Last time in bed together for quite some time, probably, he and Sydnie treated themselves to a waker-upper before arising. At breakfast, after packing, they rehashed their plans some more.

"I wish I knew," she said, "which way Griswold's going to jump. I thought I had him spooked enough to bolt, but he can't even make up his mind to do *that*."

"Always the problem with the iron heel," Sam reflected. "No good at all on slippery turf."

Okay, get on with it. "When you see for sure how the cards lie, then you pick your move." He was blathering; she knew all this as well as he did. "Oh hell; just be careful."

"And make it work the first time." Even with her hair stuck out all catawampous like a close call with an eggbeater, she looked great to him. "I have two good drill sergeant types handling the main options," she said now, "and Jules is out of the real loop, so it doesn't matter how badly he screws up."

"Try not to get him killed. As an administrator he's not much, but unless Libby agrees to take over again, we don't have a whole lot in the way of backup."

The flippancy seemed to help. "Sure." So he kissed her and toted his luggage over to *Totebag*, in plenty of time to lift with a favorable vector for a least-fuel rendezvous with *Roamer*.

Showing a deft touch, Bart Cullan took the cargo shuttle up through Magh's air and swung down-orbit. At the copilot spot, requested as a favor rather than usurped by privilege of rank, Gowdy watched the younger man play the controls like a concert musician. For once he felt no urge to take over and wring the bucket out himself; this guy was *good*.

A time later, rendezvous came with equal skill, the shuttle's rear flange mating to the corresponding fixture at *Roamer*'s stern, now cleared as *Golconda* rode alongside. Mose Tuiasso had the Gate matrices and accessory equipment in the adjacent cargo bay ready for transshipment; going aboard his ship, Sam left the man to coordinate transshipment with Cullan and proceeded to control where he greeted Charlotte Wang standing skeleton watch, as normal in rest orbit.

Gowdy needed to talk with Simone Leopold; riding the transit ring to the residence belt he found her and SuZanne Craig, among others, in the lounge and playing a new card game.

He passed the invitation to join in. "No time to learn the rules, sorry. I need to lay out a lot of sked in a hurry." So with the cards set aside, Sam spoke and Simone took notes.

First thing was to get the ship reconfigured for drive mode. "Shutting down the belt comes last, of course." Keep the comforts as long as possible. "Now the other stuff . . ."

Reseating the DV, putting the lead back in the pencil, was the trickiest job, but the laser-reflection alignment sensors at the Vehicle's stern should give SuZanne the edge she'd need. "Libby ought to have it up here, with the rest of our people, before I'm back from Yamar. You'll want to berth it fully fueled and so on." She knew that; get on with the program.

But that was about it. After checking few last details, he stood. "Say hello to everyone I missed. I have to talk with Corcoran on the miner, and then it's off to Yamar." On his way out he had the chance to thank Tuiasso for a good fast job; all the assigned gear was aboard. There weren't enough power units, and wouldn't be until Griswold's bootleg Gates were liberated, along with their pass-through field units. But under supervision of *Roamer*'s Gates expert Neville Fontaine, who with his pairmate Charlotte Wang were willing draftees into the excursion, major installation could proceed.

Anticipating Gowdy's urge to haste, Corcoran had run a tube across to *Totebag*; Sam didn't need to suit up. Their talk over coffee lasted only one cup: take *Golconda* out to the macroGate and keep the drop on anything that came through until those aboard cleared themselves of Web connections—or surrendered. "You might want to beef up at least one of your aimable side lasers, make it potent; use a spare main unit and replace the power feed. We did that one time, out in the Oort Cloud; worked pretty well, long as we didn't overheat it."

"And what are my operating restrictions?" Larry asked.

"You just heard them. Whatever it takes. I'm not going to second-guess you." Sam grinned. "I don't have to. You're not Yates; I trust your judgment." Actually Corcoran would be working with or for Pia Velucci, but Gowdy didn't figure her to be the prissy type either.

Back to *Totebag*. Pump, don't dump, and when most of the air had been retrieved, Cullan broke seal and turned the ship for Yamar.

Volunteering as an extra watch officer, during the next three days Gowdy did sit pilot on the shuttle, but his activity amounted only to minor course and thrust corrections; turnover came twenty minutes after his current stint gave way to Cullan's. He did draw the preliminary landing approach setting, but a few minutes into Yamar's air and Bart's turn came up again, enduring through a soft, sedate landing and general buttoning up.

Once down, the reason for Cullan's cautious landing became evident; one-point-two gee can punish sloppy technique. Gowdy hadn't endured this much pull for any length of time since his comet-herding days. He hadn't enjoyed it then, either.

Groundside a bit later, Sam was met by an exuberant T'phee and realized how deeply the Yainan's vitality had ebbed, separated from his own kind. He'd been putting on weight, Gowdy noticed. Especially along the thorax, at the base of his necktrunk. But it didn't seem to worry T'phee any.

And the news was good; three outlying settlements were begun, and each well situated to serve as a staging area for

Habgate influx. Accessible to ground transport ". . . although slow and tedious; roadways are not yet much improved." But between T'phee and his cohort Nahei of the second Yainan ship, six of their lander-carriers were at the ready, for airlift.

Gowdy remembered Nahei as the limp noodle who pulled out of Magh and left Sam stranded for want of transport. But that was old lines. Now, having worked and studied with someone named Cejha, Nahei would succeed to Stewardship, freeing T'phee to act as herald or envoy or something when *Roamer* reached Yain.

Through days so crowded and fatiguing that Sam lost track, things got put together: the three Yaintushes at the outlying points, then at the main colony base the Yainmouth and the pair intended for transit to and from Tetzl's Planet. Several installations would for now be only impressive shells; with only four power units currently at hand, he felt Yain had first dibs.

Not that anything would be Gating any direction for longer than he liked to consider. But this much he could do, and did.

Relayed through *Roamer*, infrequent reports from Sydnie gave little encouragement until the evening when Gowdy's people and several Yainans, plus a delegation of exiled Eamnets led by Bretl, gathered to celebrate the wrap-up of what could be done with materials at hand. T'phee was in mid-toast, or something along that line, when a woman from *Totebag* leaned over Sam's shoulder. "*Roamer* wants you."

Yamar's turning would soon block signal. So hotfoot to the shuttle and up to comm: SuZanne on the line. "Sydnie says today's the day; they're near shortdark now, so maybe we'll have more word soon and maybe not."

Gowdy thanked her; returning to the feast he decided he had nothing of real substance to announce, so he didn't. And in the brief time before departure, tried not to let his anxiety dampen anyone else's cheer. Especially T'phee's; this was his farewell celebration, before he and three others left Yamar, to go with *Roamer* to their species's world of origin.

Going back-orbit from a true planet, noon lift provided the best vee-boost. Sam didn't think he'd hinted or anything, but somehow Bart Cullan asked him to take *Totebag* up. Why, by all means! He was well outside air, enjoying the return to normal gravity and turning to set course, when *Roamer* called.

"Tell 'em I'll be there in a minute." And before turning the pilot seat over to his relief, meticulously he checked sightings.

When he heard what Marthe Vinler had to say, he couldn't believe it. "Sydnie? She did *what*?"

A cagey piece of ordure, Ames Griswold; Sydnie had him pegged on the first bounce and hadn't changed her mind since. Luckily for her, the man's superficial grasp of Gate operation fell short of reaching gut level. He knew about Gatelag but couldn't quite believe it. Otherwise, she thought, her edge as Aroka's purported *secundo* wouldn't hold up worth diddly.

But the way it was, whenever he got antsy at her nosing around, all she had to do was evoke the Spider Prince and Griswold went belly-up. That blind spot came in handy.

She had no idea where or how Aroka had rounded up his Gates crew; presumably Habegger techs were no more immune to corruption than anyone else. As near as she could tell, though, they knew their business. At least they worked on the apparatus, all circuits hot, without making a lot of sparks and smoke.

But a closer-mouthed bunch would be hard to find. Not even her best grade of industrial strength flirting educed any significant info. For one of the men, Jules said he thought she was the wrong flavor, but refused to have a go himself.

He did, however, volunteer to try with one of the two women. "Not the loud shrill one, though. There are limits." His were obvious; he drew as flat a blank as Sydnie had.

So she made do with spying—her own, Skeeter Cole's, and the occasional snoop by one of her action team, Sis Crowley who wasn't at all happy working for Griswold. A big woman with a no-nonsense look and a gift for listening, Sis had responsibility for the transmitter truck, which currently sat alongside a tool shed. Two low tires gave it the desired abandoned look.

The bulldozer, however, stood active use by its regular operator Wade McKeenan. Recruiting Wade was one of Sydnie's best coups. His obvious letch for her readied him for conversion, but what cinched it was her access to Sam Gowdy's bourbon stash on the Doodlebug. Wade was no drunk:

he merely had a strong liking for sour mash, and Jules' warehouse didn't stock the stuff.

By the time Crowley was able to report which way Griswold's plans leaned, Sydnie felt like a monkey juggling fresh-boiled eggs with a sore paw. Impatiently she heard Sis out. Then, looking from her to Wade and trying to keep straight who was in this for what reasons and under which misapprehensions of her own devising, she began.

"So Griswold fires up both Gates, his gang stands ready to bolt to the Mouth, depending on what the Tush drops. Or not. I don't see we have a choice. The bulldozer first, Wade. And if that doesn't spook 'em, Sis, you rev up the truck and get it pointed. Solid."

Unsmiling as always, Sis nodded. "And keep it there."

Crowley sometimes overdid tenacity; Sydnie told her, "But don't forget—just short of that stack of bales, you jump. And take cover behind them. Because even if we set off a stampede, there's bound to be a few who'll stand and shoot."

McKeenan took a sip. "And you, Secour; you'll be where?"

"Giving and directing cover fire; what did you think?"

Word had put activation near mid-afternoon, but dark came before Griswold strode to the Gate pair and began giving orders. Hungry and now carrying a near-empty canteen, Sydnie glowered at the unknowing Security chief as slight halos of ionization grew wavering to outline the tapering Mouth and Tush field edges.

Waiting lengthened and nothing happened. As Griswold's people slowly milled, their voices only a jumble to Sydnie's ears, she made an emphatic nod and thumbed her talkie. "Move it, Wade. Sis, hold for my mark, then go!"

Under cover of the larger group's noise, McKeenan had taken the chance of starting the dozer to run at idle. With no delay at all the huge machine, blade up but overhead clamshell now down forward and banging dirt at every bounce, lurched through the Tush egress area directly toward the Gate itself.

Bullets spanged off the heavy metal cab, but the juggernaut churned on to crash into the Gate's generating recess. Explosive disruption of the Habegger fields shot fiery bolts that clapped like thunder.

No sign of McKeenan hurt or whole; like ants stirred up by a stick, Griswold's troops moved at random, some shooting at the dozer while others looked in vain for new targets. But not hightailing it into the Mouth, dammit.

"Get 'em, Sis!" Holding one of Griswold's standard issue burp guns braced over a fuel drum, Sydnie scanned for threat as the truck's turbine whined its way toward the upper end of audibility. Dead on course for the Mouth, the lumbering vehicle emerged from shadow. Arms waving, Ames Griswold shouted orders Sydnie couldn't hear, and several guns swung toward the truck.

Take the easy ones first! She raked automatic fire across the better lit side of the clearing; two dropped, others ran. Jules on the other flank hadn't fired a shot. Well, he'd been worth a try. She moved aim to the darker side, couldn't get a fix, but let off a burst anyway, just for luck.

It stopped before she released the trigger: time to change clips. And position. Hand and foot she scrambled and flopped down, partially shielded behind a bush that wouldn't stop anything but a gunner's line of sight.

How could the truck take so long to cover so little ground? She spotted Griswold again; now he was running toward the Mouth, waving for his supporters to follow. Of those who hadn't already made the same choice without orders, some did and some didn't. Much as she despised the man, you don't shoot the Judas Goat.

Oddly, the world speeded up. *The truck:* "Sis! Jump!" Out Crowley came, not quite soon enough, slamming into the pile of bales rather than coming to ground behind it. Instinct took Sydnie toward the woman; then a *whoosh* buffeted past her and she turned to see a shoulder-held rocket launcher aiming from alongside the Mouth.

As she lurched sideward to take aim another rocket flashed; the truck's left front corner erupted into flame and the vehicle slued, pivoting off its course, jouncing to rest clear of the Gate approach. With its transmitter telling everything to the wrong planet. So Sam's plan had failed; the Web's Asian base would remain safe and undetected.

The hell you say. Whatever shape Wade and Sis were in, it would have to be someone else's problem. Against the fire of Griswold's rear guard Sydnie emptied her second clip.

Backing away now she slapped in her last one and sprayed short bursts until she was out of the light if not technically out of range.

Then she turned and ran like hell. For the Doodlebug.

It wasn't as if Sam could do anything about it, but he had to see for himself. Minutes after *Totebag* touched down he walked between Irtuk and an oddly silent Jules Perrone, leading a group through scraggly woods toward the Gates site. Even T'phee had come along, though his colleagues declined to accompany him.

When they reached the clearing's edge, Gowdy stopped and stared.

Hell in a handbasket. A Tush plugged with a bulldozer, both charred around the edges like the slapdash-bandaged driver now trying to get the machine running. A three-legged truck, itself not entirely untouched by fire. And a perfectly good Mouth in apparent working order.

But beside that Mouth, at the fringes of its entrance field, the prize exhibit: a flattish four-foot triangle of shaped metal. The honeycombed cross section showed how neatly the fin tip had sheared off the vanished Doodlebug. Habgates could do that.

Gowdy's explosive sigh was half whistle. "What a mess."

"You should have seen it before we hauled out the bodies." It was the poker-faced woman with her arm in the sling. "Seven, there were. Secour did most of them. Maybe all." For some reason she gave Jules Perrone a sour look. "Wade, he didn't like it she stayed back to give covering fire. But it sure paid off."

Sam turned facing her. "You're Crowley, right?" She nodded. "And you saw Sydnie—Secour, you knew her as—you saw her fly the 'bug through there?"

"Just the machine, I saw; not inside. But who else could it be?" Into her face crept the barest touch of animation. "I wouldn't say she flew it, exactly. It came in low over the trees and dipped down, I saw the wheels bounce just as the Gate lit up like they do, then it was gone. Hauling air on the far side, I shouldn't wonder."

"If there is any." Jules was looking at him funny, so Gowdy clarified. "Air. Instead of a cliff, or trees, or a brick wall. And the only way I could find out in less than four years is go through myself.''

Looking to T'phee he hunched his shoulders. ''No. Yain won't wait.'' *So I'll have to.*

Crowley spoke. ''I've notified Earth. Gated a message up at Admin, that she'd come out a bootleg Tush we don't know where; they should look for her. And send word ASAP.''

For that info, Gowdy felt gratitude. But the woman didn't know when to stop. ''You know why she did it, don't you?''

Sam looked at her. ''Of course.'' He gestured. ''Somebody got the truck. She figured she had to take word herself.''

''And you wish she hadn't.''

Gowdy didn't need this. But the woman obviously had feelings of her own. Gently he said, ''Yes, I wish that.''

Perrone, on the other hand, looked distinctly relieved. Either Sydnie had let him know where he stood, for blabbing, or he'd been still dreading that scene. In sudden pique Sam turned, saying, ''I guess you can rejoin the ship after all, Jules,'' and waited for his response.

''Oh, that won't be necessary now.''

Really? ''I don't believe it's your decision.''

''But *Sam* . . .''

Oh what the hell; let him off the hook. ''All right. Get whatever crew you can round up, to pull the asymptotic field adapters off all Griswold's Gates and put 'em aboard *Totebag*. And except for this one Mouth here, which might be some use to us though I have no idea how, the power units.''

''Sure, Sam; I'll get right on it.''

''Good. Now—you think you can round up any remaining Webfeet that might still be skulking around, and Gate them the hell home? By *our* Gates.''

Sis Crowley cleared her throat. ''That's my department. I'm still Security. Just not stuck with a shithead boss now. And the wrong kind of orders.''

Her face showed nothing, but likely it seldom did. ''Fine,'' Gowdy said. And then, ''Jules, I want a full report, including casualty lists, beamed to *Roamer* by the time I get there. You need to inform Glen Springs anyway, so send me an info copy.''

Perrone didn't look happy, and at first that suited Sam just fine. Then he wondered what was eating on him, that he was taking out on this undeniable schlub? No time for introspection; Gowdy looked around. "All right. let's head back."

Irtuk said, "The vessel of your construction; it is gone."

"Afraid so." But that was the least of it.

"Here it could have given much use. Not the least, in our learning."

"I know. We'll think of something else." Another loose end came to mind. "Are you ready to put Nsil's group aboard our ship? How many are there, anyway?"

"Ten in all. Their leader is called Vyorn. They are held nearby, waiting only your word to deliver them."

"Good. Thank you. And unless someone has already done so, please tell Vyorn we are returning them to Eamn."

Which should put the lot in a happy, peaceful mood. As Irtuk acknowledged, Gowdy began walking. He wasn't looking forward to his next chore. Between here and *Roamer* he had to sell Bart Cullan on a new added role for *Totebag*: combined space taxi service and training course, largely in benefit of the Maghren bearers' councils.

He didn't expect Cullan to applaud much.

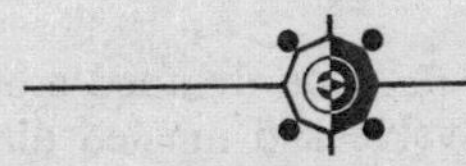

XXIII

A little faster or a little nearer, and not even Sydnie's reflexes could have dodged the building. As it was, emerging from Gate flare she hit lift and pitch and thrust all at once before she even knew what she was seeing. So instead of crashing head-on, she smashed up through a front corner of the structure's top floor and was pretty sure she could forget about landing on wheels. Or using her lower vertical fin for much of anything.

Alert or not, no Gate guards had time for a shot. But as Sydnie pushed for altitude, from her right came tracer streaks, and an explosive burst momentarily slammed the little ship's tail sideward. Aroka's trademark airstrip defense; to get it on her this fast, somebody here had to be on the stick. And now the rear of the cabin set up a nasty, whistling sort of howl.

Within seconds she was past flak range, and in case they had high-altitude stuff, she dropped to hedgehop around the flank of a range of hills. Then, safely distant, streaking topside and circling, Sydnie tried to guess where she might be.

From the airstrip she saw two jets scramble. They couldn't match the 'bug's speed, but if she ran she'd lose the Web base location. Well, when it came to upstairs they hadn't a prayer.

So she swung thrust to get there, and was doing fine until she began running short of breath and correlated that lack with the hissing sound behind her. Twisting to look around she saw not merely a hole in the hull but a major gap, and turned back barely in time to juke aside from the jets' first barrage.

No chance at all of suiting up. Snapping her belt loose she scrambled to the suit rack and popped an air tank free. The 'bug tilted; flipover with Traction lifters would rattle her around in here like a frozen turd in a boxcar; she lunged, caught the back of the pilot's seat, and reached to steady the controls.

Her strength was gone; vision dimmed around the edges. She cracked the tank's valve and inhaled directly from the hose, then clamped its end between her teeth while she managed to get back into the seat without dropping the tank. Then she belted in and looked to see what was happening.

Things go better with oxygen.

But she was still in range of the jets' rockets, once their pilots got turned and made altitude for another run, and about as far up as she dared go. Vacuum is not good for the complexion; if she stayed even this high much longer she could expect a strawberry nose and bloodshot eyes. At the least.

Now using one hand to keep the hose pinched shut or give her a whiff when she needed it, Sydnie juggled her controls with the other. Carefully banking, she achieved a downward view and spotted the Web airstrip. She wasn't exactly over it, but close enough. Firing up the 'bug's transmitter at top emission she activated a standard distress frequency.

"Mayday! Emergency! Anyone copying, take an immediate fix on my location. Repeat, take a location fix on this signal, and relay the information to . . ."

To where? "Relay these coordinates to all major law enforcement agencies in the area. Especially international. They need to hit this place fast and in force; it's a major Web base and it's well armed, including at least two fighter jets."

One of which was boosting near enough for another try, but she had to get down out of here anyway, and damn soon. "These people are setting up bootleg Habegger Gates to the Triad Worlds. I know that for sure because I just came through one. Which is why I don't know my location."

What else? Suddenly she realized she might be talking the wrong language. So as near as she could remember, only briefer, she rattled off her spiel some more, in two European tongues and three Asian.

The jet was turning to close on her. Taking an extra deep whiff of tanked air she gripped the tube in her teeth again, this time well to one side so she could still talk, and put both hands to the controls. As she gauged her next move she spoke, with less than perfect diction but maybe intelligible. First the plea for a locative fix, then, "If you move fast you can make a real haul, so get off your butts!" It sounded better in German.

In more than one way she was out of time. Trying to meter air feed with jaw pressure didn't work worth squat, and here came the Red Baron. Low air pressure evaporated much of her copious sweat and chilled the rest; she felt clammy all over.

Sydnie viewed the oncoming jet with unmitigated dislike. Here he came, Hotshot Charlie rising at one o'clock and curving with pinpoint precision to intercept. And any kind of plane he knew about, he had dead to rights.

But not the Doodlebug. Traction Drive runs by different rules. Sydnie didn't calculate; she played by ear. Twitch up, break his arc, edge to one side, now his speed's wrong, lay on major gees flashing across and past him, then flip and come back. When the pulsed downward burst from her main thrustor blew his wing off and sent the crippled duck kiting ass over teakettle, he probably never saw her coming.

For whatever reason, Charlie's sidekick wasn't in view.

Sydnie went back downstairs, low enough to breathe adequately if not comfortably. So she could close the air tank valve.

There was something funny about the controls, had been ever since she came through, but she'd been too busy to figure it out. Looking out and back she saw the stub where her right-hand fin ended somewhat shorter then the left. Another two feet would have creamed the lift thrustor supports for sure, but they'd held so far, so she quit worrying.

And for a change, absence of threat gave her time to think. She turned on the 'bug's receivers and began fishing. It had been a long while but she recognized the language; give or take a few hundred miles she was in the area of the "refugee" run, the one that had set her against Jorge Aroka.

Well, the Web had always been strong in these parts. And now she knew which way she wanted to go.

The quickest route to anywhere was a Great Circle, but lacking navigational instruments she'd have to guess and use landmarks. An azimuth of about ten, she figured, and then from somewhere along Baja she could find her way to Glen Springs.

It looked to be a fair haul. If she still had wheels, she could land someplace and suit up to take off again and make real time, suborbital. As was, she chanced leaving the controls long enough to grab a suit anyway. For the use of its amenities such as rations, water supply, and fluid disposal. It all helped.

"It's fine with me, Sam." Bart Cullan's reaction came as a surprise that Gowdy welcomed. In a surge of near-affection for Irtuk he'd gone overboard and promised *Totebag*'s services before ensuring the bargain—and as he'd told Jorge Aroka in that man's final hour or so, Gowdy had a sort of obsession about keeping promises. "I've heard enough scuttlebutt," Cullan added, "to guess which way the wind blows. And working with the locals should be interesting."

He paused. "If you could spare me a good interpreter, that would make things easier. Some of us have learned a little, but for right now we could use a bit of coaching."

They were barely out of atmosphere, turning to set course toward *Roamer*. There'd been some delay, getting all the Habgate gear packed and loaded; why couldn't Bart have mentioned this caveat before lifting? Oh well. ''None of mine, I'm afraid; we're short as it is. Back there at HQ, though . . .''

''Actually that's what I meant. There's this woman on Perrone's staff. Redhead. We sort of hit it off, talking.''

Sam didn't see a problem. ''So ask her.''

''I intend to. But Perrone has his eye on her; I imagine he'll axe the request.''

''You're his only transport link, for now, to the rest of the system including the macroGate; he has to treat you right. But tell you what: I'll give you an official reassignment order, ship's seal and the lot. Just be sure to serve it on him before *Roamer* leaves.''

''Right you are. And thanks.''

Until now, Sam hadn't found time to speak with the Eamnet group. Cargo shuttles usually carried passengers only on a short-haul basis; Nsil's ten followers were berthed in a seating area supplemented with mattresses laid along the aisles and in an open space to the front. Entering, Gowdy found most lying quietly, while Vyorn and one other slumped crouching across seats and spoke together.

Clearing his throat, Sam got their attention. ''I am Gowdy, leader of the starship. I would apprise you the status of relations between yumins and you of Eamn.'' He told it quickly and tried to keep it accurate, adding, ''Nsil could not know we posed no threat, as I cannot know what has happened when his ship reached Earth, my home.'' *Will* happen, but don't confuse them with facts. ''But with my friend Kayo to speak for him, we can be certain that accord will be reached.''

Vyorn spoke. ''The ship we brought down; it was yours?''

''It is, and now restored. I hold no malice for the deed.'' Which wasn't something he could have said at the time! ''When I have visited my greater ship, this one will restore you all to Eamn. I shall call Gvan, to inform him you return with honor.''

Come to think of it, last word to Gvan had been Nsil's escape through the macroGate. High time the Eamnet leader was brought up-to-date. So the next time that world turned to give a signal window, Sam got on the circuit and raised contact, tendering Gvan much the same assurances he'd made to

Vyorn but adding the fact that Scayna had Gated to be with Nsil.

He couldn't gauge the Eamnet's reaction, so keeping in mind that Gvan was longer on impulse than on judgment, he refrained from any mention of the Habgate time factor. And having mended all the fences he could think of at the moment, got some sleep.

The run went smoothly; approaching his ship Sam saw that the Deployment Vehicle was seated back into place, the sleek line of nose cone again complete. With *Golconda* away to the macroGate, *Totebag* docked at the ship's stern, for most convenient transfer of the appropriate Gate equipment. Cullan and the Yainans, plus a few men helping with the latter's belongings, followed Gowdy into the larger vessel. Climbing outship, Sam was pleased to see the reassembled drive mode quarters almost ready for residence.

In control, Libby Verdoorn of all people sat painstakingly checking instruments and entering the readings. ''Hello, Libby. Joining us for the long haul, are you?''

She looked up. ''Hi, skipper. Yes, I'd like to. You don't have a DV backup; SuZanne's a watch officer now. And down below, Jules is entirely welcome to all that paperwork!'' She hesitated. ''If it's all right. I mean, agency policy. Maril and me.''

''The agency's not here and it's not shorthanded. I'm both. Welcome to the clambake.'' Starting to leave, he turned back. ''Can you get me Pia Velucci at the macroGate? And pipe the call down to the lounge?'' She'd try. Okay. He did leave.

The transit ring impressed Bart Cullan; so did his first exposure to the rotating belt's Coriolis effects. Walking the corridor as far as the lounge he seemed to get the hang of it, and entered with his balance more or less under control.

Sam made short work of introductions: Simone, Mose, SuZanne, and ''Get yourself a drink or something; go get acquainted,'' as he sat with his officers. ''All right; how soon can we leave?''

Chores remaining weren't formidable; as Simone recited the checklist he nodded agreement. Then his call came through. ''Gowdy here, Pia. I need Gate techs, people who can install and fire up your pass-through fields as well as the basic units. The job's on Yamar, or maybe you still call it

Scout. I'm not expert enough to say how long it'll take; it's three Tushes with pass-through; one Tush and two Mouths without. Fairly large portal structures, so some construction types and equipment would help. Oh yeh, Bart Cullan will be out with *Totebag* to do the hauling. Too bad *Golconda* can't land anywhere, but we need Larry on watch there for out-Gating pirates, anyway."

What am I forgetting? "Anything I missed, tell me. Gowdy out, and waiting." All right; twenty-two minutes minimum, not counting the time to come up with good answers. What the hell; he'd earned a drink himself.

He was asking a lot of Velucci and maybe it wasn't entirely necessary, but somehow he didn't want to put his full trust in Gate techs recruited by Aroka & Associates. When Pia came back on the circuit she began by saying, "That was a good idea, putting *Golconda* on guard duty for now. I get the feeling Corcoran works best with a free hand, so that's what I'm giving him." Then she read back Sam's list of needs, confirming, and said, "I can do that. What I need in return is transport for some shore leave on a regular basis. My people didn't come out here to breathe canned air indefinitely—hell, neither did I."

She paused. "Hey, Gowdy, this isn't blackmail; you get your help either way. But give us a little, too."

Sam turned to see Bart Cullan near and listening. "That all right with you?"

Cullan said, "Depends on what grade of regularity she thinks she needs. We're indentured to Magh; remember?"

So to Velucci the word was, "I think that can be arranged. But *Totebag* has commitments here, too. Maybe you should send somebody along, when the ship comes back to Magh, to negotiate the sharing." And on second thought, "Quite a few of the colony admin staff can interpret for you. It should work. Gowdy out."

Now then. "Bart. Is your local vocabulary good enough to have Vyorn point out their space project site? Where Nsil's ships lifted, tell him. Just set down there, debark your passengers, exchange hellos with Gvan or anyone he sends to represent him. He may invite you to dinner; it's up to you, whether you'd feel comfortable. If not, plead hurry, my orders. In any case, nobody comes aboard without an escort."

In case Gvan got a wild hair, he meant. But no point in causing alarm.

He held out his hand. "If I don't see you before you undock, have a good trip. And down at the cargo bay, Milo Vitale will have the checklist for you."

The handshake, and Cullan left. It was time, Sam decided, for a final predeparture report to Glen Springs. For that job he went to his quarters. When he got there, he was surprised how lonesome it felt.

"Sam Gowdy's depending on us to plug the gaps for him at Tetzl's," said Jocelyn Waymire, newly flown in for a fast confab. "In return we'll expect him to plug a few for us."

Actually the senator seemed to spend at least half her time here at Glen Springs; Kayo hoped no crucial legislation needed her vote on the Senate floor. "Like what?" Kayo said.

Bill Flynn on the other hand had moved residence down here; he and his wife Mara now owned a house only a few miles off base. Flynn tapped the readerboard chart titled GATES SYSTEM. "See these Gate channels? Six pass-throughs from Yain, three each to Yamar and to Tetzl's. He supplies adapters for all but the last, which is up to us. Add single-loaders one from each world back to Yain, and two-way between Yamar and Tetzl's. All the matrices are paired and pre-activated, out of Jorge Aroka's junk box."

"So?" Kayo still didn't see it—or why *she* was being consulted. "What's not covered?"

"Between *here* and Yain," said Waymire, "would be two jumps each way, four extra years. So we want to send the hardware for the Yain end of a two-way pass-through pair, direct. Gate it aboard *Roamer* in units of manageable size, and advise Gowdy ahead of time. The Tush Gating area has to be *big*, for a project Habegger Labs is working on."

Kayo waited for more explanation but none came. "So where do I come into this?"

"We'd like you to draft the advisory." Kayo opened her mouth but the senator continued. "His own messages read more and more—uh, *independent*, lately. Independent, and impatient."

"Yes," said Flynn. "God knows he probably has reason to be edgy, and who knows how much worse it could get by the time our requests reach him? But from someone he knows . . ."

"Well, sure. Just tell me—" Outside and about a hundred yards away, an employees' soccer game had marginally caught her attention; now came yells and shrieks, players sprinting in all directions to get off the field. "What in the world?"

As all three went to the window a fuselage of sorts, sporting among other things a pair of fin-mounted Traction Drive units, lowered jerkily toward the ground. The hull showed a great jagged tear, one fin lacked a sheared-off tip, and stubs below, protruding at odd angles, might have been the remains of landing gear.

Wavering and tilting, trying to hover but jittering back and forth, the strange vehicle's movement bespoke either pilot fatigue or a sad lack of training. Waymire and Flynn ran for the corridor, but remembering that these windows opened, Kayo swung one wide and jumped down. Sprinting, she overtook the day shift comm chief, Bessie Orleans. "What *is* this?"

Short of breath, Orleans spoke in bursts. "Not sure. Call from Bangkok last night. Gated out somewhere south of there. Said it's from *Roamer*." A gasp or two and then, "Told LA this morning, she was coming here. Transmitter must've failed later."

Roamer? Then this had to be Sam's homemade spacecan! Almost too close for safety as the object skidded to a crunching halt, the two women stopped. Now Flynn and Waymire caught up; a side hatch opened and someone swung a ladder out. Then a figure emerged.

It was halfway down before Kayo recognized Sydnie Lightner.

She ran to her. Sweat-streaked in face and clothing, hair matted and one short-chopped hank standing out at an angle, sculptured features bloated and webbed with burst capillaries, Sydnie stank like a locker-room laundry hamper.

Kayo hugged anyway; they'd never really been friends, but what the hell. "Sydnie! Are you all right? What's happened?"

Lightner grinned. "Take me to your bathroom."

* * *

As near as Sydnie could put it together, the bodies were in custody but the brains got away. Acting as fast as could reasonably be expected, police agencies captured the Web base almost intact. But as they closed in, a scramjet went up; missing were two—or three, or four, depending on which witness you believed—of the top dogs. Along with any records that might have tied in to other Web groups or this one's superiors. And from what Sydnie remembered of the Web's ways, getting useful info from the prisoners would be like squeezing out a glass of rock juice.

Scramjets seemed to be the order of the day. Toward evening the deputy secretary for Interstellar Affairs landed one at the field nearest Glen Springs. Lean and mean, white-haired Crane Willigh was an old pol: ex-senator and sometime candidate for the presidency, now retired from the elective rat race to service the public in less hectic and more secure fashion.

Service, some said, as in animal husbandry.

Sydnie got her bath and some clean clothes and a meal before the man arrived, but she was nowhere near slept out when two security guards came to escort her to Willigh's plane. It took off like a screaming eagle with a hot coal under its tail, but even at night she could tell that compared to the 'bug she was riding Junior's trike.

At DC a long limo ride dumped her into a comfortable room that still spelled detention cell because the door locked from the outside, and next morning found her being sworn in at a crime commission hearing.

The audience sat sparsely scattered. Looking out at strangers, Sydnie recognized types: this one avid for some real good dirt, those two simply grateful for something to occupy their time, a pair of bored, incurious holovid reporters. With a start she saw Bill Flynn, rumpled and moving like a man short on sleep, take a rear seat. He nodded in her direction; she glimpsed a wink. Then the chairman opened proceedings and Flynn's face went serious.

Pissed off to the max, so far Sydnie hadn't raised any kind of squawk. Now as Willigh himself rose to question her, she met his predatory stare with one of her own, and held it.

For what it was worth, he blinked first. Then began asking:

how and what she knew of the Asian base, the Web, Aroka, the illicit Gates . . .

"Those Gates were no secret; Aroka's man Ames Griswold took over colony admin, including comm security; he didn't care who knew what. But I had no idea where they came out, except just Earth, until I got there. By the way, was Griswold captured?"

No answer. Instead, "You have knowledge of the Web. How?"

Merde. She could lie out of this, but not and nail the Web too. Take a chance. "Under coercion by the Spider Prince, I was at one time employed in that organization."

Commotion; Willigh's aide punished her computer keyboard. After conferring, the secretary said, "You're not in the files, Lightner."

Take a *big* chance. "Try Charel Secour."

Before the aide could speak, indrawn breath whistled through Willigh's teeth. "La Hoja Rubia! How accommodating of you to admit it." *After so many years, how does he know?* He turned to the aide. "Marie. How many murders on record as committed by that one? Listed under Klieng, Secour, Parmenter . . . who else?"

"By me, none!" Sydnie bit the words out. She'd checked the date; anything she *had* done, the statutes of limitations were long since fulfilled. This, though: "La Hoja was a job title, not a nickname. Before me was Marlene Klieng who lived up to it, and maybe others. I was a decoy; I never killed." Not as La Hoja, anyway; *Roamer* and Magh had been different situations, to say the least. "And after me, you say there were more?"

Willigh had a nasty smile. "There was you, under whatever aliases." He took a readout sheet from Marie, and read off names and dates of murder victims. After a half dozen or so he said, "Those will do for a start; don't you agree, Secour?"

"Yes, I do. When the first two occurred, I was still in high school, and the last was nearly a year before I ever heard of Jorge Aroka." She forestalled his reply: "I served as La Hoja between these two dates." Could she ever forget either? ". . . which was the night Marlene Klieng was killed, until . . ."

Here she gave only the date; if there were ever a time for that story, this wasn't it. Sydnie moved ahead. "I composed an Omnet file documenting Web activity throughout my time as La Hoja. I can produce it for this commission, and—''

Willigh cut her off. ''For security reasons, that goes under wraps. Give me the necessary coding; I'll take care of it.''

He was too eager. Play this one close to the dickey. ''Yes,'' she said. ''Hand me up that keyboard. It's easier to do than explain.'' It was also easier to key in a second copy, this one coded to Sam Gowdy's initials and birthdate, before Deputy Secretary Willigh could rise and move to see what she did.

She showed him the original codes, and said, ''There are two errors of fact. At the time I compiled this set of dossiers I thought Aroka dead. And since I was not only escaping the Web but hoped to bring it down, I documented the supposed death of Charel Secour. And returned to my own identity, which had never appeared in Web records.''

Something still had Willigh off his feed. Roughly taking the keyboard he planked it down on the table before him and struck a number of keys with more vigor than need be. Then, taking a deep breath, he sat back. Obviously relieved.

Well, he would be. Even viewing the keyboard upside down, Sydnie could follow the operation. Crane Willigh had made yet another copy and put it under his own seal. Then, overwriting with a random-generated nonsense program, he deleted the original. If Aroka could edit, why not Willigh?

Best to keep him off base a little. ''The file includes the actual perpetrators of each killing ascribed to La Hoja Rubia during my tenure. Fact is, I could pretty well reproduce the list from memory.'' She didn't like the stare that statement brought, but it was too late to take it back.

What Willigh said, though, was, ''You'll have ample opportunity to do so in your defense. I'm charging you with every La Hoja murder on *our* list. Regardless of date.''

He stood. ''Bailiffs, this woman is remanded to custody.''

Willigh wasn't the only one on his feet. From the rear, Bill Flynn called out, ''Hold up there, Crane. If you want to arrest an officer of the starship *Roamer*, temporarily on detached service, you will damn well go through channels.''

He stalked forward down the aisle to stand facing the taller man. ''Starting with Jocelyn Waymire who I'm representing here, through Glen Springs to the ship itself. You know perfectly well, Crane Willigh, you can't yank any crew member off a ship without a signed release from the captain."

Willigh's cheeks flushed. "That's ridiculous! You're asking me to wait *four years*?"

Across Bill Flynn's face a slow grin spread. "Not a bit of it, Crane. You're definitely entitled to Gate out there and back, serve the papers yourself without losing a personal day."

"You can't just take her out of here!"

"You can't stop me."

Approach of the two reporters, interest obviously aroused, drew both men's attention. Flynn beamed; Willigh scowled, saying, "All right, there's nothing here for you. Just a matter of jurisdiction."

"That's right," Sydnie put in. "Mr. Willigh thinks he owns this end of the universe and Mr. Flynn thinks he doesn't."

Flynn gave her a look of mock reproach, but his grin held. "I hope you'll dress that quote up a bit for Ms. Lightner. In his understandable zeal, Secretary Willigh was in danger of bypassing proper channels. It's settled now, wouldn't you say?"

Outside, Flynn hustled her into a drab rental car with two Glen Springs security men in the front seat. He gave no orders, but Sydnie figured airport to be the operative word. As the car moved out, Flynn said, "That was the truth, your criminal past and all?"

"Pretty much. And no killing; all my activities of that period are well past the statute." About the Omnet file, now. "First time, Aroka intercepted and changed it so he looked good. Willigh's setting up to do the same thing. But I made another copy this time, too." She gave him the password code. "He has to be Web, you know."

"No surprise, Sydnie. He's the one who got Aroka his commodore hat. But it may be a job to prove anything."

By the time they reached the plane, a small Glen Springs courier jet, the subject was pretty well talked out. Once aboard, she slept the whole way.

"You must not forget," Kaow told Nsil, "that when you emerge into your system, three Chormyears will have passed there. From what we know at this time, Gowdy and his ship will be gone to T'phee's world. Eamn and Magh should each have at least one ship much like your own; none will mount weapons. It is to be hoped that communication and trade have grown between your worlds. You will need to assess the existing situation on Eamn and determine what place you may assume in its leadership."

"Scayna and I." Nsil's forelimb clasped the bearer's shoulder. "Her part will in future be known to all."

Scayna looked up from the sleeping Nyrl. "Not with abruptness can change be achieved. The thin tip of a claw, Nsil, opens the seal."

The bearer Lightner spoke. "If one claw doesn't do it, try another. Sometimes quite a number may be required."

Nsil blinked. "You have been on my world? And on Magh?"

Her mouth took on a strange shape. "Oh, yes. And found each in its own way to be of interest."

The celebration of departure reached its end; Kaow and her seeder, Wamir and Flin of deciding authority, several more accompanied the voyagers to the ship *Hermes*. To greet them came the leading instructor Okahnr and five assisting yumins, assigned to oversee the navigating of Tasr and of Nsil himself.

Now came leave-taking with all who would remain here. To Kaow, finally, clasping foredigits and then closing embrace that also included Scayna, Nsil said, "I have come to esteem you greatly. Your absence will be pain."

Scayna said, "And your presence never forgotten." A snuffling misshaped Kaow's words, but their meaning came clearly.

Then, climbing up and inside *Hermes*: Nsil with Scayna holding the restive Nyrl, Tasr, Tirys, Duant of Magh, all ship Three's complement watched Okahnr seal the entrance before adjourning to their own residing compartments, to await the ship's rising.

One of these chambers, specially enlarged, was called Scayna's dome, though not so shaped. Leaving Tirys there with Scayna and Nyrl, Nsil returned to the navigational area and took the Eamnet portion of the secondary controlling position, beside the yumin bearer Jone. To Jone's other side and similarly paired were seated Tasr and the seeder Okahnr.

That one made the laugh sound. "Ready? We lift now."

Gently yet with growing speed, *Hermes* rose toward the great portal.

What had he forgotten? As *Roamer* built vee toward Yainstar, Gowdy couldn't get free of that worry.

To get his mind off it, once more he calculated ship's time in terms of Earth time. For him and for *Roamer* the four years of waiting, to hear what had happened to Sydnie, would be shortened. On accel from orbit to nominal cruising speed the saving was only about ninety-six days. But once up there crowding c, with t_o/t running at ten to one, things got better. As near as Sam could figure in his head, if he added in the delays between Sydnie's cataclysmic departure and his own more deliberate leaving, he might possibly get word of her around the time *Roamer* came within half a light of Yain and went back into decel. Say fifteen months from now, ship's time.

It was still no picnic, but Sam could live with it. He didn't even consider fudging extra gee force to get up to speed more quickly, or setting that speed above *Roamer*'s assigned point-nine-nine-five c. These values had safety margin built in and Gowdy approved. Several trillion miles from anywhere is no place to read the fine print in the warranty.

He was running five bodies short of normal crewing, but the people he did have aboard knew their jobs. He was also running somewhat paranoid. And knew it; after Aroka & Company he wanted no more surprises from Earthtush, so he kept that facility mostly plugged. Once each day the blockage was cleared, one party moving empty crates while two others stood braced to provide covering fire. First choice was the fire extinguisher's frigid CO_2, but one of the team had a semi-auto for backup while the day's haul was gathered and the blocking crates replaced.

Here was the thing: throughout all the piracy, fighting, the whole lot, by sheer dumb luck none of Gowdy's own people had been killed. He wanted to keep it that way.

This day's Earthtush output contained nothing out of the way: routine messages—some addressed to Commodore Aroka—and a few items of personal mail. None for him, though. As usual.

A little early for watch change, but standing not thirty paces from control and nowhere else to go, Sam went to relieve SuZanne Craig. "Anything new?"

At the instrument console Marthe Vinler looked up. "It's still too far out to be sure, but I think there's a ship coming. From Yain, probably. So we should pass fairly close."

Trying to remember T'phee's guess as to arrival of the next survival ark, Gowdy nodded. "They won't speak Eamnet, of course. Won't have heard of us, either. But T'phee can give them all the news—and get the latest from Yain, too."

He turned to Molly Abele at the silent comm position. "Set our gear to listen, and beam number strings, on the frequencies we used with the Yainan ship at Magh. No point in firing up until we're closer; make a note on the comm log, though, to begin when we approach extreme range."

Now Cole came to relieve Marthe, Libby Verdoorn replaced Molly, and from the drive room came acknowledgment that Alix Dorais was taking over for Jethro Blaine.

All shipshape, but Gowdy felt restless. How far had they come from Magh? Nearly four days now. Signal delay would be up around eleven hours; by tomorrow, forget it. He recorded one more report for pulsed burst transmission, a final signoff to the colony and to Jules Perrone.

He hoped his last talk with Jules, before leaving, had helped the man get over being so scared of his job. "You have Griswold off your back now, and Larry Corcoran's got a bead on anything hostile that might outGate." Not indefinitely, of course, but probability said any new Web troops would arrive soon or not at all.

"But there's so much I don't know!"

"Depend on your staff people to fill you in; that's what they're for. And don't think you're the first who's had to start as mostly a figurehead. The secret, Jules, is to be generous with credit—for good work, good ideas, whatever. Do that and they'll carry the hose for you. You remember Barry Krsnch?"

"Yes. But . . ."

"He did the exact opposite. And his people hated his guts."

Perrone had seemed to get the point, but his few calls since *Roamer* moved out had held a querulous tone. So, feeling a strange pity for the man who was such a pain in the butt that Sam hadn't wanted him back on the ship, Gowdy added a brief word of encouragement to the report, ending with, "Keep 'em flying, Jules. And buy Pia Velucci a drink for me."

He watched as Libby checked the circuit and fired the message off. Now what? Staring at the indicators and controls before him, gradually Sam let himself realize how thoroughly depressed he was. Had been for some time, actually.

And why? He was doing his job; faced with unexpected threats he'd managed to save the old homestead; maybe he hadn't been brilliant, or one hundred percent correct, but he hadn't really screwed up, either. Quite the opposite, he told himself.

Hell, he was even improvising a pretty fair rescue operation, on his own because Earth hadn't even heard of the problem yet. He did hope to hell they'd back him up when the word got there. But now, necessarily without authorization, he was off to spend his next several years saving more of T'phee's people than all the ships they could ever build. Surely that venture was worthwhile, something to feel good about.

So how come he didn't? Why did he want out? Because that was exactly what he damn well did want.

Not now, of course; he couldn't. But once those Gates were set up on Yain, and the refugee flow established, Sam Gowdy was going to Gate home. Probably by way of Tetzl's Planet; after all, Kayo Marlin gave it a good report. Or maybe he'd stay there, instead.

His reasons still puzzled him. It wasn't just losing Sydnie, when they'd finally begun to build something between them; he'd faced that loss, more or less accepted it. He hoped.

Then insight hit him. The killings. What he felt wasn't exactly grief or shame or guilt, but a little of all three. Even for Aroka. Even for that twisted creature Arman Lioso. And until now he'd kept himself too busy to notice.

Maybe it was time he did.

He flipped down his position's keyboard and began the letter he needed to send to Earth. When he had it the way he wanted it, he made a printout and handed it across to Libby. "Put this in today's bundle for Glen Springs, please."

For the rest of the watch he felt a little better. But not much.

XXIV

"Like any macroGate," the woman from Habegger Labs continued, "it will consist of a Tush back-to-back with a Mouth. The difference is, they'll be both ends of the same Gate."

At the back of the main briefing room, Kayo followed the presentation. She and Dan had planned to Gate out earlier today, but she was glad they hadn't; she'd have hated to miss this. "We could have produced such a combination at any time, of course," the woman added, "given a reason to do so. Now we have one. But this construct has to be much larger than any we've made before; we want to handle objects at least a mile in diameter."

So there was no question of building a solid ring. Instead, the synchronized matrix and power units would be carried by twelve individual ships and connected into a circle by cables, each approximately fifteen hundred feet in length.

Smallish, those ships—because they themselves would be taken on skids for Gating to Tushes at Yain, interconnected on the spot, then lifted off in close formation. "Only when the squadron approaches Yain's comet swarm will they assume a spread configuration and try to snare comet nuclei. Once a target inGates, the ships can reorient and move to the next one. It is hoped," the woman concluded, "that a major part of the threat to Yain can be obviated. If not the entirety."

There was more. Afterward, Kayo finagled her way into the smaller gathering arranged for the visitor by Jocelyn Waymire and Bill Flynn. Up close, Dr. Leora Crandall looked too young for her expertise; obviously, looks could be deceiving.

Over coffee Bill Flynn asked questions. "What's the disposal plan? Two years later, you're positioned to dump the entire haul into their sun? Or out to deep space?''

Crandall smiled. ''No. It's perfectly good raw material; why waste it?'' The trick was to intercept each object well out, at low velocity compared to what it was heading for. ''Then bring it in. You can close formation again for that; matter in the Aleph Continuum doesn't care about its package size in this one. But when outGating time comes, spread the circle again, and aim it tangent to a circular orbit.''

Pausing, she raised her brows and grinned. ''Because your distance to the sun is chosen so that the velocity at capture will *fit* that orbit. Of course they won't all come out circular, but close enough to constitute a loosely grouped belt.''

Right, thought Kayo; things leave a macroGate Tush at the same speed they entered the Mouth. Everything's relative.

But now she had a question. ''Dr. Crandall, if this device can clear up the comet swarm, does that mean Sam Gowdy needn't bother setting up his Gates? To evacuate the planet?''

''I'm afraid not. For two reasons. First, we're not sure how long it's going to take to develop synchronization control for a macroGate of this circumference.''

She grimaced. ''And second, until we actually try it in the field, so to speak, we can't be sure it's going to work.''

At Glen Springs they had Sydnie lying low. Lying low, and on alert to be hustled into a Gate if the posse showed up. Nobody expected Crane Willigh to roll over and play dead after only one setback; his record indicated quite the opposite. They hadn't even let her see Kayo and Dan off at the Gates room; she'd had to say her good-byes here in her carefully unlisted quarters.

So when a knock came at her door she was up, bag in hand, before she cracked the door and peeked out. ''Oh, hi, Mr. Flynn. Anything happening?''

Stepping inside, he handed her a flimsy; quickly she scanned down it.

> . . . completed such assigned tasks as were possible to achieve here . . . disruption due first to difficulties between inhabitants of Magh and Eamn as you know . . . the incursion of highly organized criminals under Jorge Aroka and Arman Lioso . . . problems disposed of as

best I could. In this system, I have finished.
I did not sign up to kill.

Damn! This was serious. Now she read more closely.

I am now committed to the Yain rescue endeavor as outlined to you earlier. I will take this ship there, see the Gates up and operating, and report my estimate of this effort's potential for success.

At that point, whatever date it may be, I intend my resignation to take effect, and will turn the Yain operation over to my second in command. At a rough estimate, four years after receipt of this request you may close my records and consolidate my accounts. Duplicate notice and letters of credit should be Gated to Magh and to Tetzl's Planet as well as to Yain; I have not yet chosen my destination.

Thank you for your consideration.

Samuel Hall Gowdy, Captain, *Roamer*

"Holy hell." Shaking her head, Sydnie looked at Flynn and saw no answers. "I don't know what did it, but he's really in the tank." And frowning, asked, "What do you think?"

Bill Flynn spread a hand. "It's in there, clear enough. See? 'I did not sign up to kill.' He's had all he can take. But he still hasn't walked off the job. Not yet."

She tried to think. "Has anyone told him I got here okay? That might help." Then she remembered: the word couldn't reach the ship for another two years. Adding up to four since he wrote that message. Oh shit.

And why did she feel to blame? Because she hadn't sensed his demons, tried to exorcise them? All Sydnie's early life, Oreadna's rules said it's always *their* fault. Now when she'd dumped her mother's ethical gestalt, it all seemed to be hers. What was the difference?

Suddenly she knew. If it's your fault, maybe you can do something about it. "Mr. Flynn?"

"Yes?"

"You don't need me on these hearings. Sam's reports detail all the stuff that happened out there, and the file I gave you the code for, it covers the old days better than I could possibly remember, after so long.''

He was going to make her say it, so she did. ''Could you get me Gated to *Roamer*, this time of night?''

When Gowdy came off watch, seeing T'phee in the lounge raised his spirits. Waving his little grasping tendrils the Yainan was explaining *Roamer*'s workings to his three cohorts. He did quite a bit of that, Sam had noticed, and seemed to enjoy it a lot. Since much of their talk was in Yainan, there was no way of knowing how much of T'phee's explanation and description bore any great resemblance to fact.

And yet—from Yainan technology T'phee didn't claim to understand in any detail, he'd made a couple of suggestions Sam wished he knew enough to evaluate. For instance: modifying ''pushforce'' units to slow time and provide a measure of artificial gravity, as on the ships *Tayr* and *L'lit*. But none of the four Yainans could tell how any of it was done. Sam had mentioned those ideas in reports to Earth and to Magh; maybe at Yamar, on the ships themselves, someone could learn more.

Now Sam hailed T'phee and told him of the possible Yainan ship approaching. ''We will try to achieve voice communication, so that you and they may exchange a maximum of information.''

''A most welcome happenment!'' Almost dancing, the squat Yainan showed excitement. He wasn't merely putting on weight, Sam gathered; he was pregnant, which should by Gowdy's lights make him a she. Except that if Gowdy understood T'phee correctly, with Yainans the concept didn't apply.

Asexual reproduction by budding? But in that case, minor glitches in gene structure would cause each line of descent to diverge from every other, and obviously this hadn't been happening. On the principle that the subconscious doesn't change its opinions unless thoroughly convinced to do so, Sam's continued to think of T'phee as male.

And currently in need of explication. ''Normal converse, you must understand, is not possible.'' The relative velocities, limiting the time between achieving comm range ahead and losing it behind, the rapidly varying signal lag, the Doppler effects: ''Tell them to record your speaking and you will record theirs. That you will speak unpausing, to give maximum information, and that they must do this also. When the time of signal utility is past, we will correct for the effects of our high rates of motion and you will hear their speaking.''

Enthusiasm less dampened than might have been expected, T'phee turned to inform the others.

Leaving them to confer, Gowdy decided to skip his usual visit to the drive mode lounge and get some sleep. He had almost dropped off when his door opened. Startled, he switched on the overhead light, but before he could register face or form the intruder cut it off with the doorside switch, and a whisper came. ''We don't need light to talk.''

Rustlings, and then someone slid into bed with him, someone as naked as he was. In dimness lit only by light reflected from the back hallway, fingers touched his mouth to silence him. Again the whisper, betraying nothing. ''You need something; I've noticed. Talk, cuddling, making love, all of the above; your choice.''

She—he could tell *that* much—waited. He said, ''What about your pairmate?'' Safe question; all but he were paired. ''A captain shouldn't—it's too much like abuse of authority.''

Her body came to touch his. All the way down their fronts, and her arms wormed around to form embrace; so much for the optional nature of cuddling, and his body voted for the full ticket. ''You're not making any advances; I am. And so?''

Then she kissed an earlobe. ''If you'd rather, you don't have to know who I am. Ships that pass in the night.''

Actually he was pretty sure already. And pleased: for this one he had considerable respect. He said, ''That part can be your choice,'' and she rolled back to spread herself.

People bring their own ways to love; those of Sam and his partner didn't always mesh gracefully; this first time, how could they? But he found the unexpected differences exciting, and their reconciliations rewarding. The time he'd been alone accounted for some of his intensity, but by no means all.

At the end of what he hoped might well be only the first of a series, he shifted his weight to ease burden from her but remained engaged. Breath halfway back to normal, he said, "So. Unmask now, or not?"

She laughed. "Maybe you didn't notice, but when you hit the rapids you were using my name in vain quite a lot."

"All right, Libby." The brief kiss was his move. "I loved this; I love you for it, you know how I mean. But why?"

"Looked like you could use some cheerin' up, podner."

First he felt insulted. Pity? And a roll in the hay would make it all better? Damn fine roll, mind you, but still . . .

Luckily he said none of that, for then it hit him: he *was* better. Not just the release; there was an ancient wisdom here. Death had weighed him down; sex affirmed life. On a very deep level. He wasn't healed yet—far from it—but his natural recuperative powers had been given one hell of a good jump-start.

"Yes," he said finally. "Yes, I could. Some cheering up, indeed. And in a little while, maybe some more, too. If it's all right."

It was. He got up and fixed them a snack; not bothering to dress, they ate and talked. He didn't tell all of it, only the besmirchment of killing, the loss of crew members, the sense of being on a blind course with no end. "Not even a real colony to show for it." Things like that. The loneliness, he knew, would be too obvious to need mention.

"No one could have done better, Sam."

Maybe, maybe not; a question surfaced. "Libby, what made you come here *now*?"

Only a little, her cheeks colored. "Your message. To Glen Springs."

"You opened it?" And then, "You stopped it from going out?"

Her vigorous headshake sent honey blond hair whipping. "I put it in the stack. But I saw how you looked when you wrote it, when you handed it over. After watch I went back, and called up the last thing entered from your position; that's how I read it."

What could he say? "I guess I'm glad you did."

Standing, she took his hand and pulled. "Come back to bed."

After a time they slept.

Before she left, a pleasant while after waking, Sam made

breakfast. Over a second cup of coffee Libby said, "I'm not sure how we should handle this. For myself, I'd like to live here part-time. Like a commuter marriage—you're making the movie, I'm doing the Broadway play and fly out for long weekends. If you think it could work."

Likely she saw he wasn't going to ask. "Maril and I, it's somewhat like that already. Except that nobody goes anywhere." This was out of Sam's territory; best just to listen. "We both wanted to try with each other, and we have. It's been nice and we're still close. But as time passes, more friends than lovers. Over the long term, it seems, she's less physical than I am."

"That could be a problem." Keep it noncommittal.

"It hasn't been, really; while I had no other interest, I didn't get antsy much." She leveled her gaze. "But now I have."

The touchy part. "What does Maril say about this? Or does she know yet?"

"I told her what I had in mind; she didn't object. After Jules, being consulted was probably a nice change." Her lips twitched. "I don't want to move out, Sam. Not entirely. She'd be left alone, and she's not the type for solitude."

Me either.

Her smile looked hesitant. "What do you think?"

Sex or no—but preferably yes—here was someone he could *talk* with. And the hell with what anyone else thought. "As long as you're happy with the arrangement."

"As long as we both are."

"That too."

Clear it was to Scayna that their return to Eamn fell far short of Nsil's expectations. In the eyes of the homeworld his daring foray on Magh had become a rash foible, forgiven if not forgotten in the new amity between worlds; his plunge into the great portal fared little better. Even his bringing of a yumin ship counted only as addition to the one already given Eamn.

Kaow had warned of such changes, but until the actuality, Nsil's thought had not accepted them. To his chagrin, Gvan showed no signs of welcoming his return, nor willingness to cede Gvan's current tenure of Nsil's rightful place in the

Overgrouping. Even Nsil's householding, nominally still his entitlement, he found given over for another to administer. In reclaiming what was his, Nsil had been in no way politic.

Now, in her dome newly refurbished with her own hangings and furnishments, Scayna roused from absorption in new study of the ancient recordances and sought to bring Nsil again to equanimity. Ever did intimacy raise his spirit, but only for the time. Now, following one such pleasuring, she spoke.

"Of all endeavors you might now essay, which could best satisfy your aspirings?"

He twitched a forelimb. "I have thought on such matters. The Overgrouping, where before our transport to Erdth I strove and achieved, now seems a nest of cluckling smofs, scrabbling for tidbits. My holdings, once a great pride, seem little more than space of land and structure—amenable to the producing of gain and displaying our preferences in design and ornament, yet hardly a nexus for serious accomplishings. No," he stated, "my interests bend toward that which I have scarce begun to know."

Of a sudden Scayna felt she sensed his wish. "Sky travel?"

"You do know me." He stroked the side of her neck. "Yes. I would hold seat on *Hermes*, in the place I occupied most often as we came here. Learning from the yumin bearer Jone to second Tasr's eventual direction of the vessel."

"Second? But by householding, by origin, your station lies well beyond that of Tasr."

"On a skyship, station matters not. I merit second to Tasr but no more, because he is the more greatly skilled and knowledged; I learn from Tasr, not he from myself."

Scayna considered. "You will be much gone from me."

"Less, in hap, than should I resume full participance at the Overgrouping. You recall how seldom I became free to visit during extended sessions. With *Hermes* matters will not be so."

"Inform me then, in what manner will I find improvement?"

"Much of our travel must go to Magh; on *Hermes* that journey becomes brief, and Tasr and I would undertake only one such voyage of each four. Or at most, of three."

"Much, you say; what of the remainder? I would hear more."

"At later time, where but Shtai the Forerunner? And to that world, Scayna, you also must come." He stood, forelimbs held wide. "To set limb upon Shtai! We must do so together."

Again she thought. "I see no hindrance. Until Nyrl ripens to readiness for the learning group, she too would be of our company."

"It is determined, then," spoke Nsil. His breath came deep. "Rather than quibble within the Overgrouping, as to rightful shares in the new commerce, we shall be those who carry it. Not the first, yet perhaps eventually foremost. And in the gains from these ventures, fewer will share more greatly."

"Then the lure of it, Nsil, is increase in holdings?"

Mirth dropped his jaw. "Cease mockery! Such gain only denotes our doing. You are wholly aware, Scayna—the lure is to be sometime paramount, among those who lead Eamn into the skies."

The Yainan ship, Sam decided, was crewed by alert optimists. With no demonstrable reason to believe their message could be understood, those aboard the *T'lais* must have begun transmitting as soon as *Roamer* was spotted; their signal emerged from interstellar background noise as the two vessels neared useful range, and continued through and beyond closest passage (a bit under fifty thousand miles), dying again with distance.

Of course Gowdy didn't know the ship's name until later, after Molly Abele and Marthe Vinler transcribed the original recordings to correct for Doppler effects, and played the resulting message for T'phee and his colleagues to translate.

"Much occurs at Yain," T'phee said after listening. "More ships are building than had been thought possible. Far too few, in sadness, to save any significant portion. Still, for each one who earlier might hope, now the number is nearer two."

Word from Yamar, of Sam's own rescue project, couldn't reach Yain for something like three and a half Earth years, eighteen months before *Roamer* itself arrived. Blessed be Lorenz and Fitzgerald, thought Gowdy; only two *ship's* years to that arrival!

T'phee continued. "Spirit and purpose maintain well, it is told here. That even though only so few escape the Swarm, Yainan heritage shall persist and survive. The maintainment of will and effort transcends the scant portioning of that survival."

"Well, we'll do better than that, old chum." Gowdy stroked T'phee's neckskin. "A lot better, in hap."

As *Roamer* built vee, Sam's morale rose with it, renewing his interest in phenomena outside the ship as caught by the sensors and logged by his watch officers and instrument techs. The drive purred, the supply Gates delivered, a dead star loomed proximate enough for a good look but safely off the ship's line of flight, nothing at all threatening outGated from Earth—and Gates being what they were, quite a lot of time remained before Glen Springs could kick back on anything he'd done. Purely hog heaven.

And this with Libby. More friends than lovers, she'd said of her and Maril. Oddly, he felt it applied to him and Libby as well. Not to downgrade the lovers part: zesty, joyous, sometimes even urgent.

But in no way did Gowdy find himself infatuated; when circumstances interdicted the physical aspect, he could wait. With the friends part, though, he was addicted; two days without a solid Libbytalk fix and Sam grew edges.

So different from the time with Sydnie, who had charmed him, more or less enslaved him, and then yanked too damn much on the choke collar and lost her hold. Before all the changes, which now looking back seemed to have happened almost at once and he couldn't sort them out.

Well, a little. She'd turned helpful just before Eamn—and Gowdy had solid suspicion as to why—but she hadn't really begun to level with him until out behind *Roamer* all in suits and the Spider Prince damn near blew his own hand off. After that, she'd never let him down. And that last crazy move, bouncing the 'bug through a Gate and no way to know what she might run into . . . !

Sam purely hoped she'd outGated in the clear.

Time reaches the need of T'phee's get to break shelter, es embryonic mandibles to rupture T'phee's thoracic integument and expose the new get's breathing orifice and sensory cluster.

Es feeding appendage is not yet opened; er still draws sustenance from the nutrient fluidities of es parent. But breathes now for enself, and most paramount, can sense selfly es newly revealed surround. Now begins the possibility and process of direct learning from that surround, most prominently therein being es parent T'phee.

Also in helpment are P'nai and R'lyt and N'tol. The lattering two retain sulkiness that T'phee provided not for *cruance* growings to be brought on this vessel. But in consult with Cejha and Nahei before enshipment, T'phee learned that neither on *Tayr* nor on *L'lit* had such growings vouchsafed notable result in zygote formation. When Yain itself is reached . . .

Acceding, R'lyt and N'tol render aid without stint.

As must any Yainan, T'phee speaks much and often to es growing yet unshed get, es goal being encouragement of communicative comprehension prior to shedding. Often, though not always, the Yainan parent can produce such height of development.

The circumstance of this shedding causes T'phee concern. Pushforce of Gowdy's ship will upon short awaiting cease, replaced by lesser force derived of rotation; T'phee does not wish es get's standings and walkings to be commenced in surround so misleadingly facile.

Yet of brief passage is such condition to be. By care, by particularity of diet and exercisings, forestallment of shedding can maintain for periods of moderate extension.

T'phee resolves dedicated adherence to such measures. Es get, which beyond all dream of hope shall see and tread es homeworld Yain, must grow without mishapness.

Yet will T'phee welcome divestment. Strain and awkwardness of the gravid state worsen much as that state reaches culmination.

Gowdy's first sight of the miniature sensory cluster peeking from the base of T'phee's necktrunk reminded him of kangaroos. Not a whole lot, but some. Though marsupials, so far as Sam knew, didn't murmur almost constantly to their joeys in three languages. Struggling with "yumin tongue" himself,

T'phee wanted to give young B'yai a head start in trilingualism. So far the small creature seemed most fluent in Blalupidadian, but maybe that was as normal for T'phee's species as it was for Gowdy's.

As *Roamer* approached its nominal time factor of ten to one, Sam called council in control and laid down some policy. "We're looking at less than a hundred ship's days at zero gee. I suggest we leave control and quarters configurations strictly alone. And not bother to upend the Gates, either."

None of his officers—Simone, Mose, SuZanne—showed any dissent; neither was any great amount of approval displayed. He said, "I do think we should crank up the belt, for sleeping and leisure time. But unbutton the facilities as little as we can and still enjoy them." He looked around, to the three and to others attending. "Does that sound okay?"

"Yeah." "Sure." And the inevitable "Fuckin' aye." So for two days after accel ceased, everyone did more work than Gowdy felt was worth it, to put the rotating belt into use. Once the device was up and running, though, he was glad they'd done it.

Unprecedented though equally laborious was the chore of laying Velcro on surfaces that ordinarily didn't need it: the control room's drive mode floor, various passages and stairs, and a certain amount in drive mode quarters. For a time Gowdy was afraid they'd run out of the stuff, but by making economies of use, all essential areas got the treatment before accel was cut.

And a good thing, too. Laying the strips in zero gee was something he'd just as soon not see, let alone try.

Keeping Earthtush blocked in zero gee was simply too much effort. Figuring time elapsed on Earth, Gowdy decided to abandon the precaution. For the same reason he'd never bothered with it on the intership Gates. Good probability estimates can make life easier, so use them.

So while the free-fall period was more than somewhat like living out of a suitcase, the three months and a bit passed quickly enough. Sam enjoyed being back in his beltside quarters, and Libby spent several nights a week there.

Remembering what Sydnie had said about her episode with Johnnie Rio, Gowdy suggested the zero gee option to Libby. Grinning like kids with a new toy, they went to his drive mode rooms. Neither of them, it turned out, had ever tried this before; when matters began to peak, both tended to forget the need to hold on securely. More than one resulting mishap derailed the big train in midair, leaving them laughing helplessly before making a new try.

"There's always glue, you know," Libby spluttered.

"Too messy." Fishing some miscellaneous gear from his closet, Sam said, "Here; let's try this. The belt on you so, with these straps down behind . . . and through . . . now up behind me and out around . . . and hold on!"

Yankee ingenuity wins every time. Later he refined the apparatus to work no-hands.

When Simone Leopold and Skeeter Cole cross-checked their separate calculations and announced imminence of the half light-year point—from Yain, that was—it was time for decel. Gowdy's policy of minimum disturbance to belt facilities made reconversion easy, and elsewhere the now-unnecessary Velcro could be reclaimed at leisure.

An hour before drive was to be applied, seeing all conditions nominal he caught Libby's attention and took informal leave inship. One last romp with no gravs; he figured they had that much coming and made the most of it.

"I've liked this," said Libby Verdoorn. "It's special."

"At Yain we'll have orbit. Same thing."

"No." She pushed back her floating hair. "By Yain there'll be changes. There always are."

"You worry too much." He reached to snag his jumpsuit and began pulling it on. Finished, he pulled her to him for a kiss. "I'm due in control; take your time."

He arrived to find Mose sitting pilot as Jethro Blaine called data up from drive. "Yaw thrustors two and three: thrust oh-point-five for eight seconds—*now*." So they'd begun turnover without him, and rightly so. Clutching a seat back and trying to remember which yaw thrustor pushed which way, Gowdy braced; unexpectedly firm (it always was), the lateral push came at an angle from behind him, lasted for the count of eight, then died.

Now the wait, while *Roamer* turned end for end, and then the command to stop rotation: "Yaw thrustor one: thrust oh-point-eight-six-six for eight seconds—*now*." Right; with three equidistant yaw thrustors you could split your vectors any way you wanted; sensibly, Jethro had chosen the simplest.

Reverse thrust came and ended, and then Mose jockeyed a bit with yaw trimmers before announcing, "Yain on target dead astern. Bring thrust up to one gee." Gradually, with no jarring, Traction Drive built strength and held level.

Leaning near the intercom Gowdy said, "Good job, Jethro," and directly, "Mose." Standing solidly now, he turned to go. "Call me if. I'll be in quarters." Drive mode digs again, now.

He was surprised to find Libby still there. But not at all displeased.

"The timing's too vague," Bill Flynn had told Kayo, he and Jocelyn Waymire at hand with good wishes for the send-off. "No way of knowing whether the ship will be in free fall or decel. So you and Dan had better lean against the back of the alcove."

It had been so *nice* of those two busy people to come see them off. Feelings mixed and mind churning, Kayo said, "Will Sydnie be all right? What should I tell the captain?"

"We'll look after her," said Jocelyn. "Tell him she's planning to Gate as soon as she's free of the hearings."

Then the Gate tech arrived, late herself but in a hurry for everyone else. As Kayo enjoyed some unexpected hugs, the tech said, "If you'll sign here . . . and step over there . . ."

Hunching against the rear of the alcove, Kayo grasped Dan Quillan's hand. "Here we go, boy." And the colors flared.

As they died, weight moved abruptly from down to backward; *Roamer* was in decel, all right. Kayo sniffed; the air had a tang, almost too slight to notice, that she didn't remember from before. Maybe she'd just been used to it.

No one in the corridor; taking the lead she walked to control and looked in. "Hi, Mose. Skeeter."

"Kayo!" "Dan!"

Leaving their seats, both men subjected the newcomers to a certain amount of vigorous greeting. Then the questions: what's happening back home, how's Glen Springs, did Sydnie get there okay, are you back for good? Regaining her breath, Kayo tried to answer as best she could, finally saying, "I have a detailed report here, for the captain. I expect he'll post it later.''

''Sure.'' Skeeter nodded. ''He's in quarters.''

Starting to turn, Kayo paused. Under drive, the belt was not in use. ''Drive mode quarters, you mean. Uh—I've never been there. They were dismantled before 6-A inGated; remember?''

''Oh sure. Well, through that hatch, you go down aft to . . .'' and he gave directions. As she left, Cole was asking Dan ''. . . back to the DV now, huh?''

She didn't wait to hear Quillan's answer; his embarrassment at being set down was painful to her, too, but this was something Dan had to work through for himself. She'd help, of course, as much as she could. But in the final analysis it was his own baby. As well as his own bathwater . . .

Skeeter was good with instructions; after only one missed turn Kayo found herself facing a doorplate that read ''S. Gowdy.'' She punched the chime button, and waited. Was he asleep? Then the door opened; there in a rumpled bathrobe stood Sam Gowdy.

''Kayo!'' And again it was hug time. ''Come on in.'' Then his face changed; still partially blocking her entrance, he stopped movement.

Before she could react, from the back hallway a voice came. ''Sam? What is it?'' A woman emerged; Kayo knew her from the Magh colony but couldn't immediately recall her name. She'd never seen her like this, anyway. Wearing nothing at all.

XXV

"The Eamnet is here," said Duant. "The bearer Scayna."

Irtuk looked up from the summary she was evaluating. "Thank you, Duant. Is all aready?"

"Of a surety. Here is my roster of your retinue for the journey. You may wish to make emendations."

The seeder's growing confidence still fell short of being a perfect fit. Irtuk said, "Your judgment suffices. Now, does your advisory council have aught to add to our agendum?"

Very little, it seemed. Yet Irtuk considered each item trivial or otherwise, approving more than not, before saying, "Do you feel this new council of seeders and adaptives provides any great advancement in overall relations?"

Diffident, the seeder replied, "As regarding increase of decisioning voice, very little. For such voice, though heretofore unacknowledged, we had not lacked. Yet in other fashion, much so. Priorly to your innovations, any influence of ours was known only within our own holdings. Now it is a matter of public view, elevating one's esteem and feelings of worth."

"This is well. Now I surmise you have much to manage, seeing that all our needings go safely aboard the Eamnet ship." To take leave of her new responsibilities so soon and for such distance was, Irtuk realized, far from orthodox. Yet here lay an opportunity not to be passed by one of her temperament.

As Duant left Irtuk's workplace, Scayna entered and Irtuk rose in greeting. With formalities given short shrift and both then seated, for a time they spoke of inconsequentials and munched on smallfoods.

Then Scayna spoke. "It pleasures me greatly that we go to stand on Shtai the Forerunner together, you and I. And that for this purpose you accept the hospitality of our yumin-given ship."

Keeping from her visage all sign of mirth, Irtuk said, "Pleasure also is mine. Though not for the first time shall I experience Shtai. Nor, for that matter, the hospitality of Nsil."

Scayna, Irtuk was certain, hid feelings similar to her own. Yet the Eamnet said only, "Our facilities have now improved somewhat. You should find them noticeably more comfortable."

No longer could Irtuk suppress her snortlings. "Forgive me, but I could not forbear . . ."

"It is well; now I may feel free to chide you also."

"Concerning . . . ?"

"The Archival panes from our householding. Had you asked, I should have so endowed you; there was no need to pilfer."

Stunned, Irtuk waited. Scayna said, "Have your devices yet unlocked their meanings?"

Quandary! Begin with truth. "To an extent. Some text has come apparent. Yet the most of each pane is filled with entrant codings of a type which exceeds our equipment's reach."

"Then you have not experienced full effect of those grisly entertainments. Although we on Eamn have no means of displaying even the text, we know that the panes once complemented machines incorporating devices such as Gowdy's viewscreens."

"Entertainments!" What was Scayna telling her? And how could she know such a thing?

"Yes. While we cannot as yet bring to view the true content of these recordances, also were found partial listings of what was stored, with brief descriptions of a given pane's import."

"And the ones I . . . need not have purloined?"

"Speculative imaginings, most possibly composed shortly after plague erupted. Their intent, it would seem from our later viewpoint, was rousing of Eamnet fury to maintain the war." Scayna's jaw dipped in amusement. "Have no such been discovered here on Magh, casting all Eamn as the embodiment of evil?''

''It may be, though not of my knowledge.'' In great confusion Irtuk acknowledged notification by the seeder Haij, that Nsil of Eamn stood ready to welcome Irtuk and her companions; accordingly she called on Duant to commence supervision and confirmation of planned loading and embarking procedures.

Then to Scayna: ''You much relieve a great trepidation I have had. Let us now go to your—to Nsil's new ship.''

Not wholly Nsil's, Scayna explained, but Eamnet-derived complexities of ownership were more than Irtuk cared to think of. With her retinue about and following, she and Scayna proceeded to the ship *Hermes*, which at first gaze could be mistook for *Totebag*, Magh's own gift—within limits—from the yumins.

Aboard, however, it differed much, largely in provision of a greater proportion of furnishings fitted not for yumins but for those who now undertook its operation. In a lounging space, Nsil greeted Irtuk and Scayna. ''Are we now prepared to voyage? To set limb upon Shtai the Forerunner, and carry new hope and nurture to Bretl and her people?''

Irtuk moved to clasp limbs with her former abductor. ''I hold warmest joy that we have gained understanding to join in these endeavors.''

''And I joy to welcome you here, Irtuk the Elect.''

Oh *jeez!* Looking from Kayo to Libby and back, Sam Gowdy felt like seventh grade and caught behind the bleachers with Lauranna Sprague. Also like that time, just now he hadn't been doing anything. Yet. He said, ''Uh—''

Vanishing into the bedroom momentarily, Libby reappeared shrugging into her jumpsuit. ''Hello, Kayo. It's good to see you again. I expect you have a lot to discuss with the captain, so I'll go now.''

No ''later,'' no kiss good-bye, no help at all. As the door closed, Sam breathed a deep one. ''Sit down. We need a drink.''

Getting out the fixings he gave Kayo a quick lookover. She hadn't changed much. How long had she been on Earth, anyway? He couldn't remember. Long enough that now she could tie her hair back at the nape. Just barely; at one side a strand fell loose to wave down across her cheek. Drinks made, he handed one over and sat to face her.

When they'd touched glasses and taken first sips, he said, "Libby helps me be not so alone. Now, what's the word from Glen Springs? More than just the official reports, I mean."

"Libby Verdoorn," Kayo said. "That's who she is. Second in colony Admin under Barry Krsnch. Only he went back, didn't he?"

The four-year comm turnaround date from that caper, with its potential for repercussion, had passed without Gowdy's notice. Cautiously he asked, "What did ol' Barry have to say about it? Did you see him?"

"I think he'd Gated out somewhere, to a new job."

So far so good, but this was all side stuff. "Sydnie. Have you seen her? The last we know, she flew my homemade space can through a bootleg Gate to Earth. Did she come out okay?"

Now Kayo grinned. "Mostly. Your Doodlebug had a big hole shot in it, and she lost the wheels and part of one fin. But she plunked the rest of it down in one piece. Smack on the Glen Springs soccer field."

The intensity of Sam's relief shook him; with a sort of gasp he mumbled thanks—to Whom, he wasn't exactly sure. Kayo gave him an odd look. "I hadn't thought you two were all that close."

"A long time there, we weren't. I'm not certain we will be. But we went through a lot of wringer together. Since you—uh, left, that is." Too much to try to tell, and entirely too personal. "Let's say I value her for different reasons than I did at first. Better ones."

He leaned forward. "Now tell me things." She did, and he listened. About Nsil, and Scayna, and the ship they had taken back to Eamn. The furor when Commodore Aroka & Company outGated, all dead. The support for, and additions to, his Yain rescue plan. Habegger Labs' projected scheme for comet catching, ". . . but that's a maybe; we can't wait for it. Meanwhile you're going to need interpreters; that's what I'm here for. To learn Yainan from T'phee before we get there."

Lastly she told of Sydnie's predicament with the crime

commission. "Bill Flynn's keeping her under wraps; the first sign of real danger, I expect he'll Gate her here. Otherwise she'll stay through the hearings. But sooner or later, Sam—won't you have a problem?"

Ignoring Kayo's use of present tense for events two years past on Earth, he thought about the question. "Maybe I will. We'll see when the time comes."

The problem wouldn't be Sydnie; at least he didn't think it would. She'd been gone a long while, after all, and him with no way of knowing she'd ever be back. What was he supposed to do—burn a candle every night to her spare jumpsuits?

Libby, though: thanks a lot for filling in, but the first string's coming back on the field? Fine grade of appreciation. Maybe he'd better talk with her right away, before . . .

Thinking these matters through, after Kayo left to arrange drive mode quarters for herself and Dan, Gowdy shook his head. In terms of what he and *Roamer* needed to do, this personal stuff was cracker crumbs.

Which might have been just as uncomfortable to sleep on.

The shedding of get brings sensings of undue intensity yet not without pleasure. The building and then easing tingles as connections disengage with excruciating slowness, the inrush of cool air to recesses long filled hotly to distention, the overdue contraction of sinews likewise maximally stretched: each release signaled by a pang preceding gradual ease and growing comfort, each such process ending with warmth and quivering, wholly freed of stress.

Until small B'yai stands unsteady upon es own four limbs, with T'phee's aid freeing es weakly straining manipulars from adherence to the slowly extending necktrunk, turning es sensory cluster in newly aroused curiosity to es surround, unclosing for the first time es feeding orifice for T'phee to introduce the morsels of es initial separate nutriment.

Congratulatory now, T'phee's companions cosset the get also.

For a time greater than optimal, until Yain itself is reached, B'yai's surround is limited to little more than this residence compartment. As in lesser extent, once again as was true in building of the vessel's pace, are those of T'phee and es colleagues. Under pushforce, activity of any Yainan is as though taking place on a world, and nowhere has the species built or utilized stepstairs. Here on Gowdy's vessel T'phee and the other mature Yainans negotiate these devices only when truly necessary. And difficultly; in example, all descent proceeds hindfirst.

As before, however, Gowdy provides special quartering, whereby both the ship's directive compartment and the place for feeding may be reached without recourse to stepstairs.

The time to Yain is yet long, but T'phee waits with the utmost of serenity here achievable.

To announce the hope that Gowdy brings.

Coming off watch Skeeter Cole took a detour to the drive mode lounge, noting that Blaine and Craig and Tanacross had the poker game going while at another table Libby Verdoorn held a darker drink than usual. Fixing a mildish one for himself, he sat across from her. "Cheers."

"If you say so. Kayo Marlin just outGated."

His brows raised. "That's bad?"

"Caught me at Sam's, in my nekkids."

He took a cool swallow. "Nem'mind; she's a big girl."

"It's not that; she and I are friends and you know it. It's Sydnie Lightner."

"Come again? I thought you said—"

"If Kayo's had time to get here, Sydnie's next. And I don't think I can stand seeing what she does to Sam. Not again."

This was none of Skeeter's business and he said so. Except, ". . . what's so terrible, anyway?"

"She's all take and no give. In everything. Sex—I heard her brag once, a little drunker than she thought—all the kinky extra things she keeps her men eager to do for her in bed, but never any payback."

What the hell. "You always go even-steven, then."

She glared. "Now that *is* none of your business."

Instantly contrite, Skeeter grabbed her hand. "You're right; I was out of line and I'm sorry. Anyway, what you figure to do about it—besides pickle yourself for posterity?"

"Not a damn thing except stay with him while I can. And when Lightner outGates, tell her a thing or two."

"Good luck with that project." Glass empty, Cole patted

Verdoorn's shoulder and headed for quarters. By this time, Alix should be up and around.

For sure, she'd be in a better mood than Libby right now. She always was; one reason he and she got along so great.

Next day Verdoorn bore a look of greater cheer. In a brief passage over coffee she confided, "I'm okay with it now, Skeets. If he needs me I'm here; if he doesn't it's not all that long to Yain. Once we get there and the tech help starts Gating in, we won't be stuck in this goddamn ingrown mess anyway. Any of us."

She grinned. "But I'm still going to tell that bitch."

Everything always takes longer and costs more. Before Sydnie could inGate to *Roamer* she had to sit with Waymire and Flynn, going over her old Web file point by point and filling in additional info from memory. "There was always some skivvy about big shots in the background," she told them. "Higher-ups in various governments, with a finger in the pie and maybe giving some protection behind the scenes. Nobody knew for sure, though. Well, Aroka, probably, but not the foot troops. *I* sure didn't."

She looked through various references from files Waymire had brought. Here and there vague correlations seemed to appear, but nothing she could validate for sure. Nor could she pinpoint with any exactitude the times when Aroka had gone away to meet with his own boss, the mysterious Connection.

"Too bad," said Jocelyn Waymire. "We can nail down several of Crane Willigh's overseas trips, including three to southeast Asia. Now if only you could peg some of it from your end . . ."

But Sydnie couldn't. She'd kept no journal of her time with the Spider Prince; even if she'd thought of doing such a thing, the risk would have been too great. By now, of course, much of the period blurred together in her mind. Too bad, indeed.

Well after dawn they finished. Fatigued, unready to face greetings and the like on *Roamer*, Sydnie postponed Gating and opted for sleep. By evening, refreshed and then fed, she called for escort to the Gates room.

Bill Flynn led the group and took her bag. "Jocelyn had to return to DC" he told her, "and says she's sorry she can't help see you off."

"Tell her thanks anyway."

At the Gate he surprised her with a hug. "And you tell Sam Gowdy we're behind him here, whatever he needs. If he still feels he has to resign, then of course he can, but make sure he knows we hope he doesn't. *I* hope he doesn't."

"Sure." Braced against the rear of the alcove, she sat and watched the air go iridescent and opaque as weight pull shifted abruptly from down to backward.

Vision came clear; within her view, no one stood or moved. She climbed to control and found Simone Leopold on watch with Skeeter Cole. "Hi, folks."

Talk happened, lively and lots of it. If Simone still had a down on Sydnie she wasn't showing it. Skeets seemed friendly but strangely embarrassed, maybe even guarded. Still and all, Sydnie stayed longer than she realized or intended. Until Cole said, sounding somehow awkward, "You'll want to get down to see Sam. Your same old quarters, from when we came in to Magh."

Right he was. "See you later, then." Inship, turning to the last flight of stairs she met Libby Verdoorn. "Hi, Libby. I made it."

Verdoorn's eyes narrowed. "You may as well know, I've been with Sam a lot, this trip. And treated him better than you ever did. Now I suppose you're taking him back; he seemed to think you would, if you ever did return."

No way to answer that. Brushing past, over her shoulder the woman added, "But if you start crapping on him again, I don't think he'll take it this time. And he won't have to."

Standing a little shell-shocked, Sydnie wasn't angry at Verdoorn; the woman made a valid point. Libby couldn't know how Sydnie's feelings had changed, how she saw things differently now. Still, whether she could keep up these new ways—playing things straight, discarding forever the loaded rules of her mother Oreadna—all that was a proposition yet to be proved.

But she owed it to Bill Flynn to bolster Sam out of resigning. For that matter, she owed it to Sam. After all it was *her* past that had risen from the pit so to speak, and run with spiked talons over his personal codes and feelings.

If only she'd thrown that damn knife a little better.

Now, though, could she do what she needed to? Finding

out was going to be interesting. At the very least.

Well. Sydnie went on down. At their quarters door she punched the chime. In the old rhythm: shave and a haircut . . .

By the time Dan came in, Kayo was mostly unpacked. Gazing up from the drawer she was arranging, she tried to appear unconcerned. Quillan, though, seemed chipper enough. She said, "Well. How's it feel to be back aboard? About the same?"

"The people, yes. Except that a lot's happened while we were gone; we can compare notes later. The ship, though—in drive mode it's like a whole different place."

He shrugged. "We'll get used to it."

As he set to work emptying his own luggage, Kayo felt she was waiting for the other shoe to drop. But either he'd speak up in his own good time or he wouldn't. Actually it was only about five minutes before he said, "I talked with SuZanne Craig. If I don't have any further reflex lapses between here and Yain she'll post me for full DV duty on her own chop."

Kayo didn't ask the alternative but maybe her face did. "If I do have another flatout, or more, it's like they said on Earth; I can drive the little beast but not solo."

Kayo went to him. "And that fills your glass again?"

He hugged her. "Half, anyway."

"But now it's half-full, not half-empty?"

"Why either-or? Maybe it's just, the glass is too big."

With the chuckle they shared then, a load left her. He was going to be all right.

He didn't expect Sydnie because why would she ring the bell at her own digs, but he opened the door and there she was. He didn't even get her name said all the way before she grabbed on and kissed like shouldn't we stop the car first; when he pulled free to breathe she said, "We all need you. You *can't* quit."

Stepping back he damn near fell over the bag she'd dropped, but caught himself. "You," he said. "The Doodlebug. Through a f'Chris'sakes *Gate*! Are you crazy or something?"

"Something." Except for the big unfamiliar grin that

wouldn't seem to stop, she hadn't changed enough to notice. She went on, "A lot to tell you. Now or later; your choice."

She probably wasn't too surprised he picked later. Until they finally got back up, not even so much as a homecoming drink. Then, both unclad but sitting on towels so as not to stick all sweaty to the plastic, she was telling about Earth and he about the time from Magh and Yamar to here. Between them it all got considerably mixed up but he thought he was getting a pretty fair picture and if not they could fix it later.

Before going back to bed they showered and changed the sheets. For what good that might do in the long run. Next morning by Gowdy's schedule, at breakfast he tried to explain how he saw the situation:

No war in the Triad Worlds, and Larry Corcoran hanging near the macroGate with the only big daddy laser in the system could get the drop on any contender, local or outGating. Ames Griswold's Web contingent gone from Magh. So far so good.

Yain, now. How many live bodies per day could be passed through six thirty-foot Gates? With luck, a whole bunch. But what about the mechanics of assembly, the migrations? And at Yamar and Tetzl's, the dispersion and absorption into new living space? Well, he couldn't be everywhere at the same time.

He'd forgotten how long Yain had left before Doomsday. He did remember the old line that if all Chinese lined up to march past a certain point at such and such speed the parade could never end; population increase would outpace it.

Yainans, though, had cut back on breeding. And then there was the macroGate comet snatcher which might work and might not. Whenever. Anyway, he knew what the problems were.

"You're going to oversee all that?"

Even to Gowdy his laugh sounded thin. "Umpty years watching T'phee's people hustle their four-legged butts to get out alive? Not a chance. We set it up, see it working, leave competent personnel in charge, that's all folks."

"To any reasonable onlooker, I should think it's enough." And she took him back to bed. He wasn't quite past his normal recovery time, but a little unprecedented aid helped it all work.

Sam roused to the door chime, accepted a message copy from Marthe Vinler, and read it before he noticed it was addressed to Sydnie. So, "Here; see if you can figure this out."

What it said was:

> Crane Willigh led a sizable armed group to storm macroGate Two and forced a tech there to Gate them out. Seems he didn't take time to ask where. The Mouth feeds a general supplies hold in the Liij Environ. Humans cannot survive more than minutes on Liij air.
>
> Willigh may have gone desperate when he saw his name in a copy of your Web file which I apparently left unprotected by password. I should be more careful.
>
> All best regards, Bill Flynn

"That's the bird who was trying to nail you in the crime hearings?" He had to ask her twice because unaccountably Sydnie was almost choking with laughter. "What's so damn funny?"

"Bill Flynn." The laughing spree ended in a hiccup; then she said, "Willigh's name wasn't *in* the file I made on Aroka, way back when. Flynn did some editing on his own hook."

And left it out for bait. Right. "Remind me never to get in that man's bad books."

"No danger." But now she looked serious. "Sam. Can we pick up where we left off? The new start we were making?"

This was what he'd hoped. But why was she asking? He said, "Any reason why not? I mean, am I in for any more surprises? From the past—the time of La Hoja Rubia?"

She gripped his hand. "I swear I never killed then." An incongruous bubble of laughter escaped as she added, "Hell, if I'd had any practice I wouldn't have botched Aroka when I made a break for it. No; stopping Estilete, that was the first. And however many it was, when I was firing to cover Wade and Sis at Griswold's bootleg Mouth, I hope they were the last."

Then her mouth twisted. "I forgot. When I outGated, at the Web base. They sent two fighters up after me and I knocked a wing off one. I expect he splattered."

Gowdy squeezed the hand that held his. "Self-defense. The

lot. Same as me on *Golconda*. But still I found it damn hard to live with."

"You think I don't? Now that it's had a chance to sink in?"

"I hadn't known, is all." Sam thought about it. "I'm sorry if you're hurting. But doesn't a person have to? Or else be like Aroka."

Drawn and looking somehow needful, Sydnie Lightner said, "I don't know if I can be what you want. What we both want, on here and then at Yain."

One side of her mouth made a sort of grin. "Libby Verdoorn thinks not. She's letting go without a fuss, but she'd still like to see my head on a pole. That's not mutual, mind you; if she's been good for you, I owe her."

"Too right; we both do. My own head was in bad shape." And how could he ever repay Libby? There had to be something. . . .

Sydnie shook her head. "What I do know is, I'm going to give that project one hell of a try."

"Cheer up," said Gowdy. "It might even be fun."

XXVI

Nothing in Kayo's experience had prepared her for the chaos that followed *Roamer*'s arrival at Yain. How Sam Gowdy kept his head on straight she had no idea, but over a hectic period his plan got results. Gazillions of Yainans gathered to leave for Tetzl's Planet, nearly as many to Yamar or Scout or even Shtai the Forerunner, depending on who told it.

At the six assigned staging areas, Gate construction had continued 'round the clock; then as each pre-activated matrix fired up, Yainans began inGating. The parades moved slowly, but over time the numbers mounted.

The comet swarm surpassed human expectation; interspecies communication was never great with quantities. Word of the twelve ship macroGate stirred more curiosity than hope. For starters, a mile wasn't going to be big enough; at least four nuclei over that size were sure strikes.

At Gowdy's heartfelt urging, relayed by Kayo and T'phee though some expletives would not translate, considerable Yainan effort went toward manufacture of thermite and the like; *Roamer* and the Deployment Vehicle slammed large amounts of the stuff into the backsides of several iceballs too bulky for netting. The resultant gas jets gave only minor extra push—but enough, out in slow country, that those chunks would reach Yain's path too wide and early to hit anything. Well, that's what Gowdy said.

Long before his estimate could prove out, he and Sydnie were gone from Yain, commanding the *Arrow*-class ship *Valkyrie* which had arrived by what looked quite a lot like black magic.

"Not really," Gowdy said. "Glen Springs had our ring of Gate ships swallow *Valkyrie*, converge and land to be Gated here, then lift and spread again. So our ship could pop out." Which it certainly had, so apparently the trick didn't really violate the Blocked Tush Principle after all.

Once in action the Gateship ring bagged considerably more cosmic missiles than anyone had a right to expect. But a lot of debris got through anyway. You win some, you lose some.

Regardless of Crunch Day's approach, not all Yainans planned to Gate free. Some would ride ships well clear of the Swarm, observing. And the least strike-prone side of the planet mounted shelters, stocked against prolonged siege conditions, for a surprising number who chose to weather the debacle.

The great quakes and tsunami were bound to level coastal cities and even alter coastlines. But eventually, when the blanketing dusts of impact settled, many refugees would return.

To join in Yain's rebuilding with T'phee's cadre of stubborn survivors, the self-styled Chosen of Gowdy.

"Speak this to en, Kaow," said T'phee, "that er may know es place among us."

"So I shall, Steward of Yain," said Kayo Marlin. Well, she could Gate the message on datacap. "Sam will like that."

She wasn't sure where he and Sydnie were headed, along with several more from *Roamer*'s original complement, on *Valkyrie*. One of these days, when Simone qualified Libby Verdoorn to succeed Dan as DV Chief, maybe they could Gate aboard and find out.